# *Mending Stone*

*a novel*

# Mending Stone

*a novel*

## Sharon Duerst

Three Towers Press
Milwaukee, Wisconsin

This novel is a work of fiction. Names, characters, places, and incidents are either the product of the author's imagination or are used fictitiously. All characters are fictitious, and any similarity to people living or dead is purely coincidental.

Published by
Three Towers Press
(a division of HenschelHAUS Publishing, Inc.)
2625 S. Greeley St. Suite 201
Milwaukee, WI 53207
www.henschelHAUSbooks.com


ISBN:    978-1-59598-134-9 (paperback)
         978-1-59598-135-6 (Kindle)

LCCN: 2011931262

Library of Congress Cataloging-in-Publication information available on request.



Cover design by Daniel Fleming.
Author photos by Tullisphoto.



Printed in the United States of America.

*To  Carolyn, my sister,*
*Who dares to dream and create.*
*You lead the way!*

# $\mathcal{A}CKNOWLEDGMENTS$

This book has been a labor of love involving many people. All of your insights and encouragement have helped me so much along the way. Without you, I couldn't have done this. To Lisa Anderson, Anna Arem, Pat Armstrong, Lois Berreman, Kathy Bingham, the Bunko Girls and Beading Babes, Maria Carlos, Kathy Cascade, Julia Chapman, Diane Conroy, Debbie Dalton, Erica Davido, Paul and Kay DeBast, Carol Duerst, Roy and Lavona Duerst, Vicki Dyrdahl, Richard Falxa, Sandy Fischer, Velvet and Doug Foster, Richard and Susan Funk, Josefina Nunez Herrera and Jose Jarmillo Rivera and family, Roxanna Hill, Mollie Jurgenson, Carolyn Kortge, Susan Kurtz, Jan Lindner, Karen Liska, Brad and Debora Lorang, Janet Lorang, Mae Lorang, Mike and Cindy Lorang, Tim Lorang, Kathy Lorensen, Karen Martell, Jet McCann, Janet Mead, Carolyn and David Nau, Debbie and Mike Plaia, Ingrid Preston, Cameron Prow, Charla Ranch, Ann Robinson, Dusty Varburg, Kathy Whittington, Debbie Wiemeyer, Shelby Zacharias—my most heartfelt thanks.

Special thanks go to my grandmother, Faye, and parents, Albert and Georgia—though they have passed, I continue to feel their influence.

Additional thanks go to Janice M. Jefferson, editor, whose well-placed suggestions enhanced the clarity and beauty of the story.

Special appreciation goes to my beloved husband, Jonathan; and children, Gretchen and Joseph—you sustain and inspire me. My life and words are richer for the love we share.

Sharon Duerst

# RUNNING

*Orange tongues licked the sky. The fire crackled, filling the air with smoke and the smell of burned flesh. Frantically, a woman tried to push through the crowd but they held her back.*

*"My baby!" she screamed. "Do something!"*

*But they did nothing—only watched as the fire burned. Already it was too late. She dropped to the ground like a stone, and they left her sobbing.*

*Ay...ahuehuete...why devil take my sweetness...*

Mia's eyes snapped open. Her heart was pounding. She pushed back her tangled hair, struggled to get free of the down comforter, and stumbled from the bed to the windowed wall. Mia pulled back the drapery then opened the door. Stepping out onto the patio bricks still damp with night rain, she breathed.

A breeze lifted her hair and fluttered the leaves of a Japanese maple in the yard. Red and weeping, the tree reminded her of the distressing dream filled with fire and loss and so much pain.

Mia rushed back inside. Pulling on her robe as she moved quickly toward the kitchen, she tripped on the belt and stubbed her toe on the doorframe.

"Owww!" Mia whimpered as she limped to the cupboard for a mug. She reached for the coffee pot but her hand stopped mid-air; the pot was empty. Her brow furrowed. Tim always made the coffee before going to work—though lately he'd been going earlier and earlier, and it'd cooked down to sludge by the time she dragged herself from bed. But he always made it for her. Always. Until now.

Disturbed and shaking, Mia filled the coffeemaker. She watched as the amber brew began to drip then she glanced out the window at her neglected garden. Tim wasn't the only one letting something slip. Blooms on the Christmas rose hung from the thick dark foliage in wisps of shriveled brown, and the flower beds were still covered with soggy leaves from last fall.

Mia sighed and watched water dripping like falling tears from the wide bowl of the mossy fountain. The coffeemaker sputtered and gasped. Startled, she turned from the window. Mia poured sugar and milk into her mug and filled it with coffee then gulped down the burning liquid. Her mind filled again with frightening images.

*Whipped by the wind, the fire burned hot and fast,*
*sending curls of black smoke into the darkening sky.*

She scribbled the details of the dream onto a scrap of paper, but the words in her mind would not be quieted.

*I can do nothing...only cry...*

Mia began to cry. Tears fell from her eyes and blurred the ink that ran from the page in a river of blue. She blotted the paper but the ink smeared and more tears fell. Choking back her tears, she crumpled the page, and tossed it into the trash on her way to the shower. Stepping in before the water had warmed, Mia gasped.

*Ay...my heartbreak...is you...*

Hands braced against the marble tiles, Mia wept as the water poured down over her. "Why can't I just be happy?" she sobbed.

"Happiness is yours to find," her counselor had said at their last visit. "You won't find it outside yourself—not in a husband, not a career. Not even a baby. You must find your own sweetness, something to make you smile."

So many tears had fallen these past months. Now Mia's plaintive cries echoed in the large shower, "My heart hurts! I'm tired of being sad. But what can I do?"

*Grandmother say beauty steal heart...*

Suddenly Mia stopped crying. Maybe she could recapture Tim's attention. She drew a breath. Maybe romance could be rekindled. Maybe recapturing Tim's heart would help *her* heart heal. Mia drew another deep breath and grabbed up a loofah; she scrubbed at her skin as if disappointment, anger, and sadness could be washed away. She pumiced her feet, shampooed and conditioned her hair, shaved her legs and underarms, then lavished her skin with glistening almond oil—perhaps a smooth body could make their lovemaking, and their life, smooth. Mia drew another breath and stepped from the shower.

The heat lamp and fan scattered the steam like clouds in the wind. She dried with a plush cotton towel, wrapped her hair, and pulled on her terry-lined silk robe. Considering her reflection in the mirror, Mia forced a smile. "See? Better. Smile and feel better." But her words were as shaky as her brief smile.

Back in the kitchen, she glanced out the window. Tall white irises and lilies in the garden reached toward the sun just breaking through the clouds. Maybe that was all she had to do: reach for the warmth she needed. Mia poured another cup of steaming coffee and wandered to the living room. Light angling through the leaded glass windows illuminated dust on the glass tables. The wool rug was in need of vacuuming and the umbrella tree in a large Italian ceramic pot was pale and limp from lack of watering.

Sinking down on the sofa, Mia picked up a book. She thumbed through several short stories but could not settle her emotions enough to read. She shoved the book aside, gulped down the last of her coffee, and moved toward the kitchen. Glancing into the nursery as she passed, Mia suddenly halted. Surprised smiles were frozen on the faces of furry animals peering out from the shelves above the antique chest of drawers. Sunflowers and bumblebees dangled silently from the musical mobile above the crib. Wispy, white clouds lingered on the sky blue walls, and the sheepskin rug in front of the rocking chair was un-trampled. She entered the still room and went over to the crib. Her hands rested on the smooth, white rail.

Her eyes fell on the face of the brown bear. She reached for it and cradled the soft body in her arms. Her voice was barely more than a wavering whisper as she sang, "Mama's here, Mama's here, Mama's here, Mama's here..." A tear slipped down her cheek. Another and another fell.

*I cry and wait...*

"No," she sighed. "I've cried too much and waited too long. Now I...have to go on." Mia wiped her face. "No more crying. No more waiting for things I can't have." She put the bear down and placed a fleecy lamb beside it then pulled up a handmade quilt of soft, organic cotton. Pastel squares, bordered in flowers, were exquisitely embroidered with darling depictions of mothers and their young: foxes and squirrels, quail and ducks, skunks and tabby cats, doves and bluebirds. Bluebirds of happiness. Mia blinked back tears. The quilt had been purchased many months ago when she still had hope, when she still anticipated the joy of bringing forth a living, breathing form from her womb. That small sweetness would have changed everything.

*I pray...*

"No," Mia whispered, "no more praying either." She closed her eyes and a tear splashed out from her lashes. "Praying didn't make my dreams come true."

As a child, Mia had believed her heart's desires were only prayers away. Under a canopy of flowering cherry trees at the sanctuary of her school, she had prayed fervently: "Hail Mary... full of Grace...the Lord is with thee...Blessed art thou among women...Blessed is the fruit of thy womb..." She had stood before the concrete statue of the Virgin Mary and prayed for happiness to fill the empty ache inside her. And, looking up, Mia had felt something. But when she'd looked more carefully, Mia saw that Mary's dark eyes were unmoving and that her sweet smile did not waver. But the pink roses on Mary's pale feet had seemed somehow promising. Mia had wished then that the flowers were real—that Mary was real and alive, and that she listened.

But did Mary listen? Maybe no one listened. Not even God. Not then, not ever. And maybe Mia's wishes only scattered in the wind like the hope-filled poems she'd written on scraps of paper and placed at Mary's feet.

*Every wish…is hope…*

"Hope," she now whispered bitterly, "gets me nothing. No happiness comes from crying and waiting, or praying. It's up to me. I have to make my own happiness." Mia turned and closed the nursery door with a resounding thump.

Her bare feet slapped the hardwood floor as she moved quickly down the hall to the linen closet. Armed with fresh linens, she went to the master bedroom. Mia pulled off the comforter and dark winter sheets, then dressed the bed in white Egyptian cotton sheets edged in romantic eyelet and a creamy damask cover. Her hands smoothed down a few bumps. Extra pillows completed the look of a fluffy cloud on which to land. Spraying the bed with vanilla scent, she paused to breathe in the sweet aroma, and a sly smile spread across her face. "A woman can do more than issue fruit from her womb!"

Mia turned and headed into the kitchen to dash out a shopping list. "I will make *my* happiness another way!"

Determination in her movements, she went into the spacious master bathroom. While drying her long hair, Mia examined her dark roots in the vanity mirror and sighed loudly. She fussed with her hair: pulling it up into a clip, letting it down, making a messy ponytail, and finally just tucking it behind her ears. Eye cream and foundation dabbed on the dark circles under her eyes, she finished her makeup with shadow, liner, mascara, blusher and lipstick. Appraising the results in the mirror, she practiced an alluring smile.

*Grandmother say beauty steal heart…*

Mia blotted her long un-kissed mouth with a tissue.

*Why I no listen…*

Her smile faded; she turned from the mirror. Mia went into the closet and started dressing: first in a navy blue sweater and slacks, then a red blouse and black flare-legged jeans, then a rust-colored tweed jacket and brown pants. Dropping them to the wardrobe bench, she sighed. "I need something pretty."

She searched the closet again. "Aha!" Mia pulled the silk camisole, tan slacks, and petal-pink linen shirt from their hangers and dressed. She adjusted the collar and cuffs of the blouse and slid her feet into brown leather sandals with three-inch heels. With mischievous anticipation, Mia smiled as she pulled out a little black dinner dress; its thin straps crossing low in back would leave no doubt where she planned for the evening to lead.

After choosing a purse from a shelf of contenders, Mia tossed in a hairbrush, makeup bag, and wallet. She retrieved her keys from the dish on the hall table, and went out, closing the door behind her. The key turned in the lock with a solid thud.

The sun was high, and flowers bloomed in a medley of colors along the walkway. Mia paused to breathe in the moist, warm air. At last, at last, the long winter had passed. But as she moved through the shade of a towering Douglas fir, a chill swept over her. Mia hurried to the car and started the sputtering engine.

She let it idle several minutes before backing down the driveway and into the street. Steam rose from the wet pavement like breath and words flowed into her mind.

> *All my tears*
> *wash away to the distant tide*
> *and whispers on the wind*
> *call to my heart*

# PARIS

*I*t was only five miles to Portland's downtown, but the traffic was moving so slowly Mia barely traveled a mile in ten minutes. She craned her neck and looked for the cause of the congestion but could see nothing. Losing patience, she took an exit off the freeway and tried another route, but the winding side streets were no faster. Perhaps the "Rose City" was filling with tourists for the month long Rose Festival that'd been heavily advertised in nationwide travel magazines. Previously named America's "Most Livable City" and fifth in one magazine's list of "100 Fabulous Places," Portland was getting a big share of Oregon's tourist dollars. These late spring days of bright blue sky made a stunning backdrop for the snowy peaks, flowing rivers, and evergreen covered hills.

After forty minutes of driving, Mia reached downtown. Looking for parking, she circled several blocks, but all the street-level lots were full. She might have driven to her space in the dank and distant parking garage, but after a few more times around, she lucked into a space just being vacated at the curb. Mia parked and deposited coins into a parking meter. She checked her watch; already it was one o'clock. Quickly walking a half-dozen blocks, she came to a large, brick building and pushed open the door. Startled by people rushing out with coffee cups in hand, Mia glanced up at the sign in the window; the artisan co-op gallery that'd been there only months before had been replaced by a coffee shop. She went inside anyway and eased through a cluster of chatting customers.

"Help you?" Behind the counter, the spiky haired, pale faced, nose-studded, chin-pierced clerk rolled her eyes while waiting for Mia's slow response.

"Double-shot espresso with extra hot water, please."

"That *all* you want?"

Mia was fumbling with her wallet and looked up suddenly. "What?"

The girl sighed loudly and asked impatiently, "Just coffee?"

She nodded, moved to the back of the long narrow room, and waited. Sounds filled her ears: sputtering and whirling machines, newspapers rustling, phones ringing, patrons laughing and talking loudly. When her drink order was ready, Mia carried the cup over to a shelf and yanked off the top. She added multiple packs of sugar and a long pour of cream—so much that she could barely stir without spilling. Mia took a sip, tossed the wooden stick and sugar wrappers into the trash, and went out the door. When she glanced back through the window, she noticed the lid left behind on the shelf.

Just as Mia was passing a group of people gathered around a dog roped to a tree, a guy with a long skateboard under his arm stood up and bumped into Mia as he turned suddenly. Coffee spilled onto her shirt.

"GOSH!" Mia grumbled, but the skateboarder only shrugged and rolled away. She gulped down the rest of her coffee before continuing down the street. Becoming increasingly discouraged as she combed through numerous little shops, Mia searched and searched but found nothing captivating to create a mood of romance. Deflated but still determined, she returned empty-handed to her car. A slip of paper, along with a blob of smudgy white stuff, was on the windshield.

"Shit!" she sighed, stuffing the parking ticket into her purse.

Mia drove to her favorite "natural" foods store, but was edgy and irritable by the time she reached the crowded parking lot. Narrowly escaping a collision with a mini-van, she pulled into a space and hurried into the store.

Her cart squeaked and wobbled up and down the aisles as Mia hunted for items on the list she'd made earlier but now could not find in her purse. She debated at length over each selection as if the outcome of the evening would somehow be affected by brand choice or nutritional content. Many minutes later, she pushed her full cart toward the front of the store.

Lines at the registers inched forward. Mia nearly screamed, "Hurry up!" as the clerk phoned for price verifications, exchanged a leaky carton of milk, mishandled bulky items, and repacked bags for slow moving customers. But at last Mia was checked out. She hurried to her car, stuffed her grocery bags inside, and drove away reviewing the shopping list she found on the seat. Risotto: Parmesan, imported raw rice, dry white wine, onions, carrots, chicken stock, butter, and saffron. Chops: bread crumbs, mozzarella, oregano, and thick-cut pork chops. Artichokes. Hazelnut gelato. Wine. She'd forgotten the wine.

It would have been faster to go back to the grocery and endure the lines but Mia avoided that aggravation by driving out of her way to a wine shop to purchase Tim's favorite Pinot Noir.

He'd sampled it once in Paris, before they'd met, before he'd given up expensive vacations and an ever-changing array of women.

*He smile to me and I think of nothing else...only him...*

Mia smiled and also purchased one of *her* favorite wines; it was sweet and light like the first kisses Tim had given her so many years ago on the day they had married.

Distracted by these pleasant thoughts and details of meal preparation as she drove toward home, Mia barely noticed a bicyclist swerving over from the bike lane. She let off the gas just in time to avoid hitting him. Mia rolled down the window and yelled, "Stay where you belong!"

The bicyclist's fist shot into the air, fingers clenched tightly, save for one.

"Right back at you!" she yelled, but was shaking and nervously checked her rear view mirror as the bicyclist sped up behind her. When the traffic slowed, he passed her car without incident and she let out a long, loud sigh.

A few miles down the road, the traffic condensed and stopped, then inched toward a control light allowing cars to enter the freeway one by one. Mia checked the clock on the dash: 4:15. Where had the day gone? She'd be late getting dinner prepared. Her brow furrowed. Maybe Tim would be even later if he went to the gym after work as he often did. Her carefully prepared meal would be less than fabulous, if not ruined. She fumbled through her purse then dumped it out on the seat. Pawing through the pile, she searched but found no cell phone.

Mia smacked the steering wheel in frustration. But she soon had an idea and turned the car around, heading toward the gift shop they'd recently purchased fifteen miles southeast of Portland, in Oregon City. Tim had been going to work early and staying late: shouldering the renovation of this new space and also running the other store in her absence. Swallowing a hard lump of guilt, she whispered, "I'll make it up to you, Tim. I promise."

*He say he make me woman...his woman...*

Mia pulled into the parking lot of their new store and scanned the vehicles. Tim's car wasn't among them, nor was it parked at the curb out front. She frowned, checked her lipstick in the mirror, and stepped out of the car.

A flashing "OPEN" sign shined through the shop window. Mia paused, then pushed the glass door open and walked in.

"Oh, hi," Margo purred, looking up from a gleaming gold necklace she was placing on a leopard print velvet "neck" in the showcase.

Mia eyed the opulent displays. "The store looks beautiful!"

"It's been a bit rushed and crazy! Too bad you couldn't be here for opening day," Margo purred but her red lips closed suddenly. "Mia, I am so sorry! Really. I heard about your loss. It must have been terrible. I can't blame you for taking time for yourself!"

Mia blinked her glassy eyes and managed to ask, "How's it been doing?"

"The store? Oh, great! I'm giving it everything I've got," Margo boasted as she swept a black tress from the shoulder of the blue paisley polyester dress that covered her more than ample figure. "I've been calling into the radio stations with daily 'flashy' specials. And how do you like the flashing 'open' sign in the window? That was my idea to attract more customers! Soon there'll be so many we'll have to hire more new help!"

Mia's eyes turned suddenly toward the office.

"Did you know Oregon City was the first incorporated city west of the Mississippi and was once the state capital?"

Mia looked back at Margo. "I didn't. No."

"The waterfalls are just gorgeous! Our advertising campaign for the grand opening could be tied to a blue theme for the rivers. They meet here, you know."

Her attention had strayed again to the tinted window of the office. Mia's head whirled back around. "Who meets here?"

"The Willamette and Clackamas rivers."

"Oh," she stammered. "Is Tim here?"

"He's back at the downtown store," Margo replied abruptly.

"Oh. Sure," Mia managed to say as she eased toward the front door. "Just thought I'd stop by, while I was...out." Her hand found the handle, and she pulled the door open.

"Don't forget my ideas for the grand opening! We can make a big splash if you know what I mean!"

Mia nodded and hurried out to her car. Hands clamped to the wheel, she sped from the parking lot and whined to herself, "I should have stopped in to see him when I was downtown before." Tension inched down her spine with each passing minute as she wove through lines of slow traffic. The digital clock was glowing 5:25 when Mia finally pulled into the empty space next to Tim's car in the parking garage. Almost closing time. Perfect. With luck, there'd be no distracting customers or interrupting phone calls while she gave Tim an enticing preview of the night's possibilities.

*How I want him…*

Mia's feet quickly covered the blocks to the building. Her hands were shaking with anticipation as she unlocked the back door but her footsteps barely made a sound through the darkened storeroom and up the hall. Mia paused outside the office, drew a breath, and prepared a radiant smile. She took a step and glanced through the open doorway. Her eyes riveted to the scene inside.

Valerie was perched on the edge of the desk. Tim's back was to the doorway and his hands were on Valerie's hips. Valerie breathed something into Tim's ear. He responded with a throaty moan. Their lips met. The kiss deepened.

Mia did not utter a sound. Her heart pounded and her legs shook, but her eyes did not look away and her ears did not stop listening.

"I promise," Tim said brushing a long strand of blond hair from Valerie's young face. His hand moved to her flawless white neck. Their mouths met again. His arms pulled Valerie close and his hips pressed into the space of her skirt.

Repulsed, fighting panic and nausea, Mia spun around and stumbled forward, knocking over a glass statue in the showroom. She lifted the figure and hurled it away. The showcase cracked and shards of glass flew out, littering the dark floor like glittering stars.

Valerie's shrill screams punctuated the air.

Tim burst from the office yelling, "What are you doing?" He grabbed for Mia's arm as she passed him in the hallway.

She pushed him away, dshed out the door and down the street to her car. Mia jammed the key into the ignition and pressed the accelerator but the engine sputtered. She pressed the accelerator again and the car suddenly squealed backwards, nearly hitting Tim but he jumped out of the way. She kept going.

Mia looked back to see if he followed. He didn't. The traffic light turned red and pedestrians stepped out into the street. She slammed on the brakes. Her heart hammered in her chest and she took big gasps of air.

Another block was covered before flashing lights closed in behind her. Shaking, Mia pulled to the curb, but the police cruiser sped right on by.

She drove on as if in a trance, her car in tow behind other cars. Through neighborhoods and back downtown again she drove, but her mind dwelled on the shocking scene of Tim with Valerie. Her hands gripped the steering wheel, but they ached to slap Tim's handsome face, to bloody his adulterous lips and claw his eyes. Her heart pounded and her chest hurt as if crushed by an invisible weight.

Hours had passed when Mia discovered she was nearing the airport. She parked and walked toward the terminal, but people stared at her disheveled appearance. Her eyes were red from crying, and her cheeks were streaked with blood and tears. She ran from their prying looks.

*Mother say he want too much...*

Mia blinked back her tears.

*Why I no listen...*

After avoiding her parents for months, could she have just shown up in Austin and told them everything—every heartbreaking thing?

*I can say nothing to her...maybe she say what I do is
wrong...*

Mia's jaw was clenched tightly as she drove the freeways in the
direction of home, but as the turn-off neared, she started to cry
again and kept driving toward the coast. She would face the night
alone, alone with swelling waves rushing the shore. She would
walk in the sand, and the wind would blow, and her tears would
dry, and maybe then she would know what to do.

Towering fir trees and dense shrubs beside the road
formed a cocoon of darkness around the narrow highway. She
would have liked to have just stopped there on that road and
wrapped that darkness around her like a blanket to seal out the
cold, the heartache, the doubt.

It was long after sunset when Mia reached a deserted
beach, but the moon was shining brightly and glowing white
lines of surf rushed the shore again and again. Her ears listened
to the waves crashing, and words were in her mind.

*Maybe Mother say something more...words I no want
to hear...maybe sadness come with love...but I listen
only to him...sweet words he say to me...and I go with
him...*

How could everything have gone so wrong? These last months
were like a bad dream. This morning was a nightmare and today
that scene with Tim and Valerie was unbelievable! Mia drew in a
sudden breath. Of course! *All* of this was part of the nightmare! If
she went home, and went back to bed, and went back to sleep,
tomorrow she'd wake and everything would be different. There

would be no lost baby. No cheating husband. No ache in her heart like a piece of it had been torn away.

Mia blinked back tears of relief. Waves rolled onto the shore; water slid back into the ocean. She drew another breath and started the car. She'd go back home; she'd go back to bed. She'd call Tim to tell him she was on her way. A few miles up the road near a dilapidated market, Mia stopped next to a phone booth. Dialing her home number, she waited for Tim to answer, to tell her everything was fine, to tell her he waited for her, wanted her…but the machine answered with his cool, recorded voice. Tears stung her eyes. This was not a dream. This was her life. Mia growled a message into the phone, "I'll be in *touch* with *you* when I'm ready!"

Her hand slammed the receiver into the cradle several times then she turned from the booth, leaned over a filthy waste can chained to a pole, and vomited.

Mia returned to her car and an hour later was on the outskirts of Portland.

Golden lights streamed from windows of houses where families gathered around tables and televisions. Mothers, fathers, children, aunts, uncles, grandparents spending time together. Families. Friends. She had none of that. She was alone in a car heading nowhere.

# SPLIT

*L*ike a mannequin propped on the seat for looks—looks Tim once said he would never tire of—Mia drove through neighborhoods, onto the freeway, into industrial areas and back to the suburbs. Her mind returned again and again to the sight of Tim with his hands on Valerie, his lips on Valerie, his hips all too familiar with Valerie.

It was late; she was driving mindlessly, her car tailing other cars across a bridge over the Columbia River into Washington. Seattle was several hours north: it was a beautiful city near water, like Portland. And beyond Seattle was Vancouver, British Columbia. Another stunningly gorgeous city on water—but in another country. Would she ever go to another country? Mia sighed. Perhaps someday, not now. She turned onto an exit to the east, away from city lights, away from Tim, away from her empty house and the business where she had worked herself into exhaustion—and for what?

*Everything I give for him...*

The freeway narrowed to a rural highway. White fog clung to the forested hills of the Cascade Range and the gray Columbia cut through the mountains like a blade of steel. Her tears rained down. Shivering, Mia turned on the heat but the windshield fogged. She gripped the steering wheel with one hand and was swiping the glass with a soggy tissue when a strong gust of wind pushed the car toward a dented guardrail.

Mia pulled hard on the wheel, and the car headed toward an embankment on the opposite side of the road. Somehow she managed to keep it on the pavement and drove on, but she could not stop shaking. Her mind began spinning images of danger around every curve. Curves in the road. Curves on the desk.

"I was Tim's woman. His 'Italian Beauty'," Mia cried. "I gave everything for him, our future. How could he do this to me? How could he?" she sobbed.

Just ahead, Beacon Rock jutted 850 feet above the river. Dark and imposing, it had been a guide for travelers for hundreds of years. If Mia had been strong like that basalt, could she have been a navigation point keeping Tim on the right course?

Tim had taken Valerie into his arms and kissed her and pressed his body against her. Valerie with the fresh face, blue eyes and blond hair like his.

Mia had tried so hard for so many years. And yes she had recently been in a slump, but just today she had vowed to ignite a fire in Tim. Now she seethed in anger and wished he would *burn* in his desire! That would teach him not to stray. No one would want him with a scarred face! Horrified, Mia gasped and suddenly turned the car into a wide pull out. She opened the door, and vomited on the ground. Rain was drumming down. She climbed out and stood in the downpour with her head tipped back, her mouth open—letting the rainwater rinse out the bitter taste she then spat on the ground.

Mia stomped back to the car, grabbed the sacks of groceries and hurled item after item into a large metal garbage can: thud, thud, thud, thud.

"There's your dinner, Tim! Cheater. Liar. You said I was all you'd ever want, all the family you ever needed!" She pounded the bottles of wine against the inside of the trash can until they broke. "Why didn't you help me, Tim?" Mia sobbed, "I needed you and you did nothing—nothing but help yourself to someone else!"

Her clothes soaked through with rain and tears, Mia shuddered and drove farther from Portland, farther from their shop filled with baubles and gems and sparkling gifts given with hope and love, respect and appreciation. Mia had none of that; she had only the car and the road.

Signs for the Columbia River Gorge National Scenic Area, Bonneville Dam, the Bridge of The Gods, tidy upbeat Stevenson, and White Salmon glowed brightly in the headlights. Deserted-looking hamlets clung to the windswept edge of the dark river. Rain showered down and rocks slid from muddy hillsides. Near Wind Mountain, a boulder rolled into the road. Too late to swerve, the car struck the rock with a loud thump but kept going. If Mia had swerved, would the car have gone through the rusty guardrail and plunged into the river? Would she finally have been filled with something other than longing?

Wind gusted and the sky ahead cleared. The moon emerged, shining down on angled hillsides that reached like fingers into the river. Inside short tunnels carved through those rocky hillsides, the wind was quiet but was it Mia's heart she heard pounding loudly?

Further east, the hillsides flattened out where the water of the Columbia had once flowed. A metal bridge and a massive hydroelectric dam spanned the river at The Dalles, but she did not cross over there to Oregon. Mia shuddered: the dam's monstrous concrete gates were clenched tight like teeth holding back the water.

Celilo Falls had once thundered over nearby rocky ledges. Salmon had jumped those falls and Native Americans had dipped their nets from wooden fishing decks for hundreds, if not thousands, of years. But now the falls were covered by the back waters of the dam. Some said, during the construction of the dam, the Army Corps of Engineers had dynamited those rock ledges. The river was now quiet, but wind whispered over the water in ghostly gasps.

The sloping hills beside the river were bare here except for sagebrush, bunchgrass, and occasional trees. Perhaps in the dry climate east of the Cascade Range, with the wind blowing so hard and so often, nothing grew except where planted and tended like new vineyards perched on the hillsides. Who tended those plots and nurtured those delicate fruits to ripening? Who touched that sweet flesh and turned it into lovely wine? "Tim loves wine," Mia sobbed. "Wine and pretty things."

Her clothes had dried with the heat turned to high and now her tears dried in streaks on Mia's face. As she passed the Maryhill Museum of Art, she peered across the shadowy grounds to the concrete mansion silhouetted eerily on the bluff above the river. A piercing cry rang out. Mia gasped and goose flesh rose on her arms. Maybe it was only a peahen calling at the lights of her car, but she pressed the accelerator to the floor and raced away.

*So far from home…I cry…*

*A* fork in the road soon forced a decision: north into central Washington; or south, the direction of Texas. She drove downhill toward the Samuel Hill Memorial Bridge that arched over the dark water of the Columbia River.

Mia had wanted to be arching with desire under her husband's hands. But it was too late. Too late. Tim's hands were on someone else.

Stopping the car halfway across the bridge, she yanked the wedding ring from her finger and threw it out into the depths of the dark water. Perhaps it would be swallowed like a lure by some ancient fish—a sturgeon with leathery white skin and fins like wings.

Across the bridge, a truck stop restaurant and gas stations were crowding the junction of the highway and the I-84 freeway. Bright lights flashed on a sign: JIM'S QUICK MART. The sign reminded her of Tim—Tim who had taken Valerie in his arms and moved his body against her like a promise. Repelled, Mia turned the wheel and entered the freeway heading east.

Hands clasped to the steering wheel, she hovered in the windless void behind a double-trailer truck driving to somewhere across a sleeping nation. Mia's head bobbed in weariness; she rubbed her neck. Unable to maintain the high freeway speed, she veered onto an off ramp, across railroad tracks, and through a dark hamlet squeezed onto a steep hillside beside the river. She passed old cottages, mobile homes, and several businesses. Turning south again, Mia followed a narrow road set in a ravine. Away from the river, between the hills of earth, it was windless and quiet except for some sound thumping loudly. Was it her heart beating too hard? A train rumbling down the tracks?

Mia pushed down the gas pedal; the thumping grew louder, but the car did not accelerate. She pressed the accelerator to the floor, but the car slowed to a crawl. All she could do was steer toward the narrow shoulder and stop.

Leaning her head against the steering wheel, Mia cried, "Mother of God! Why is all this happening to me?"

There was no answer.

"Mary, do you listen? God? Can you help me? Please," she begged.

There was only silence.

Mia got out of the car. She started up the road in the darkness but stumbled in a pothole and fell hard to the pavement. She rubbed her scraped and stinging hands on her shirt; her knee bled through her pants in a dark, sticky spot. Limping, Mia left the road and crossed a dry creek bed. Lashing branches caught her clothes and scratched her skin. She pushed through to a thick patch of tall vegetation that stung like electric fire.

*I can do nothing...only cry...*

"Stinging nettles?" Mia sobbed and scrambled out of the ravine.

The hillside was steep; rocks and sand slipped beneath her feet but Mia grabbed at clumps of grass and brush for support, and climbed. A barbed wire fence snagged her shirt. She cursed and cried in frustration then yanked it free and moved on.

When finally reaching the top of the hill, Mia gasped for breath. Down below, lights of the John Day Dam upriver and cars on the freeway blurred in her tears. She cried in exhaustion. She could do nothing more. She wavered there at the edge. Maybe it was the weight of her heart pulling her down, nearly causing her to topple over the brink, but a gust of wind pushed her back. Her body was heavy, heavy as stone. She sank down,

down into strange dreams with words and images stretching like roots to a distant land.

> *Ahuehuete...ay ahuehuete...why you let me dream...*
> *why you listen to my wishes...why you say nothing...*
> *why you no tell...maybe some dream come true...but*
> *then devil take everything...every sweet thing...and*
> *leave me...alone...*

# CHAIN

*M*ia woke in confusion. She studied the abrasions on her palms. Her hands were shaking as she pushed back the covers and gaped uncomprehendingly at her soiled clothes. A chill went down her spine. She glanced up to see a large man standing only ten feet away.

Her muscles tensed, ready to fight or bolt for the door, but the man only moved toward the kitchen in the corner of the one-room cabin. She stared at his back and the thick black pony tail hanging between his wide shoulders. He turned and moved toward her with something in his hand. Mia pulled the covers to her neck.

"Hungry?"

She could not find her voice.

He set a plate of food next to her on the bed and crossed the room to a large chair where he sat down and picked up a book. Mia's eyes searched the walls for an exit, but the only door was near his chair. She glanced down at the plate of food and was considering the eggs when a loud rumbling outside approached the cabin.

The man got up and went out, leaving the door slightly ajar. She listened to his footsteps crossing a wooden porch. A vehicle pulled around to the back of the cabin. Metal scraped and chains rattled. She waited. And listened.

Mia sneaked toward the door and had only just reached it when the hood of a truck suddenly rounded the corner of the cabin. The screen door snapped closed as she bounded back to the bed and quickly pulled up the covers.

The man's footsteps sounded on the porch, and he came through the door. "Where were y' headed?"

She watched him move closer.

"Last night?"

Her voice came in barely a whisper, "South."

He raised an eyebrow.

Her heart beat loudly in her ears.

He looked as if he would ask something else, but then he pointed to a partitioned corner. "Towels're under the sink."

Mia waited until he went outside again before tiptoeing to the bathroom, closing the door and quietly locking it. She moved to the window of frosted glass, slid it open, and peered out. He was sitting on the porch. Mia quietly closed the window. She undressed, scrubbed the stains from her clothes and hung them to dry in front of a space heater turned to high. She had just stepped into the old porcelain tub when the man's voice sounded outside the bathroom door. "Okay, in there?"

She peeked around the shower curtain at the door knob, but it didn't move. When she heard him return to the porch, Mia lathered with a hard cake of lemony soap and washed the blood and dirt from her body. She dried off with a stiff, line-dried towel. The scrapes and bruises were hurting and bled a little but she gently patted them dry with tissue. Shivering, Mia slipped on her damp clothes and glanced into the small mirror. She collapsed down on the toilet lid and buried her head in her arms. A dark fan of wetness spread from her hair across the fabric of her pants and tears fell from her eyes.

*I can do nothing...*

"Find what y' need?"

Mia sucked in her breath and waited. When the man went outside again to the porch, she sneaked from the bathroom. Quickly searching the room, Mia didn't find a phone but she did find her sandals under the bed. She slipped them on and moved quietly across the room to peer out through the screen door. The man was sitting just a few feet away, his hand motioning to her.

Reluctantly Mia went out. She sat down stiffly at the edge of the porch. Her sandaled feet plopped onto the ground and powdery dirt puffed up in a whisper.

The man pushed a cup toward her.

Mia did not look at him, but she picked up the cup and breathed in the warm aroma of strong coffee.

"Not as good as Portland brew."

Her head snapped around to look at him. He was holding her purse. When Mia grabbed for it, the cup fell from her hand. Coffee ran off the porch and disappeared into the soft dirt.

"Checked y'r license."

"Oh," she breathed, staring down at her purse as if she could see through the leather to the contents inside. What else had he checked? Maybe he helped himself to her credit cards. She could report them stolen if she could get to a phone. If she had her cell phone she could've called for help, but so far from a sizeable town the service would have been questionable anyway. A sickening wave of worry swept over her.

The man went inside with her empty cup, and Mia hurriedly looked through her wallet but found nothing missing.

He returned with fresh coffee and set the cup down. "Where'd y' get the name?"

She looked up at him, noticing his dark brown eyes, and whispered, "Mia?"

He shook his head. "Maria Isabel Angelina Casinelli Edwards."

"Family names. But..." she picked up the cup... "I go by Mia. Edwards."

"Y' married?"

She nodded, but the frown on her face was hidden behind the cup as she took a long drink of the reviving coffee.

"No ring."

Mia glanced down at the bare finger where her heavy diamond-studded filigree band had been. "I threw it out the window last night," she said, struggling to keep her voice from wavering.

His eyes were on her face.

"What's *your* name?" she barked accusingly.

"Gerald," he replied, his voice calm and slow. "Call me G. if y' like."

She looked away and drank down the rest of the coffee.

He went inside and came back a few moments later with a full cup he set beside her. Gerald pulled up a sit against the cabin. "Mechanic in town's not good. Had y'r car towed here. I'll fix it."

"Oh," she sighed, blinking back stinging tears. Now she couldn't leave.

"I heard it coming up the road last night. Followed y' up the hill."

She looked over at him.

"Y' almost went over the edge up there. That y'r plan?"

"No! I was just driving. My husband..." Mia stammered, her eyes searching his face. "I wanted to...surprise him...with a special dinner." She took a drink, and a breath, and then the story spilled from her mouth as if the coffee was truth serum, as if she could not stop the flow of words.

Tears rolled down her cheeks, but Mia wiped them away and kept talking, telling this Gerald everything. Finally she did have to stop and bolt for the bathroom.

He was walking down the driveway when Mia came out. She might have darted around the corner of the cabin but Gerald turned, and his hand motioned for her to follow. She went with him down the road and up a steep hillside. Her muscles ached and several times she stumbled, but Mia kept going until they reached the summit.

The river below stretched out in a band of flat water like a ribbon in a child's crayon picture. Faintly green, rounded hills tumbled down from a sky impossibly blue.

How slowly time moved. Wind had worn away mountains, and water had carved a channel through the rock to make a path to the ocean. Her problems were meaningless to this landscape. And she was so very small.

Fluffy clouds were pushed across the sky. Like a hand, a gust of wind forced Mia back and she sat down abruptly. She glanced around; Gerald was sitting cross-legged on the ground a short distance away. She watched as he tossed twigs and pebbles into a pile. Was that all he meant to do up there?

Mia lay back with her arms folded under her head. The wind, and traffic on the freeway below, roared in her ears like an ocean tide. The sky was swaying. Or maybe it was only the earth turning, spinning her around and around like a spot on a swirling sand picture. Closing her eyes, the warm sun on her face, she drifted off.

A hand smoothed back a wayward strand of her hair. Soft lips brushed against her skin and her body moved with the touch. Heat rushed through her and tears fled from her eyes. The world spun around and shards of crystal flew through the air. A cry rang out.

*He make me feel something...*

Startled, Mia sat up and looked around. Clouds filling the sky blocked the sun like a thick blanket. Gerald was sitting where he'd been before, but the pile of pebbles and twigs was now larger. She fled down the hill to the cabin, soaked a cloth in cold water and pressed it to her burning cheeks.

When she came out, Gerald brought her a plate of cinnamon toast; the smell of warm butter and sugar wafted in the air. He was standing close—close enough to see a new tear threatening to break over the brim of her eye. But Gerald said nothing, and he only set the plate on the table and went out the door, leaving her alone.

Mia did not eat. She went to the bed and climbed under the covers. She looked out the small window on the wall next to the bed. Tiny stars were appearing in the darkening sky. Maybe those first stars were actually planets. Maybe wishes made on planets did not come true. Not ever. She drew a breath, and sighed.

Across the room, the river stones at the base of the woodstove looked pretty in the soft light from the front window; colorful, hardbound books filled tall bookshelves nearby. Maybe there was some book Mia would like to read—if only she could keep her eyes open, but they were too heavy. Her hands smoothed back the bedcover. Her fingers traced swirling stitches through faded fields of yellow, red, and blue on a black background as dark as night. Around and around she followed the lines. Her eyes closed.

*How I want him…*

# WHEATEAR

Filled with late afternoon sunlight, the room was warm and smelled of coffee when Mia opened her eyes. She watched Gerald chop zucchini and tomatoes he put on to cook. He started grilling sandwiches and when he turned to retrieve a spatula, he noticed her looking. "Y'always sleep so much?"

Mia only looked back at him.

"Hungry?"

She shrugged a shoulder.

He pointed at the coffee pot. "Fresh."

Mia pushed her hair from her face, got up, and fixed a cup. When the soup was ready they sat down at the table and began eating. Warm cheese oozed out from between slices of the browned oatmeal bread. She sighed, "I could live on cheese."

"Thought only coffee."

"Coffee and cheese. Bread. And pizza," Mia said with a smile.

Gerald chuckled, "Gourmet or take-out?"

"Any. But I especially love homemade with fresh mozzarella, tomato, and basil. What kind do you eat?"

"Frozen." Gerald licked his fingers as he finished his sandwich.

"No pizza parlor nearby is there?"

"Nope."

"You must drive a long way to work."

Gerald raised a shoulder. "I worked at the aluminum plant across the river a few years. Now I do odd jobs, construction and clean up. Have to drive a bit, but it's not bad, except for the price of gas."

Mia nodded, swallowing her last bite of soup. "Doesn't sound like much fun."

"Hobbies are fun," he offered.

She eyed his muscular arms. "What hobbies do you like? Weightlifting?"

Shaking his head, Gerald scowled as he got up from the table. "Refinishing and restoring. I'll show y'." He carried their empty dishes to the sink while Mia put on her sandals. She followed him outside to a metal building where he pulled back a rusty hasp and pushed open a large door that squealed loudly. A flip of a switch brought fluorescent lights to flicker overhead, illuminating a room full of wood furniture.

Her hand glided over the surface of a chest of drawers. "Did you do this?"

He nodded, satisfaction showing on his face. "Took a while."

"Beautiful," Mia exclaimed. "Where do you get the furniture?"

"Yard sales, junk shops, estate sales," he explained.

"Oh, sure."

He moved toward her, his hand reaching out to switch off the light on the wall behind her. "Y' don't salvage?"

She shook her head and looked up at him. "Maybe I will… sometime."

They went out and Gerald showed her a small orchard of fruit trees: plum, apricot, cherry, and apple. "They're ugly apples, but pure heaven inside. Especially good in Brown Betty."

"I've never heard of that. How is it made?" She didn't ask if it was a Native American dish, but she wondered.

"Break up dry bread, add butter, milk, sugar or honey, apples, raisins, cinnamon and bake it all." He licked his full lips, "Soft and sweet; good warm with milk on top."

"Mmm, I like anything with cinnamon," Mia replied smiling. Her eyes scanned a row of rusting cars and trucks: some were missing doors, hoods, engines, or upholstery. "Saving those for scrap metal?"

Gerald shook his head. "Restoring."

"I've never known anyone that does that; looks like you'll have decades of work."

"Been needing doing for decades, that's for sure," he chuckled.

They were quiet a long time then. Mia sat in a metal lawn chair with frayed plastic webbing while Gerald methodically weeded and watered his vegetable garden where green fingers of growth were poking through the soil in neat rows. Last year's giant sunflowers leaning against a fence of woven wire looked like lanky guards with large, drooping heads.

When the sun fell down behind the hills and the sky paled, Gerald finished in the garden and came over. He squatted with one knee on the ground while he pulled dandelions from the sparse grass. "Y' garden?"

She nodded.

"Do y' have a favorite plant?"

"If I had to pick one I'd say my Christmas rose. I like the blushing edges of the white flowers, and that it blooms in winter."

"*Helleborus niger*. It's poisonous."

"Is it?" Mia's eyebrows raised in surprise.

He nodded gravely. "Causes heart palpitations, respiratory failure, convulsions. It was long used as a medicinal for mental illness, as an abortant, or to hasten death like hemlock and nightshade."

She shuddered. Night shade. Was there shade at night? She looked up to the sky where lights were beginning to shine: the moon, a few stars, and Venus. Venus—a symbol of love, fertility, and the Virgin Mary. Mia sighed inwardly. Love and fertility had failed her.

*I pray* La Virgen *listen...*

Mia blinked back tears and turned her head. Gerald followed the direction of her gaze to a tall tree with grayish bark near the shed. "Honey locust. White clusters of flowers smell heavenly in summer."

"Reminds me of something I've dreamed..." she mused. "A tree with craggy bark and spreading branches so wide it could shelter a family."

"Mother of all trees." Gerald stood to turn on the hose and rinsed his hands.

"Yes," she sighed.

Stings of mosquitoes forced Mia to retreat to the cabin. She soaked a while in the old porcelain tub. The sweet citrus soap helped ease the irritations, but later, as she tried to get to sleep, she scratched the bites. They swelled and itched more. Mia wrestled with the covers and whined to herself, "Why does everything hurt so much?" Painful thoughts of Tim with Valerie intruded and kept her awake for hours.

Angry and tired when she woke late in the morning, Mia gulped down a coffee. She grabbed her purse, dug around for paper, jotted a few choice words to Tim on the back of a credit card statement and shoved it back into the envelope. Her feet pounded the pavement down to Rufus, and she sent the forwarded bill off with a smile. Her satisfaction was brief, however, for the trek back up the hill was hot and she winced as blisters rose on her sandaled feet.

Gerald would fix her car once the ordered parts arrived, perhaps in a week or two, but Mia was in no hurry to return home. The Cascade Range standing between here and there seemed as impassable as the situation with Tim.

While Gerald was away at work, Mia filled the hours with self-assigned chores. Lined up, one after another like words of a poem, knots in a string, or beads on a rosary, they gave her a focus. When finished with all she could find to do, Mia climbed the hillside. Up there, on the screen of bare blue sky, it was easy to review her life.

All fifteen years in Oregon, Mia had poured her energy into long days at the store, renovating the house, and laboring in the garden. Work was the only thing to dull a burning ache inside her that could not be extinguished. She ached for some absent thing. Deciding it was a baby she needed, Mia pushed at Tim to start a family. He resisted but eventually yielded saying she could go ahead and have a baby if that was what she must do. After months and months of trying, she conceived, only to lose the pregnancy again and again. After the first trimester this last time, Mia had decorated the nursery and filled it with every item a baby could possibly need. Each purchase shored up her shaky hope and confidence. But this baby, too, was lost, and doctors said it was unlikely Mia would ever carry to term.

Devastated, unable to make herself return to work, she had moped about the house with bitterness like a heavy stone inside her. Nothing helped. Not counseling. Not exercise, television, or prayer. Mia tried to find solace in reading stories of how other women coped and recovered, but she could not seem to rally. She might have lingered longer in that limbo, but the frightening dream forced her to take action: Mia did not want to be like the devastated and sad woman in the dream. But it was too late.

Many tears fell from Mia's eyes up on that hillside, and when she could cry no more, she ran down the hill to the cabin, and stayed.

*G*erald barbecued one night on a charcoal grill he'd fashioned from a large can topped with a metal grate. He coated chicken in sweet and spicy sauce made from his home-grown tomatoes. The smell of it cooking over the coals was incredible! Mia sliced cucumbers from Gerald's garden, and prepared macaroni salad. Plates on their laps, they sat on the porch, and ate enthusiastically.

"Y' larned bar-bee-cue real good," Mia said in exaggerated Texas drawl. She finished a thigh and licked her fingers. "The smoky flavor from them apple wood chips is just delicious! Mmm."

Gerald smiled and dropped a bare bone to his plate. "Good for y'."

"What?"

"Tearing meat from the bone with y'r teeth."

Mia laughed and kept eating. When she had cleared her plate, she wiped a splotch of sauce from her cheek, and groaned, "You made it too good! I ate too much!"

He chuckled affably.

Mia set her plate aside and leaned back on her hands. Kicking the dusty earth beneath her feet, she let out a sigh. "Don't you ever get bored living out here—so cut off from the rest of the world?"

Gerald wiped his hands on a paper towel. "I read, listen to radio."

"Wouldn't you like to go somewhere fun? Or watch something on television?"

"Like what?"

She shrugged. "Sports, documentaries, nature shows?"

"Never developed the habit."

"How about movies? Don't you like movies? I'd love to see a movie. Even one I've seen before. There are so many good ones," she sighed. "Like *Pleasantville!*"

"What do y' like about it?"

"The story! How they struggled to find the color and passion that was missing in their lives!" She glanced over at him; his deep brown eyes were looking back. Her cheeks warmed. She took their empty plates inside and began washing the dishes.

Gerald helped finish up the dishes then he sat down to read.

Mia plopped down at the table. She ran her finger through a layer of dust on an old camera he'd unearthed from a box beneath the bed earlier in the day. She sighed.

He lowered his book and turned to look at her. "That camera's like me: simple."

"That's one word," she said dryly but his gaze was steady and she looked away.

"What do y' do for recreation besides watching movies?"

Mia shrugged. "The usual: shopping, reading…"

He raised an eyebrow. "Got lots of friends, do the social scene?"

"Working takes most of my energy," she replied slowly. "I see a lot of people, but I'm not close to anyone really."

"Got hobbies?"

"Well, I…" Mia fumbled for a response. "I garden."

"Plant seeds?"

"No. But I take care of everything." She looked down, her fingers poking at the tear in her linen shirt where it'd snagged on the barbed wire.

"Creating is good. It's restorative." Gerald stood up. His eyes were on her hands that still fiddled with the hole in her shirt. He went to a cupboard and brought back a needle, thread, and scissors. "Y' sew?"

"I can, I think." She unwound a length of thread, poked it through the eye of the needle, and tied a knot.

"Something to drink?"

Beginning to stitch, she mumbled, "Sure."

Gerald filled glasses with ice, rum, and cola. He brought them over and sat down opposite her at the table. He took a long drink.

Mia paused in her sewing to take a sip. "I'm surprised you drink this."

"Men like me only drink beer or whiskey from a bottle?"

His tone hinted at something, but she ignored the implication and finished stitching. She took another drink from her sweating glass.

"Let's see y'r handiwork."

Her cheeks warmed but she raised her shirt so he could see the crude stitching. "It's not very good."

"Not so bad."

"Mother tried to teach me," she sighed. "But I thought I had better things to do."

Gerald switched on an old radio atop the refrigerator and found a station playing oldies from the 60s, 70s and 80s. Mia listened to the music. She took a drink, savoring the sweetness and sting of alcohol in her mouth. Sweetness. She had planned to make sweetness with Tim.

Now she was here. Gerald had carried her to safety and he let her stay, but he asked nothing of her. Was there nothing he wanted? Was there nothing *she* wanted?

Her body answered with a rush of warming to delicate places. She gulped down the last of her icy drink.

Gerald fixed more drinks, returned to his chair and resumed reading.

Mia stared at his thick pony tail hanging over the back of his chair. He was nothing like her well-dressed, athletically-driven husband, or anyone else she would have wanted any other time, anywhere else. But Gerald had a steady presence. And when he spoke, the deep tone of his voice made her ache for something she could not, would not, name. She examined the skin exposed on his neck; it was tan and smooth. If his head turned, if their eyes met, if his gaze was welcoming, she might go over to him. Her lips might fall onto his. Her mouth might open, tasting his sweet breath.

But his head did not turn, and she looked away. Mia placed her lips on the glass instead and gulped down the sweet liquid. A deep voice and the heartbreaking lyrics of a song playing on the radio seemed to reach inside her. Mia blinked back tears, and without meaning to, she sighed aloud, "I wish I could make things different."

"Haven't y' already?"

Mia stammered, "I was just...driving. I'm just waiting... for my car to be fixed."

Gerald turned in his chair, and his eyes rested on her face. "That all y're doin'?"

She lifted her glass to her mouth. He couldn't see the longing in her eyes or the desire coursing through her body like a swooning dance. He couldn't hear her mind's questions: did he dance, or want to do something more with that muscular body of his?

Mia pushed herself up from the table and her head spun a little. She stumbled over to the bed, curled up, and rode the swaying mattress into heavy dream-filled sleep.

*How I ache for him...*

*L*ate in the morning, light was pouring in through the small window by the bed and it was warm, very warm, but Mia buried her head beneath the covers. Her heart hurt and her eyes burned. She cried pitifully until she could cry no more, then she wiped away her tears, and got up. While fresh coffee brewed, Mia contemplated a note Gerald had left on the table. It said simply: "Feel better. G." A lump was in her throat as she whispered, "G."

What would make her feel better?

Mia looked down at her shirt. She went to a drawer in the kitchen and pulled out a knife. She slowly worked the tip of the knife through the threads she'd previously sewn. Mia fixed a cup of coffee, gulped it down thirstily, fixed another, and settled down at the table with the needle and thread. She slowly sewed a chain stitch circling the hole and an artful web of stitches that looked very much like the branches of a tree.

Encouraged, Mia downed the cold coffee and went to the kitchen. She searched the well-stocked cupboards for ingredients. Finding all she needed, Mia began making bread as her Grandmother Angelina had taught her. She measured flour into a large shallow bowl and sprinkled salt around the periphery. Then she made a hollow in the middle of the flour where she poured in softened yeast, melted butter, two beaten eggs, and a dab of scalded milk. Gently mixing it all together with her hands, she kneaded the soft dough into a smooth mound. Mia placed the dough inside an oiled ceramic bowl as aged and crinkled as a grandmother. She turned the mound to coat its surface with oil and gave a loving pat to the dough as a mother would pat a baby's behind. She covered the bowl with an old, white cotton cloth and left the dough to rise.

Outside in Gerald's garden, Mia cut two small heads of escarole, which she washed, steamed, drained, and cooled. She browned garlic, onion, and celery in butter, then added cannellini beans and chicken stock to the heavy pot. On a whim, she peeled a carrot, chopped it, and tossed it into the pot.

Mia wiped sweat from her brow. She fixed a glass of iced coffee and drank it down. The creamy liquid cooled her stomach. As she chopped the escarole and tossed the tender leaves into the pot, her mind filled with childhood memories of being home in the kitchen in Austin.

*"Do all Italians eat escarole soup? Is that Papa's favorite? How do you make it?"*

*Sighing heavily, Victoria answered, "Quiet. Watch me. Beat the eggs, beat in the cheese and gradually add the mixture to the soup."*

*"What if you add it too fast?"*

*Victoria shook her head. "Questions will not make soup. Wait. Watch. Listen."*

*"But what if..."*

*"Mia! Always questions, too many questions! You must wait for answers," Victoria snapped.*

*Stung, Mia stormed to her backyard tree swing, kicked her feet in the air, and pumped her legs as hard as she could.*

*A*lone in Gerald's kitchen now, Mia stirred the soup slowly, her eyes watching the escarole leaves go around and around in the broth. She whined to the soup, "Why is it wrong to wonder and ask questions? Why must I always wait for answers?"

A sudden wave of nausea washed over her.

Mia turned off the soup and rushed from the hot cabin. She walked out to the road, placing one foot in front of the other and pulling in breaths of air. Each step, each breath brought a sense of calm and her stomach settled.

A yard sale at an old farm property attracted her attention.

Plywood boards on saw horses displayed glass dishes and scratched kitchen pans, ugly lamps with misshapen shades, dog-eared books, and outdated record albums. Mia eyed them all. She picked through a rack of clothes and found several things that might work for her and also a pair of worn but comfortable athletic shoes. Moving toward a dilapidated card table where a skinny teenager was manning the money box, she noticed a blue Schwinn bicycle leaning against a shed. "$25.00" was scrawled on cardboard taped through the spokes. She examined the bike that appeared to be in working order.

"New tubes, pumped 'em up myself. Go for a spin," the kid suggested.

Mia dug in her pocket and pulled out a $20.00 bill. "Would you take this for the clothes, shoes, and the bike? It's all I have with me."

He shrugged, placed the bill in the metal box, and stuffed her items into a plastic bag. Looking out to the road, he said, "I could load the bike into your car for you."

"I'll ride it. But thank you." Mia wrapped the plastic bag around the handlebars. She pedaled shakily down the driveway and turned onto the road. Momentum gathered on the hill and taking a corner too fast, she nearly skidded in the gravel beside the pavement. But laughing with a mixture of fear and elation, she kept going.

Back at the cabin, Mia put the bread in the oven to bake. She wiped down the countertop, and was washing dishes when Gerald came in from work.

He took a big whiff of air. "Mmm! Bread?"

Mia pushed back a tendril of damp hair. "Did you see what I bought? Out front?"

"Gonna ride it?"

"Already did," she grinned. "And it was so much fun!"

He smiled and held out a bag. "Brought y' something to help sort things out."

"What *things* would that be?" she snapped, barely glancing into the bag before placing it atop the refrigerator. "Thanks," she muttered ungraciously.

A shadow crossed his face, but he only turned and went to wash up.

Mia removed the bread from the oven and cut the steaming loaf into thick slices. She ladled the re-heated escarole soup into bowls, sprinkled Parmesan cheese on top, and brought it all to the table with butter and milk.

They ate. When Gerald finished his soup, he said enthusiastically, "Good!"

"Like it?" Mia sounded grumpy and tired.

"Yeah!" He got up and helped himself to another bowl. "Y' like to cook?"

"I'm Italian," she answered, gesturing with upturned palm as if that was explanation enough.

"But do y' like to cook?"

She shrugged. "It's expected. Every Italian woman has to cook; bake; take care of the house, the husband, the family."

"But do y' *like* doing it all?"

Mia pushed crumbs around on her plate. "I never wondered about that but I guess I do. Cooking anyway. Especially for an appreciative diner." She looked up at him.

"Oh, I'm that." Gerald squirted a dribble of honey onto a crust of bread and popped it into his mouth with a smile.

"I could make gnocchi for you."

"I don't know what that is; I bet y' make it good."

"I do, but I haven't for a long time," she said quietly.

They finished eating and did up the dishes. Gerald went outside and Mia retreated to the bed with a book on Oregon history. She tried to read, but her eyes became heavy. She reread the same page several times before falling asleep with the book still open on the pillow beside her.

*M*ia slept poorly and woke in a foul mood after Gerald had gone to work. Standing in the kitchen, she gulped down two cups of coffee but felt no better. She ate a crust of bread with honey.

Her eyes wandered to the top of the refrigerator. Mia stomped over, grabbed the bag, and took it to the table. Her hand pulled out a sheaf of paper and a slim satchel of stiff leather. A single flower with five petals was tooled onto the flap. Her fingers traced the petals and then the braided handle that was surprisingly supple, worn soft by the grip of hands. Hands that grip and fondle and stray where they do not belong. Hands like Tim's. A sob crept up her throat, and tears threatened but Mia blinked them away. She extracted a pen from the bag and scribbled his name. Other words followed in a torrent.

> *Alternate actions fill the day:*
> *Taking a bath, plunging over a ledge into the river*
> *Peeling apples for a pie, chopping flesh into*
> > *tiny little pieces*
> *Hanging linens in the sun, tearing clothes from*
> > *his body*
> *Rolling down a hill of grass, throwing stones at him*
> *Riding naked on a bike, running until breathless*
> *Calling Tim, hitching a ride to somewhere*
> *Reaching for him, pushing his head into the wall*
> *Inviting him near, pulling him to my breast*
> *Caressing his smooth cheek, pinching his lips*
> *Asking for what I need, pleading for his kiss*
> *Taking him in my mouth, holding back hurtful words*
> *Telling him to leave, begging him to return with*
> > *more love than he's taking*

Stirred emotions and restlessness forced Mia from the cabin; she climbed the hillside. Picking up a rock, she bobbled the weight in her palm. She threw the rock, and another and another; fury flew from her arm until she was breathless and sweating in a hot wind.

Mia ran down the trail and kept going, up the asphalt road that wound the hills like ribbons. She drank in calming views of old farms. A golden sun was shining down on green fields of young wheat undulating like water in the wind. So much promise, so much hope in those swaying stands.

On the ridgeline, dozens of white wind turbines looked like giant skeletons. Mia's heart pounded with sudden dread. She retched in a gulley, wiped her mouth, and ran down the winding road to the cabin with words rumbling in her mind.

*Wind turbines dress the hill*
*turning, turning*
*marking time*
*death come like wind*

# $S\,H\!A\!D\,OW$

*T*ired and sweating, Mia limped into Gerald's yard, turned on the hose and let the sun-warmed water run out. She took a sip from the cool stream then drenched her sweaty hair. Dripping and shaky, Mia sat down on the porch to push off the rummage sale shoes. She drew several breaths and her shoulders sagged. She was tired, so tired she could cry. A breeze blew across her wet skin. She watched a lone Ponderosa pine swaying. It answered the wind with whirring, longing sighs. Mia sighed. Such a peaceful, praying pine. But did the tree "pine" to move its roots, to bend its trunk and stretch its branches beyond the limits of stiff bark? Did she?

When Gerald drove in from work, Mia dashed inside. She splashed her face with cold water and pressed a rough, line-dried towel to her cheeks until the urge to cry had passed. She went back outside and stood on the porch, watching as Gerald filled his rustic bird feeders with seed. Soon birds began appearing.

"Yours?" Mia pointed to a large gray and black tabby cat eyeing the birds from a crouched position beneath a bush.

Gerald looked over and smiled. "He keeps the mice down."

"I've never had a pet. Cats are independent aren't they? Is yours friendly?"

"Sometimes." Gerald snatched up the cat and motioned her over to him.

"Oh," she cooed, petting the loudly purring cat in his arms. "Softy, aren't y'?"

Her eyes glistened. "I love his striped legs. What's his name?"

"Boy."

"Imaginative," she laughed. The cat raised his head suddenly, launched from Gerald's arms and ran off. Mia returned to the porch and sat down; she dragged her toe back and forth through the soft dirt below.

A bluebird appeared at the feeder. Gerald pointed to its mate hovering on the low branches of a bush nearby. Mia looked and said, "Reminds me of my parents: always together." She kicked her toe through a heart she'd drawn in the dirt.

"Y' go back to Texas much?" Gerald sat down on the porch

"No," she replied slowly. "And they only came to Oregon once. It's difficult. With Tim. Things were said."

"Kind of self-important, isn't he?"

Her eyes shot to Gerald's face. But then Mia sighed, "They *were* right. It *did* take a long time to build our reputation and clientele. I thought we'd starve before we broke even. When I finished renovating the house I sent them pictures. And I thought they'd come. Mother said she liked my arched front door that reminded her of the cathedral in the village where she grew up. But that didn't convince her to make the trip."

"Maybe they dislike travel," Gerald suggested.

"They must."

"What'd they do for a living?'

"Papa worked in my grandparents' Italian market in San Antonio. Grandfather died, the store was sold, and we moved to Austin."

"What do they do now?"

"Oh, play golf. And they spend a lot of time with Grandmother Angelina. She's over ninety, and quite capable, but she does need help with her garden. I don't know why they don't hire someone..." Mia shrugged. "I guess they like working and keeping busy."

"Do y' talk much?"

"Nooo," she sighed.

"Y' mad at them?"

"What would we say? Probably everything is just the same as always with them."

"Kind of self-centered, aren't y'?"

"Kind of a *know-it-all*, aren't you?" Mia snapped. "Who do you keep in touch with? *You* don't even *have* a phone."

He pulled a thin cell phone from his front pants' pocket and held it up.

"It never rings, you never talk on it," she sputtered.

"Don't have much reception here."

Mia stared at Gerald and fell silent.

He breezed on, "Y' go to college in Texas?"

Reluctantly she replied, "UT, Austin. I loved school. But I couldn't settle on a major. I was restless, I guess. I followed some of my interests to different jobs—at a bakery, a clothing store, a gallery/gift shop. That's where I met my..." Mia frowned suddenly and turned the question back to Gerald. "Did you go to college?"

He nodded. "Y' have a favorite course?"

"Ancient literature. I like stories: how culture, beliefs, and even landscapes influence lives—especially lives of women."

Mia glanced over at him and their eyes met; she drew a deep breath. "I dream about a woman. Maybe in Mexico. She struggles, and suffers greatly, and yet she's filled with so much love, and desire. I feel her, hear her words in my mind, as if she's…with me," Mia barely whispered.

"How long she been there?"

"I'm not sure," Mia sighed. "A long time."

"Think she's a ghost?" he asked gently.

Mia shuddered and rubbed goose bumps from her arms. "A strange word just popped into my mind: *lil*. What do you think it means?"

He shrugged. "Y' have a good imagination?"

Her brows furrowed. "As a kid I was very imaginative. I dreamed up stories and acted out little dramas I called 'trage-mia's'. Roses in the garden were ladies with petal skirts; bushes were thorny devils. The characters were friends, family. But they suffered terrible calamities. I don't know how I dreamed up such things! I should have written them down, so I wouldn't forget."

Mia rubbed her arms again and changed the subject. "What college classes did you like?"

"History. Photography."

"I probably would have loved photography, or art," she gushed. "I'm such a visual person. I love textures and color. And I have a lot of ideas. Maybe too many ideas." Mia glanced down at her hands. "I do love being active."

"Like to swim?"

She smiled and nodded. "I love the elements: water, air, earth…"

"Y' left out fire."

Images from the nightmare flashed into her mind. "Fire's destructive!"

"Just part of life. After fire come new beginnings."

Mia looked down and rubbed her thighs that were suddenly aching from her run.

"What'd y' want to do after college?"

Relieved to move from talk of fire, she breathed, "Oh, I didn't know. When in literature class, I daydreamed of being a poet. In business courses, I fantasized about opening an Italian gelato stand, or a natural foods grocery. I had lots of ideas, but nothing stuck. After a while it didn't seem as important *what* I did, as *who* I did it with."

"Tim who y' wanted to *do* it with?"

She glanced up at Gerald. But with a slump to her shoulders, Mia replied, "Seemed so. Everything just fell into place."

"*You* included?"

Her face reddened.

"Y' always go along with him?"

"I didn't just GO ALONG," she snapped loudly. "I made a choice."

"Get what y' wanted?"

Mia dragged her toe through the dirt. "I was excited to move, buy the store and start the business. And it was fun, at first. Everything was new. It was summer: so pleasantly warm in Portland, not at all like Texas with oppressive heat and violent storms! I fell in love with downtown. I like the hilly streets and all the unique little shops and galleries that keep multiplying. I love how the ships move along the river, and in winter, their lights seem to glide across the water like stars streaking the sky." Her eyes gleamed. "But the overcast sky is the color of concrete—for months!"

"Kinda dramatic, aren't y'? Not all Oregon's like that."

"I see that now," she replied, scanning the dirt at her feet. "My flowers do love the rain, even if it drizzles day after day." She looked up at him and laughed suddenly.

"Yeah," he chuckled. "Green's good. Feel like a change of scene?"

Her face lit with a smile. "The river?" Mia hopped up and headed inside. She changed from the sweaty t-shirt she'd worn running to a bright paisley halter top from the yard sale. Tuna sandwiches made and wrapped in waxed paper, she put them in a big bag with apples and chips. Outside, Mia started to put on the athletic shoes but they were too smelly so she pulled on her sandals.

Gerald soon emerged from the cabin dressed in frayed cut-offs and canvas boat shoes with large holes in the sides.

"Won't something get in there?" she laughed.

"Maybe fish."

"Slimy fish? Ew!" Giggling and shuddering, Mia turned and noticed the bike leaning against the cabin. "I'd love to take a quick ride. Could I pedal you down the driveway?"

He smiled. "Y' can try." When she pulled the bike up, he put a leg over and sat down. Mia got on. Her feet were on the pedals but she was unable to move her legs. They laughed and she hopped off. Gerald lifted her up and set her on the crossbar sidesaddle. Mia grabbed the handlebars at the center and he started pedaling. They had covered only a few feet before the bike tipped precariously.

Mia jumped off laughing. "Yeow!"

He handed the bike over to her. "Better take it y'rself."

"Back in a jiffy," she called, riding away and out of sight. Moments later Mia reappeared: legs pushed out to the side, an arm thrust in the air, head thrown back laughing with glee.

As she hopped off her bike, Gerald asked, "Want to see my bike?"

"Why didn't you say you had one?" she whined, but she followed him to the back of a shed where he pulled a dusty tarp from a lumpy form. Leaning down, Mia studied the scratched and faded image on the gas tank. "What kind of motorcycle is this?"

"1951 Indian Chief."

"Oh." Mia looked again at the logo then Gerald's face. "Does it run?"

"Needs hard-to-get parts. I'll fix it eventually and sell it."

"After all the work and time spent, won't it be too precious to part with?"

"Like a lot of things," he answered, his eyes steady on her face.

A rush of heat went through her. They were standing very close and Mia barely resisted the urge to reach for him. She turned instead and went out of the shed.

# BLANKET

T hey rode in Gerald's old two-tone Ford down to a mini
-mart in Rufus. The clerk behind the register grinned
and flirted playfully with Gerald while ringing up his
items. "Hey, G. I hear you're doing some painting at my aunt's
place. Maybe I'll see you there."

"Yep." He smiled and laid down several bills.

"Can I give you a bag or something?" the girl purred.

Gerald shook his head. Her hand lingered above his then
opened, and dropped his change. He deposited the coins into a
collection box for homeless veterans and walked away with the
girl's eyes on his back.

Mia stepped up to the counter with her selections and
opened her wallet. The clerk rang up and sacked the items,
collected the money, and slid the change across the counter
without looking up. Mia snatched up her bag and pushed past
Gerald who was waiting by the door. He followed her out, and
they drove away in silence.

Miles rushed by. The wind blowing through the cab of the
truck was hot; Mia was drowsy and inattentive until colorful
movement on the river caught her attention. Dozens of bright

parachute-like kites attached to boards hopped and twisted in the air. "Look!"

Gerald smiled, glancing over at the boarders moving like toys across the choppy blue water. "They come from all over the world."

"Imagine the strength it would to take to hold those sails steady in the wind! Amazing. Crazy or courageous, I can't figure out which!"

Soon they were arriving at Heritage Landing on the western shore of the Deschutes River. Gerald parked in the sparse but welcome shade of tall poplars. He got out and came around to Mia's door as she slipped off her dressy sandals and slid her feet into the flip-flops she'd purchased at the mini-mart. She placed their purchased snacks and drinks into the big brown bag with the sandwiches and rolled the top down into a lip for carrying.

"Clever," Gerald remarked as he tucked a green wool blanket under his arm. He led the way down a dirt path alongside the river.

Mia moved hesitantly, warily eyeing the rocks and dry grass beside the trail as if something might creep or slither out.

"Probably no snakes," Gerald said, but he, too, scanned the ground.

Every ten feet or so she paused, and shook dirt from between the flip-flops and her tender feet. Upriver a quarter mile, they stopped at a grassy spot where the water swirled in a deep pool lined with rocks and lush green vegetation. Wiping sweat from her face, Mia set the bag down.

Gerald placed the cans of pop between two rocks in the shallow water, shook out the blanket and it settled flat on the ground.

Mia kicked off the flip-flops, then splashed into the cold water. She sat down quickly, leaned her head back to dampen her hair, and sprang to her feet.

"See any fish?"

"NO!" she sputtered, scrambling to the shore. She shivered convulsively, but sat down. The hot sun soon warmed her. Gerald pulled off his shirt. She watched as he waded into the water and dunked under the surface. He stood up a few moments later and moved toward the bank. Water streamed down his muscular torso; his heavy denim cutoffs clung to his muscular thighs. Gerald pulled two sodas from the water. He moved toward her and held out a can. Cold water dripped onto Mia's shoulder. "I just got warm!" she whined, wiping the droplets from her skin.

"Poor baby," he teased. Gerald sat down beside her on the narrow blanket and took a long drink of his soda.

Mia took a sip of her drink. She watched the water of the river slide by. Sunlight danced across the surface and grasses on the far bank rustled in the breeze. Words filled her mind.

*Wind whispers...*
*tugging my ear...*
*urging me: listen...*

Mia took another few sips of her drink. Unsatisfied, she rummaged through the bag for her package of gummy bears. Mia popped several into her mouth and chewed. She leaned back on her hands. Her eyes followed a rivulet of water running down Gerald's back. Heat rushed through her. She dashed to the water, plunged under the surface and swam around until cooled. "It's silky cold heaven!" she called.

Gerald smiled and laughed. He took a drink of his soda and sampled a few of her cinnamon gummy bears.

"Spicy, huh?" Mia returned to the blanket and sat down. Her eyes were drawn again to Gerald's smooth back glistening red in the sunlight. Sudden thoughts of his warm hands reaching cool spots beneath her wet clothes made her almost forget there was somewhere else she should be, and someone else she should be with.

Mia sat up and stole a sidelong glance at him. "Gerald, are you seeing anyone?"

He turned and his eyes rested on her face. "I see y'."

She met his gaze but glanced away. Her words were barely more than a whisper, "Have you...ever...fallen for someone?"

"Don't y' know?" The deep tone in his voice was like a caress.

She searched his face. "I think..."

He shook his head but a smile was on his lips, "Some things y' just feel."

Mia looked down at her hands. "Have you...had many...'relationships'?"

"Been burned plenty of times," he sighed. "Gets old; like me."

"You're not old," Mia objected, but she looked into his face and studied the small lines crinkling at the corners of his eyes.

He watched a wisp of her hair catching at the corner of her mouth. "Old enough to know what I want."

She brushed the hair away and shifted uncomfortably. "When's your birthday?"

"Spring. End of April."

"Mine's winter. December 23rd. I never liked it then."

His eyes were on her downturned lips. "Did y' get lost with the holidays?"

Her brow furrowed. Wiping perspiration from her neck, Mia shifted her gaze to the water. A dragonfly with iridescent blue wings hovered near the bank. "Look at that!"

"Beautiful. *Odonata* order. Lots of myths and meanings associated with it. Depends on the country and culture, but it represents change, renewal, sense of self."

Words darted into her mind as quickly as the insect flitted away.

*Dragonfly*
*humming stirs the air*
*Warm hands upon my heart mend the break*
*mysterious ways on shifting wind*
*of a long hot summer day*

The water moved on past the shore. Seagulls having flown up the Columbia from the ocean circled overhead. The sun was hot. Mia flipped over onto her belly and rested her head on her arms. The heat and the sound of the rushing water soon lulled her into drowsiness.

It was evening when they walked back to the truck. It was hot inside; Mia rolled down the window and rested her arm on the door. The metal burned. "Owww," she whined and brushed away a sudden tear. She glanced over at a sign marking the turn to "Fulton Canyon" and "Wasco." A tractor ahead crept up the narrow road and blind curves prevented passing, so they settled in behind and viewed the scenery. They passed an old wooden church nestled between bare locust trees with bark as gray and weathered as the peeling boards of the church. Preservation had been attempted by covering the shake roof with corrugated metal, but the gingerbread detail on the steeple was beginning to fall off and the peaked window frames were empty where stained glass may have once been. A stirring gust of wind rustled the branches and shriveled leaves of the old trees. A swallow swooped through one glassless window of the church and out the other side.

"It must have been beautiful here once," Mia breathed.

Gerald nodded. "Methodist Church. Built in the late 1800s."

Methodist. Tim was Methodist. Mia sighed inwardly. She leaned her head back and closed her eyes on stinging tears. Hot air rushing through the open windows blended with the soothing sound of the truck's engine. Lulled into sleep, Mia missed seeing the small town of Wasco. The next thing she knew, the truck was stopping and Gerald's voice was in her ears. She sat up, rubbing her eyes. "What'd you say?"

"Visit my gram?"

"Your grandmother? Where does she live?"

"Chenowith. West of The Dalles. Twenty-five miles or so from here."

She stared at him. "What's her name?"

"Charlotte. Charlotte Mary."

"Oh!" Surprise was in her voice. "That sounds…"

His glance was piercing as he interrupted, "White?"

"No," she stammered, "that's not what I…"

He pulled his keys from the ignition and got out, shutting the door on her words.

Dumbfounded, Mia watched him walk away. She had wondered but didn't ask if he'd grown up at the nearby reservation at Warm Springs. He looked Native American, but he didn't act it—if there was a "Native American" way to act. There was so much she wondered but didn't ask—that'd be rude, too personal, intrusive and intimate. But the time spent with him was intimate in a way. A disturbing way.

Mia remained in the truck for a long time before going into the cabin. She changed her clothes, turned on the radio, sat down at the table. Her fingers drummed the smooth surface of the wood. Reluctantly, she retrieved the satchel from atop the refrigerator and sat down again. She ran her fingers over the raised tooling of the flower. It was stark and sensual—like something Georgia O'Keefe would paint. If only Mia could create something so simple, so beautiful…but her mind was on something else and the words exposed thoughts she would not claim.

*Oh my red skin*
*burns like my heart*
*in a thunderstorm of emotion*

It was nearly dusk when she climbed the hillside. Mia leaned against a large, sun-warmed rock and cried. She glanced through her tears at the fading sky just as a downy feather floated down. It came to rest on her open hand and she studied a hint of blue on its edges as if that faint color might reveal something.

Mia tried to push down rising feelings of anger. More anguished tears fell. She paced the ridgeline, back and forth, back and forth. A breeze spinning dust devils in the dirt exposed two smooth stones. She picked them up. They were warm in her hand and their shapes, rounded and familiar, were somehow settling. She sat with them a long time before heading down the hill. Stars lighting the way down the now familiar path were a reminder of all she still wanted.

Mia pushed open the door to Gerald's workshop. "Southern," she stated.

Gerald looked up from a table he was resurfacing, but he didn't say anything. He just kept sanding with quick sweeps of his hand.

"Southern," she repeated loudly, her eyes steady on his face. "I'm from Texas. Charlotte sounds Southern to me. Especially Charlotte Mary. *That's* what I meant to say."

"Oh," he replied gruffly.

"I know what you thought," Mia snapped.

He said nothing more.

She turned and closed the door, leaving emotion hanging in the air like dust beneath the fluorescent lights.

Mia went back to the cabin, collapsed on the bed, and fell into dream-filled sleep.

*He kiss me and I can think of nothing else...*

# SATIN

Gerald poured coffee and the rich aroma permeated the air.
Mia sat up suddenly in the bed. Her wild eyes scanned the
room.

"Y' okay?"

Tears welling in her eyes, she stammered, "I dreamed...I
was standing on a ledge above beautiful blue-green water like
glass. I was filled with awe. It was as if I'd waited all my life for
that water, to be in that place..."

Mia clutched her empty arms to her chest and drew an
uneven breath. "I felt her...a baby in my arms...she was soft and
warm. Her hair was damp and dark and wrapped her head like
petals," Mia sobbed. "I...looked into her eyes so much like my
own...and my heart filled with love. But," Mia fought the tears
and struggled to speak, "she was taken from me and I could only
cry. Every happiness was taken from me!"

She looked helplessly up into Gerald's eyes that were dark
and steady and looked back at her with tenderness. Oh, how she
needed some of that.

"Only a dream," Gerald said quietly.

Tears rolled down her cheeks. Mia pushed at her damp hair and whispered, "Her skin was like satin against me. It was... so real."

Gerald brought her a cup of coffee.

Mia looked up into his warm face. His leathery skin was the color of caramel. As she reached for the cup, her hand brushed against his. A wave of emotion and desire washed over her. She could have pulled him down, wrapping her arms around his neck, pressing her body against him, but Mia only glanced into the cup and took a sip. She took another long, energizing drink and cleared her throat. "Thank you, for the coffee. I'll finish it and get ready so we can go see your Gram." He nodded and she watched him turn and cross the room; her eyes were on his broad back and hips as he went out the door.

They drove down the Columbia River past landmarks and landscapes: Stonehenge, Samuel Hill Memorial Bridge, Maryhill Museum of Art, the rumpled hills on the Washington side of the river. Mia's stomach was still a little upset, and her emotions were high after the tumultuous dream. As they passed Celilo Village where the falls had once been, she shook off a chill and asked in disbelief, "How could something so stunning be destroyed?"

"Not destroyed. Sleeping. Someday she returns," Gerald replied confidently.

She turned to look at him. "When they built the dam, didn't the Corps of Engineers dynamite the ledges under the falls?"

He shook his head. "Still there beneath the water. Someday Sister Celilo will return."

A haunting presence did seem to linger there. *Could* the falls reappear if the dams were removed? Saint Anthony is often asked to intercede with God for lost things and missing persons. Mt. Adams and Mt. Hood, ancient, snow covered volcanoes to the north and south, looked like ghosts watching the strangely still river. Perhaps they called to Saint Anthony. Perhaps the wind whispered prayers. Perhaps even what was long lost could be found…

"Wire men," Gerald was saying. He pointed to metal towers supporting wires coming off The Dalles Dam in every direction like rays from the sun. "Power lifters."

Startled from her reverie, Mia looked: the towers did resemble supermen with broad shoulders and wide-spread legs. Her eyes surveyed Gerald's smiling face. "You're funny," she laughed.

Just outside downtown The Dalles, Gerald pointed to large, white, cylindrical storage bins. "Old Sunshine Biscuit Mill, soon to be renovated, maybe made into condos and artisan shops."

Mia nodded. Change. Nothing stayed the same. Her mind and eyes drifted to a sign for a cherry processing plant. Cherries. Sweet cherries. Oh, how she could use some sweetness.

They passed an old building with colorful murals depicting historic scenes of pioneers and industry. History. Heritage. Mia sighed inwardly. Heritage was more than bloodlines and places of origin. Heritage was connection. It was important to feel connected to a place. But where did she feel connected?

A lovely clock tower was a reminder of the passage of time. They passed a red brick church with an iron rooster atop a tall steeple. Mia wondered if faith could be found inside those walls. They passed a sign for the Columbia Gorge Discovery Center and Wasco County Museum. What might she discover? They passed a pizza parlor with oddly pitched roofs and the sign out front had a ghost wearing a hat like the roof. Mia shuddered.

But pizza was comfort food. She could use some comfort now, for she was disturbed by questions and emotions she struggled to contain. Attempting distraction, she pointed to a school. "Did you go there?"

"Nope."

"What kind of student were you?"

Gerald shrugged but offered, "Quiet."

"Did you like school?"

"Some of it."

She might have asked something else—something to push away her distress—but Gerald turned the truck onto a short gravel road and stopped in front of a small house. Dull fuchsia paint barely covered the warped siding; turquoise paint on the trim peeled in long curls from the window frames.

Mia drew a breath and followed Gerald up a concrete walkway. He rapped once, then opened the door to a small living room furnished with only a low slung sofa covered in a bright wool blanket and dated imitation wood side tables. Beyond the living room, a small woman sat at a chrome and Formica table. Hanging over the back of the red vinyl chair, her single gray braid nearly touched the floor. She pushed herself up and turned as they approached.

"Gram, Mia. Mia, Charlotte." Gerald patted his grandmother on the shoulder.

"Nice to meet you," Mia said offering her hand.

Charlotte only nodded, her wrinkled face crinkling into a smile with few teeth. She stepped over to an old refrigerator and extracted a full pitcher of dark amber liquid. Charlotte filled three glasses which Gerald placed on the table. They sat down: Mia squeezed between the table and the countertop, Gerald on the side, Charlotte in her chair closest to the living room.

Sipping the bitter, unsweetened tea, Mia listened while Gerald and his "Gram" caught up. They talked of his latest construction job and someone named "Unc."

Finally Charlotte asked, "How'd y' meet?"

Looking up, Mia answered, "My car broke down. Gerald's fixing it."

"Where'd y' come from?"

Mia swallowed the last of her tea and stammered, "I, ah, came to Portland, from Texas, about fifteen years ago."

"Go back soon?"

"Texas? I don't think so," Mia replied uncomfortably.

Charlotte poked Gerald who got up and fetched the pitcher of tea to re-fill their glasses. Charlotte slipped over into Gerald's chair and grabbed Mia's hand. She closed her eyes and cocked her head as if listening. Then Charlotte said, "A woman cry."

"Who is she?" Mia whispered.

Charlotte clucked her tongue, "Y' know. Another place. Another time. Pain. More pain. Horror. And sorrow." Her pale eyes rested on Mia's face. "So much sorrow."

A chill rushed down Mia's spine.

"Death come like wind. Later, by water. Wind whisper name."

Her heart pounded. Mia pulled her hand from Charlotte's grasp and stood up. Glancing out the kitchen window, Mia asked, "Can we go outside? I need some air."

Charlotte pushed up from the table and, brushing her hand along the wall, she led the way to the back door. Gerald offered his arm. They walked along a worn dirt path to a weathered bench in the shade of a crabapple tree. Charlotte sat down and her short, bare legs dangled, the toes of her flat sandals barely reaching the ground. "Better find what y' look for."

"I'm not looking for anything," Mia replied. She sat down heavily on the bench and drew several long breaths. Her eyes turned to a colorful garden. White alyssum bloomed in thick tufts. Delicate blue delphiniums and red bleeding hearts hung like ornaments from slender branches. White lilies trumpeted blasts of gold. A leggy, purple clematis twined around a rough ladder leaning against a weathered cedar fence. Pink roses with spots of red were achingly beautiful. "This is heavenly," Mia gushed. "It must be a lot of work."

"Good gittin' hands in dirt. Y' could use some earth on y'," Charlotte replied and playfully pinched Mia's midriff.

Mia giggled uncomfortably. She looked down at dense green foliage with small blue flowers beneath a concrete birdbath. "What's that plant?"

Gerald followed her gaze. "Forget-me-nots."

"Oh, I've seen that flower somewhere before..."

"A gardening book?" He leaned down to pull a few weeds and grass stragglers from the flower beds while Mia tried to recall where she'd seen the flower before.

The heat of afternoon soon intruded and Charlotte stood up. "Let's go in." She reached for Gerald's arm then swatted his backside and laughed devilishly.

"Y're in a mood!" he chuckled as they went back inside.

"Yep! Can't help myself when a handsome man's around."

"HA!" he snorted. "We'll be going now."

Charlotte wrapped her arms halfway around his waist and squeezed. "Too short!"

"Y'r arms?" he asked playfully and patted her shoulder. "Be seeing y' soon."

"Could stand to see more of y'," Charlotte scolded.

Mia had moved on into the living room and noticed a single framed photograph by the door. She was leaning in to examine it when Charlotte came up behind and barked, "Glad y' came?"

"Yes. Thank you for the tea," Mia managed to say while following Gerald out. She turned to wave goodbye, but the blistered and peeling door was already closing.

They got into Gerald's truck and drove to the freeway. The air moving through the cab was hot like a furnace blast. Wiping sweat from her neck, Mia gazed across the river to a freight train passing by a house with windows and a door like a face.

"Take a detour?"

"Oh, sure," she answered, distracted by the house that seemed to be watching and waiting by the water.

Gerald turned off the freeway. He drove up a winding drive to a viewpoint at the crest of a hill. They got out and walked to the cyclone safety fence atop a high wall.

"Wow! You can see how the river carved through the land. What a curve!" Mia exclaimed, looking out over the town and the Columbia River below.

Gerald pointed to the west, "Gram's house is there at Chenowith. Cherry Heights is between here and there. See the orchards?"

"And look, the red brick church with all the steps out front."

"Old St. Peter's: granite steps, lots of marble and stained glass inside." Pointing at a large rectangle of bright blue water a block from the church, he said, "Natatorium."

"People are jumping from the high diving board! I could never do that."

"Need a little coaxing?"

"I would need a lot of coaxing," she laughed. "Heights make me nervous."

"Good berry picking over there on the Klickitats," Gerald said nodding north, to the hills across the river near snowy Mt. Adams.

Mia shook off a chill. She moved suddenly toward Sorosis Park on the other side of the street.

They wound around a three-tiered concrete fountain at the center of a rose garden. Every few feet, Mia stopped to admire the flowers.

Gerald held still the head of a giant yellow *Floribunda*. "Smell this one!"

She leaned down to breathe in the perfume, and smiled. Mia moved along the gravel path. At a bush of silvery pink roses. she exclaimed, "*Love* this one!" As she reached for the identification card, Mia read aloud, "Our Lady of Guadalupe." She inhaled deeply.

Gerald bent down to smell the flower. His face was very close to Mia's. "The lady is pretty," he said, smiling, but she moved away.

They crossed a narrow asphalt lane to the park with acres of grass and hundreds of towering Ponderosa pines. They stood there beneath the trees, not talking, not moving, just looking out while the river flowed toward the ocean and a cloudless blue sky hung overhead.

When they left the park, Gerald took a different route down the hill on a winding drive past tidy older homes with manicured lawns and small colorful flower gardens. A cyclone fence surrounded an asphalt playground of an old two-story stucco school. "Colonel Wright Elementary School" read the sign on a postage stamp lawn.

"Wright commanded the army post here a century or more ago," Gerald said.

A jungle gym of steel pipes and an old slide with steep stairs stood beside a row of swings. How many small feet had played on that ground where soldiers had once marched? Mia wiped perspiration from her neck. "How hot it'd be playing on asphalt!"

"Hot just driving! Want to swim?"

"Definitely. But *not* at the Natatorium. No high dives!"

Laughing, he asked, "How about Horsethief Lake? It's just across the river."

Mia breathed and words rushed into her mind as she glanced warily at Mt. Adams.

> *White mountain watches*
> *distant water laps the shore*
> *again and again*
> *while she waits*
> *beneath a blue blue sky*

# ROPE

Strong gusts of wind buffeted the truck as they crossed the bridge next to The Dalles Dam. Mia stared straight ahead and clutched the seat; she barely breathed and her heart pounded. "This wind is fierce! What do you think it is saying?"

Gerald shrugged and kept driving. Away from the water, the wind was calmer. Several miles down the road, he turned in at the Columbia Hills and Horsethief Lake State Park. "Site was a Native American encampment and burial ground."

Distracted, Mia nodded. Her hand was on the door handle. As soon as the truck stopped in the parking lot, she pushed hard on the door and hopped out. Crossing the wide green lawn, she walked quickly to a narrow sandy beach, kicked off her flip-flops, then stepped into the green water. She waded out fifteen yards, dunked under and came up sighing, "Ah. That's better! Sooo much better."

Treading water, Mia watched as Gerald pulled off his shirt and dove in. He swam toward her with effortless, powerful strokes. When he got near, she skimmed the heel of her hand across the surface of the water, splashing him.

He laughed, delivering a fan of water to her face. "Give up?"

"No! Girls rule!" she chortled. They splashed back and forth. She pounded her hands and feet. Their laughter echoed across the water. When tired, they swam side by side for shore.

At the truck, Gerald pulled a small ice chest from beneath a tarp in the truck bed.

"Whoa! That's new," Mia observed as she wrapped a towel like a sarong around her wet clothes.

Smiling, Gerald carried the chest and a wool blanket over to a grassy spot beneath intersecting lines of poplars and maples. He spread out the blanket and they sat down.

Children were running up and down the beach after a giant, tan dog with drooping black muzzle. No matter how much they coaxed, the dog only sat and barked. It wasn't until they gave up and jumped into the water that the dog ran after them.

Mia laughed. "I was a lonely 'only'. Were you?"

He shook his head.

"I've longed all my life for…something…someone," Mia sighed. "I have no siblings, no aunts and uncles, or cousins. Mother said, 'Less pain leaving small family.' She left her family and never talks of them. Maybe she was glad to leave."

Gerald watched Mia closely as she continued, "When I was little, Mother wore her hair long and loose. It was so lustrous and thick; I loved to watch her brush it. Once I swooped up, and wrapped my arms around her hips. I breathed in the smell of her hair and her freshly starched apron. I squeezed her soft middle and I never wanted to let go. But Mother pushed my hands down saying, 'Mia! You spoil my clothes. Let me be!' I'll never forget her look: like I was just too much to be endured."

Eyes glistening, Mia glanced over at Gerald. "I was just crushed. I ran out to my rope swing. Pumping my legs, going higher and higher, stomping my feet down in the soft dirt, I cried and mimicked her: '*Mia! You spoil my clothes! Let me be!*'"

Her mouth struggled to continue. "She was so concerned with her looks: how a 'lady' should act, how I should act. And she was always correcting me! But not Papa; he would just smile and say, 'Don't bother our Little Miss Perfection'. For years I thought he meant miss-perfection…like I was…flawed."

*Such small sweetness…*

Mia rubbed her feet together as if to alleviate the sting of painful memories.

"Easy to get it wrong when y're small."

Mia sighed. "I didn't fit. I don't know why. She didn't feel like…she just didn't seem to know how to…mother me."

"Kept y' safe. Cared for y'…"

"It seemed that I…wasn't what Mother wanted. But still I tried to do what was expected." Mia looked up to the sky. A string of sing-song words began playing in her mind.

> *My Momma told me to be a good girl*
> *a nice girl, a do-as-I-should girl*
> *Momma told me, "Be quiet. Be a lady:*
> *thoughtful, kind and sweet."*
> *Momma told me what I should not be*
> *what I could not be*
> *Momma told me everything*
> *I thought*
> *except what I could be*
> *and the possibility*
> *I could be more*
> *than a GO-ALONG girl*

Mia turned suddenly and asked Gerald, "Am I difficult? To live with, I mean?" But then she blushed at her own words and squirmed under his look. "Not that we're living together really."

"No," he answered, shaking his head, his eyes on her hair that was shining in the sun like burnished wood. His voice came deep and slow, "Not difficult."

She fished a cold soda from the chest and gulped it down. He lay back and closed his eyes. After a while Mia whispered, "Gerald..."

He opened his eyes.

"At your Gram's house, I saw the picture of her with a baby. Was it you?"

"Uh, huh."

"You don't talk of your life or say anything about your parents."

Gerald sat up; he exhaled a long breath. "Mom got pregnant, dropped out of high school, got married. Dad worked fruit harvests all over the Northwest."

"Must've been a rough life."

Gerald shrugged, "Kids are durable. They can make fun wherever they are."

Surprised, Mia looked at him. "Kids?"

He nodded. "We lived a while on an alley. Often played out there in the dirt. I went inside to get water to make a moat. Neighbor came out, got in his car and backed up. My brother, Henry, was run over. Thought he might pull through, but he didn't."

"Oh, my God!" Tears flooded Mia's eyes. "I'm so sorry! I didn't mean to go on and on about my stupid little problems."

He shook his head. "Not y'r fault."

"I know," she whispered, voice quavering.

"After that, the folks were drinking even more than usual. Dad beat up the neighbor. Cops came and took Dad to jail."

"It must have been so hard for your mother." Tears spilled from Mia's eyes and she dabbed at them with her towel.

"Time Dad got out, she was running around. About the last time I saw her."

"But you were the only son she had left! How could she leave you?"

Gerald shrugged. "Maybe like y'r mother said, 'Less pain leaving small family.'" He looked out to the water. "Mom said I'd be like Dad, just a 'big dumb Indian'. But he said we were better off without her 'big mouth and skinny white ass'."

Surprised, Mia glanced over at Gerald and asked quietly, "Where is he now?"

"Dead by the time I turned ten."

"I'm so, so sorry," Mia managed to say, her eyes blurring with tears. "How?"

"Heart attack. I got tough then. Gram sent me to live with Unc at Wasco. He taught me woodworking, mechanics, self-respect. Good man. Good father figure."

"That's where you went to school? In Wasco?" She stood up, stretched, and bent down to pick up a stick. "I wish I'd seen it."

Gerald nodded. "Went to high school just a few miles south of there, at Moro."

Mia tossed the stick toward the water. "After that, what did you do?"

"Went into the service, then college. Moved to Rufus after divorce."

She did not turn to look at him as she sat down. "How long were you married?"

"Not so long. Five years more or less." He downed half a can of soda. "How about y'? How long y' staying married?"

A gust of wind suddenly blew hot and dry. Maybe it was the wind that brought tears to her eyes.

Gerald persisted. "Y' date much before Tim?"

Mia blinked. She looked down at her hands, examining the indentation on her finger where her heavy gold ring had been. She sighed, "Mostly losers not knowing where they were going, what they wanted to do. But Tim was full of plans."

"That what y' wanted: plans?"

"Yes, something to count on," she snapped.

"That all y' wanted?" He looked at her and waited but no answer came, and the question hung between them.

Mia took a breath, forced a smile, and gushed, "We had the most beautiful wedding. Dozens of flowering dogwoods filled the air with perfume. It was just how I wanted. Heavenly."

"Honeymoon? That heavenly, too?"

Her face fell. "Not at all. I hoped we'd go somewhere romantic like Hawaii or Paris, but we used the money to move to Portland. Since then, we've worked six, seven days a week to keep it all going."

"That why y' don't have kids? Too much work?"

"Why don't you?" she bit back, her eyes blazing at him. "Or do you have one hidden away like your cell phone?"

Gerald replied evenly, "Hasn't been right yet. Maybe someday. Hope so." His dark eyes settled on the curve of her lips that was pretty, even when she frowned.

"Hope," she said bitterly, "that'll get you nowhere." Mia sprang to her feet and walked away from Gerald's piercing look. She crossed the parking lot to a display of petroglyphs lining a rock cliff. When The Dalles Dam was built, these rock carvings were cut from the river bank and moved here, away from the rising backwaters.

Mia read a sign on a gate blocking a path. "*Tsagaglalal*, She Who Watches," was available for viewing only by guided tour due to vandalism near the site. "I wish we could see her," Mia sighed heavily as Gerald came over.

"*Tsagaglalal*'s both petroglyph and pictograph: carving and drawing."

"I've only seen pictures. I imagine she'd be looking down with kindness and warmth radiating from her broad red face, and a sweet smile would be on her lips."

"*Tsagaglalal* watches."

Mia looked up at Gerald. "Sad they had to move her and the other artifacts."

"More than artifacts. Ancestors. Still here." He patted the center of his chest.

She blinked away tears, turned, and went to the truck. Mia pulled the door handle. "Sorry, about before," she said as Gerald came up beside her.

"Don't fight much, do y'."

"Fight?" She shook her head. "I never fight."

"Explains a lot."

"Like what?" Mia barked, giving the handle another yank.

"Why y' struggle."

"I *don't* struggle." She pulled again.

"Good to clear the air."

"I can't clear the air of every emotion that plagues me! I feel too much!"

Gerald reached around her, pressed down the button of the handle, and opened the door. "Not healthy keeping it in," he said kindly.

They left the park and were driving down the highway before Mia spoke again, "I am so sorry about your brother. I always wanted a brother, or a sister. But I don't think Mother ever really wanted *any* children." Mia looked out at the river and words moved through her mind.

> *'She Who Watches'*
> *wide eyes open*
> *what does she see*
> *is she our mother*
> *does she watch for my return*

Suddenly Mia turned to Gerald, "Charlotte's like *Tsagaglalal*: a little old grandmother with eyes watching everything."

He shook his head. "Gram's nearly blind from diabetes and cataracts."

"But she poured our drinks! How does she do things if she can't see?"

"Uses other senses. Got the 'gift', too."

"Oh," Mia nodded. "As in psychic? Is that a skill she developed, or a God-given gift?" Mia didn't wait for his response. "I don't know what I believe. I was raised Catholic, but I haven't been to Mass in years."

"Me either."

"*You're* Catholic?"

"Unc made me. Said it was good to have faith in something."

"That's probably true." Mia glanced out at the river bank where rocks jutted from sand covered hills and clumps of grass clung for dear life in the gusting winds.

Gerald pointed to trees ahead in the distance. "Y' know the story of the castle?"

"Not much. It was built by Samuel Hill and is named Maryhill, after his daughter—or his wife, also named Mary?" Mia's eyes lingered on the building as they passed.

"Hill was a lawyer, railroad executive, philanthropist. He bought 6,000 acres in Klickitat County in 1907. But he couldn't make his dream of creating a utopian community materialize. He donated the mansion and died before it opened as a museum."

"It's such a lonely looking place...so far from any city. I haven't been inside but I...passed by..."

"Interesting works of Auguste Rodin, furniture from Queen Marie of Romania, lots of artifacts of historical significance. Samuel Hill had another concrete house: in Seattle; it's on the National Register of Historic Places."

Snapped from her reverie, Mia smiled. "You like history, don't you? I like stories, dramas."

"His-story: just dramas from the past."

"His-story," she smiled again. "I'm more interested in 'her-stories': women's struggles and the dramas of their lives."

He pointed to the east. "Hill built that war memorial, a replica of England's Stonehenge, to honor the soldiers of Klickitat County."

Mia's eyes studied the circular concrete structure on a nearby hillside. Soldiers died. Their names were carved in cement. Letters they had written to loved ones left traces of who they were, what they did with their lives. Gerald refinished furniture and restored vehicles. What would she leave behind? Not a child. A husband, parents, satisfied customers decked out in jewels and surrounded with elegant possessions?

"The phrase 'What in Sam Hill?' came from articles about him," Gerald was saying as they wound down the road toward the arching bridge named for the man. "Quite a few people thought he was crazy doing all that he did."

Mia was not really listening; she was looking down into the water for the sparkling wedding ring she'd thrown into the river.

When they arrived back at the cabin, though the day was still warm and her clothes had dried in the sun, Mia was shivering. She ran water as hot as she could stand in the bathtub and leaned her back against the slant of the old porcelain tub. Mia closed her eyes. The heat soaked into her. Her body began to relax, but her mind was not yet quiet. Maybe it was only sweat that poured from her eyes.

Later, tucked in the bed under Gerald's old quilt, leaning up against the headboard with pillows cradling her back, she let odd expressions pour from her mind onto the page.

*Clear water moves across dry land, etching a channel through rock, carving a place to be. Where is my place?*

*A ribbon of water cuts through pale hills; a slice of blue like a knife through cake...Where is my sweetness?*

*Wind moves clouds over the land and rivers flow to the sea. Does something, someone in the sky guide us? What is it that tugs at my heart? How do I find where my heart can settle—where I belong?*

Mia sighed. Was there no way for her ever to be happy? What could she do?

*Grandmother say hands busy with work keep trouble away...*

With sudden sense of purpose, she started copying her poems onto clean white pages and she labored over cover letters to send to magazines. Perhaps some publication would like her poems so much that her rookie presentation would be overlooked. It had been a long time since her desire to be a writer had been squelched, but now Mia smiled a little: perhaps it was not too late for some long unrealized desires to be indulged.

Satisfied with her efforts, she tucked the papers into the satchel. Mia settled down in the bed and was just beginning to drift off to sleep when Gerald came in from working in his shop. She watched him wash up at the kitchen sink. Their eyes met. Her hand turned back the covers.

Gerald slowly approached the bed, took off his shoes, and lay down beside her. His arm slid beneath her neck. His other hand gently stroked her head.

Tears slipped from Mia's eyes. She turned her face toward him. Her fingertips gently traced the line of his jaw, the velvety ridge of his ear, the smooth skin on his cheek. Calmness swept over her and the sensation was like falling through silken water. Then, with careful movements as if venturing onto sacred ground, their bodies found each other.

$\mathcal{M}$ia was alone when she woke in the morning. She breathed deeply and gazed out the window to the small square of blue sky then reluctantly rose from the bed. She fixed a cup of coffee and sipped it slowly, savoring the sweetness on her tongue. Mia had wanted sweetness. But now what? She set down the cup, dressed, and hurried outside.

Gerald was weeding his garden. He looked up.

"Let's go to town; I need some addresses to mail letters."

He set aside his hoe. "Need envelopes?"

She nodded.

"Stamps?"

Again she nodded. They went inside. Her hands were shaking as she slipped the folded letters into long envelopes affixed with stamps Gerald gave her.

They didn't speak on the drive to The Dalles but undecipherable looks passed between them. Mia watched the river of choppy water that mirrored her mood. As they passed a large sign painted on the side of a building, she sighed, "I like signs; they're easy to understand."

Gerald flashed a quizzical look her way but did not comment. He parked, and they walked to an old brick building separated into narrow storefronts. A placard on the sidewalk outside Klindt's Booksellers and Stationers claimed the store was the oldest bookstore in the Pacific Northwest. Tall display windows of heavy glass stair-stepped back to a centered glass door framed in wood. A brass bell above the door rang loudly as they entered. Worn plank floors creaked under their feet and dozens of clocks ticked loudly on high shelves lining the narrow space. Long glass showcases down the center of the room displayed rare books, monogrammed pen and pencil sets in gift boxes, paperweights, pen holders set in marble, and globes of the world showing countries no longer in existence.

Gerald spoke quietly, "Opened in 1870."

"Smells like it," Mia whispered, eying the attentive saleswoman who might've stepped out of an old book herself. The woman's hair was tightly curled as if put up at night in pin curls. Her mid-calf woolen skirt and heavily starched beige blouse with buttoned collar and cuffs were long out of style and out of season. Her flesh-colored hosiery was coarse like cotton; her serviceable black shoes looked as if they'd been polished and re-polished for decades.

The woman spoke knowledgeably, however, with Gerald about newly acquired books on digital photography, and as they talked, Mia wandered away. Her eyes scanned the titles of numerous writing and publishing books. She pulled out a book and quickly jotted addresses of poetry publishers onto her envelopes.

Moving to the spiritual section, she was immediately drawn to a book about Inanna, ancient Sumer's most beloved and revered deity. Mia had studied her years ago in Middle Eastern literature. She thumbed through the photographs of cuneiform writing: pictographs inscribed on clay tablets. Many of these, unearthed and now housed in museums all over the world, had been deciphered. The myths, hymns, psalms, love songs, and laments had been combined into poetic stories of the goddess. Mia studied photographs of ancient art: depictions of trees and flowers, grains and fruit, sun and stars, mountains and water, even a lovely rosette. Inanna, queen of heaven and earth, was shown with large eyes and a sweet smile; her face was regal and kind like the Blessed Mother.

Mia scanned several books. She found a picture of Venus, a symbol of the Virgin Mary; in a book of famous paintings of the Virgin Mary, there was one with tiny blue forget-me-nots, like the flowers in Charlotte's garden. Somehow these things seemed connected, and were speaking to Mia—of something. But what?

A chill ran over her skin. Mia turned and looked up and down the aisles. She sighed and wandered toward the front of the store. She slid a dime into the slot of a gumball dispenser, pulled the lever, and a ball rolled down the curved metal tube. Red. Mia slipped another dime in. A purple ball appeared.

Finishing his transaction, Gerald dropped his change into a depository for missing children. "Thanks, Mable."

The woman smiled broadly, "Glad to be of service."

As he moved toward the door, Gerald watched Mia pop the gumballs into her mouth. "They'll make y'r teeth dark."

"Don't look," she laughed as she chewed the stale gum. She slipped another coin into the slot. "For you," she said. He popped the green gumball into his mouth as they went out the ringing door. While on the way to the truck, Mia stopped at a large mailbox. She placed her letters on the tray, tipped it up, and waited as they dropped with a thunk to the bottom of the metal bin.

"Hungry?" Gerald asked.

"A little."

"We could go to the Baldwin Saloon. Their French onion soup is almost famous. It has Gruyere cheese. And they have homemade bread and coffee drinks…"

Mia sighed, "Oooh, a caramel latte and a bite to eat would be good!"

They walked several blocks to the historical brick building and went inside. Before sitting down, Mia studied the numerous Englehart oil paintings on the walls, the long mahogany and stained glass bar, the big brass cash register, and an antique clock. Finally sliding into their booth, Mia remarked, "I like this place—the sense of history, the beautiful woods and all the colors in the glass and paintings."

Gerald only nodded as he looked over his menu. They ordered, their food was delivered quickly, they lingered over a flavorful meal and went away satisfied and smiling.

Later in the cabin, as she struggled toward sleep, simple words for complex feelings flashed through Mia's mind.

*Like sun*
*he warms me*
*chasing clouds from my heart*

# BACK

Morning came far too quickly for Mia had been awake and fretting most of the night. She splashed her face with cool water, looked into the mirror and ran her hands through her wild hair to tame the fly-away strands. She drew a deep breath, and went to the door. Peering out, she saw Gerald leaning against the porch post, shoulders looking broad in his thin, white t-shirt tucked into faded jeans. His hair hung loosely with an indent and deep wave where his pony tail had been. Her hand pushed open the screen and her feet moved across the porch.

"Mia. Don't go." The gentle tone in his voice nearly melted her resolve.

Her legs were shaking as Mia moved toward her car with his eyes following. She got in, started the engine, and drove out beneath an overcast sky.

Mia's hands clamped the steering wheel as if the slightest relaxation might cause the car to veer through the concrete divider into oncoming traffic or through the guard rail into the river. A barge was being pushed upriver by a five-tiered tug boat. Windsurfers and kite-boarders zipped across its path, but it pushed on, and so did she.

She passed a sign for The Columbia Gorge Discovery Center and Wasco County Museum. Gerald talked of going there together "sometime", but they hadn't. There were many things they hadn't done. Some things they had. Some things she could not erase from her mind, or her body. But Mia tried not to think, or feel, anything.

The river and the road beside it made a sharp turn just west of The Dalles. A dangerous wind gust struck the car, nearly forcing it into the next lane. Mia gripped the wheel tighter and kept going as the sky darkened with leaden clouds.

It started raining in splatters at Mosier and was coming down hard by Hood River. Mia turned from the freeway at Cascade Locks and passed by a cheerful and fun-looking art gallery: Lorang Fine Art & Gorge-ous Gifts. She passed a park with enormous maples and firs shading a wide expanse of grass; beside it, a paddle-wheeled boat sat motionless in the river. Mia pulled into a gas station and rolled down her window. "Fill it up, please."

The freckle-faced attendant swiped her card and put the nozzle to her car; he picked up a squeegee and started to wash the windshield with dirty water.

*I cry…*

"NO!" Mia said smacking her hand against the wheel. The attendant froze mid-swipe.

"Oh! I didn't mean you," she said with a forced smile.

The kid shrugged, finished the windshield, and handed her a receipt for the gas. "Thanks for coming," he offered politely.

Mia drove out to the freeway muttering, "I will not cry." She soon reached Multnomah Falls; plummeting more than 600 feet from Larch Mountain, it is the fifth highest waterfall in the nation. She pulled into the parking lot and waited. The historic stone lodge nestled in the trees at the base of the misty falls beckoned her, but Mia fought the urge to go inside to putter in the gift shop and read from books. She forced down the desire for a hot drink of cocoa or creamy, rich coffee to melt the chill settling over her.

The windshield steamed up as minutes passed. Mia was wiping it with a tissue when she noticed the familiar car pulling into a space a dozen yards away. She drew a deep breath, pulled her keys from the ignition, and stepped out of the car on shaky legs. She listened for the final click of the door lock before moving ahead.

Tim spotted her as he emerged from his car. He scowled as he approached.

Her feet stopped. Her heart pounded and a sudden downpour beat down on her.

"*WHAT* are you wearing?" he asked loudly.

"Oh, I, uh…" Mia looked down at the cargo shorts, paisley halter, and work shirt from the yard sale. Every word she'd planned to say evaporated from her mind.

"We'll talk in the car." Tim grabbed for her elbow and tried propelling her toward the passenger side of his car.

Mia jerked her arm from his grasp. "Wait," she shouted. "Tim, PLEASE."

"GET IN! We have to GO; Victoria's ILL." He reached for her arm.

"I'll have your car picked up," he yelled while trying to open the door against a strong gust of wind.

Jolted by emotion, Mia gasped and doubled over.

There were loud footsteps on the wet pavement and Gerald stepped between them. He raised his large hand to shield her face from the pelting rain. "Y' okay?"

She looked up at him. "What are you doing here?"

"Don't go, Mia. Tell him y'…"

"Tell me what?" Tim demanded to know, his face red with anger.

"We *have* to go," she said to Gerald, her words flat with resignation.

Tim grabbed Mia's arms. "What have you done, Mia? Were you shacking up with this *Indian*?" Tim spat the word out like a bitter taste in his mouth and he squeezed her arms as if he could extract answers from her flesh, her defiant bones.

She pulled and pushed and finally escaped Tim's grasp, but Gerald did not see this. He was already walking away with tight fists at his sides: fists that could have smashed Tim's smug smile and his perfect white teeth. Gerald got into his truck and drove past the blur of figures standing in the rain; water from his tires splashed up, drenching their feet.

"Gerald, wait. You don't understand," Mia yelled, but the truck did not stop. Reluctantly, she got into Tim's car, jerked the seatbelt around and snapped it into the buckle. The car sped away down the rain-slicked pavement.

Angry and unwilling to look at Tim, she closed her eyes. Her ears were fixed on the hum of the engine and the sound of the wipers slapping the windshield. Mia shivered. She kicked off the wet flip flops and pulled on her sandals. Grabbing Tim's trench coat from the back seat, she draped it like a blanket over her and slipped her arms into the sleeves.

Later, as the airplane flew high above the clouds, the words she meant to say returned and Mia whispered them with venom into Tim's sleeping ear. When she tried to sleep, other disturbing words were in her mind.

*Ay…ahuehuete…how I cry…*

# PEARL

hen they landed in Austin, Tim rented a car and drove toward the hospital with the radio tuned to a classical music station. Mia dozed a little and was startled when the car abruptly stopped. Crossing the street, a Latina woman and a young man were swinging a little girl between them. The plaid ribbons in the girl's hair flapped in the breeze. Mia sighed, "I wanted a family like that."

Tim tapped down the volume control. "What?"

"Like that!" She pointed. "I wanted that."

He shrugged as if not understanding.

"A MOTHER! A FAMILY!" she yelled.

Bitterness laced his quick response, "Always 'Suffering Mia'! Mother of Christ!"

"At least she was a mother!" Mia replied caustically.

He turned up the radio as if to signal the end of the exchange. Mia brooded in stony silence until they neared the hospital. "What's wrong with Mother this time? She's had so many ailments that amounted to nothing."

"Angelo didn't say but she hasn't been very well since winter."

"Winter? When did you find this out? You should have let me know!"

"How could I? The rude note you sent included no address or phone number."

Mia's face paled. "I knew something was wrong. I had the worst feeling and I kept thinking…"

"That attitude will be no comfort to her," Tim replied coldly.

"Attitude?" Mia blinked back tears.

"Everything is not about *you*."

"Something has to be about me," she whispered. "It's my…" she stifled a sob. "It's Mother." Mia was on the edge of her seat and her hand was on the door latch as if she might suddenly jump from the car and outrun the danger Victoria faced.

"Done feeling sorry for yourself? Christ! All winter I had to put up with your negative attitude. You could have called them. You could have talked to someone besides the damned counselor."

Shock and dismay showed on her face. "The counselor was your idea!"

"I thought she'd snap you out of it. You aren't the only person who lost a baby."

"As if you cared! All you did was go to work!"

"Someone had to! What were you planning to do, Mia? Stay home forever and saddle me with all the burden of the businesses? What else could I have done? You were like stone." He swerved the car into the parking lot. "There was no room for my grief."

Charlotte's words rushed to her mind: "Death come like wind."

Mia's head was spinning and her footsteps were loud in her ears as they hurried toward the hospital entrance. Bitter bile swelled up her throat. She bent over and retched into a potted tree beside the walkway. Pressing a limp tissue to her lips, she moved through the snapping glass doors into the crowded lobby.

Boisterous kids burst from the gift shop while wrestling with a newly purchased stuffed monkey. Mia grabbed Tim's arm. "Wait. We should get something."

But he only flashed a look of irritation and continued toward the elevator. He punched the button. They squeezed inside. Mia pulled the belt of the trench coat tight, straightened the collar, and fought a wave of nausea as they moved upward.

When the doors opened, the crowd filed out. Mia looked up and saw Angelo standing in the hallway only a few feet away. His hair was neat and smooth, his camel slacks and cream shirt were crisply pressed, and his doe suede shoes were brushed and spotless. Everything about him was perfect except the new deep lines she saw in his face.

"Papa," Mia breathed.

He stepped toward her and his arms reached out to her. He kissed her forehead. "Darling Mia, you're here."

"How is Mother?"

"Not so good." He pulled a perfectly pressed handkerchief from his pocket and wiped the tears misting his eyes.

"What's wrong? Is it pneumonia again?"

"We'll talk later. You go see her." He pointed to the nearest doorway.

Mia crept forward. Taking a deep breath, she pushed open the door to the private room and moved toward the bed. Victoria faced the window; her head rested on the pink satin pillowcase she used to keep her hair from going flat. Mia stared at the tangled mass of dull strands and for a moment believed it wasn't Victoria at all, just some other woman in a lifeless wig.

Victoria's eyes opened and her voice rasped, "The missing girl appears." Her hand reached out from the covers.

Mia clasped the thin hand and blinked back tears. "I'm sorry I...wasn't here sooner, Mother."

Victoria nodded with a hint of a smile and closed her eyes.

Mia was standing, leaning over awkwardly to hold Victoria's hand and her back began to ache. She knelt down beside the bed and rested her head on the mattress, but soon her knees began to ache. She extracted her hand but still Victoria slept. Mia sat down in a chair. Her eyes wandered the room of neutral beige; every surface was sleek and easily cleaned, ready for the next human frailty.

When Angelo came in, he smiled lovingly and went to Mia's side. He rested his arm on her shoulder and she leaned her head against him, breathing in the familiar scent of his cologne. "You go over to the house with Tim," he said gently.

"I don't want to go."

"You get some rest. Come back in the morning. She does better then." He reached for Mia's hand to help her up from the chair.

"But what's wrong with her?"

"Too many possibilities to say until more tests come back." He escorted her to the hallway and her waiting husband.

Lights along the streets blurred in Mia's tired eyes. As they drove up to her childhood home, the house looked strange and unfamiliar. Inside, Mia went directly to her old bedroom, stripped off her clothes, took a shower and slipped into her double bed. She curled up, cradling a pillow next to her body, then fell into an exhausted sleep.

Sometime later, Mia awakened to the feel of Tim's hand. He smelled of Scotch. "Get away from me!" she snarled and swung her arm at him. "How dare you!"

He deflected her blow and shouted, "Cut it out, Mia! Jesus Christ! I was just trying to comfort you!"

"Don't touch me! Cheater."

"Look," he yelled. "What you saw that day was a mistake."

"It did not look like a mistake! It looked like you were planning to spend plenty more time at it!" Springing out of the bed, Mia grabbed an old robe from the closet and stormed into the bathroom. She thrust down the toilet seat lid and sat down with her head on her arms. She couldn't talk to Tim. Not now. She could deal with only one withered relationship at a time. They could hash it all out later, after. After what? Tears of fear and dread fell, and then Mia started to pray.

*I pray...*

*T*im left for Portland early the next afternoon. She all but lived at the hospital. Waiting for more tests to be taken. Waiting for test results to be shared. Waiting for doctors to give opinions, nurses to come, suffering to be alleviated. Mia spent hours at Victoria's bedside, sometimes retreating to the waiting room where she lingered on a long purple couch next to a shiny glass table with a gleaming silver lamp. The bright décor did little to calm her restlessness. Mia paced the halls, ran up and down the stairs, and eventually gave in to her cravings at the cafeteria in the bowels of the hospital basement. Her spine pressed against the back of a molded, lime green plastic chair, Mia sipped coffee and ate a piece of apple pie.

The swing-shift cook on break at a nearby table glugged down a cup of coffee and crunched through a pack of crackers.

The busboy came over and struck an indignant pose with thin hands propped on imaginary large hips. He pointed an accusing finger at the cook, "ROBERTA! Wat did Momma Potts tell ya? Stop gabbin' an' git up an' do some cookin'!"

Roberta doubled over, her wide shoulders and the ample, freckled cleavage heaving with laughter. "Oh, Anthony!"

"As if I don't have 'nough to do! Girl just look at this mess!" Anthony complained with a laugh and pointed at the crumbs and wrappers on her table. "As if I didn't have 'nough trouble this mornin'. No coffee to drink. Had a flat tire comin' in. Didn't even have a jack! Thank goodness somebody stopped to help. But the spare's already almost flat." He shook his head. "Shit never ends."

"It's the shit-shift," Roberta cackled. "Or the shift of shaft!" she added, barely able to speak the words through her laughter.

"You name it, I got it," he quipped with an impish grin.

Watching tears of laughter roll down Roberta's cheeks, Mia stifled a giggle. How could they laugh with hardship of their own and all the suffering at the hospital? Where did one get that kind of courage if not in oneself?

*Maybe* La Virgen *listen...*

*T*he next day, after a lengthy vigil at Victoria's bedside, Mia's restless wanderings led her past the hospital chapel. She paused at the door, pushed it open, and stepped inside. The walls were beige; the carpet was beige. There were no statues, no crosses, no stained glass windows, no hymnals or prayer books—only sleek modern seats with low backs and stiff cushions in beige vinyl. A narrow pedestal at the front of the room held a round candle shaped like a pearl but it was covered with a thin layer of dust and the wick was unburned. Nothing about the room was warm or encouraging, but it was quiet. It was a sanctuary acceptable to all: just a place to pray or meditate or have a private moment.

Mia knelt at a pew in the back and closed her eyes. She recalled the twice-life-sized statue of the Virgin Mary in the Catholic church of her childhood. Mary's long, auburn hair waved around her face, her blue cloak pooled on the ground, and two pink roses rested on her bare feet. Mary's pink lips were curved in a sweet smile. Her cheeks glowed, and Mary's eyes, dark like the night sky, seemed soft with understanding. Mary too had lost a child. But how had she accepted her loss so gracefully? Was the honor bestowed on her so great it kept her heart from sadness?

"Mary, do you listen? You have a kind heart. You know sadness. You know pain. Did you have someone to tell your secrets, or share your load? I wish I did. Please Mary, can you help me?" Mia prayed and a tear rolled down her cheek. "Dear Mother Mary, I ache...for something...someone...somewhere. Can you help me find what I am missing?" Gripping the back of the pew in front of her, Mia put her head down and tears flowed from her eyes.

The roses on Mary's feet came suddenly to Mia's mind, and the calm that washed over her carried a hint of fragrance. She wiped her eyes and whispered, "Are you here?" But there was no sound, no movement. She hurried out to the hall but there was no one. She rushed down the stairway to the basement, her footsteps echoing on the hard floor.

Mia picked up a plastic tray, a glass of orange juice, coffee, and a frosted cinnamon roll that looked like a mountain covered with snow. She moved to the register to wait for the attendant and absently glanced down at her tray.

A woman waiting behind her said, "Long day? I know the feeling."

Mia nodded and smiled. "Maybe all this sweetness will help." She paid for her food, and went for a napkin. The woman caught up, and Mia looked around the cafeteria. "We almost have the place to ourselves. Would you like to sit with me?"

"Sure," the woman answered smiling.

They walked to a yellow table in a sea of empty white tables, set down their trays, and sank onto the stiff plastic chairs as if they had just completed an arduous journey.

"I'm Joyce Campbell." The woman offered her hand across the table.

"Mia Edwards." They shook hands. Mia drank her juice and a few sips of coffee before asking awkwardly, "Who do you have here?"

Joyce chewed and swallowed a bite of carrot cake. "My neighbor. And you?"

Mia's mouth quivered. "Mother; she's wasting away before our eyes and the doctors can't seem to find the reason. I want to scream, 'Hold on! Fight whatever it is!' but she doesn't seem to want to."

Joyce sighed sympathetically. "My neighbor's fighting cancer. I know how helpless it can feel."

Mia blinked back glistening tears. "How's your neighbor doing?"

"Louise's trying to beat it. Eighty years old and still full of spunk. She doesn't expect a miracle," Joyce sighed. "It'd be nice, though."

Nodding, Mia took a drink of her coffee. "How long have you been coming?"

"Years. Just about every day. I also volunteer on the children's wing."

"You're very generous with your time."

Joyce smiled. "It lifts my spirit as much as theirs. And I'm working toward a degree in social work. Getting credit for the time is an added bonus."

Mia was finishing her cinnamon roll and only nodded.

"I'll have my MSW in the spring. Then…" Joyce shrugged, "anyone's guess in this job market. Really, you'd think someone could create more jobs and address the problems in our communities!" Joyce's chuckle rang pleasantly through the large room and her green eyes sparkled. "Sorry. I'm sometimes a little outspoken! If you want to hear more just meet up with this wise old 'sage' again tomorrow."

"Maybe I will. But I should be going now," Mia said rising and Joyce followed. They deposited trash and trays at the receptacle, walked down the hall and rode up together in the elevator. "Nice talking to you, Joyce Campbell, Sage of the Cafeteria."

Joyce laughed. "Best wishes to you and your family."

"Thank you. And also good wishes to you and your friend."

They parted, heading in opposite directions down the long hall.

Victoria and Angelo were sleeping, so Mia wandered over to the lounge area and slumped down onto the couch. She soon slept and words were in her mind.

*Why life so hard...?*

# CORAL

*A*ngelo's hand gently patted Mia's shoulder. "We have news."

Mia struggled to get to her feet and rushed into Victoria's room.

The doctor was pressing Victoria to accept some kind of treatment, but she resolutely refused. "No cutting, no chemicals, no radiation. I live or I die. It is out of your hands." Later discussion with a hospital social worker was no different. "Only I want no pain. No more pain," Victoria kept repeating. When she lapsed into sleep, they went out into the hallway and conferred in hushed voices.

"Perhaps the best thing would be to take her home," the social worker suggested.

"And do WHAT? Watch her die?"

The social worker glanced at other families walking down the hallway and spoke quietly. "Each case is different, and each outcome."

Mia's eyes grew large. "She's more than A CASE!"

"Yes. I'm sorry. Of course. Perhaps at home Victoria will be more comfortable. Perhaps there you could convince her to try some intervention."

Mia looked to Angelo, but he was shaking his head. "She is comfortable here. If there is to be healing, it will come."

"Papa, you can convince her!" Mia implored, but he was shaking his head.

"Mind if I ask her again, just for documentation sake?"

"Documentation? Isn't there an alternative treatment? We can't just stand by watching and waiting and praying!"

Angelo put his arm across Mia's shaking shoulders and pulled her close.

The hospital social worker went into Victoria's room. There were murmurs from inside then Victoria's loud exclamations. "No! No procedures, no experiments. I want only something for pain. It is too late to go back home."

Mia pushed through the door, pleading, "Mother, please. Being at home with all your pretty things will be so much more cheerful and we'll take such good care of you."

Victoria shook her head. "It is not for you to bear. If death comes for me, after all this time, it will not be again where I lived."

"Please," Mia begged. "For me? At home I can cook all your favorite dishes and you'll be right there to tell me again how to do it right." Her eyes sparkled with tears.

Victoria's look softened, "You can cook and bring it here. That would please me."

Mia's mouth fought for a smile.

The social worker jotted something on a sheet of paper, then silently exited.

Angelo sat on the bed and stroked Victoria's hand soothingly. "If you are comfortable here, here is where you shall be. We will do something to brighten your stay. We can bring more of your lovely linens, a reading lamp, a vase of roses from the garden. Yes, that is just what we shall do," he announced triumphantly.

But Victoria did not look at his smiling, and determined face; her eyes were on the window. "I am sorry…for putting you through this…and for so many things." Closing her eyes, she was silent a few moments. When she spoke again, Victoria's voice was barely more than a whisper. "You give more than I deserve."

"You should have so much more…" Mia's voice broke with tears.

"Sshhh. It is life only. Be happy we lived it well."

"You always say that! How can we be happy if you give up? I don't want to lose you like this. Why won't you do something for me for once?" Mia whined.

"I did something for you once that changed both our lives," Victoria replied, but her eyes registered a look of surprise she exchanged with Angelo.

Mia did not seem to notice. "Please, Mother, you can't give up."

Victoria's thin hand patted the mattress. "Come here."

Angelo moved over to the window; Mia took his place beside the bed.

"Now listen: some things cannot be changed. And you, my dear, cannot keep fighting the world."

"I don't fight," Mia declared weakly.

"Maybe not outwardly, but here," Victoria tapped the center of her chest, "here is where you need acceptance."

"I can't accept what you're doing! You've lost hope!"

"*I* have never lived on hope. I have lived on what I *plan*. I accept whatever is to come, and I want you to do the same."

Eyes glistening, Mia whispered, "How can I accept it?"

"Find a way. Ask Our Lady to help you."

Mia blinked back tears, "Does she listen? Does anyone? If they did, how could they let there be so much pain and suffering and sadness?"

Angelo's eyes met Victoria's. He said evenly, "We raised you in the Church so you would have faith to rely on."

"Is that what you're doing—relying on faith for healing? You said you don't *live* on hope. You have to *do* something! You can't just go to sleep! We can't just…wait." But there was no following response. Mia sighed loudly, collapsed into the chair and after some time, suggested brightly, "Let's play rummy. Or solve word puzzles."

Victoria shook her head. "My brain is foggy. Angelo, go home, make my hot chocolate just the way I like it with cinnamon, and really hot. Bring it in the thermos."

"You know I will do anything for you. Always." He kissed Victoria's smiling face and left the room.

"Mia dear, read me some gossip from the magazines."

"You don't want to hear all that, do you? Lying and cheating, weight gain and tragedy, pain and anguish…" Mia struggled to keep her voice steady.

*I cry for Mother…Grandmother…*

"No," Victoria sighed, "not if you put it that way." She clicked on the television, and ran through the channels, stopping on an old western starring John Wayne. But she turned it off when the title *Angel and the Bad Man* flashed on the screen.

"Let's tell stories," Mia suggested. "Tell how you met Grandmother Angelina."

Victoria gazed out the window as if seeing the past unfolding. "Angelina frightened me so back then…"

*Victoria tapped her foot against the curved leg of the brocade chair as she waited. Her eyes wandered the room. A crystal chandelier hung low over a dark mahogany table set with a gleaming vase of roses. Long, velvet draperies graced tall windows that opened onto a garden. Leather bound books filled shelves flanking an ornately carved fireplace. Red oriental rugs covered shining hardwood floors and an exquisitely crafted grand piano stood in the corner.*

*Angelina Casinelli sat opposite Victoria in a matching brocade chair, only a small table separating them. "So," Angelina said abruptly. "You have found yourself a husband."*

*"Yes," Victoria answered meekly, struggling for her voice.*

*Angelina poured hot tea from a gleaming silver tea service into delicate porcelain cups and handed one to Victoria. She fixed a cold stare on the girl. "My son has made a hasty commitment he may regret."*

*Victoria's cup rattled on its saucer.*

*"Thankfully, Angelo had the good sense to bring you to me before word gets out. We have time to talk, just the two of us. Yes?" Angelina raised her eyebrow, but her mouth, as stiff as her back, was unsmiling.*

*"Yes," Victoria whispered. She raised her cup to her lips but was unable to drink.*

*"So, you say you come from Salina, Italy."*

*Victoria nodded.*

*"And the name?"*

*"Victoria Maria Bar...Bartolome...o." She squirmed under the heavy scrutiny but met the older woman's gaze.*

*Angelina studied the girl: long dark hair, brown eyes with light flecks, good skin, straight teeth. Pretty. Angelo could have done worse. But there was something else, something Angelina did not let go unnoticed. "I see, Victoria, what you are."*

*A cold chill went down Victoria's spine, but she did not look away.*

*"My son may have been fooled, but I am not. Angelo does not see with his eyes. He does not hear behind your words. Only desire guides him." Angelina let her words hang like dirty laundry between them. She set her cup deliberately onto the saucer. "He is a good man, yes? You will do anything to protect his good name, yes?"*

*Victoria nodded.*

*"Family far away? You wish to keep it so, yes? There will be no more trouble?"*

*"Yes," Victoria stammered. "I mean. No, no trouble,*
*I hope."*

*"Hope?" Angelina raised an eyebrow. "Hope will have nothing to do with it."*

<br>

*V*ictoria sighed, not realizing she'd fallen silent before finishing the telling of the story. "We made our peace in time. And Angelina shared a wealth of information; she was like a mother to me in so many ways."

Mia's attention peaked. "You don't talk of yours. Was she like Grandmother?"

"My mother was meek, hard-working."

"You left home when you were so young."

Victoria nodded, her voice barely a whisper, "I wanted nothing of that life: aching backs and tired hands scratching out a living. So much hardship and struggle for so little happiness." She looked down at her pale hands. "Tradition was not enough to keep me. I did what I had to do...to leave."

"Didn't you miss your family?"

Victoria looked up suddenly. "Of course, but...more than miles separated us. I...was afraid...I couldn't go back..."

Mia's brow furrowed. "Even after I was born?"

Victoria's lips stiffened. "Especially then. It was too... difficult."

"Sorry I made it so hard for you," Mia said with a snide tone to her voice.

"No, I am sorry...You...were so unexpected..." Victoria's voice faltered. "I did what I could...to keep you safe, and then... Angelo and Angelina became our family."

Mia troubled over those words, but Victoria had closed her eyes and soon only quiet rhythmic breathing came from her thin body. Slumped down in the chair, Mia slept until Angelo returned with the thermos for Victoria and a foam cup of coffee for Mia. She smiled and took a drink. "Ugh. That is horrible! It tastes like the inside of an old shoe." Mia glanced up at him. "I'm sorry, Papa, if I hurt your feelings."

He chuckled. "I purchased it from the machine down the hall. Why don't you go to the cafeteria; perhaps they'll have better. Have a bite to eat. Take a break."

"Mother doesn't get a break," Mia whispered. But the look in his eyes was insistent and she relented, "I guess I could go for a few minutes."

Angelo sat down in her vacated chair and sighed, "We'll be here."

A patch of sky showed through a small window on the wall of the stairwell. As Mia started down the stairs, she glanced up at the blue sky and her mind drifted back to the window by the bed in Gerald's cabin. Sudden words were in her mind.

*In summer sun*

*pine scent rises where I step*

*layered needles crackle, advising*

Mia paused to look back at someone puffing down the stairs behind her.

"Going...for...coffee?" Joyce managed to say.

Mia shivered and shook her head, "No more, please!"

"You didn't...try the...machine...did you?"

"Terrible!" she laughed. "How's your neighbor today?"

"Louise is sleeping...I saw you in the hall...thought we could...go somewhere."

"You should breathe first," Mia chuckled. "I'll tell Papa we're leaving."

"Sure." Joyce leaned on the hand rail and followed Mia up the stairs.

Pushing open Victoria's door, Mia peered into the light-filled room. She turned to Joyce and whispered, "They're sleeping." Mia jotted a cheery note on a slip of paper she left on the nightstand, and tiptoed out.

"Mind if we take the elevator?" Joyce huffed.

They passed Victoria's nurse, who remarked, "Don't spend too much, girls!"

"Shopping? What a good idea!" they chimed.

Getting into her Oldsmobile Cutlass, Joyce apologized for hamburger and fry wrappers littering the back seat. "Comforting don't you think: the smell of old food?"

"My favorite," Mia laughed.

"Been a while since I cleaned. I'd blame it on my kids, but it's all me! Since I went back to college, I eat too much on the run," Joyce chuckled, shaking her head. "I do eat too much, but I NEVER run!"

Mia laughed again. "How old are your kids?"

"Susan's twenty-one, just finishing her Bachelor's Degree; Matt's a freshman at the university. Both still live at home." Joyce shrugged. "It's a mixed blessing."

"A blessing for sure."

"They *are* great kids. They make good grades, keep busy with jobs and activities, but also help me with the house when I insist!" Joyce laughed good-naturedly.

Mia rolled up the sleeves of her denim shirt, and put down the window. She drew a few deep breaths and sighed, "Ahhh, I needed this air."

"Me, too!" Joyce drove to the Arboretum Shopping Mall in northwest Austin. The sumptuous displays in the stores were a pleasant diversion from the hospital dreariness.

Mia bought a bottle of perfume and had it wrapped in gold paper with a huge bow for Victoria. As she contemplated buying a soft blue blanket for the bed, questions formed in her mind. Did Victoria refuse to fight the cancer because she was afraid of losing her hair from the chemo? If she lost her hair Victoria could wear a wig, or a peasant style scarf like the flowered one she wore when gardening and over the plastic cap on hair coloring day. Victoria prided herself on her looks, to be sure.

And she dressed impeccably, although a bit old-fashioned, like Angelina. But was Victoria sacrificing her life for her looks?

"You okay?" Joyce asked kindly.

Mia sighed, "I wish Mother would fight. If only to stay a little longer with me."

"Maybe she can't. Maybe it's too hard. My husband was in his forties when colon cancer took him. He fought for three years through multiple treatments and surgeries. It was so exhausting and, in the end, we still wanted more time. I'm not sure his struggle was worth all the sickness and sacrifice."

"I'm sorry," Mia whispered.

"Thank you," Joyce replied quietly and wiped away a tear.

They were walking through a department store and Mia caught a glimpse of herself in a mirror. "What was I thinking? This looks like a denim uniform!"

Joyce laughed, "Not that bad. Let's check out the sale racks for something cute."

Poking through summer items, Mia found a pale blue and green print shift with a wide belt; Joyce bought a pair of lightweight gray slacks and bright coral blouse.

They changed into these purchases in the ladies' lounge. "You look fantastic!" Mia said as Joyce emerged from a stall. "I love that color with your hair and eyes."

"Thanks." Joyce tugged at the hem of her plus-sized blouse. "I'd look better if I lost a few pounds. Quite a few."

Tying her hair in a double knot at her neck, Mia smoothed a few wild strands. "You look good. I on the other hand need some attention. Quarter of a century and I've never let my hair go this long without coloring!"

"You colored as a toddler?"

"I was fifteen," Mia laughed, "and awkward, self-conscious. 'Time to make you a lady,' Mother said. She lightened my hair, showed me how to apply makeup. From then on, my clothes were purchased instead of home-sewn, and Mother insisted I practice walking and sitting properly."

"Do you always call her Mother? It's rather formal."

"Is it?" Mia was examining the dark circles under her eyes and sighed, "I look as tired as I feel. I could sure use some coffee, *good* coffee!"

"And something to eat?"

"Definitely something sweet!"

As they walked through the mall, Mia's attention was drawn to the vibrant window display of an import store with a large sign of scrolling letters: *A N G E L I T A*. She turned to look and nearly ran into a shopper exiting the store. "Oh! Sorry," Mia exclaimed. She stared at the woman, who looked vaguely familiar.

"Excuse me, please," the pretty Hispanic woman apologized.

Already having breezed on in search of a restaurant, Joyce called back to Mia, "There's something! Thank goodness! I am famished!"

Mia peered ahead only briefly, but when she looked back, the woman had vanished.

Settled into a corner booth of the restaurant near a bright window, they waited for service. Admiring a large potted plant on the windowsill, Joyce remarked. "I love kalanchoe for its hardy, thick leaves and so many cheerful little flowers."

Mia nodded and smiled. "Especially yellow: it's warm like sun. I like sun."

"What'll y'all have?" the approaching waitress barked.

"Coffee and cheesecake," they said in unison and laughed.

The waitress retreated but returned quickly with their desserts and poured coffee into their waiting mugs. They drank and ate and didn't speak until only crumbs were left on their plates. Pushing hers aside, Joyce giggled, "That was good! A little caffeine, a lot of fat and sugar, I'm sooo much better!"

Taking a sip of her coffee, Mia smiled in agreement. "Just heavenly."

"So, tell me about your other life, in Portland. How'd you meet your husband?"

Mia's face sobered. "We met here in Austin fifteen years ago. We married only a few months later."

Joyce's eyes widened, "Oh, a whirlwind romance!"

She shrugged. "Tim had an opportunity to buy a business; we jumped at the chance and have been working at it ever since."

*Mother say he want too much…take too much…but I no listen…*

"Hmm," Joyce said in a diagnostic tone. "You must be really close spending all your time together."

Mia frowned. "Well, we don't spend all our time together. We…" she swallowed hard and stared down at her empty plate.

"Sorry. Just tell me it's none of my business," Joyce replied, waving at the waitress, who then came over and filled their empty coffee cups.

"No. It's just …" Mia took a deep breath. "We've been having a hard time. Last winter I miscarried, again. And I found out I probably can't ever have a baby."

"Gosh, that's rough. I'm so sorry!"

Mia nodded. "I was really depressed; I couldn't make myself go back to work. I watched TV, read story upon story of women triumphing over terrible, tragic things, but I couldn't get myself together. I was having nightmares about a woman..." Mia blinked away tears. "The woman's cries sounded so much like my own. I just could not be that sad any longer. I decided I had to change things." Mia's eyes glistened with unshed tears; she took a drink of water.

"You don't have to talk about it," Joyce said softly.

*I cry for him...*

Mia's words rushed out. "I planned to mend the gap between Tim and I with a special dinner. But I was too late." She took a deep breath and her next words were laced with bitterness, "I found him at the store...he was...*kissing* Valerie, a girl he hired to 'help out' while I was off work!"

Wide-eyed, stirring her coffee, the spoon going around and around in her cup, Joyce asked gently, "What did you do?"

"I turned and stumbled into a statue. I picked it up and thrust it away! It crashed into the showcase. Glass was everywhere..."

Joyce's spoon dropped to the table.

"Valerie was screaming..." Mia put her hands to her ears.

"What did your husband do?" Joyce's eyes were wide.

"He yelled and tried to stop me but I pushed him back, ran out, and sped away. I didn't know what to do or where to go. I just kept driving until my car broke down. I scrambled up a hillside and wavered at the edge of a cliff. I might have fallen to my death but for the wind...and Gerald..."

"Ah."

"Gerald fixed my car. Eventually I sent Tim a note to arrange a meeting, but I didn't know if he'd even show. He did, and that's when he told me Mother was sick. We were standing in the rain...and then Gerald was there...but he...left."

"Where is this Gerald now? Is he tall, dark, and handsome?"

Sighing, Mia said, "In Oregon. He...he's..."

Joyce waited.

"He's different. From anyone I've ever met. He's...sharp."

"Oh! A smart guy, huh?" Joyce smiled.

Shaking her head Mia said, "No! I mean, he is smart, but he...needles me with his words, his looks..."

"Oh, is that all?" Joyce laughed suggestively. "Sounds like an interesting guy."

Mia's face warmed. She glanced around, leaned forward, and whispered, "I had a dream about him that felt so real I couldn't get him out of my mind. And before I left I..."

Joyce's expression lit up. "A sexual dream, you mean? I'd love one of those! I *wish* my husband could come back to me like that again, even if only in a dream. He was sick for so long. That part of our life just slipped away. We were happy just holding each other but..." Now Joyce blinked away tears.

"I'm sorry. That must have been so hard." Mia drank down her coffee. "The Church says even *thinking* about committing adultery is bad and I feel so guilty."

"Oh, guilt schmilt."

"And I wonder if Tim feels guilty for what *he* did."

"How old is that little vixen?"

"Twenty-three," Mia sighed heavily. "I don't blame her. I was the one who..."

"Tim was the one who put his hands on the help!"

"But I pushed him so hard to have a baby and then I wallowed in self-pity."

Joyce scowled. But her look softened. "I'm sorry for the loss of your babies, those miscarriages. Understandable you'd be depressed, but it's no excuse for his behavior!"

"But I can understand why he turned to her. I was angry: at God, at Tim because he wasn't sad, at myself for waiting too long to even *try* to get pregnant. It was a difficult time; I wasn't easy to live with." Wiping away a tear she managed a rueful smile.

"Still." Joyce patted Mia's hand. "How old IS he? I mean really, how selfish."

"*I* was selfish…not helping him at work, not paying attention to his needs…"

"Oh, COME ON!" Joyce exclaimed loudly, her green eyes flashing.

People at nearby tables turned to look.

Joyce leaned forward and said more quietly, "He should've been there for *you*. He left you at home when you needed him and now he has left you here."

"But I told him to go," Mia argued.

"Are you saying you don't feel abandoned? Even a little?"

"I feel so many things. I'm all over the map. Sometimes I'm not even sure if what I feel is my own emotion or someone else's. The woman's lament is as deep as my own."

"You should take a class," Joyce responded enthusiastically. I've heard of one called 'Finding Voice'. Women translate feelings into words that speak to other women." Stirring her cold coffee, Joyce raised her hand to catch the eye of the waitress again. "Many writers find being in the company of other writers, or going on retreat, is helpful."

Mia nodded. "It *was* easy to write when I was with Gerald, and I felt on the edge of some discovery."

Joyce was thinking aloud, "Edge of a cliff, on the edge of discovery. Some kind of symbolism there. Maybe counseling would help, or analyzing your dreams."

"I *did* see a counselor; I *was* writing every day. And Gerald gave me paper and pens with a pretty leather satchel. It's old—maybe something he picked up at a yard sale—but I like it. Especially the flower emblazoned on the flap."

"Emblazoned? Like a burning heart of desire?" Joyce mused. "Did writing help?"

"With desire?" Mia looked confused. "I have been writing about the woman: she's so passionate, so filled with longing and sadness."

"Psychologists say every woman you dream is really you."

"No, she's a Mexican woman. I haven't even been to Mexico. Strange, huh?"

Joyce said excitedly, "Bring the woman to life! Write her story. If you don't, maybe she'll leave you."

Mia smiled uneasily. "I have the sense she's always been with me. She's so intense, sometimes it's too much to feel. Maybe it would be a relief if she left."

"Maybe she'll cheer up if you give her voice."

"Maybe," Mia laughed and gathered up her things. "You're kind of odd, but I like you." They both chuckled.

As they headed back to the hospital, Joyce drove along in congested traffic, and was humming softly. When a car suddenly squeezed over into her lane, she only shook her head and slowed down to avoid a collision.

"Yikes! That was scary! But you are so patient!"

"Eh." Joyce shrugged a shoulder and smiled.

"How do you stay so upbeat? How do you keep from getting depressed at the hospital? I think it is so hard!"

"I find encouragement in so many places: sometimes just what I need to hear is said by someone in the line at the grocery, or I read it in an article I happen upon. Sometimes I find it unexpectedly in a book someone has recommended. Words we need just come to us. I try to practice positive thinking. I believe we attract good things to ourselves when we put away doubt and worry. I try to live as if all the good I'm hoping for is already on its way. And I try to bring some cheer to each situation." Joyce sighed, "It has been more difficult since Louise became ill. Still, she has so much courage and is fighting so hard. And she reminds me to be thankful for each day. Doctors say 'hope for the best, prepare for the worst.' I say 'hope for the best, prepare to learn.'"

"What are we supposed to learn?"

Joyce's eyes gleamed, "Love. You never know who you might care for, what you might find in them. Maybe you have only to look at them differently, or on another level."

"But how *far* must we go?" Mia asked dramatically.

"Maybe you have to really dig: go all the way down to the basement. Maybe subterranean," Joyce answered in a deep and dramatic voice.

Mia was still laughing as they entered the hospital. "Want to try the stairs and work off the cheesecake?"

"Lead the way!" She climbed the steps behind Mia, and reaching the top, Joyce huffed, "You…do have…an influence… on me!" They exited the stairwell; she walked a few steps away, then turned and asked, "See you tomorrow?"

Mia shook her head. "When I get back."

"Where are you going?"

"Oregon. I refuse to let anger and guilt take away the good things in my life."

Joyce looked as if she was about to say something but only nodded somberly. "Good luck. Thanks for coming out with me."

"It was a good distraction. See you soon," Mia answered smiling.

Back in the hospital room, Mia glanced down at Victoria sleeping and had second thoughts. "Papa," she whispered. "Maybe I should I stay."

Angelo's dark eyes looked weary, but he encouraged her to go and she finally relented, "Call me if…" she swallowed the lump in her throat, "if you need anything."

# LOOP

Rustling papers, carbonated drink cans snapping open, snack carts thumping down the aisle: all those sounds irritated Mia on her flight to Oregon. She tried, but she could not sleep. Her nerves were on edge and jarring thoughts were in her mind. She switched on the overhead light, pulled out some paper, and wrote down the odd words.

> *How much was given and sacrificed*
> *while dulled down in the hum drum whirl of work*
> *without wondering*
> *how much is too much to give*
> *how little is too little to receive*
>
> *I cry and cry for home...*
> *and something...someone...somewhere...else*

It was eerily quiet when Mia unlocked the front door of her Portland house and stepped into the hallway. She dropped her keys noisily into the black bowl on the table below the antique mirror; she switched on the lamp and golden light flooded the space. She turned on more lights and the radio in the living room.

Everything was immaculate: the cleaning service Tim hired in her absence was doing a great job.

"Good at getting others to do what he doesn't want to do," Mia remarked bitterly. But she checked her attitude, and said with satisfaction, "Clean. Just how I like it! And I don't have to do it."

She lit scented candles, breathed in the musky vanilla aroma, and smiled. At last she was home in her beautiful Tudor cottage. She loved its steeply pitched roof, the leaded glass windows, and the beautiful arched door with its lovely etched glass inset. Constructed around 1930, the house had fallen into disrepair by the 1990s. But Mia had seen promise in the quaint structure. She poured her heart, and many thousands of dollars into the renovation. Each piece of furniture, each accessory, each detail in her now elegant home had been painstakingly selected or designed by her.

Mia wandered through the house to the master bedroom. She stripped off her clothes and paused at the mirror: she was still slender, attractive. Perhaps even beautiful. The thought made her smile. She stepped into the steaming shower, and luxuriated in the use of her favorite mango shampoo and conditioner. She dried off, wrapped her hair in a dry towel, slipped on her green silk robe, and sat down on the king-sized bed. The bedroom's understated décor of pale neutrals was soothing, but boring. Was that part of her discontent: desire to create something new, something beautiful? A baby would have been beautiful.

She sighed loudly and turned on the radio. A captivating song with a Latino beat filled the space. Mia began swaying with the music; she moved energetically through the room, then jumped up on the bed. She gyrated in passionate response to the rhythm and the towel fell from her head. Her robe gaped open as she whipped her hair around in an undulating dance.

Tim came into the house. He blew out the candles and switched off the radio in the living room. Following more loud music, he went to the master suite. "Mia!"

She screamed, and spun around to see him in the doorway. Mia pulled her robe closed and jumped down off the bed. "I didn't hear you come in!"

"Oh, really? I thought that dance was *for* me," he responded suggestively while loosening his tie and moving toward her.

"I was just livening up the room! It's so boring. We should redecorate and paint—red maybe." She waved her arms as if it could magically be done.

"Red, huh? A little wild." He studied her look. "Maybe I'd like *you* a little wild." Tim stepped closer, took hold of her robe and walked her backwards to the bed. Mia's knees gave way and he sprawled out, covering her with his need.


*L*ater, she made their supper: Chicken Parmesan, thick toasted bread with garlic butter, and tossed salad. They ate outside at the table on the deck. A warm summer breeze was blowing beneath slightly overcast skies.

A sweet after-dinner drink loosening her tongue, Mia was emboldened to say, "So…Valerie…"

Tim's face twitched, but he responded quickly, "I let her go."

"Quite a sacrifice for you," she cracked.

"Wasn't worth the complication." He raised his glass, rattled the ice cubes, and drank down the last of his Scotch.

"Ah." Mia added under her breath, "I should have guessed. Dollars and cents make you tick."

He put down the glass and stared at her. "I don't want to fight."

"Neither do I. But something had to be said."

Tim shot her a piercing glance. "What about the *redskin*? I can't imagine what you were doing with someone like that."

Her eyes blazed at Tim, but then Mia looked away and fixed her gaze on the Christmas rose. "I can't imagine you wasted time…with Valerie."

"That's behind us now. Let's don't rehash."

"Fine," she answered.

They talked of changes at the shops, financial goals, and strategies. Ideas flooded Mia's mind and she spilled them out. Tim refilled his drink. The sky darkened, the air cooled, and a breeze rustled foliage in the garden. Tim shifted in his chair and sucked liquor from the ice cubes in his glass. Finally he stood and headed inside. Following him into the bedroom, Mia silently stripped off her clothes. She pulled him toward the shower and had her way with him while the water beat down on them.

Lying next to him later as he slept, she listened to Tim's rhythmic breathing and darkness settled over her like a blanket.

*M*ia was startled awake by the light coming from the dressing area; she watched Tim head out the door in his running clothes. She jumped up, dressed quickly, and hit the road. At first, he didn't seem to notice that she followed, but she ran hard and was gaining on him when he looked back. Tim increased his speed and looked back again. She sped up and laughed when he looked back yet again. She kept his pace for nearly a mile, but Mia finally eased up. She walked then, and breathed in the warm air. She looked around, enjoying the pleasant sights.

Early risers in the neighborhoods were out. Dogs sniffed, cats darted across lawns, and fluffy gray squirrels crossed the streets on power cables. Beautiful Portland: abundant, tall leafy trees and evergreens, neat rows of grass, brilliantly flowered rhododendrons. People nodded polite "hellos" as Mia passed on the loop back to her house, but there was no one she knew.

Limping and tired by the time she reached home, Mia retrieved the newspaper and went inside. She was sitting in the kitchen, eating a toasted cinnamon-raisin bagel and reading the paper, when Tim tromped down the hallway from the front door. He tossed a pile of mail onto the table in front of her, filled a glass with cold water from the fridge tap, took a long drink, wiped his mouth on his wristband, and belched.

"Good run?"

"Christ! I thought you meant to run me down."

She laughed, "Maybe I did."

"When'd you start running?"

"A while back."

He flashed a speculative look her way. Sitting down, Tim began reading, holding the paper away from his arms that were dripping perspiration onto the table.

Mia's eyes narrowed, but she took a deep, slow breath. After reading the community, real estate, and home improvement sections, she asked, "Want something to eat before you go? I could make omelets, potatoes, bacon?"

Tim lowered the paper and shook his head.

"Can we meet up later this afternoon? I want to go downtown anyway."

He drained his glass and grunted a response on his way to the bedroom. The shower started; ten minutes later he was dressed and leaving the house.

Mia went through the stack of mail. She ripped open a self-addressed envelope. Two lines of print on a small slip of paper rejected her poems. She balled up the paper and tossed it into the trash.

Downtown later, Mia scrutinized numerous oddities and handcrafted items in the outdoor public market. She looked at buildings, signs, and new businesses. She wandered up and down the streets until ending up at Powell's City of Books, the largest independent bookseller in the country. Mia examined books in various sections: metaphysics, religion, history, writing, and poetry. Hungry for expression, wit, and insight, she filled a basket and carried her weighty selections to the check out. Her large bag of books barely cleared the ground as she returned to her car.

Mia drove to a wine shop; she selected bottles of Pinot Noir from the Willamette Valley, Syrah from Walla Walla, Pinot Grigio from Italy, and a sweeter Pinot Gris from Alsace, France.

It was late afternoon by the time she finished shopping for food and headed home. She stowed the groceries in the pantry and refrigerator and started washing vegetables in the sink. Outside the window, a neighbor's cat made a dash across the grass. Gerald had a cat. Why had she never considered getting one? Why had she never considered many of the things that had been occurring to her lately? Things like having music in the kitchen. Evenings after work, Mia had labored over suppers in silence, or with the sound of a ballgame Tim watched in the den.

Pushing down the faucet handle, Mia turned off the water, dried her hands, and retrieved a small radio from the nursery. She turned the dial to an "oldies" station, and smiled.

As Mia grated fresh Parmesan cheese onto a bamboo cutting board, she paused to admire her kitchen. She had all the best utensils, knives and cookware. It was a "cook's kitchen" and such a pleasure: so beautiful and convenient.

The door swung open suddenly.

"Oh! I didn't hear you come in," she said.

Tim turned the radio down. He pulled a bottle from the wine refrigerator, glasses from the frosted glass cabinet, and a corkscrew from the drawer. He opened the Syrah expertly, poured a taste, licked his lips, and filled two glasses. "I can sure pick 'em," he said, self-satisfaction oozing as he sauntered out the swinging door.

"I picked it," Mia grumbled, putting the bottle back in the wine refrigerator. She heard Tim plop down in his leather chair, slam his feet to the ottoman, and turn on the television in the den. She turned up the radio volume.

Opening the French door to the deck, Mia stepped outside, and breathed. The air smelled of summer. Her mind shifted to Gerald's garden and the swaying, praying pine whirring in the wind. She went back inside, drank down her glass of wine, and cooked the rice: stirring, stirring, stirring.

A Neil Diamond song she'd heard at Gerald's cabin came on the radio just as Mia was heading into the dining room with several dishes. "G., dinner's ready," she called.

Tim clicked off the television in the den, tossed down the remote, and came through the French doors. "What'd you say?"

"Gee, dinner's ready. Better eat." Mia went back to the kitchen and snapped off the radio. Tim was already serving himself when she returned with a bottle of Pinot Noir and the opener. She sank down onto her chair and pushed a damp tendril of hair from her face.

Tim got up to fetch the opened bottle of Syrah. He filled his glass then resumed eating his risotto taking a sip after each bite.

"I thought you liked my cheesy rice."

He shrugged. "Sure. It's fine."

Mia cut her pork chop into tiny pieces and pushed the food around on her plate. When Tim had finished eating, he left the table. She cleared the dishes, washed the cooking pans, and loaded the dishwasher. She joined him in the den where he was watching a movie from the late 1970s: *Days of Heaven*. Mia poured herself a drink of brandy. Savoring the sweet and lingering taste of butterscotch on her lips, she sat down and leaned her head back. She closed her eyes on the sweeping views of rolling hills, golden grain ripening, and love blossoming for a young Richard Gere.

When the movie ended, Mia went over to Tim's chair, straddled his legs, pulled out his tucked shirt, and caressed his chest. Unbuckling his pants, she showed him just how interesting she could be when she set her mind to it.

Later, unable to sleep, Mia stared for a long time at the shaft of moonlight shining through a gap in the drapery onto Tim's pale skin.

She got up and wandered to the kitchen to search the refrigerator. She took out a block of mozzarella, sliced off a hunk, and began to eat it as she went down the dark hallway toward the living room. Mia stopped outside the door to the nursery. Going back to the kitchen, she tossed the cheese into the garbage, and pulled a box of heavy-duty garbage bags from a cupboard.

Returning to the nursery, she stuffed the bags full, then lugged them to the garage. She dragged out pieces of furniture on a throw rug. When the room was emptied of all the things she could manage alone, Mia went back to bed.

Morning dawned, warm and overcast. Mia woke with a sharp pain behind her eyes. There wasn't much time before Tim had to take her to the airport. He pulled up to the curb. She leaned over, kissed him on the cheek. Her head pounded and she barely managed to say, "See you soon."

As the airplane climbed and flew out over Portland, Mia's headache also lifted. Down below, the tips of fir trees covering the mountains looked like green serrated edges piercing the white sky. Her eyes followed the blue line of the Columbia River beyond the Cascade Mountains to the dry eastern lands the color of honey. Her mind turned to Gerald and rivulets of water running down his sun-warmed back.

*He can do nothing for me…*

Sighing loudly, Mia pulled out some paper. She sketched layouts for repurposing the nursery into a private writing retreat. She listed items for the new décor: potted Norfolk pine, river rock fountain, comfy chair, rustic bookcase, and a writing desk of thick planks sanded smooth as satin. She'd paint the blue walls a warm tan. And she could use watercolors in sepia tones to paint words: thought-provoking, moving, worthy words like gratitude, love, kindness, wonder, and creativity.

Mia jotted down other words that came uninvited into her mind.

*My heart packed away*
*waiting, watching*
*my body left wanting*
*longing for you*
*I sigh*
*and dream of you*

Sighing, she twisted her hair and bunched it behind her head. Mia closed her eyes but could not sleep. She pulled out a book of word games and crossword puzzles bought for Victoria. Tears welled in her eyes. Even if Mia did pray, would it make any difference?

*B*ack at the hospital in Austin the following day, Mia caught up with Joyce.

"I'm in a rush to turn something in on campus. Want to come with me?"

Mia went along and they chatted all the way. They were walking down the grass-lined sidewalk near the English building, when they encountered an attractive, gray-haired woman.

"Hello, Dr. Farnsworth," Mia said suddenly, recognizing the woman. "I took a class from you years ago. I'm Mia Edwards. I was Mia Casinelli. This is my friend, Joyce Campbell. She's in the MSW program."

They exchanged greetings and Dr. Farnsworth said, "I remember you were a good writer, Maria. Are you writing still?"

Startled, Mia replied, "I do. But I haven't published anything."

"I'd love to read your work. Always looking for a new voice with a Latina perspective," the professor replied.

Mia flashed a look of confusion. "I have been writing of a Mexican woman that I...dream. I've written some of her lament, and some poems."

"I'll look at whatever you like. Shall we meet for coffee tomorrow morning?"

"Yes. I'd like that very much. Thank you."

"It's a date: restaurant around the corner, say ten-thirty? Nice to meet you, Joyce." Dr. Farnsworth shook their hands good-bye and walked away, her long legs striking the pavement with fast, even steps.

Chuckling, Joyce remarked, "Interesting. I've heard she goes on tangents talking of the mystical universe. Our paths cross. Desires are woven together into a tapestry, so to speak, of opportunity that becomes the fabric of our lives. No coincidence we ran into her today. Thoughts, like energy waves, create possibilities for fulfilling our desires. We're really creative beings."

Mia sighed, "Great. So I've created all my troubles?"

"I don't know. But I do know we can invite things to happen when we're very clear what we want. I'll give you an example. A few years ago I had a plastic fit."

"What?" Mia laughed.

"Plastic stays around for who knows how long or what toxins are emitted. I decided to get rid of all my plastics: wastebaskets, kitchen containers, closet organizers. The kids helped me fill the trunk of my car and we headed for a donation center. On the way, they begged me to stop to rent a movie. It'd been a little dull around our house, but I had no extra money and payday was days away."

"I can't imagine anything dull around you, or your house!" Mia laughed.

"Aw," Joyce smiled. "You're sweet! Anyway, outside the second hand store, we were loading the plastics into a cart when an elderly woman approached. She'd recently moved and was looking for just such items to organize her sewing room. We loaded them into her car. As we shook hands good-bye, she pressed several bills into my palm and would not let me refuse. It was just enough for candy and a movie."

"That's odd!"

"Our desires intersected: I wanted to get rid of something, the woman wanted something to organize, and the kids wanted fun." Joyce paused in the middle of the sidewalk to ask in an ominous tone, "What is your desire?"

"Desire," Mia sighed. "I have a lot of that..." Thinking a moment, she said, "I do want to improve my writing. Maybe I could take a seminar."

Joyce grinned. "See? Opportunity."

Across campus at the Administration Building, Mia filled out a registration form and waited for a clerk to waive her forward.

Checking his computer screen, the clerk said, "Sorry, the class is full. I can put your name on a waiting list; if anyone drops out you might get in."

"Any other poetry classes still open? Or any writing class?"

"Nope." He yawned, drumming his fingers on the keyboard. "Next."

Mia turned to Joyce. "I'm too late."

"Maybe your desire will be fulfilled another way. Maybe with Dr. Farnsworth."

Mia flashed a doubtful but amused look.

"You could take some other kind of course; you never know what might positively influence your work. How about a drumming class?"

"As in making irritating clacking noises on computer keyboards?" Mia's head nodded toward the clerk.

"As in letting the 'rhythm of life' lead you somewhere," Joyce suggested with raised eyebrow. And walking toward the car she asked, "When girl? When will you find a new rhythm?"

"Oh, I worked on that this weekend," Mia replied suggestively. They were laughing and rounding a corner when a wild-haired kid on a bike appeared suddenly. He nearly crashed into Mia, but kept going, and they turned to watch him ride away.

"Strange. As if you were drawn together by an invisible force!" Joyce offered.

Shaken, Mia drew a deep breath. "Did you see the tattoo on his arm? It was '*VIRGEN*' in blue, with a pink rose."

*T*he next morning, Mia greeted Dr. Farnsworth at the café. They were seated in a comfortable booth by a sunny window. They ordered coffee, and she told Dr. Farnsworth about the closed classes.

"Call me, Diana, please. Let's see what you have written. Perhaps there will be other opportunities for you."

Surprised by the comment so like what Joyce had said, Mia handed over several of her poems for them to be read. She gulped down her coffee while waiting.

"Wonderfully expressive," Dr. Farnsworth stated after a few moments. "Definitely publishable."

Mia smiled. "One publisher rejected them with just a slip of paper! And I haven't heard from the others."

Diana was nodding, but her eyes had returned to one of the poems. "This is particularly intriguing."

Mia glanced at the words on the page.

*Sheltering*
*blankets for thin legs*
*cool words for burning cheeks*
*protecting*
*warning of danger I can't see*
*instructing*
*correcting*
*holding me at arm's length*
*in my mother's shadow*

"Mother and I...we...struggled as if not knowing how to be with each other. She's very sick right now and I...," Mia stammered.

Diana pointed at the last lines. "Are there *two* women?"

Mia glanced again at the words and her brow furrowed. "I don't know...I can't explain that. It's just...how it came to me."

"Have you taken many writing classes through the years?"

"I've enjoyed writing, but it has only recently become something more serious."

"There's a writing program that might interest you. Sponsored by a private foundation, it is very competitive, but we do highly encourage minority interests and perspectives." Diana paused, as if waiting for some response.

"Oh," Mia answered. "Good."

"Stop by my office later, pick up an application, return it as soon as possible. Of course, I can't guarantee anything, but you may find it worthwhile to apply."

"It sounds intriguing. I'd be honored to be considered," Mia gushed and her face warmed. "Thank you, Diana. You're very kind to take this time with me."

"I appreciate the opportunity to read your work. It has been a pleasure."

# THORN

*A*ngelo was rushing from Victoria's room when Mia arrived at the hospital. His voice was a mixture of anguish and relief, "Oh, thank goodness." He wrapped his arm around Mia's shoulders and propelled her forward. "We've been waiting for you."

She hurried inside and held Victoria's hand. "I'm here, Mother."

"I wish…was true," Victoria whispered in a rasp. "So much I…didn't tell…"

Tears stung Mia's eyes. "There's so much I didn't tell you. I wanted so much to be a mother but I…couldn't…"

Victoria pressed Mia's hand as if squeezing in understanding. "Remember…what I love…meaning…there…" Gasping, Victoria closed her eyes as if to gather her strength, but her breathing became ragged.

Angelo stroked Victoria's other hand and tears glistened in his eyes. He said soothingly, "We were so lucky to find each other in San Antonio. How you captured my heart. And with Mia to love I was all the more lucky. From that first moment, you have both been my joy and delight."

Mia kissed Victoria's warm cheek and whispered, "I'm sorry if I wasn't what you wanted, Mother. I didn't mean to be a bother to you. I love you."

Victoria's eyes opened suddenly. Her breath came in slight puffs as if she was trying to say something. Then her eyes closed and there was no more movement in her.

They waited, holding their breaths as if by doing so, hers would return. As if the still body, that only moments before had been alive, would start moving again.

Angelo finally said softly, "Sleep now, my beauty. Remember only love."

Letting go of Victoria's hand, the hand that had cared for them throughout the years, Mia whispered, "I love you." She waited and listened to hear the words whispered back, but there was only silence.

The nurse was summoned. Victoria was dressed in clothing selected for leaving the hospital. Angelo and Mia said good-bye to her again, then went silently down in the elevator. They slowly walked out to the parking lot and stood there for a long time with their arms wrapped around each other while their tears fell.

A blur of activity filled the next days. Victoria was cremated as requested, and no picture of her or obituary was published in the paper. There was no funeral or memorial, also at Victoria's request, but the following Sunday, her small family attended Mass together. Angelina sat between Angelo and Mia, her bony hands gripping theirs tightly. Tim, at the end of the pew next to the aisle, looked somber and handsome in his dark suit and blue shirt that matched his eyes.

After Mass, Mia rushed back to the house and into the garden. Hastily clipping long stems of roses, she was pricked deeply by a thorn; her tears fell freely then and she struggled to regain her composure before the guests arrived. Neighbors and acquaintances of Angelina acknowledged Victoria's passing and expressed their condolences. What a shame it was that she'd passed so quickly—at least she would suffer no more, they said. Mia troubled over that statement, realizing for the first time that Victoria had lived in near isolation, as if she suffered from some unspoken ailment, as if she feared becoming known.

When the guests had departed, Angelo took Angelina home. Tim had offered to stay another day, but Mia told him she could manage. No sense in missing more work.

"Mia, are you sure you don't need me?" he had asked, but she'd given him a peck on the cheek and turned back to the leftovers she was wrapping for the freezer. A cab arrived soon after, and she watched at the window as the car disappeared down the street. She washed the crystal by hand in hot, soapy water and was sweating by the time she finished. Petals from the pink roses, Victoria's favorite, had fallen on the dark wood table. Mia swept the petals into her hand, crushed them in her palm, and breathed in the sweet fragrance.

Still wearing her simple black sheath dress, Mia went to her old room and lay down on the bed. Her fingers stroked the decorative metal pin at her shoulder. The Mother's Day when Mia had given it to Victoria, roses were blooming in the garden and the French doors out to the veranda had been open. The scent of roses and a kind of magical suspense filled the air as Victoria had un-wrapped the silver pin with a small, blue, five-petaled flower that Mia now recognized as a forget-me-not. Victoria had pinned it immediately to her sweater, and said, "Only a mother can say how much she thinks of her daughter." And the smile she wore was not proud, as Mia had thought then, but wistful.

"Oh, Mother," Mia now cried. "Why have you left me? What can I do? I have so many questions without answers."

*Sister say be strong...do the work of women...*

Mia dwelled on that line and more strange expressions came to mind.

*Truth and pain run deep*
*can we atone for sins of omission*
*can we ever go back home*

Memories flooded into Mia's mind: Victoria dressed in a brightly embroidered apron preparing one of Angelo's favorite dishes. *Capelletti* in *brodo*, dumplings in cheese, is made with ground pork and veal, diced turkey, and *mortadella*, Italian sausage. Mia begged to be allowed to help but was told to sit quietly. She'd watched with her feet wrapped around the smooth cherry legs of a chair that was passed down, like most of their furnishings, from Angelina. Once, Victoria finally let Mia roll out the pastry, and Angelo had claimed it was the flakiest, most delicious pastry he'd ever eaten.

"It's the Italian in me!" Mia had remarked proudly.

But what was the look that'd passed between Victoria and Angelo? Mia had glanced back and forth but could not read their secret exchange.

They had often told the story of how they met in San Antonio near the River Walk at a festival in La Villita, the little village, one of San Antonio's original neighborhoods. Angelo had been instantly captivated by Victoria. "Her hair was pulled up in old-fashioned combs, and one long curl brushed her shoulder, tempting me," he had said.

Inseparable from that first meeting, their lives had been so entwined Mia could not imagine how Angelo could now go on without Victoria. He was in his late seventies and his health was good: he might have many years yet to live. But now he was alone like his mother. It was so unfair! Mia had wanted change— but not this much, not this way.

Filled with anguish, she dressed in her running clothes and went out of the house. She ran down the street and kept going until she was sweaty and tired. Mia limped back to the house and went inside. She slipped off her shoes and headed for her room but paused in the doorway of the master bedroom. Switching on the light, she glanced into the still room. Mia crept across the carpet to Victoria's bureau and slowly opened a drawer, peering in as if some piece of Victoria might suddenly pop out. Her eyes ran over the neatly folded and stacked articles of clothing.

Pulling out a sweater, Mia put her cheek to the soft angora. Her eyes fell to the exquisite initials Victoria had embroidered in swirling blue letters on the tag: "VM" for Victoria Maria. "VM" like the Virgin Mary. A chill washed over Mia; she set the sweater down and closed the drawer. She looked through Victoria's closet which was also ordered neatly: outfits paired with coordinating shoes and matching handbags. Victoria had always dressed finely, as if intending to go somewhere grand, but she never went to more than a handful of places and was always accompanied by Angelo.

Behind a rack of shoes at the back of the closet, beneath a stack of old books, Mia found a small photo album. Opening it, she tried to study the photos but the plastic pages reflected the overhead light. Pulling back the brittle plastic, Mia studied several pictures that were peeling away from the sticky background.

One snapshot was of Victoria dressed in a Spanish costume. Beneath festive, colored lights, her smiling face seemed to glow. It might have been taken the day Victoria and Angelo met. Another photograph was taken outside a church: the sky was robin's-egg blue and Angelina looked proud and somewhat triumphant standing between the couple. There were no notations or imprinted dates on those pictures. Another photo showed Mia wearing a red velvet dress and standing in front of a studio background of snow. "1968" was written on the back. Mia stared into the eyes of her younger self and wondered about the wary look on that young face.

Mia pressed the photos back onto the page in the album and smoothed down the plastic. She turned the pages and studied other photographs arranged in chronological order. Mia's clothes had been made for her by Victoria and were somewhat old-fashioned in style. At fifteen, she had started coloring her hair, but in all the pictures taken before that, Mia's hair was dark and hung plainly.

Sighing, Mia took the album over to the bed—the painted iron bed given to Angelo and Victoria by Angelina—perhaps it had been Angelina's own marriage bed. This iron headboard had large curves like rams' horns linked with trailing vines and flowering roses. More than once when Mia had been ill—strep throat or flu on the wane—she had recuperated in this bed with a hot water bottle, and Victoria had fixed her a bowl of sugared peaches with cream. How sweet that had been: enjoying the brief, nurturing care of Victoria.

Mia got up from her parents' bed and went to her own room. She fell asleep with the photo album in her arms but she tossed and turned all night. When she woke in the morning her heart was racing. She glanced at the floor; the three photos were lying loose on the carpet beside the album. Mia shook off a chill.

*So much pain come from loving...and such small sweetness...*

ngelina lived nearby. When Mia arrived, Angelina was in her sitting room with a fresh pot of tea, two cups, and a plate of sweets. Perhaps Angelina was always ready for callers: that was the way of a good hostess, the old way, the way of a lady. Maintaining a formal elegance with manicured nails, fresh coiffure, and finely tailored clothing, Angelina looked the part of a ninety-eight-year-old matriarch.

The exquisitely carved grandfather clock in the hallway ticked and bonged loudly in the otherwise still house. Mia smiled at the sound as she entered. "Grandmother, this house is beautiful and always the same."

"Yes, dear, it is," Angelina replied, the corners of her mouth curving upward. "Reminds me of one I long admired in the King William District near the River Walk of San Antonio. Keeping it just so is my habit."

"You are a creature of habit," Mia laughed.

"Yes, good habits are the hallmark of a lady."

"There's no one more a lady than you, Grandmother."

Angelina nodded and smiled, but her face looked tired.

"You work too hard," Mia sighed. "I guess I come by that habit naturally."

Angelina's eyes keenly considered her.

"We're a family of hard workers—so busy we barely have time to record events."

Angelina's face dimmed.

"I was looking in Mother's photo album. There are no baby pictures of me. And no pictures of Mother and Papa in San Antonio except outside the church with you."

"It was a difficult time."

"Too difficult to snap a few pictures?"

Her lips pressed into a thin line, Angelina stared down into her cup of tea.

"Mother was so much younger than Papa, and they married so quickly after meeting, you must have been quite surprised."

"Yes."

"They had their heritage and religion in common; surely that made it easier for them." Mia looked into her grandmother's face as if searching. "Do you think it's wrong for *different* people to mix? Or is it enough that they love one another?"

"Always questions, Maria."

Mia winced as if she had been scolded, but she kept on. "Do you think people are naturally drawn to the land of their ancestors, some force pulling them back, some history, some irresistible longing calling them home? Did you ever return to Italy? Did Mother ever explain why she didn't go back?"

"Perhaps someday you will find your own answer," Angelina replied, glancing down at the leavings in her tea cup. Her eyes lifted to the curtained window. "Heritage matters. Religion and custom influence a life, how it is lived. The blood of one's ancestors is thick with knowledge and tradition. Much sickness comes from denying that connection. Denial and secrets, like sickness, kill."

Taking a sip of her hot tea, Mia was not warmed.

"As a boy, Angelo fell sick with a fever so high the doctors said he was 'damaged', perhaps never to father a child."

Mia looked up suddenly and stared as Angelina continued, "Federico, bless his soul, and I prayed for a miracle: just one grandchild to carry on the family heritage. It was not to be as we wished."

"I have the family name," Mia managed to say. "And I would pass it to my children…"

Angelina raised a penciled brow, and the look from her small brown eyes was piercing. "When will that be? Perhaps you are like Victoria: interested more in the man and the 'deed' than in his seed."

Mia's eyes grew wide but she could utter no response to the shocking words.

Angelina only dabbed at her mouth with a lace handkerchief and continued, "Angelo was afraid no woman would have him. Victoria was afraid of something else. I, on the other hand, was afraid of nothing."

*I pray* La Virgen *keep safe…*

Still as a statue, Mia listened.

"We are proud women, yes?"

Mia nodded woodenly.

"We take care of our own, for the good of the family, the men we love. These things we do not discuss openly; you understand?" Angelina pierced Mia again with a glance. "I taught Victoria to be an *Italian* wife. It is the woman who guides the home, molds the man into what he wants to be, what he can be, with her help. A smart woman can make a good man, yes? But the wrong kind of woman that comes from the wrong place can bring a man down. When a man falls, he is not alone. Down comes his heritage, his name, his blood, his family. We would not want that, would we?"

She shook her head.

"Angelo could have done worse. And of course, we were thankful to have you. Named for your aunt, your grandmother, and myself, you were baptized in our church and then so loved."

A crease formed between Mia's brows.

Dabbing her handkerchief to the corners of her dry eyes then pouring herself more tea, Angelina continued. "I thought Victoria wanted only our money, our family name. She'd come so far already; clever that one: naming her life as she wished with a map." Angelina paused and sighed audibly. "Her secrets, she kept to herself. I respected that, and grew to love her, in time. I will miss her."

Mia took a shaky breath. "I miss her now, too."

Angelina studied Mia's face. "Don't look so sad; be thankful you live. You still have two of us who love you and would do anything to keep you safe." Angelina refilled Mia's cup. "Drink your tea, dear."

Blinking back tears, Mia took a sip.

"Will you leave soon for Portland?"

"Probably."

Angelina raised an eyebrow. "A man has needs."

"So does a woman," Mia snapped, and her grandmother's face stiffened. "I'm sorry. I'm worried about leaving—I'm afraid Papa will have a hard time." Her eyes brimmed with tears.

*I cry for him…*

Angelina clucked her tongue. "Do not worry about Angelo. He is my son, strong like his father and I. He will bounce back soon. He accepts what comes. Something you might yet learn: giving up laments for what cannot be changed. Finish your tea, dear."

But Mia was disturbed. She gave an excuse for leaving abruptly, and as she walked the short distance back to her parents' house, her mind mulled over the conversation with Angelina. Her steps quickened. She hurried into the study and scanned the books on the shelves. Mia stood on her tiptoes to reach the red atlas on a high shelf. Her hand bumped one of Victoria's black ceramic pots; it wobbled then settled. She breathed a sigh of relief but words were in her mind.

*Danger come like wind...*

Mia carried the atlas to the desk. She thumbed through the pages and stopped at a map of Italy. Perhaps she would visit there someday. Perhaps she could find the place where the blood of her ancestors flowed. She turned the pages to maps of other countries and came across a raveled scrap of cloth. Mia fingered the satiny stitches of a flower and traced the curvy letters of "*Angelita*" embroidered on roughly woven fabric. She slipped the scrap into her pocket, and returned the atlas to the shelf. Mia wandered back to the desk and sat down. Her hands stroked the polished dark wood.

She glanced about the room. The books were arranged neatly on the shelves. The fireplace was spotless and the mirrored service cart was cluttered with full crystal decanters sparkling in a shaft of sunlight from the window. It was all so perfect, and lonely. She lay down her head and cried. Perhaps she slept.

When Mia wiped her bleary eyes, her mind filled suddenly with words. She extracted a pen and paper from the drawer and began writing.

> *My mother*
> *where do you go*
> *will I ever find you again*
> *do you wait for me still?*
>
> *How you love me*
> *praying me to safety*
> *waiting for my return*
>
> *How I long for your sweet smile*
> *and embrace*
> *melting me into your softness*
> *where I fit*
> *sheltered in Mother's shadow*

Mia puzzled over the words and the subtle and odd changes to the lines of the poem she'd written before. She pondered the meaning of those changes, and feeling lost, she cried helplessly.

> *Ay...ahuehuete...*

# PETAL

ngelo came into the house. He set his keys in one of Victoria's black ceramic bowls on the hall table. "Are you here, darling Mia?"

She stuffed her poem into her pocket and wiped her eyes.

"Sweetheart, were you sleeping?" Angelo entered the study and stopped at the service cart. "Do you care for a brandy? I know it's early, but I believe I'll have one. I doubt anyone would find fault with us at such a time..." he paused, looking her way.

She declined, moved from the desk to give him a brief hug, and collapsed into a wing-back chair in front of the fireplace. Mia leaned her head against the back of the soft chair. Though the tapestry was old and slightly faded, it was still beautiful. As a child she had traced the intricate design of alternating threads with her finger, imagining some mysterious spell, some secret message was hidden in a code of colors and design.

"Darling Mia, I wanted to talk to you about something." Angelo removed a sheaf of papers from the inside pocket of his jacket. "As you know, we are not extremely wealthy, but should I live another twenty or thirty years we have sufficient funds."

"Don't talk like that," she protested.

He held up his hand. "I've set aside some money for you. You may draw the interest from it until such time as you have greater need or want. Should you ever be alone; heaven forbid anything happens to Tim, it is there for you."

"I don't know what to say," she stammered.

"Money can be a comfort," he sighed. "I've been fortunate and so very happy. Now, without my dear Victoria filling my life with beauty, I don't know how I shall live."

Mia's voice wavered as she looked into his misty eyes. "I hate for you to be alone, Papa; maybe you could live with Grandmother!"

Laughing, he protested, "She's an old woman!"

Her brow furrowed with concern. "Do you think she's all right?"

"If Mother suffers, she does it quietly."

"She seemed strange today. And she…said odd things."

"Oh?"

"I was asking about heritage."

"Mother is proud of her Italian heritage," he replied stiffly.

"I'm proud, too. Remember when we had culture month at school?"

He looked out the window.

"Remember the report I did on Italian Americans?"

Angelo glanced down at the papers on the desk.

She persisted, "I wrote about Mother and Grandmother teaching me to make our favorite Italian family dishes. Remember the club I wanted to join: the 'Talians'?"

He shuffled the papers in front of him.

"Remember?" Mia implored, staring intently at his face. "The 'Talians'?"

He raised his eyes. "The 'Talians'? Oh, yes."

"I thought someday we could go to Italy, find our families," she sighed. "I would have been so excited to meet them. I'm so proud of our heritage."

He said nothing, only looked at her.

"It would have been fun! I'm so proud of our shared heritage," she repeated.

"Yes, Darling," he managed to say. "We wanted you to feel a sense of heritage, some family connection."

Her brow furrowed anew and her eyes studied him. He got up suddenly, moving toward her as if about to say something requiring closer proximity. But instead, he sank down into the other wingback chair and sighed heavily.

"I'm sorry, Papa. You must be exhausted." Mia got up and settled on the floor at his feet as she had done as a child.

His hand patted the top of her head. "I'm sorry we could not keep every heartbreak from you."

A tear slipped down her cheek. She rested her head on his knee. Maybe Mia drifted to sleep, for she was very stiff when she finally rose from the floor. She kissed Angelo's bare, warm forehead and retired to her room. Colors blended in a blur through her half-closed eyes as she lay face down on the comforter that had been on her bed since her tenth birthday.

That year she had fallen in love with a giant teddy bear at the department store. He had glassy, warm brown eyes, and a pleasing smile of embroidered threads. Imagining how his big arms might wrap around her, Mia had hoped and prayed he'd soon be hers. When her birthday arrived, hidden behind the Christmas presents in the study, there was a big, soft package wrapped in bright blue foil paper. Mia had torn a tiny hole and poked her finger inside to feel the bear's fur, but there was only fabric.

Victoria had announced, "A perfect comforter to replace your little girl quilt of drab little bears. Now you are a young lady."

"It's pretty," Mia had managed to say.

The new comforter was placed on her bed and Mia had dragged the old quilt into the closet to her secret place behind the hanging clothes. Crying with disappointment, she had clung to the teddy bears on her "little girl" quilt.

Rummaging now behind boxes in her closet, Mia reached into the dark corner and pulled out her old quilt. It had that dusty smell of being too long without fresh air, but she placed it on her bed and drifted to sleep.

She dreamed of a brown bear in a feathered headband holding her in his comforting arms, and she woke in the morning with an aching heart. Mia got up, poured a large mug of coffee, and wandered to the study. Alarmed to see Angelo sitting in the wingback, she asked, "Papa, were you here all night?"

"No, no. I woke early. How was your sleep, my darling Mia?"

Mia sat down in the other chair and yawned, "I slept." After several sips of coffee she asked, "Papa, do you know anything about Mother's life before you met?"

"Rather early in the day for questions," he said, eyeing her.

"Mother was young when she left her family. Something very compelling must have happened to keep her away all those years. Was there someone before you that..."

He sighed loudly as if to interrupt but he only said, "She would not speak of it."

"But…" Her eyes held him. "To never go back, to never speak of her family, it must have been something devastating!" Mia's eyes were wide with imagined scenarios.

"You know how she was," he sighed. "Victoria was a mystery even to me. Such a woman! Everything she touched was made beautiful," he said, his voice wavering.

Mia's eyes were filling with tears. "Remember how she made me over when I was a teenager? I'm not sure I ever thanked her. I can't believe she isn't coming back."

"I expect at any moment to see her; everywhere there are reminders."

"I could pack away some of her things," Mia suggested gently.

"Perhaps. But where to start?" Angelo's eyes moved around the room. "Victoria lingers in everything she touched."

"Oh," Mia said, jumping up and rushing to her room. She returned with the cloth she'd found in the atlas. "See the flower and the curve of the letters? Did Mother make it? It looks like the style of her embroidery."

He barely gave it a look. "It is only a scrap of forgotten cloth."

"I found it stuck between two pages in the old atlas," she said, pointing to the high shelf of books.

His eyes darted to her face. "Which pages?"

"I didn't notice."

He shrugged dismissively. "Wondering about every little thing won't bring her back." But his eyes softened as they rested on her face. "We said that often about you—after you married and moved so far away. We wondered how you were but didn't want to bother you—two lonely old fuddy-duddies disturbing your happy little life."

"It wasn't that happy," she replied offhandedly. But then Mia asked, "You wondered about me, and *wanted* to call?"

His head bobbed up and down. "We had to let you go, have your own adventure, even if it was with someone we weren't sure about. You seemed sure."

"I wasn't," she admitted. "But I had to go and make my own life. I tried to be independent, but I missed you so terribly I couldn't call. Just hearing your voice made me miss you even more." Her eyes filled with tears.

He smiled sadly. "That's how it was with Victoria. Whenever the phone rang, she'd answer, thinking it was you. But her tone would change, and I knew it was Mother calling, peppering her with questions: when did you call, what did you write, what gifts did you send?"

"Oh," Mia exclaimed. "That must have been terrible getting the third degree from Grandmother! I did send nice gifts, though."

"Every one was treasured."

"I should have done more. I was selfish, and too absorbed by my 'little life'."

"We did wish you and Tim were more comfortable with us. We might have grown to care for him, at least a little, if we'd seen more of you together."

She sighed, looked down into her cup, and was silent.

"Are you all packed and ready to go?"

Mia looked over at him. "Almost. I feel guilty leaving. Will you be okay?"

"Yes," he answered. "But it will be very quiet."

Reluctantly she stood up.

"Darling, I wish you would let me drive you to the airport."

"No, it's silly; the shuttle can pick me up. Besides, I don't think I can stand parting in public." Her voice quavered with emotion.

"I will miss your pretty face, my dear."

"I'll miss yours, too." A tear broke over the rim of her eye, and he handed her a perfectly pressed, monogrammed handkerchief. Mia dabbed at her eyes. "Thank you, Papa. Even with Mother at the hospital, with all she went through, it was good for us to spend the time together, however heart-wrenching, and short."

"Yes, Darling," he said gently.

Mia hugged him, and went to her room to finish packing: the scrap of cloth, photo album, puzzle book, a piece of Victoria's favorite black pottery, and the teddy bear quilt.

*W*hen she arrived in Portland, Mia caught a taxi at the airport. She tidied her makeup and hair on the drive home and glanced up just as the taxi pulled to the curb.

Tim had come out of the front door and was moving quickly down the walk toward the cab. He pulled the door open. "I would have come to get you."

"Oh, I didn't want you to bother," she answered, smiling sweetly up at Tim.

He took the purse from her hands, opened her wallet, and paid the driver while Mia headed for the house with her suitcase. Tim followed with her other bags and set them just inside the door. Mia sank heavily onto the living room sofa and closed her eyes.

"I have some business to finish," Tim announced, standing above her.

Her eyes opened.

"I'll be back at seven-thirty. We'll go out for dinner." He started to walk away, paused as if meaning to say something else, but then he turned and left.

She closed her eyes again, slept, and dreamed.

*Too long I wait...*

$\mathcal{M}$ia woke in a sweat and her heart was beating wildly. The clock on the mantel bonged seven o'clock. She hurried to the shower and whispered resolutely, "I've worked too hard to give up. I will make things better. We will make a new, different future."

Tending her appearance, Mia blew her long hair dry, massaged vanilla-scented lotion into her skin and sprinkled powder on the hot creases of her body. She dressed in a dark red satin sheath, accessorized with sandals and the pendant of Tim's birthstone he'd given her for their first anniversary. Makeup meticulously applied, she was putting a finishing spray on her hair when Tim's car pulled into the driveway. Mia threw a shawl over her arm, grabbed her evening bag, and hurried to the hall just as he was coming through the front door.

Tim stopped in his tracks. "You look great," he remarked with obvious surprise.

"Thank you," she replied, a warm glow spreading over her. She flashed him an alluring smile.

"Let's go," he barked. Tim waited for her to exit, locked the door, and moved down the walk behind her. His eyes were on the fit and shimmer of her dress as Mia got into the car. She smiled up at him but he did not meet her eyes, and he did not turn to look at her as he started the car and backed down the driveway.

The restaurant was elegantly decorated with evergreens and ivy, rose-colored linens, sparkling crystal glasses, and gleaming white china. "This is pretty. It can be our new place, for our new life," she said smiling. "I think I'll have champagne!"

Tim ordered Maker's Mark.

Their salads arrived quickly and they ate. Piano and cello music played in the background. When their entrees came, Tim devoured his New York steak and a baked potato he smothered in butter and sour cream. Mia picked at her overcooked hazelnut-crusted halibut and limp asparagus. She sipped her champagne, and her mind wandered to after-dinner intrigue: Tim's wet tongue exploring her mouth, his hands caressing her back and removing her slip of a dress, his fingers searching for her sweetest spot, his mouth making her believe he wanted her and no one else.

*If only...*

Tim pushed his plate aside, wiped his mouth, and placed his napkin on the table as if signaling the end of their meal. But when the waiter came over to retrieve their dishes, Mia ordered raspberry sorbet. Tim ordered another drink. He watched as she began to eat her dessert. "You seem well," he remarked.

"Life goes on. I am thankful I live." She smiled and licked a drip of sweetness from her lip. "And now we can make a new start."

His mouth turned to a thin slit, and his head moved slowly side to side.

"We can make a happy new life together," she said, ignoring his expression.

He shook his head. "No."

Her heart pounded. Her breath would not come.

"Valerie…"

Her hair tingled. An alarming chill raced down her spine. She struggled to find her voice. "You said you let her go. 'Not worth the complication,' you said."

He looked at his hands. "Valerie," Tim looked up, his eyes level with hers, "is pregnant with my child." He shrugged. "You were gone so long."

"With Mother dying!"

"Valerie's having difficulty. The doctor says she needs bed rest. I want to help."

"Playing nursemaid is not your style, Tim," she replied hotly.

His hands pushed down the air as if to push down the volume of her words and the level of her emotion. "Look," he said reasonably. "You're strong. You can handle it."

"I have to because *you* mishandled it?"

"Valerie and the baby need me."

"You didn't do a thing for me when *I* needed your help, when I lost *our* babies. All you did was work. You said you didn't even care if we had a baby. And you didn't seem to care at all when they said I…" Tears welled in her eyes.

"Mia," he said solidly, reasonably. "You don't know what I felt."

"And I thought we were putting the past struggles behind us that weekend I came home…" her voice broke.

Tim replied evenly, "We both know what that was."

"We do? What?" Mia snapped.

"Victoria was dying: you needed the comfort of the familiar and you wanted to believe there was a chance for her, and us."

Blinking back tears, she said bitterly, "What do you plan to do now, Tim?"

"Valerie's not as capable as you; I want to step up and be a real husband, take responsibility."

"You're MY husband!" she practically shouted. "What about your responsibility to ME?"

People nearby turned to stare.

Tim squirmed in his seat. "Things change."

Her eyes studied his face as if seeing it for the first time. Throwing her napkin to the table, pushing her chair back, Mia stood up and stormed toward the exit.

He tossed bills down for the check and hurried after her, reaching the door just as it swung back in his face.

They drove home in silence. When the car stopped, Mia jumped out and went up the walk, unlocked the front door, and marched into the master bedroom closet. Tim followed and froze when she reached up to the shelf where he kept his gun. "Mia!" he exclaimed, flinching as she turned suddenly.

"Get going," she said acidly, tossing something to his feet.

He stared down at an overnight bag. "Let's talk about this, Mia. Nothing has to happen right now."

"Want change?" she growled. "GO!"

He didn't move. "But I…"

She shook her head and laughed harshly, "Unbelievable! Always about you!"

"Get real, Mia! You weren't happy. You never really wanted me—just someone. I actually thought you'd be relieved. I didn't think you'd be unreasonably mad."

Her eyes blazed. "You mean mad like a crazy woman? What's the matter, Tim? Afraid I'll do something rash? Tear up the house, break some glass?" she laughed harshly. "I'm not mad." Mia drew a breath and her voice calmed. "Done. That's what I am, Tim. Done."

Glancing around the room at all the possessions she'd lived without these last few months, she said, "On second thought, Tim, why don't you just move Valerie in here, then you won't be inconvenienced at all?"

A look of relief spread over his face. "That would be easier."

Mia smiled, stepped toward him, and whispered sweetly, "I'll be out of your way in no time." Her lips were almost touching his.

He smiled.

"You know, Tim," she looked up at him and placed her hands on his chest, "you're a self-absorbed jerk!" Mia pushed him away. She turned, and started throwing her clothes into suitcases.

"Don't go like that," he barked from a position of retreat in the doorway.

"How would you like me to go? Huh, Tim? Happy-go-lucky, skipping down the walk with suitcases in hand?"

"But I don't want…"

"*YOU* don't want?" Her voice lunged at him, and he disappeared down the hall. "I don't know why I didn't see it before," she yelled. "You're not just self-absorbed. You're selfish! I can't believe I ever wanted you to father my children! You'll be a terrible father—just like your father! No wonder your mother left you both!" Mia wiped away angry tears, and filled more suitcases.

When she had finished packing, Mia lugged her bags to the front door. Tim was in the den, drink in hand, watching a ball game on television. She stared at him, but he did not look over. Mia walked silently back into the bedroom, took off the pendant and placed it in his box of cufflinks and tie clasps. She did not need his birthstone hanging around her neck and dragging her down any longer.

Mia walked into the den. When he looked up, she smiled and said, "You will pay for this, Tim. Dearly."

"Wait," he said flatly. "I didn't want it to go like this."

"No, TIM, NEITHER DID I!" Mia yelled, and she smiled when he flinched and put his hands to his ears. She dropped her house key noisily into the bowl on the hall table. "You can pick the car up at the airport tomorrow," she growled before going out the door.

After shuttling her bags from the house to her car, Mia stopped. She walked over to Tim's shiny black BMW. Keys firmly in hand, she walked alongside his car and imagined scraping through the paint.

*M*ia caught a lucky flight to Austin and, hours later, was sitting in a café drinking a big mug of steaming hot chocolate when Joyce came in and sat down. The waitress came for her order.

"Tea, please." Joyce studied Mia's appearance. "I'm glad you called. Pretty dress. Bit fancy for this place."

Mia only sighed and asked how Joyce's neighbor was doing.

"Hospice house is making her as comfortable as possible." The waitress delivered her tea, and Joyce stirred in several spoons of sugar. "So, how are you? I thought you planned to go back to Portland."

"I went. Something happened. Tim and I are through. I had to get out of there."

"You weren't in any danger, were you?" Joyce's voice registered alarm.

"Not me!" Mia laughed, "Maybe he was."

Joyce spooned ice from her water glass into her hot tea. "What happened?"

"While I was here, Valerie called him."

"Oh, no." Disgust showed on Joyce's face. "That makes me so mad! You're with your dying mother and he's messing around? What a selfish creep!"

"That's not the worst of it," Mia added. "She's pregnant."

Joyce shook her head. "I am so sorry. What does he have to say for himself?"

"He says he wants to take responsibility, step up and act like a real husband and father," Mia said bitterly.

"*You're* his wife! What about his responsibility to you?"

"That's what I said."

"The jerk! My poor husband would have done anything to be with me, even one more day, but he was taken away. And I would have given everything to keep him."

Mia blinked back tears. "I'm so sorry for you. It must have been terrible."

"It was! But as much as it hurt to lose him, it wasn't his fault, and I had no anger at him. It's worse for you! You have someone to blame! And that's torture!"

Forcing down a sob, Mia groaned, "It is! But...here I am." Her palms turned up as if she had just magically appeared.

Joyce nodded soberly. "What will you do now?"

She shrugged. "I have no plan. I need a few days before I can even begin telling Papa all of what has happened. We were so focused on Mother, and I had already kept so much from them, I didn't say anything about any of it."

"I have an idea! Come home with me. Stay as long as you want. I have room, if you don't mind a few sewing things in your way. Maybe I'll even clear out a closet!"

"It would be much friendlier than a hotel," Mia replied.

Joyce drank down her tea, and threw down several bills. "Come on, let's go!"

# BASKET

*T*he Campbell's house was an inviting, yellow bungalow with Dutch blue shutters and window boxes filled with Texas petunias. Joyce had her hand to all the soft surfaces of the interior: slipcovers, curtains, and table cloths she had sewn. The small guest room had a few sewing things indeed: piles of fabric, numerous spools of thread on pegs, notions in baskets, and many other useful items stowed on a wall of shelves.

Clearing out a drawer in a large chest and a space in the closet, Joyce filled a cardboard box and pushed it under a small table in the corner. They made up the twin-sized bed in clean sheets of candy-cane stripes and a pink gingham coverlet.

"Get some sleep. I'll have coffee in the pot whenever you get up."

"Thank you," Mia said yawning and gave her a hug.

"Happy dreams." Joyce went out, quietly shutting the door.

Mia changed into pajamas, snuggled down into the soft bed, and dropped into heavy sleep.

*What I can do…only work…pray…*

*W*aking late in the morning, Mia lingered in bed and listened to the house noises. She gazed around the bright room. A postcard on the bulletin board caught her attention: *La Virgen de Guadalupe.* The figure depicted stood resplendent in a gleaming crown and a long, deep blue cloak covered in stars. Mia got out of bed, turned the card over and peered at the typed description on the back: *Templo de Santo Domingo, Oaxaca, Mexico.*

She pulled on a lightweight sweatshirt and went out to the kitchen for coffee. Joyce was just taking a pan from the oven.

"Smells heavenly," Mia remarked.

"One of my favorite recipes." Joyce brought the pan and a jar of home canned peaches to the table. She served generous pieces of warm coffee cake into bowls.

Mia took a bite. "Oh, Joyce, this is scrumptious!"

"Try it with peaches. That's yummy, too! I just love to bake. Do you?"

"Not so much. Grandmother likes to bake. I do love to eat sweets, but I had to break the frequent consumption." Mia patted her slender belly.

"Obviously, I haven't broken the habit!"

She took another bite. "Mmm. Sooo good!"

"Louise's recipe. She was full of good ideas. Some of the fabric in the spare room was for a quilt we planned to make." Letting out a sigh, Joyce said, "Such a bummer."

Mia started laughing and tears filled her eyes. "I haven't heard that word in ages." Waving a hand at her face to dry the tears, she managed to say, "Sorry." She ate another bite of cake, and mumbled, "Joyce, this is so cinnamony! That's not a word, but it's true. Mother would love this recipe; she loved cinnamon in everything, even hot chocolate."

"They do that in Mexico." Joyce turned and checked the clock. "Want to come to class with me?"

Mia shook her head. "I couldn't sit still. I'll take a run to calm my nerves."

"Do you ever meditate? It can be helpful, and illuminating. A few years ago, before I sold my flower shop, my employees were tattling on each other, and I didn't know who to believe. One day I put my head down on my desk and asked, 'What can I do with my trust?' Impatiently a voice in my mind said, 'Put it in a basket and throw it off a cliff!' So, envisioning a big-handled Easter basket, I put my worry and mistrust inside. I stood at the edge of an imaginary cliff and threw the basket out over a canyon. And the most amazing thing happened..."

"What?"

"The basket tumbled out into a cloudless sky, but before descending, my emotions transformed into a white dove, flew up and disappeared."

"Oh," Mia sighed.

"'What do I do with myself?' I asked, and the voice said, 'Jump off after it'. So I imagined I took a running leap off the imaginary cliff. I sailed out into the air but before I started to descend, I became white light and floated up into nothingness."

"Oooh."

"After that, everything was easier to manage. I reclaimed my strength and took charge of the situation at the shop," Joyce said, her face aglow.

"Nice symbolism: basket with a big handle, you get a handle on your emotions."

"Now who's the 'Sage of the Cafeteria'?"

"'Sage of the Kitchen' to you," Mia chuckled. "You believe in miracles, too?"

"Miracles and blessings. We get them every day. Louise has lived next door since the kids were little. She's been like another mother, or grandmother to them. Even while she was taking care of her own elderly mother deteriorating with Alzheimer's, Louise always had time for us." Joyce paused, swallowing hard before continuing. "When she was stricken with cancer, my spirits got so low. I prayed for someone to cheer me, and then there you were in the basement cafeteria, asking if I'd like to sit with you."

Mia nodded, her eyes glistening. "I had just prayed to Mary for someone to talk to, someone to help me find what I am missing."

Joyce gestured with open palms and smiled, "She listens: Mary, the goddess, creator—whatever you want to call her."

"I saw the postcard in your sewing room. What do you know about *La Virgen de Guadalupe*? Is she the Patron saint of Mexico?"

"Oh, isn't she lovely? She's so much more than a saint. She's our Mother."

"Like Mary?"

"*La Virgen* watches over us, helps us." Looking at the clock again, Joyce jumped up. She grabbed a set of keys from the rack on the wall by the door and gave them to Mia. "Take the spare car anywhere you want. It's kind of a beater but it goes. And so must I!" Joyce dashed out the door.

Mia finished eating, cleared the table, squirted soap and ran warm water into the sink to do up the dishes. After sweeping and mopping the kitchen, and vacuuming the living room, she made the call that had been on her mind all morning.

"*E*nticements Boutique. How may we help you?" Tim answered smoothly.

"Tim…"

"You sure don't waste any time," he snarled.

"What do you mean?"

"That redskin called."

"What did he say?" she asked breathlessly.

"He said he wanted to get hold of you. I told the son-of-a-bitch to keep his grimy hands to himself."

"You didn't keep your hands to yourself!" Mia snapped.

There was silence on his end.

She spoke loudly, "I *called* to give you a mailing address."

He took it down and said in a more subdued voice, "Mia, I'm sorry things took a turn."

Startled, she managed to say, "I thought we were good partners; what happened?"

"Something was missing."

"I thought it was a baby," she sighed. "I thought if I had a baby I would feel better, *we* would be better."

"It just played out."

She could almost see his shoulders shrug nonchalantly. "*Played out*? Our marriage, our partnership, wasn't an exercise, A GAME we were playing!" Mia responded caustically.

"So that's how you're going to be? Always 'Suffering Mia'!" There was a moment of silence before his clipped words, "I've got your address. Expect papers."

"What papers?"

"I've filed for divorce."

"Speaking of not wasting any time yourself, huh? Guess you have a timetable to keep, a new family to plan for…" her voice faltered.

"Christ!" But Tim's next words were matter-of-fact. "One last thing I meant to say: thank you for all your work through the years."

Mia did not hear what else he said because she pushed the button on the phone and ended their connection.

*Every happiness go from me...*

*H*ours later, when Joyce arrived home, Mia was still in the living room where she'd slumped to the floor. "What are you doing here?" Joyce sat down on the sofa.

"I called Tim to let him know where I was and..." Mia's voice broke. "He's filed for divorce. Everything is lost: my babies, Mother, my career, my marriage..."

"I'm sorry. I'm so sorry."

"And the final insult?" Mia stared up at Joyce, her eyes ablaze. "Tim *thanked* me for all my work through the years. Like I was an employee he was letting go to retirement!" she snapped bitterly.

"Ohhh," Joyce sighed sympathetically.

"And you know what the worst is?"

"No, honey, I don't."

"He had the audacity to say something had been missing with us! I felt it, too. But I've been missing something all my life. I thought I was missing Texas and my family. And then I thought it was a baby, if only I had a baby I'd feel more... more..." Tears streamed down her cheeks and Mia wiped her face on her sleeve. "Shit."

*Why he go from me...*

"Ain't it the truth? Ain't it the truth?" Joyce just shook her head.

Slamming her fists to the carpet, Mia railed, "I'm so angry! This isn't how I wanted my life to be! I'm torn from my roots! How do I go on from here?"

"Get the best attorney you can afford and fight for what is yours, what you've worked so hard for!" Joyce advised.

"I can't believe this is happening to me. My whole life has gone off track."

Joyce suddenly stood up. "We need food! I'll make something."

Mia followed her to the kitchen.

"Want some hot tea? No, coffee!" Joyce filled the coffee pot and turned it on. She rummaged through a tall cupboard and pulled out a nearly empty bottle of Irish Cream. "Oh! That would've been good!" She looked again into the cupboard and pulled down an air popper. "Let's make popcorn! Chewing always makes me feel better!"

Leaning against the cupboard, Mia watched the coffee maker dripping. "Who am I? I don't know any more. I have no job or home, no husband or baby, no mother or…"

Interrupting, Joyce said, "Those are just the details of your life, not who you are."

"I guess," Mia sighed. "But I feel so lost. Where do I go? What do I do?"

Joyce poured popcorn into the whirring air popper, melted butter in the microwave, and poured it over the popcorn when all the kernels had popped merrily out into a large bowl. Mia filled large mugs with coffee and added extra sugar and dollops of whipped cream. They went into the living room, sat down and started eating.

"Tim is so confident, so separate, so comfortable in his own skin," Mia complained. "It irritated me no end how he would sprawl out on the furniture and watch sports on television without a care in the world while I flitted around doing chores. I was so wound up, always going, going, going, running on an empty heart that ached for something, someone…and I…"

Joyce listened while chewing her popcorn.

"I worked and worked to build the business, make a home, keep myself up and interesting and involved. What is my reward? Now I'm alone. No one wants me."

"That's not true. And it's not so bad being alone," Joyce said softly. "There will be someone else for you. Can you envision ever dating in the future, or are you sour on men for all time?"

Mia sighed. "I can't imagine who I'd find interesting enough."

"What about Gerald? He sounded interesting and fun."

She shook her head. "He's just not…"

Joyce's eyebrows arched melodramatically. "Not what?"

"How could there be anything between us anyway? He's in Oregon. And I'm here in Austin."

"Is this where you want to be?"

"Yes," she said with a nod. "Definitely. With the best friend in the world."

"Good save," Joyce chuckled.

Later, snuggled down in the bed in the cozy sewing room, Mia slept deeply and dreamed of rose petals falling like rain from a blue, blue sky onto a sandy beach.

$\mathcal{T}$he next morning, after dressing and consuming several cups of coffee, she dialed the number on the paper in her wallet. "Hello, Dr. Farnsworth, uh, Diana? This is Mia. I was wondering about selections for the residency."

"Final decisions are still pending for next summer's spot, but you stand a good chance of being selected. You *are* still interested?"

She took a deep breath. "Actually, my situation has changed and I wondered if there might be something sooner."

"Are you available now? Our selected resident withdrew only yesterday. A family emergency of some kind. We contacted others already accepted into the program, but no one is available on such short notice."

"When does the residency start?"

"As soon as possible," Diana answered.

"That's perfect!"

"You realize the cabin is in the Piney Woods of northeastern Texas?"

"That's fine. In fact, I think it's just what I need. Can you tell me more?"

"Rent and utilities are paid, but you must supply your own food, paper products, linens, etc. There are two separate living units with a shared kitchen and laundry; locking doors on either side provide security. It's completely, though sparsely, furnished. Televisions are discouraged. The reception would be poor anyway, and we recommend using headphones for music so as not to bother the resident in the adjoining unit. And the stipend is quite small."

"Stipend? We get paid to live and work?"

Diana clarified, "Only $300.00 per month, to help with food costs, etc. Anything you write will most likely be published within a year."

"I'd be thrilled to be selected. I'll be anxious to hear from you, Diana."

Unable to contain her nervous energy after the call, Mia went for a run through Joyce's neighborhood, Hyde Park, where children played in front yards in easy view of parents relaxing on shady porches. Mia ran on to the campus. She stopped at Battle Hall and stared up at the old building. It was beautiful Spanish Mediterranean Revival architecture with a red tile roof, limestone walls, blue ironwork balconies, and high, arched windows under wide eaves. It hadn't changed at all; it was just as captivating as ever. She loved the stone architecture that was so solid, so enduring.

After finishing her run, and a shower, Mia sat down in Joyce's living room and turned on the television. She soon fell asleep, but was startled awake by her ringing phone.

Later, she told Joyce of her selection for the residency, and then said, "I'll cook for you, as a thank you, for all you've done. I'll make gnocchi!"

"And that would be?"

"An Italian potato dish with Parmesan; it's delicious served with gravy, spaghetti sauce, or pesto if you like," Mia answered.

"I don't want you to slave in the kitchen. Let's really celebrate and go to the *1886 Bakery and Café*. The three-cheese crab pasta, and the apple pie, is scrumptious."

Dressed up, their hair and makeup done perfectly, Mia and Joyce enjoyed a delicious meal at the café. Afterward, they stopped by a little club Joyce suggested for a celebratory drink. The live music, by an up and coming singer/songwriter, was captivating. "She must be thirty, right? Not so much younger than us but she has so much confidence. And her voice just reaches down into my heart," Mia said.

"Let's toast to strong, talented women!"

They clinked their glasses together, sipped the good house wine, and then headed for home with satisfied smiles.

*T*he next morning, when Mia had finished packing, Joyce walked her out and handed Mia a brown bag. "I made you some goodies for the road. Drive careful! I hope this old car won't give you any trouble. And let me get a note from you once in a while."

"I'll call you at least. Thank you, Joyce. For everything."

"I wish you great luck, fruitful dreams, and the power to make them come true."

Mia laughed, "All that? I'll do my best to make us proud." She hugged Joyce good-bye, and got into the car. Mia rolled down the window, breathed, and said, "I can hardly believe this is happening."

"It's happening for a reason: because you want it. You created the opportunity with your desire and action."

Mia smiled and blew a kiss. "See you soon, Joyce, a.k.a. 'Sage'. Take care of yourself and the kids. I'll be thinking good thoughts for Louise's recovery."

Nodding, blinking back tears, Joyce replied, "And I'll send *you* some positive energy for writing."

They waved, and the car pulled away from the curb.

*M*ia's mind wandered as she drove the miles of highway toward northeast Texas. Already she was considering what to write. Maybe something about how heritage influenced lives. Or how faith, or the lack of it, changed things. She blinked

back tears as surprising lines came to her mind. She repeated
them over and over so they would not be forgotten.

*Would my words be any clearer*
*if another color was my skin?*
*Would my voice be any stronger*
*if another self joined in?*

*If I cast my genetic make-up*
*like dice upon the felt,*
*would the pot be any sweeter?*
*Or would I simply melt?*

*What is it makes us separate?*
*Our color or our fears?*
*If we were just the same,*
*would it banish all our tears?*

*If we were free to love*
*each one we see in passing,*
*would it change the way we speak*
*if each was for the asking?*

# FERN

ervous anticipation filled Mia as she drove down the country lane lined with trees. She turned into the driveway, and through a clearing, saw a cedar-sided cabin on a stone foundation. She pulled up to the railed front porch complete with rocking chair and neatly stacked firewood. Stomach aflutter, Mia got out, mounted the stairs to the porch, unlocked the wooden door, and stepped inside the cabin. The entry was slate, the floors hardwood.

A river rock fireplace dominated the end wall and bookcases framed a window on the door wall. A farm table with benches, a cushion-style sofa, and a trunk for a coffee table furnished the main room. There were two standing lamps but no pictures or adornments. The bedroom was small, but it had a high bed and a long narrow chest of drawers crafted in golden pine. There were no rugs to collect dirt and only metal blinds on the windows but the rooms seemed cozy. Knotty yellow pine wainscoting wrapped the rooms. The walls were painted pale yellow, the color of dried grasses.

Mia opened a closet door and was peering inside when she was startled by the sound of another door opening. She turned and looked through a doorway to the kitchen.

A wiry man with a boyish grin and a Disney character wave said in deep baritone, "Hi! I'm Rick. Welcome to the 'cabin of creativity'. I'm your mate."

Mia was so surprised by his words she could utter no response.

He smiled apologetically. "Your cabin-mate."

"Oh, sure." They stood awkwardly staring at each other until Mia remembered to say her name, and they shook hands. Rick bounded out the front door to her car, carried in her suitcases, and rushed back out for the boxes in her trunk. When it was empty, he slammed the lid shut and dashed back inside.

"Thank you for your help, Rick."

"No problem. I wondered if anyone would show. I'm a musician, songwriter. I play with headphones so if you make noise I won't hear a thing and neither will you."

"Oh. Good." Mia looked down at her boxes. "Thanks again for coming over; now I can get right to work putting away my things," she said politely.

He nodded and headed for the kitchen. "I fix supper around five, five-thirty. I wouldn't mind co-operative meals occasionally, if that appeals to you. Otherwise, I'll clean up by six o'clock every day. The cupboard on the right is for you," he said turning and pointing.

A silver and blue medallion on a short chain at his neck distracted Mia. She took a step closer for a better look but Rick gave a wave and said, "Best of luck in your writing endeavors." He went out and closed his door.

Mia stood in the midst of her boxes for a few moments then opened one and began unpacking. When finished, she made hot tea and cinnamon toast and went outside to the porch. Rocking in the chair, she ate her toast, and watched birds landing in the trees. Reminded of Gerald and how he liked to feed the birds at his cabin, she sighed and tossed her crust onto the ground.

"I'll get nothing done if I think about him," Mia chided herself. She walked down the driveway to the road and followed it to where it dead-ended at the driveway of a well-kept, two-story white house. "Debbie and Steve Barber" was stenciled on the mailbox. Debbie was the Associate Director of the program, Mia had been told; Debbie's husband, Steve, had built three cabins in the woods and all the furniture inside.

As she headed back toward her cabin, Mia noticed a trail veering from the road. She followed it across a meadow and over a mossy log that lay across a small creek lined with ferns. Her mind flashed back to another trail: the one up the grassy hill near Gerald's cabin. And then her mind moved to Gerald. Gerald. Gerald. Not the time to be thinking of him. She ran the trail looping through the woods back to her cabin, bounded up the stairs, and quickly shut the door behind her.

> *Words...so many words*
> *needle me*
> *stringing me together*
> *mending my heart*

She wrote the words on a blank page and tried to force away the thoughts of Gerald. Aimlessly flipping through old magazines, Mia avoided going to bed. She fixed some soup but ate only a little and finally gave in to sleepiness. She lay down and covered up with her old teddy bear quilt but only dozed lightly and tossed and turned all night. When the sun sent its first glimmer of light through the windows, Mia made a pot of coffee and settled down at the table.

Her paper, pencils, and ink pens were lined up. Her elbows were bent, hands ready to write. Minutes passed but no inspiration came. Mia carried her satchel of supplies to the sofa, the bed, even the bathroom. She made lists, pulled words from the dictionary, wrote descriptions of her walk through the forest, but nothing led to a story. After several cups of coffee, she went for a long run, took a shower, and put in several more hours of uninteresting writing. She prepared pasta, grated Parmesan, roasted garlic bread under the broiler, and made a salad. Mia sat down on the sofa with a full plate. She ate slowly, slowly, and every time she thought of Gerald she forced the thought away with another thought. But all those thoughts left her feeling empty and alone. Mia tried to sleep, but it was another night as restless as the one before.

The next day, and the next, Mia put her unique spin on stories from magazines: changing characters, inventing new scenes and different endings. After three days, she still hadn't written anything particularly original or creative.

Down on the floor, Mia placed her head on a pillow, put her knees on her elbows, raised her legs up, and balanced. Even standing on her head did no good: no fresh ideas fell into her brain. Why had she believed she could do this with only store advertisements and a few poems to her credit? Mia's legs fell heavily to the floor. What could she do if she failed at this? She had nowhere else to go.

Thoughts of Gerald popped again into her mind. Mia pounded the pillow on the floor. She wiped tears from her face and went through the kitchen to knock on Rick's door. But Mia held her breath, and sighed with relief when he didn't answer. With months of this solitude to get through she'd have to find a way to cope without crying like a lonely child and reaching out inappropriately.

With a cup of coffee fixed extra sweet and white, just how she liked it, Mia went into the bedroom. She sat down on the bed and pulled the photo album from the bedside drawer. Mia flipped it open. Dressed in Spanish costume, Victoria stared up at her with mysterious dark eyes. "Oh, Mother," Mia whispered, "I wish you could tell me something. Anything. I feel so lost."

Closing her eyes, Mia lay back on the bed but was too restless to sleep. She donned her headphones, turned on her new i-Pod, and her mind drifted with the music. A Latino beat with lyrics of passion played in her ears and words were suddenly in her mind.

*Everything I give for him…*

Startled, Mia opened her eyes and jumped up from the bed; she grabbed paper, and wrote the words. Pen poised and ready, she waited, but no more words came.

"Talk to me. Please? Come back to me," she begged with sudden tears slipping down her cheeks. Still there was nothing.

She splashed her face with cool water and brushed her hair. What else could she do? She couldn't just wait for words to come. She had to do something different. She slipped her feet into clogs, grabbed her keys and purse, and went out.

Mia drove a few miles back to a rundown store with a rusting, metal roof. A wood-framed glass door squeaked on old hinges as she entered. Her footsteps echoed on the graying wood floor. The room was dimly lit, and the windows were covered in old posters for tobacco and fishing lures interspersed with handmade signs for bait and garage sales. Mia selected several food items and set them on the counter before surveying a rack of publications and pulling out several.

The clerk, watching from behind the register, spat into a grungy foam cup long overdue for tossing. He smiled at her, showing stained and missing teeth. "That it?"

She nodded uneasily.

He set down the cup, rang up her purchases, bagged them, and slid her change across the counter with a grimy hand. "Thank y', Ma'am."

She reached for the grocery bag.

"Have a NICE day," the clerk said, grinning. He leaned over and spat into his cup.

"Thanks," she mumbled.

Unnerved for no obvious reason, Mia got into the car but didn't drive away. She pulled a piece of paper from her wallet and studied the barely legible number on the slip that'd been folded and unfolded many times. Suddenly determined, she walked to a pay phone in the parking lot. After taking several long, slow breaths, she dialed the number and waited through five rings before there was a click. She said loudly, "It's Mia."

"What's that?"

"Mia. I'm in Texas. Sorry, it's a bad connection."

"Uh, huh."

Her mind raced, searching for words. "I'm surprised you answered." She tried to envision where he was—if he was standing in his cabin near the table, or perhaps on the porch. "Gerald, I…"

"Y' alone in Texas?"

"No more Tim, if that's what you're asking." She swallowed and breathed. "I…wanted to hear your voice. And to say thank you for all you did to help me. It really meant so much to me."

"That it?"

Words froze on her lips as she tried to decipher his tone.

He spoke again, but Mia did not hear. She set the receiver in its cradle and fled the phone booth. A cry was in her throat and words rushed into her mind, filling her like breath. Mia hurried back to the cabin and began writing.

*Devil take every happiness from me…*
*I pray* La Virgen *help…but she no listen…*

# STEM

everishly writing over the next weeks, Mia completed many pages of her yet untitled manuscript; a short version was sent to Dr. Farnsworth as a report of progress.

*Mexico 2005*

*Water rushed the shore, and retreated in rhythmic movement like breath: inhaling, exhaling. A slight breeze was blowing, but the air was heavy with humidity. Rosa wiped a bead of perspiration from her neck. Her shoulders ached from sitting for many hours and sewing. She paused, her eyes peering through a gap in the trees to a patch of blue sky turning pink. Soon the glowing sun would fall behind the finger of land reaching into the ocean. Rosa sighed. Another day was winding to a close.*

*Many years ago, in the village where she was raised, Rosa had not minded evening. But now it was a reminder of time passing, of dreams still unfulfilled.*

*Back then, she and her sister had made wishes on the
first star appearing in the darkening sky. Perhaps it
was not a star they wished on—perhaps it was only
Venus in a glowing gown, but the air was filled with
magic, and their make-believe seemed real.*

*"I will have a handsome husband and many
children," Rosa claimed.*

*Maria said, "No babies to spoil my looks! I will
marry for riches and travel far away."*

*"No, you cannot leave me," Rosa protested. "I
will come with you."*

*But Maria shook her head. "Our parents will cry
too much for us. You stay behind. They will help with
your children and you will help with Grandmother."*

*Arms across her chest, Rosa huffed, "I will make
beautiful stitches and teach them to my daughter. We
will make much money!"*

*"Little sister," Maria scolded. "You spoil our
dreams with ambition!"*

*"You spoil our dreams with talk of leaving! I cry
for you."*

*"Do not cry for me. Sadness haunts like ghosts
from ancient places."*

*But Rosa retorted, "If you leave, regret will
haunt you!"*

*Years had passed; the sisters no longer played at make
believe. They were older, and there was work to be
done. All the women and girls of the village worked
together but the sisters did not quite fit in. Maria had
grown to be exceptionally pretty. Her hair and eyes*

*were light—perhaps passed down from some conquering Spanish soldier. And she was smart, talented in anything she set her mind to. But Maria had no patience for the work and crafts of the women of the village. Her mind was elsewhere. She wanted to be elsewhere.*

*Wherever she went, Maria attracted much attention. As is often the case of pretty women, she fell for the wrong boy. He was from another village, and it was said the family of Guillermo was lazy, shifty, dangerous: that they would do anything for money. But Maria did not care about this. Guillermo said they might go far together with her good looks and his daring. But her family did not like the family of Guillermo, and they did not want that kind of life for their oldest daughter.*

*"It is my life to live how I want!" Maria exclaimed. "And I will see who I want."*

*"Not under this roof!" her father yelled. "Guillermo will meet with trouble if he comes again!"*

*Rosa cried, frightened by the heated exchange. After that, their parents were vigilant; there was no obvious discord, and no sign of Guillermo. Maria was strangely silent and obedient but she spent more time with Rosa and this made Rosa very happy. But one day, Maria was gone.*

*How they cried for her. Especially Rosa cried. They feared some devil had taken her. Sometimes it happened—a pretty girl just disappeared in the night. There was talk in the village that Maria had gone with Guillermo. Guillermo was lazy, but he was no devil. At*

least, that is what they hoped. They prayed for her
safety. Months passed and Maria did not return. Rosa's
family met with Guillermo's family but they came away
with no information, and no better impression of that
family.

Rosa grew up to be much like her sister: pretty
and fair and full of ideas. While Maria had been a
good cook; Rosa had unusual talent for sewing. Hoping
to keep Rosa safe from temptations, the women of the
village taught Rosa secrets passed down through the
generations: special stitches they hoped would keep her
in their midst. But Rosa had her own mind, and she did
not always do as they said. Her hands were kept busy,
but they could not keep her eyes from looking, or her
mind from wandering.

Rosa first saw Manuel walking with his friends
at a weekly market in the city of Oaxaca. How easily he
shelled roasted peanuts and tossed them into the air,
catching them in his laughing mouth. She glanced up at
him through the veil of her thick lashes, and he smiled
at her, but she bowed her head, feigning interest in her
sewing. When Rosa looked up a moment later, he was
gone. But his smile stayed in the blush of her cheek.
Whenever she recalled Manuel's smile, Rosa flushed
with excitement. She prayed she would see him again,
and one day her wish came true.

Manuel caught her eye as she sat sewing at a
stall in the market, but she warned him away with a sly
nod toward her mother. He pointed to a fountain and
waited there until she slipped from her mother's
watchful eye.

"*What is your name, little girl?*" *he asked playfully.*

"*Rosa,*" *she answered, smiling up at him.*

*His eyes sparkled with merriment.* "*Rosalita,*" *he teased.* "*Little Rosa.*"

*She retorted boldly,* "*I am too young for you? Maybe you are too old!*"

"*You are so pretty! You should be mine. My cousin Guillermo said your sister...*"

*Her eyes widened in surprise and her smile faded. She turned and hurried away.*

"*Bonita Rosalita! Pretty little Rosa!*" *he called after her. His laughter rang like music in her ears as she ran.*

*Rosa tried to keep her mind from Manuel but her face colored whenever he appeared. Others began to notice and had much to say.*

"*The price of good looks is too high,*" *commented one woman.*

"*A good looking man thinks he is always good. He spreads his looks around!*"

"*Ah, yes!*" *agreed the women. Their heads in brightly patterned scarves bobbed like a moving flower garden.*

"*A woman's looks fade and a good-looking man leaves. A woman keeps a man only with what she puts in his belly.*" *Again sighs of agreement were heard.*

"*Rosa won't keep a man,*" *said her mother.* "*Her mind wanders and her food turns black!*"

*The women laughed, and Rosa pouted, but it was true.*

*"Pretty girls must also be smart," her mother offered more kindly.*

*And Grandmother added, "Beauty captures heart, but a good mind keeps it."*

*There was much discussion of this. Finally, someone shrugged and said, "Love? Life? Is all mystery. Who can say how it happens?" The women nodded again.*

*"I dream of a sweet, handsome man who will do anything for me!" Rosa pronounced.*

*"Daydreaming does not make it happen," Rosa's mother stated. "I pray someday Rosa finds a good man. I pray he works hard and takes care of her."*

*"And she takes care of him!" one bold woman quipped suggestively. The others giggled, their hands hiding embarrassed smiles.*

*Rosa did not care about all this talk. Her mind was on Manuel and what she might do when she saw him again. And it was not long before she had her chance.*

*One day Rosa begged to stay behind from a trip to the market in another village. Worn down by Rosa's persistence, her mother relented, but also assigned her many chores. Rosa rushed through them, and she met Manuel in secret.*

*How thrilling it was! Hiding beneath the sheltering branches of the ahuehuete, Manuel held Rosa's hand. He smiled at her and said, "I dream of you every night. And every day, I hope to see you. I think I would do anything for you."*

*How sweet and surprising were his words! But Rosa sighed, "You can do nothing." She looked into his dancing eyes and could not tell him what her family said of his family. "My family...objects..." she stammered.*

*"Ah, Rosa! Don't worry about them." He kissed her ever so slowly. "We can do what we want." Manuel kissed her again.*

*His lips were soft like bedding on which to fall and she struggled to pull herself away. "Manuel, I...I want you and I...dream of nothing else! But my family..."*

*He shook his head. "You can leave behind the ways of a child. I will teach you to be a woman. My woman."*

*He kissed her again, and his hands gently touched her face, but Rosa was a little frightened by his words. She pulled away and hurried home. And yet it was not long before they met again in secret. Each time, parting was more difficult. Manuel had captured her heart with his smile, his sweet words and kisses.*

*Each time Manuel held Rosa, he spoke to her with more passion, "Every day I long to see you. You are my reason to live. My pretty, Rosalita, you save me."*

*"You save me!" she claimed, clinging to him. "Every day, every breath is for you. But how can it be for us? My parents give no consent...they will send you away..."*

*That is when Manuel suggested they go away together.*

*It was exciting to consider, but then Rosa became quiet.*

*"Perhaps you are too young to leave your family," he pouted. When she did not reply, he said angrily, "Perhaps you care too much what they think."*

*"No!" Rosa protested and reached for him. "I love my family…but I love you more! It is only…" she looked up at Manuel with tears in her eyes. "I am afraid to go without their blessing."*

*"Surely God will honor our pledge to each other. He is our witness; and our cathedrals are much the same, we can go to either…"*

*But Rosa shook her head and folded her arms across her chest. "We pledge our love at both cathedrals!" Manuel beamed and said they would marry soon. Rosa smiled weakly, yet her kiss was sweet with promise. Her heart pounded: maybe with joy, maybe fear. It was not to be the marriage she'd hoped for.*

*At first, it was exciting being with Manuel. They had little money, but he made friends easily, friends who let them stay a few days, a week or more. Sometimes with these friends Manuel drank too much, and he acted with them as boys do in the practice of their manhood: they said shocking things and put on tough faces. But when he was alone with Rosa, Manuel had only kisses and sweet words for her. And the touch of his hands almost made her forget how she longed for home.*

*Manuel was good at love making, and he worked hard, when he found work. They had food, and Rosa thought life was good. But as the months passed, she grew thin everywhere except her belly. Sometimes she was sick, and they worried what would happen to her. But what could they do? They had no money for medical care. And they could not return to her family in shame. Even his family might not help them.*

*Rosa tried to be strong, but she was only a girl, and the burden of worry was too heavy. She cried and prayed to* La Virgen *for assistance, but no help came. Then Manuel had an idea: they could find Guillermo in the north. And he said something else surprising: perhaps Maria would be there.*

*They traveled a great distance walking and hitching rides. At last they arrived in a town where Manuel and Guillermo had relatives, but Manuel did not know where to find his cousin. They asked at house after house, but wary eyes turned them away. Finally, someone gave directions but also warned, "Be careful."*

*Rosa did not know what danger to fear but they had traveled too far to turn back. She leaned heavily on Manuel, and they walked to the place where Guillermo might be found. Manuel knocked at a shack door. A cloth hanging in the only window moved. The door opened a crack. A woman asked, "Who is there?"*

*"Rosa. Rosa and Manuel."*

*The door flew open. "Ay, Dios! I think I never see my sister again!" Maria exclaimed. Pulling them inside, she shut the door quickly. Maria offered food and they had rested only a short while, she said they must go. "It is dangerous here."*

*Rosa was too weak and could not rise from the pallet on the floor. Maria paced anxiously. When Guillermo arrived, he peppered Manuel with questions. Unsatisfied, he said they must leave. Maria pleaded with him to let them stay, but he was fierce in his refusal. She persisted, and he became angry. He struck her hard on the mouth, but Maria would not be silent. Guillermo struck her again and again but she would not be silent.*

*Rosa cried in distress and begged Manuel to do something. He was smaller than his cousin, but Manuel grabbed Guillermo by the shoulders and pulled him aside. "Women make trouble. Let them be. We will go to the cantina for drink and the talk of men." That was enough persuasion and Guillermo strutted away with Manuel, leaving the women huddled and crying.*

*Late in the night, after many beers, Guillermo offered work to Manuel. It was not good work but the money was plentiful. Manuel was a good man, but he must do what he could for his family. That is what Rosa told Manuel. And she hoped her prayers were strong enough to keep harm away. The men left and were gone many days. When they returned, Manuel would not say what they had done, but he talked in his sleep of frightening things.*

*The men left again and were gone this time for many weeks. They missed the mid-December Feast of Our Lady of Guadalupe. Rosa was sad to be so far from home at such a wonderful time, but it was some comfort being with Maria. Still, she missed Manuel. She longed to see him, to kiss him and feel his body*

next to her. And as the days passed, her longing grew
along with her stomach.

"Ay, ahuehuete, why you let me do this? What
will happen to me?" When terrible pains came, Rosa
cried for her mother, grandmother, and La Virgen.
Maria said she must be strong. But Rosa cried again,
this time for Manuel.

"Men can do nothing in this! You must do the
work of women," Maria snapped.

Rosa was young and her pain was great. How
could so much pain could come from loving? Rosa
screamed in terror as blood gushed from her. Maria
spoke soothingly now. She held Rosa's hand and wiped
her brow. Encouraged, Rosa worked hard, and finally
the sweet reward for all that suffering was in her arms.
Rosa cried tears of joy and her heart swelled with love.
Dark hair wrapped around her daughter's head in
swirls like petals of a flower, and her ears were perfect
spirals like shells from a beach.

The men returned. Manuel kissed Rosa and cried
for her great suffering. He held their baby, stared down
into her beautiful face, and wept with happiness. "Ay,
Rosalita, we have been blessed! God has sent us a tiny
angel!" The baby was sleeping peacefully between
them. They kissed her cheeks and then each other. It
was a sweet time.

But sweetness fades. The men soon had to leave.
"I will come back soon!" Manuel claimed, smiling
encouragingly as Guillermo pulled him away.

It was lonely for Rosa and Maria. They did not
gather with others in the village—they stayed in the hut

*to avoid inquiries into the work of the men. Weeks became months. The house was small and hot. The women fought over small things. Even the baby did not smile. She cried and could not be soothed except when held tightly and walked around and around.*

*Rosa's nerves became frayed, and she, too, began to weep. "I want Manuel! I miss him! If only he would come..." she wailed. "Why is life so hard?"*

*"Why must you cry?" Maria said with much irritation. "Go to the market and come back without tears!"*

*"But the baby..." Rosa objected. "If she cries?"*

*Maria snapped, "If she cries she will be like her mother!" But seeing Rosa's concerned face, Maria added more kindly, "Enjoy the fresh air, but don't be gone long. And bring me something sweet and spicy!"*

*Rosa reluctantly went. Every few yards she looked back with worry in her eyes, but as she neared the marketplace, her spirit lifted. The vegetables and fruits were so colorful and the chatter of the villagers was like music in her ears. Rosa dawdled over the shopping, and then she lingered by the fountain in the courtyard where children laughed and played.*

*Not so long ago Rosa had been young. She had played with Maria in their village in the green valley at the base of the dark mountain in the south. So much had changed since then. Rosa sighed. She ate a mango and chili candy and was cheered. She kept eating until even the candies for Maria were gone. Rosa hurried to buy more candies, and with arms laden with packages, she walked toward the hut.*

*But Rosa's belly was on fire, and she was tired. She went inside a small church. It was not grand like the cathedrals back home, but inside it was cool. Catching her breath, Rosa knelt down and began to pray her rosary—something she had not done since meeting Manuel. The words felt good on her tongue, and the rhythm was pleasant and familiar in her ears. She breathed in the scent of old roses left on the altar. Sudden tears were in her eyes and her heart pounded. Rosa prayed harder, but a sense of foreboding crept over her.*

*She sprang to her feet, grabbed her bags, and rushed outside. There was a commotion in the village. Rosa stared into the distance and gasped. Orange tongues of fire licked the sky. She dropped her packages and ran.*

*A crowd had gathered. Rosa tried to push through, but they held her back. She screamed in anguish, "My baby! Do something!"*

*"Too late," one woman said scathingly, "bad things happen to those who do it."*

*"I have done nothing!" Rosa wailed. But then she was silent with the lie still on her lips. She had sinned. She had gone against her parents' wishes. She had let Manuel do things they knew were not good. And there were small things: she criticized Maria's cooking though it was better than her own. And Rosa had grown irritable, crying like a child, thinking she was ill-equipped to care for her own baby. She had left her small daughter in a dangerous place while she lingered over sweet pleasures and indulgent prayers.*

"Ay!" Rosa cried, lashing out at the people,
"You watch and do nothing! Why do you let this
happen?" She collapsed to the ground, and they left
her there alone in the dirt. "Ay, ahuehuete, why you let
me do it?" Rosa wept, tears streaking her soot covered
face.

When the snakes of gray smoke had faded and
the embers no longer glowed, Rosa put a cloth to her
face and poked through the ashes with a stick. Her eyes
burned and the acrid smell of charred flesh nearly
caused her to turn away in horror, but she persisted.
She nudged a large lump on the floor and dragged the
stick across it. The stick caught on a blackened string
of metal. Her eyes strained to see through her tears; it
was the chain worn by Guillermo! Rosa wept in relief.
She had not liked him.

Frantically, she poked again through the ashes.
She coughed and cried and could not catch her breath.
Someone grabbed Rosa from behind and a hand was at
her mouth, another around her waist. She flailed her
arms and tried to escape the grasp, but the man was
strong. He pulled her far away from the debris. When
he finally released her, Rosa turned, and looking into
the man's face, saw it was Manuel. Weeping, they
clung to each other, and then they ran.

They did not stop until they reached the place
where Maria said they should meet if trouble came—a
place with a name like their home villages. Perhaps it
would be a good place. Manuel bought an ax, a rope,
some nails, a small amount of food, and water jugs.

*Beyond the village, they found a seasonal stream. They rested and washed, filled the jugs, and moved on. They came to a trail winding up a hill covered with ahuehuetes. Perhaps this also was a good sign. They searched the hillside and found a piece of metal, an old can, and a bottle. They carried these things up to a flat spot beneath a large tree.*

*Rosa gathered rocks and made a fire pit. Manuel cut down some trees and built a frame for a hut. He nailed found wood to the frame; Rosa made a pallet with bits of cloth and plastic—whatever she could find for cushion. Afraid to be separated while they slept, they tied their bodies together and wept in anguish and exhaustion. What had happened to their baby? What had happened to Maria? They cried and waited and prayed, but days passed, and Maria did not come.*

*When their money was nearly gone, Manuel left to find work. His search took him farther and farther away. Rosa did not want to stay behind but she had to wait for Maria. Time passed slowly. Rosa endeavored to do what she could. She scoured the area and found materials: a flat stone for preparing food, metal to cover holes in the roof, an old burlap bag. She unraveled several strands and threaded them through a loop of found wire to sew a curtain.*

*Each time Manuel returned, they wept and clung to each other—renewing their love and hope in each other's arms. It was, at least, some small sweetness to share.*

*Often when Manuel returned from working, he brought Rosa presents—sometimes only found items: a pan, a piece of clothing still good for wearing. Special times, he brought candy they savored, laughing and grinning like children. Once he brought Rosa a sickly tomato plant. She did not think it would survive, but she cared for it anyway. She planted it and sheltered it and carried water to it. What else could she do? It had a strong will. Though the stem was spindly, the plant grew and blossomed and made small red fruits. She nibbled one like it was sugared candy, letting it linger in her mouth until only the thin skin remained.*

*One night, she dreamed Manuel dripped sweet juice into her mouth from the fruit she saved for him. They kissed beneath a shady tree and sweetness lingered. But when Rosa awoke from her pleasant dream, she found the plant broken and bare: some cruel thief in the night had stolen her fruit. Rosa wept for lost sweetness but finally she scolded herself: what did she expect? Christ suffered, the Mexican suffered. That was life—especially the life of a woman. She wiped away her tears. What else could she do?*

*Grandmother had said hands busy with work keep trouble away. Rosa summoned her courage and walked to the village to buy needles and thread and a bit of cloth. She smiled shyly and asked the vendor if anyone needed help with mending. "I work fast for only a bit of food, if it can be spared."*

*Impressed by Rosa's pleasant ways, the elderly woman gave her the name of someone who would pay money for mending, and perhaps sewing, if Rosa could do it.*

*"Yes, yes!" Rosa responded eagerly. "I was the best seamstress in my village..."*

"This is not your village!" the woman said brusquely.

Rosa's smile faded. She bowed her head. "It is a good place and you are kind."

The woman softened. "See what you can do for Agraciana. Perhaps I will have some work for you also."

"You will see my excellent stitching. And the first piece for you I will do for free," Rosa offered and hurried away.

Rosa mended late into the night. Satisfied, Agraciana asked her to make a bag. She then made a blouse, and requests poured in. Rosa purchased more supplies. She sewed diligently, sometimes working until she was so tired she cried big tears that fell in splotches onto the cloth she sewed. It was not much of a life just working and crying and waiting and praying beneath the windswept sky, but what else could she do?

Sometimes as she sewed, Rosa imagined her thoughts were carried away by the wind to her mother, grandmother, and other family and friends left behind. Perhaps they would breathe in this wind and know she was safe. Perhaps Manuel's family could know this. Perhaps even Maria could breathe in Rosa's hope and follow it back—bringing their beautiful daughter with her. It was a sweet hope.

Sometimes Rosa imagined her life was different, that her parents and Manuel's had given permission for their marriage. She imagined great celebrations for their wedding and the welcoming of their baby who was dressed in a beautiful garment sewn especially for

her blessing. But Rosa's imaginings were only a
fleeting respite from loneliness. Eventually sadness
always returned, and her tears fell like a drenching
rain.

Time passed and months stretched into years. No
other babies came to Rosa and Manuel, and the burden
of grief lined their faces. Still Rosa clung stubbornly to
her hope that someday Maria would come, that
someday their daughter would be in their arms again.
It would be an answer to her many prayers—and Rosa
still had faith.

Rosa lost track of time but still she waited,
always hoping. What else could she do? She sat on the
stoop of her hut and sewed. One day, a strong breeze
stirred the branches of the ahuehuete trees. She paused
to watch dust devils whip up their tails on the road
below. Rosa sighed and blinked away tears. If only the
wind would bring Manuel home. How she missed him;
she hungered for his touch and longed to see his smile.

"Ay, ahuehuete," Rosa sighed. She bowed her
head and said another prayer. Her prayers were like
roots stretching across the miles to a distant land,
always searching.

Rosa let out a ragged breath. She raised her
head, and her eyes were drawn to something moving in
the distance. Someone was coming. Her heart pounded
in excitement. How she had prayed for this day! But as
the figure drew closer, Rosa saw it was only the woman
for whom she sewed. Rosa greeted her and offered a
drink of water.

Agraciana shook her head and an ugly glint was
in her eyes. "Your Manuel was seen in the city. He was

*in the company of a young woman he gave a lot of money."*

*Rosa shook her head. "Manuel has no need to pay a woman! And he has little money. He sends the rest to me!" She could prove Manuel's faithfulness. Behind the hut, Rosa searched for a buried jar; she scraped at the dirt and dug a hole with a stick. At last it was found. Triumphantly she held up the jar but it was empty.*

*Agraciana laughed cruelly. "Manuel took your money. He has left you. Why should he come back? Your beauty is gone, and your food is not good!" Agraciana laughed cruelly. "A man wants family, a comfortable home. You have none of this."*

*Rosa could not believe Manuel would take the money. It was not from his labor alone. She had sewn until her fingers were stiff and her eyes stung. She had saved for when they would be too old to work. It would have been a sweet time: passing the days together and finding comfort in each other's arms every night. But now the jar was empty. She showed a brave face to Agraciana. "I will work harder and make more money. And Manuel will return soon!"*

*Agraciana only grunted and left Rosa with a bag of mending and orders for more sewing. Rosa threw the bag to the ground and stomped on it until her anger had passed. "It is life only," she sighed. Then Rosa drew a long breath, and began to mend. When the sun had gone soft behind the hill, Rosa struggled to see in the failing light. Tears burned in her eyes. "Sadness is life, especially life of a woman," she told herself, but alone in the darkness, Rosa wept in despair. Was there no one who cared for her? She prayed to La Virgen for help to bear this sadness. The Virgin Mary was a wife, a mother. She knew pain, she knew loss. Surely she would send relief. Wouldn't she?*

*Tortured by doubt, wringing her hands in anguish, Rosa paced the small hut like a caged animal. Where was Manuel? Tears poured from her eyes like rain. Rosa thought of La Virgen weeping at the feet of Jesus who had suffered and died. Manuel was a good man, perhaps he suffered. Perhaps he was sick. Perhaps that is why he did not come. This thought made Rosa weep with relief. But Agraciana's cruel words again pierced her heart with doubt.*

*Had Manuel taken the money? Perhaps he paid for a surprise! Perhaps he paid a woman to search for Maria and their baby who would be grown by now, perhaps with a child of her own! Ay, such a miracle that would be! But if Maria was safe, wouldn't she have come back? Even Maria was not so selfish, was she?*

*"Ay! My heart hurts," Rosa wept in desolation. If only Manuel would come. But if he still cared for Rosa, wouldn't he have come by now?*

*What did Rosa expect? A man needed a woman in his bed. Manuel was still handsome. If he spread his good looks around, as the women of the village said he would do, it did not matter much. But had he left Rosa when her looks had faded? Bitterness filled her with fury. She threw dishes to the hard dirt floor and tore fabric from the windows like she was tearing meat from*

*a bone. Had his desire turned to someone else? Rosa
wished he would burn in the heat of that desire! But
then Rosa wept with horror and begged forgiveness for
this evil wish.*

*She lit candles, and light flickered on the
porcelain face of La Virgen de Guadalupe on her altar.
Was there a trace of sympathy, some slight softening in
the stiff countenance of the statue? Rosa looked again
but saw no change. She lifted a dried flower and faded
petals fell to the altar cloth.*

*Tears fell from her eyes. "I failed Manuel: I
doubted his love and wished evil on him. But he is
good. My parents are good. Maria is good. Especially
my sweet baby," she sobbed, "is good. I am not good
enough. I sinned. I am not worthy of forgiveness. Every
small sweetness has been taken from me." Rosa laid
her rosary beads at the feet of La Virgen. A pain like a
burning knife sliced through her chest. She gasped, and
clutched the fabric on the altar. A candle tipped and its
flame spread quickly, racing over the dried flowers and
across the littered floor. She did not care if she was
burned, scorched to a crisp and blackened like her
broken heart.*

*Rosa gave herself over to the flames, but some
force, perhaps Jesus himself, pushed her out of the hut,
out into the night air. The sound of screams she did not
feel in her own throat rang in her ears.*

*Down the hill, she stumbled. Looking back, her
eyes played tricks: beside the burning hut, Manuel was
etched in red against the night sky.*

# HEM

*M*ia cried as she wrote those words. How she cried for the tragedy and torment of Rosa. She cried for the lost baby and the lost husband. She cried as the words flowed from her heart onto the page. And then as quickly as they came, the words stopped, as if inspiration had burned away like oxygen gone from a flame.

She tried everything to bring them back: running, cooking, listening to music. Even re-reading what she had written. Again and again. But still there was nothing. When she was able to sleep, Mia only thrashed in the bed, tortured by dreams she could not remember in the morning.

Coffee fueled her with energy but not words. Mia thumbed through the fashion magazine she'd bought and stared disinterestedly at the odd styles on the glossy pages. Wardrobe and makeup had been important to her once, but out here in the woods, the only clothes she cared about were the ones for running or sleeping.

Perusing her other magazine, the *Texas Travel Guide*, Mia scanned the colorful photos and read of activities within a few hours of the cabin: Angelina National Forest; the Big Thicket;

Montgomery—the birthplace of the Texas flag; a balloon race in Longview; Kirbyville's exotic cat refuge and wildlife orphanage; Caddo Lake State Park—an area once occupied by the Caddo Indians; cheese making in Cleveland; a crocus farm harvesting saffron. Mia used saffron in her risotto but hadn't known the stigmas of 70,000 crocuses made only one pound of saffron. Grown in Texas and other places like Italy, it was the most expensive spice in the world.

Mia pondered the interesting facts on the pages of the travel guide. Perhaps a change of scene could incite new creativity and a return of words. She snapped the magazine closed, shoved some things into her bag, and set off in the car. Mia drove south, and when she stopped for coffee, she dialed Joyce's number. The phone rang several times before it was answered.

"Joyce?"

The reply was slow, "Uh, huh."

"Are you okay?" Mia asked with alarm.

"Yes," Joyce sighed. "Just very sad. My friend Louise is gone."

"Oh, I'm so sorry."

"We had a nice service for her this morning. She had many nieces and nephews and friends who came. It was really lovely."

"How are you holding up?"

There was a long pause. "I'll be okay. I'm glad she's no longer in pain."

"I wish I'd gotten to know her," Mia said softly.

"You would have enjoyed her tremendous humor."

"How are the kids?"

"They'll miss her. But they're very busy with school."

"Do you feel like getting away for a day or two?"

Joyce's voice perked up, "Where do you want to go?"

"The beach; let's go down to the Gulf. I want to smell the air, feel the wind in my hair and sand under my bare feet."

"My brother has a charter fishing boat; maybe we could go out," Joyce suggested.

They made arrangements to meet the following day in Galveston.

It would be a long drive, but after the seclusion and difficult writing at the cabin, Mia welcomed the diversion. She drove to Tyler and drank in the verdant sights: flowers, fruit and shade trees, and expanses of green grass in numerous parks. She took a walk down a long trail and feeling refreshed, went to lunch at *Bruno's Pizza*. It was tough to choose from the tempting items on the menu but she enjoyed a cheese pizza and went on to the Rose Garden.

The annual mid-October rose show was approaching, and the view from the balcony at the Rose Garden Center was already intoxicating with over 30,000 bushes and 500 varieties blooming. In the meditation garden, flowing fountains and sparkling pools enhanced the serenity. Mia sat down on a bench in the shade beneath flowering trees. She breathed in the beauty and her mind filled with thoughts of Charlotte's garden—and Gerald. Remembering the honey of his voice and the touch of his hands brought tears to her eyes, but Mia wiped them away, left the garden, and wandered around the town.

Later in the day, she purchased a bowl of minestrone soup and fresh bread from a little diner then checked into a reasonably priced motel. She tucked pillows behind her on the bed and ate while watching television. Every program was a reminder of Gerald: a backyard make-over and his yard with rusting vehicles, a fountain installation and the rose garden in The Dalles, a car tricked out and his motorcycle waiting for restoration. Mia sighed loudly, oh, how she could use some restoration. She pulled the covers over her head, and went to sleep to the sound of an old Western.


*P*acing in the steady mist and blustering wind at the 61st Street pier in front of the Captain's Dory, Galveston, Mia blew on her cupped hands to keep warm.

"I'm sorry, I'm sorry," Joyce called as she got out of her car. "I drank too much coffee and had to stop too many times!" Hugging Mia, she hung on a long time and their cheeks were streaked with mascara when they parted. "All made up and full of tears," Joyce laughed.

Mia offered a tissue and dabbed at her own face with another. "I doubt the fishermen will notice in this weather."

"No, they definitely won't. A storm's coming and the boats can't go out."

"What a relief!" Mia exclaimed. "I love being in water but not when it rocks!"

"I was nervous about it, too! Spending time here with you is all I care about."

"My stomach is so glad!" Mia said, patting her rumbling middle. "I saw a restaurant down the road. Would you like to get a bite to eat?"

"Always!" Joyce chuckled. "You look fit! What have you been doing?"

"Running every day on a trail near the cabin."

"I should," Joyce sighed. "But alas I spend my time running for food!"

After a meal of pancakes drenched in syrup, hash browns, eggs, and plenty of coffee, they stepped outside again into a light drizzle.

"What shall we do now?" Mia stared up at the gray sky.

"The only thing left to do is walk, but it's too blustery for sand on bare feet."

"There's plenty of wind for our hair, though!"

They walked some distance up the beach. Mia studied the line of gray water where it met the cloudy sky.

Stopping to pick up a pretty shell, Joyce said, "You're quiet."

Mia only sighed and picked up a smooth dark stone. "Maybe it's the weather."

"Feeling low and wearing sorrow on your sleeve?"

She glanced at Joyce. "That reminds me of Mother. Once while marking a hem, she said, 'Long sleeves, long face; maybe if I cut them short you'll cheer up.'"

"That's funny."

"Strange to think of it now," Mia laughed, her eyes pooling.

"Memories are like that," Joyce sighed. "They come when they're ready."

Mia nodded and wiped tears on her sleeve.

"How's your writing coming?"

"I've been suffering! I'm writing the Mexican woman's story. I feel her pain and lament. She's so real to me." Mia stopped walking and looked at Joyce. "But why?"

"Not so strange imagining someone in similar circumstance."

"Do you think something's wrong with me?"

Joyce studied Mia's face. "You're a sensitive, creative person. Maybe what's wrong with you is what's right with you. And maybe she brings more than story."

Mia shivered, and her eyes gleamed with tears. "I didn't plan to...lose so much."

"No," Joyce sighed sympathetically. "We can't plan everything in life. We can only figure it out as we go."

"I have so many questions, so much I wish I could ask Mother."

"Ask. Maybe she listens. Maybe odd occurrences, coincidences, even dreams, are angels leaving signs that they're here with us."

"I'd like to believe that," Mia sighed.

"You believe in guardian angels don't you?"

"I used to. I feel so out of sorts now. Maybe the seclusion is getting to me."

"Maybe something *else* should get to you," Joyce quipped suggestively.

Walking ahead quicky, Mia called over her shoulder, "I did talk to Gerald."

"You sly dog!" Joyce ran to catch up to her. "And?"

"And nothing. I couldn't say a thing."

"So filled with passion you couldn't speak?"

Mia turned her eyes to the leaden sky. "I can't stop thinking about him."

"Why try?"

"I'm still married to Tim and he..."

Joyce exhaled loudly, "And what are we thinking about Tim?"

"He was my tether."

"Holding you back, or keeping you at a distance?"

Mia shook her head, "Keeping me from flying off wildly. He was steady. Like Mother: a master of emotional containment. I tried to be like that, tried to close the door on my emotions, but I failed. It hurts to feel so much." She scanned the waves that rushed the shore and receded, leaving residual lines of foam on the sand.

Joyce replied softly, "You should embrace your feelings, not hold them back.

Emotion is energy in motion, moving us toward something. If we hold back, we prevent ourselves from reaching our potential, our destiny, what we were meant to do, where we were meant to go, who we were meant to…oh, sorry. Tell 'Sage' not to be so preachy."

Mia laughed, "You're right. I'm talking about my heartache and you have just lost your friend and your husband before that. You have had plenty of your own heartache."

Joyce's eyes sparkled with tears. "Maybe Louise and Neil are up there right now looking down on us and wondering why we aren't having a good time."

They smiled and walked until the moist salt air turned their hands red and gusts of wind blew sand in their faces.

Shielding her eyes, Mia said, "Life stings."

"Sometimes it does," Joyce chuckled and turned to walk backwards against the wind. "I could sure use a hot drink."

Mia brightened, "We could go to the Bar Witch Hotel; I saw a flyer for it at the restaurant. There might be music later: drumming!"

"I do like rhythm!"

*L*ater, after dinner and drinks and some enjoyable but strange music, Mia put new words to the page.

> *In the small space between booming thunder*
> *and the strike of lightning*
> *there is stillness*
> *and thought*
> *condenses*
> *into water for a parched soul*

# FEATHER

*B*ack at the cabin, autumn was soon aloft. The trees were changing color and strong winds were tearing leaves from branches, dressing the forest floor in a kaleidoscope of yellow, orange and red. Red like fire. As Mia ran down the winding trail, her mind filled with Rosa's lament.

> *Had her evil wish come true? Was it Manuel burning?*
> *Rosa scurried away in horror. She did not want harm to come to Manuel, even if she did wish it in a moment of weakness. She had prayed and tried to make up for that evil wish. But was the devil listening instead of* La Virgen?
> *Even through the long years of waiting, believing Maria would someday come, believing her child was alive, Rosa had not lost hope. Life was hard. Everyone suffered. At least she had Manuel to love all those years. Her beauty had faded, and she did fear he had left her, but even as she offered up her own life, Rosa did not believe she would die there. She still hoped he would come. Had he pushed her from the*

*flames, sacrificing his safety for hers? Was it him?*
*Could it have been?*

> *Rosa wept and ran. She ran until she fell and*
*could not get up, then she crawled. Rosa set her eyes*
*on the highest peak in the distance and inched toward*
*it. When daylight came, she kept to the shadows. Her*
*clothes tore on bushes and her skin was scraped and*
*bruised but still she dragged on. Her mouth was dry*
*and her lips cracked but she pushed on, tormented.*
*Regret tore at her heart. Tears poured from her eyes*
*until she was dry as a bone, until she could only*
*crumble and fall to the earth like dust.*

Nights were growing longer and cooler. As the end of November neared, Mia woke up one morning shivering. She put on socks and her robe. She drank hot tea and ate a piece of sugary cinnamon toast while burrowed beneath the comforter. She slept again, got up long enough to make hot oatmeal, and then returned to bed.

Maybe she was sick. Or sick at heart, tormented like Rosa, adrift on a sea of devastation. Thanksgiving Day arrived, and Mia was no better. She pulled a TV dinner from the freezer and warmed it in the oven. Tearing back the foil, Mia took a whiff of the food; her stomach turned over. She dropped the dinner into the garbage with a clunk.

There was a knock at the front door.

Wrapping the comforter around her pajamas, Mia went to the door, opened it a crack, and peeked out at the porch.

"Hello," said a smiling woman. "I'm Debbie Barber from down the road."

"Oh," she opened the door a little wider, "I'm Mia."

"I apologize for not comin' long before this! I've gone back to teachin' high school English. Boy! What an adventure," Debbie laughed. "I've been so busy! Finally with a few days off for the holiday, I can catch up a bit. Steve and I had all the family over for dinner earlier today, but we have so many leftovers. I got to thinkin' about you here and I thought you might like some. I brought you a plate." Raising her arm to show the basket dangling from it, Debbie smiled. "A bit more than a plate. Hope it's not too presumptuous of me."

Mia shook her head and pushed back a lock of hair. "I look a mess. I've been…sick."

"You poor thing! Gosh! I am sorry! I should've been here sooner! I apologize."

"Oh. No. Come in." Stepping back in her stocking feet, Mia nearly tripped over the comforter dragging the floor.

"No, no, sweet thing!" Debbie smiled, holding out the basket. "I'll just leave this and you can bring it back anytime you feel up to it."

Mia accepted the basket. "Thank you, Debbie. It's really thoughtful of you."

"You're quite welcome! If you're still feelin' a bit on the down side tomorrow, mix some of that gravy and turkey with noodles and make yourself some soup."

"That's a good idea," Mia smiled.

Debbie started off the porch and chirped, "Happy Thanksgivin'."

"You, too. Thank you. Nice to meet you," she said closing the door.

Already smelling the food, Mia carried the heavy basket to the kitchen. She opened foil-covered dishes of turkey, mashed potatoes, yams, gravy, cranberry sauce, homemade rolls, and pumpkin pecan pie with real whipped cream. Staring down at the colorful display of food, Mia bent over and wept. Then she dried her eyes and fixed an immense plate of food. She warmed it in the microwave, lit a candle, and sat down at the table. Saying a prayer of thanks for the care of strangers, she began eating her unexpected feast. Later, sated and smiling, Mia put new words to the page.

*Jaime traveled in the mountains and along the rivers in the state of Durango. There was abundant wildlife for a hunter; he often traded dried meat, feathers, bones, hides, and even horns he carved into beautiful figures. And Jaime had the freedom to enjoy beauty all around him: the undulating grasses of the hills, the twisted piñon cones, the colorful feathers of birds. He was thankful for all of nature. And he was thankful to be able to go wherever he wished, whenever the desire struck him.*

*One day, as he walked along a dusty trail, he paused to listen to the call of a bird. A heap of rags caught beneath a bush attracted his attention. Jaime was in the habit of salvaging and was often diverted from his path to retrieve found items. He had noticed a slight fluttering—like a breeze playing at the fabric— but when he reached down to scoop up the tattered cloth, he recoiled at the feel of a body! Regaining his composure, he pulled back the cloth and was shocked to see a woman. There was not much life left in her, but he lifted the woman gently and set her on his burro. Slowly, he made his way back to his hut. Jaime cleaned the woman's damaged skin, and dressed her wounds with cool cloths and herbs. He spooned water into her mouth and set her upon his bed of straw. He did not think she would live, but he prayed, and his faith was strong.*

*Every day, the woman grew stronger in his care. Soon she was able to sit, and stand, and then to walk. Jaime talked to her in Spanish, but she said nothing in return, only did as he indicated. Perhaps she knew only the language of her village, he could not be sure, but he kept talking. And he began to enjoy her company, even if she was silent.*

*A* few days after Thanksgiving, Mia drove to Dallas and flew out. She turned to the window and her eyes drank in the landscape below: emerald green fields, rugged brown hills, khaki sagebrush, snow dusting the high peaks of the Rockies. When the plane neared Portland, her eyes followed the blue strip of Columbia River threading along the highway toward Gerald's cabin. Mia imagined visiting him.

His familiar figure would emerge from the cabin; he'd sweep her up in his strong arms and carry her inside. They'd drink icy sodas around the kitchen table and watch birds outside the window gathering seeds for winter. Much later, with old songs playing on the radio, they'd find each other under the quilt of blue, yellow and red on the black background as dark as night.

In the morning, he'd make coffee and cook breakfast: whipping eggs, chopping onion and tomatoes, grating cheddar cheese for omelets, toasting bread. They'd eat in the bed, their crossed legs covered with blankets to keep the crumbs out.

"Stay," he'd say.

She'd bow her head so he wouldn't see her eyes telling him she couldn't. He was a lone pine in a field of grass, separate from the world. She longed to be the grass, surrounded by others, with the wind sighing through her.

He'd needle her with words, "Running away again?"

She'd shake her head, "I have to go."

"Always do what y' have to?"

She'd nod. "I...had to see Mother...see it through with Tim. And there's nothing here for me." She'd try to rephrase. "I mean, I can't just hang around here with nothing to do and nowhere to go." She'd try to soften her words, let him down easy.

He'd turn away, no longer listening to words he did not want to hear. She'd leave with the screen door snapping shut behind her, the sound of her footsteps hollow on the wooden porch.

That imagined scenario prevented Mia from going to see Gerald: the gap of time, the distance in miles, the differences in their lifestyles stood in her mind as obstacles too large to overcome.

Rain swished loudly beneath the wheels of the airplane as it landed in Portland. She was reminded of the rain at Multnomah Falls, the last time she saw Gerald. Maybe it would be the very last time she would ever see him. Mia quickly pulled out paper and put new words to a page.

*When summer came 'round*
*When the sun stood high*
*I looked upon your red tanned skin*
*With glad and favoring eye*

*Now winter wind cools me*
*Time for other things*
*But I hold you in my mind*
*And thank you for my wings*

*T*he next day, Mia's legs were shaking as she entered her attorney's office in a dark and sleek building in downtown Portland. Her hands held the pen tightly as she signed Mia Edwards for the last time on the Dissolution of Marriage papers. She'd receive half the fair market value of the house, half the replacement cost of all joint belongings including vehicles, half the retirement savings, half the value of the business real estate and contents of the stores, and a large sum of money as compensation for her loss of career. Guilt had a price, and Tim had paid, dearly.

"Good luck to you," her attorney said kindly and his look was almost fatherly.

She nodded and smiled but was on the verge of tears as she left the office. Mia gathered her wits and rode the elevator up to the restaurant on the top floor. Seated at a table next to the window, she looked down on the gateway to Old Town Chinatown where male and female lions, like yin and yang, guarded the arched entrance. Drenching rain fell on their grimacing faces.

Mia picked at the vegetables in her pasta primavera, ate a few bites of crusty bread, and paid the bill, leaving her glass of wine untouched on the table. She rode the elevator down to the street. Her feet moved toward the galleries in the Pearl District. The bright paintings and intricately designed sculptures failed to shake her mood, but Mia pushed on, trying to make the most of what might be her last hours ever in Portland. In the far corner of one small gallery, a wooden table captured her attention. Its satiny smooth surface glowed in golden light from a sparkling chandelier. Her eyes searched for the name of the artist on the tag, but it was not Gerald. A black ceramic bowl stood in the center of the table. Her finger traced the rim and a draft swept over her. Mia turned to look, but no one was there. She rushed out of the gallery.

Undeterred by the inclement weather, Mia walked several blocks to the Pioneer Courthouse Square. Standing in the steadily falling rain, she watched water cascading from the tall concrete fountain and tears poured from her eyes.

Tim and Valerie now lived in the house Mia had renovated. They had her fountain and flowers, her arched front door with beveled glass and etched rose design. Was any amount of money enough compensation for her labor, her lost love, her dashed hopes and dreams? Why had Tim turned his heart away?

*I wish he burn...then I cry...but* La Virgen *no listen...*
*devil take every sweetness...*

Fueled by the words, Mia walked to a discount fashion store and on to a hardware store. She stowed her packages in the car and drove toward the house. She parked down the street. She slipped on the trench coat, tucked her hair into the brimmed rain hat, and pulled on the heavy rubber boots and rubber gloves she'd purchased. Walking past the house, sliding her eyes over the unlighted windows, Mia moved stealthily along the driveway. She slipped through the hedge gate into the back yard. She knelt down in the garden, pulled the knife from her pocket and cut into her Christmas rose, careful not to drip any juice from the poisonous plant as she placed pieces into a plastic bag.

After cautiously creeping back around to the front of the house, Mia stepped up onto the porch and took out the knife. She ran it along the molding and tried to pry the etched glass from the front door but it held fast. She considered breaking it so Valerie would not have it, but the noise would attract attention and the window was still dear to Mia's heart: she didn't want it damaged.

The point of the knife was sharp: sharp enough to carve anything. Mia examined the door and imagined how the knife might scrape the finish. Her mind jumped to how the knife might plunge into something soft like flesh. She shuddered and used the knife to pry at the door lock, but it did not budge. She tried the locks on windows near the back deck, but the dated hardware held secure. She'd been safe in that house. Mia turned her eyes to her garden: all the plants she had placed with such care would go on living without her. Her absence, her pain, her lost time and plans were nothing to them. Her flowers would drink in the rain and they would wait for sun.

Sighing, Mia walked back to the car.

This time, as the airplane pulled up and away from the emerald green landscape surrounding Portland, Mia did not look out the window. She did not follow the Willamette River into the Columbia and out to the ocean that lapped at some distant shore. Her eyes did not turn to follow the Columbia upriver to the eastern side of the Cascades where the falls waited beneath the water. Mia drew down the blank shade and closed her eyes. Words filled her mind.

*Rosa was angry Jaime had saved her. She did not deserve it. Her heart was heavy, broken, and black as stone. She should have been put out of her misery like a chicken: neck cracked, skin peeled away, bones left to*

*rot in the sun or picked clean by some scavenger. Stiff
and silent, she would have stayed that way until all life
had left her. But Jaime prodded her with food and
questions. He coaxed her into activity, and her body
slowly healed. But Jaime could not reach her heart.*

After arriving back in Texas, Mia got into the car at the airport, but her hand would not turn the key. Her foot would not press the gas pedal. She stared out the windshield at a fading sky. Was she also fading? Who was she now? Not Mia Edwards. And she was not Mia Casinelli, either. That girl had been left behind years ago.

Mia shook herself and swallowed the bitter taste in her mouth. She started the car and drove away, but not toward the "cabin of creativity", as Rick had dubbed it. Instead, she drove up to Grapevine, a little town to the north of Dallas with many old buildings listed on the National Register of Historic Places. Grapevine called itself the "Christmas Capital of Texas," according to the *Texas Travel Guide*. Its stunning holiday lights and decorations did not disappoint and there were many charming retail stores to explore.

Downtown, at a specialty kitchen shop, Mia found an adorable timer shaped like a small angel she bought for Joyce. For Angelina, she purchased an elegant hand-blown vase at an artisan gallery. And for Angelo, she decided to buy a gift certificate for a round of golf at Bear Creek Golf Club. She knew it had been selected by the *Wall Street Journal* as one of the "Top Ten Courses You Can Play in America." Perhaps the gift would entice him out of his lonely house, perhaps even to make some friends.

Mia thought of buying something fashionable for herself. Now that she no longer needed to dress for business, she could wear whatever she liked—she just wasn't sure what that was. Mia shopped in a charming boutique and tried on some bright, retro-boho clothing. But she imagined the disapproval of her grandmother Angelina and lost interest.

Dining later in an Italian café, Mia ordered pasta Parmesan, garlic bread, and a cup of luscious chocolate hazelnut gelato. After dinner, she walked the short distance to a bed-and-breakfast where a white picket fence surrounded a tiny yard. Mia pushed open the gate and stepped up to the wide, white porch lined with wooden rocking chairs. A sparkling chandelier over the stairway inside shined brightly through the leaded glass transom above the door. It was lovely, warm, and inviting: just like home. Someone else's home but comforting nonetheless. Going to bed early, she slept well.

Late the next morning, Mia went for a massage at a nearby spa and afterward, strolled through downtown. She surveyed a line of shining motorcycles parked outside Willhoite's Restaurant, but there were none like Gerald's with the logo of a stunning man with feathers in his hair. Lunching inside, she lingered over fried cheese sticks and an old-fashioned charbroiled hamburger and her eyes watched the motorcycles coming and going, but there was no one familiar.

As Mia set off for the cabin, words began pouring into her mind and she sped down the highway. Writing late into the night, and through the next days, she barely gave a thought to the approaching holidays.

*Jaime had often traveled to one village or another for supplies. But now he went only to the nearest village;*

*he did not want to leave Rosa alone for long. But extra purchases he made delayed his return, and this time, the stars were already shining when Jaime reached his hut. He found her sitting in the darkness. He lit new candles and grinned at Rosa in the golden light, but her eyes remained expressionless.*

*"I brought something for you to pass the long hours."*

*Still she made no response.*

*He tore open a large package and drew out a length of cloth, a needle, and several bright colors of thread. "Do you hunger as I do for beauty? We need something colorful for our table. Please, can you stitch something for us?" Jaime smiled with hopeful anticipation as she shifted her gaze, but the lines of her face deepened and Rosa turned away. Exasperated and hurt, he blew out the candles and stomped outside to his hammock.*

*The next morning when he rose, she was already sewing! Jaime's face was all smiles as he went about his chores. By nightfall, Rosa had finished a long table runner.*

*"Ay, Rosa," he exclaimed. "You have done it!"*

*Jaime marveled over the intricate design of tiny stitches: yellow, purple, and blue flowers with green leaves and stems so delicate they brought tears to his eyes. "Ay, this day, this day I am happy! We have undying flowers for our table!"*

*Did he see a slight upturn on her lips? He believed he did! Later, as he washed up, Jaime sang. And that night, alone in his hammock beneath the stars, he allowed a wish to fill his heart: that someday she would share more than his food and the passing of time. Jaime looked forward to that day; he was a patient man.*

*While her hands were busy, Rosa's mind was free from the sad thoughts that had tortured her. She recalled the fragrance of the flowers in the meadows and gardens of her youth, and she was calmed by the steady rhythm of her stitches. Jaime bought Rosa more fabric and colors of thread, even a thimble for her finger that was sore from pushing the needle. She did not thank him then, or even smile, but she put the thimble on her finger and sewed faster. And she noticed how this filled him with pride.*

*Rosa sewed hour after hour, day after day. She worked colorful threads into ever more complex designs and yet, to Jaime, it seemed she sewed with indifference.*

*"Why do you work with no happiness?" he asked in frustration.*

*Her mouth struggled to speak, "I sinned. There is no forgiveness.* La Virgen *does not listen. Devil takes every happiness from me. My heart is black and heavy like stone."*

*Still he did not understand.*

*"My heart is broken. I have no hope of ever mending stone."*

*Her words were like a drenching rain but still Jaime persisted. "Life is to enjoy. There is beauty all around, and you make even more. Be thankful! You live!" he replied excitedly. "I saved you."*

*"For what?" Rosa sighed inwardly as she turned away from his hopeful, smiling face. Late into the night, she sewed by candlelight, and he muttered, "A fortune in candles she will burn."*

*At first, Rosa sewed only to keep busy, and to keep Jaime from cajoling her into doing something more, like walking with him to the river, or watching with him for a bird with a dark coat of blue, or listening for some animal or other creeping through the brush. But something shifted in her—maybe some spirit began to heal her pain. Maybe it was Jaime's steadfast optimism and care that began to work its magic in her.*

*One night, coming up from the stream where he washed, Jaime heard Rosa calling to him. He ran as if some catastrophe must be at hand. But he found her in the hut, holding her most stunning creation yet: a shirt bearing a brilliant bird in a sky of blue.*

*"Ay, Rosa!" Jaime exclaimed excitedly. "A man I know in Durango will pay a lot of money for this! Rosa, come with me to the city. You can choose your own threads and fabric! I will buy you anything you need," Jaime offered.*

*Rosa drew a breath. She glanced up at him through her lashes, and her head nodded ever so slightly!*

*Jaime burned much wax that night making ready to leave at first light before she could change her mind.*

*They traveled to the city of Durango and sold the shirt, along with other fine pieces she had made. They explored the city that had many beautiful colonial buildings and churches like those in other cities she and Manuel had seen. In the plaza, there was a four-*

*tiered fountain and a round gazebo with a domed roof where a band played. They stopped to listen awhile to its happy sound. At an aged cathedral with twin towers, she hovered a moment, imagining she might step through the arched, amber-colored wooden doors to the interior, where the air would be cool and still. Perhaps the saints would look down on her and they would not turn away. It was a small thought, but it filled her with the tiniest glimmer of something that felt strangely like hope.*

*There were many towns to see and so they went on, traveling south. They visited the village where Jaime was born in Michoacan. A white church stood high on a rumpled hill covered in prickly pear. Angled roofs of thatch and tile covered stone and stucco houses that were perched on the hillside. It was a pretty sight, but they did not stay long.*

*Rosa had stayed so many years in that one place—as if her feet were rooted in the dusty ground—and still Maria had not come. Now Rosa was free and her body moved as if pulled by some force she could not resist. She longed for something...*

*As they traveled, Jaime began to see a change in her. He tried not to notice Rosa's beauty, but his eyes could not help looking. His herbs and gentle care had restored her skin, taking years from her face. Perhaps he was younger than Rosa, but it did not matter. Perhaps she had been another man's wife, maybe she had children. Jaime did not care. He cared only for the rounded shape of her head and the chestnut color of her hair under the bright sun.*

*When her tiny fingers worked the needle, he imagined how they might touch him. His manhood rose at the sight of the smallest wisp of hair fluttering near her cheek. And Jaime longed to brush his hand against that cheek, to feel the silk of her hair on his skin. He wondered why her man ever let her go, how harm had come to her, and why she had been in the road for him to find. At night he dreamed of her, and by day he feared she would capture his wandering spirit, making him settle with her in a place impossible to leave. But he did not fool himself: even now, he could never leave her.*

*A woman could see Jaime had appeal. Rosa tried not to like the look of his smiling face, or the way his eyes brightened when he brought her something, or how his ears stuck out beneath a brimmed hat pushed down too far. Her eyes tried not to see the muscles of his strong legs through the thin cloth of his wrinkled pants. She tried not to notice his broad shoulders in a denim shirt with sleeves too short for his arms. And Rosa appreciated how he provided for her the way a man of the country could. He made a pleasant sight returning from a hunt with his rifle hanging from his shoulder and a bag of birds slung across his chest.*

*Rosa longed to see the ocean, so they journeyed down the western coast of Mexico. There were many fishing villages and more popular beaches for tourists and travelers. They stopped in San Blas. At the edge of town, a paved street split off in one direction and a narrow, dirt road veered in another. Between the roads, a square white stucco house faced the sun. The windows were covered in lace and the door between*

them stood open like a mouth. A woman sat in the
doorway. Perhaps she was watching a cat creeping
past, or someone placing flowers at the shrine across
the road where plastic flags on a rope surrounded a
pedestal holding the plaster bust of General Simon
Bolivar. He was a hero to many. But he was only a
man. And Rosa did not like stiff, uniformed men who
did not smile, so they went on.

They roamed through the town and discovered a
circus. A round tent made of alternating triangles of
blue and white canvas was topped with a flag and
secured to the ground with ropes coming off in every
direction. Beside the tent, a bright silver trailer with
rounded top gleamed beneath the high sun. Another
trailer, much larger and smelling of animals, had a
picture of a tiger and "CIRCO," circus, painted on the
side.

Jaime convinced Rosa to see the show. Though it
was several hours until the performance began, they
sat in the front row and watched the preparations. They
ate palomitas *(popcorn), and candies. It was hot and
crowded, but Jaime did not care—beside him sat a
pretty woman and his belly was full of sweets. Finally
the performance began. The costumed handlers and the
animals were magnificent to see! And even Rosa
laughed and clapped her hands together like a girl
when the clowns cavorted in the ring.

San Blas was a pretty place, but there were other
towns to visit. Everywhere they went Rosa looked at the
faces of women. But there was no one she recognized,
and she only wanted to push onward to somewhere
else. They traveled to Acapulco but even that splendid

city could not hold her for long. A restless wind blew, and Rosa was filled with longing she could not put away.

Farther down the coast, where the rock-lined shore stretched east to west, they found a captivating place with perfect blue-green water. Fishing had once been the main attraction, but now world-class surfers flocked to the beaches with stunning waves. There was a construction boom, and Jaime found work easily. Tourism was also bringing money to the area. Rosa set up a booth and found many customers willing to pay a great price for her intricate designs and fine craftsmanship. A man from the United States even proposed selling her work in stores there. Eventually, he invited Rosa to travel to Texas for the grand opening of a new store he would name after her label: ANGELITA.

Rosa walked on the beach and her feet sank into the sand. Waves lapped the shore again and again like a heartbeat, and she was soothed. There was something different here. It was in the wind, in the water, in the sky of this place. This place was growing, changing, and she with it. All her sorrow and grief and even guilt flowed out in her tears that fell like rain. Her heart, once impermeable stone, was softened by those healing tears. And each stitch was settling, mending stone: putting together the pieces of her broken heart. Each breath she drew restored her hope. Rosa found a voice for prayer, and she began to believe again that anything could happen, perhaps even a miracle.

# $\mathcal{V}\mathcal{AND}\mathcal{YKE}$

ecember had nearly slipped away when Mia closed the door on the cabin and drove away. Passing small towns still decked out in holiday décor and lights, she wound through the countryside beneath an overcast sky. Disinterested, grass dangling from their chewing mouths, cows munching in fields glanced up at her passing car.

Mia drove to the house in Austin. She went inside. "Papa?"

Angelo hurried into the hallway. "My Darling Mia! You look wonderful!"

Mia hugged him with a quick squeeze, "It's good to see you."

"My goodness, we have catching up to do! We missed your birthday!"

She took a deep breath. "I was not in the mood to enjoy it anyway."

"Has it been so hard for you?" His voice was soft with consideration. He wrapped his arm around her shoulders and walked her toward the kitchen.

"Wow! All my favorites," Mia exclaimed at the sight of chopped vegetables, meats, cheeses, sliced fresh bread, dip and condiments on plates covering the island. She nibbled a slice of mozzarella.

"Yes, I remember." Angelo began constructing a thick sandwich.

"Will you even be able to eat that thing?" she laughed.

"We shall see!" Angelo sat at the bar; he pressed down the sandwich and asked playfully, "What do you think of your papa in golden bronze?"

Mia appraised his newly acquired tan and the radiant look in his eyes. "Maybe everyone should go on a long cruise for the holidays."

Trying to take a bite, he chuckled as his sandwich slid apart and fell to the plate. "You haven't told me about your writing. What title have you chosen for the work?"

"*Lamentation.*"

"That sounds very sad."

She looked over at him and nodded. "The losses and laments of a woman. A Mexican woman."

He seemed to choke on a bite but managed to say, "I'm surprised you didn't write something city-savvy and modern."

"At first I struggled, unable to write anything! But words came, combined with the dreams I have, and the story just gelled. It's a story of lasting love—the kind that reaches across time and distance."

Angelo watched closely as Mia continued to talk and eat.

"I'm not sure when it will be published. The committee is reviewing it. They'll make recommendations and suggest changes; I'll do some rewriting probably. It could take months actually, and there is no guarantee of publication. But Dr. Farnsworth read the summary and says it's good." Mia smiled and breathed. "In the meantime, while I'm waiting for the review, I'll research marketing ideas, and I may enter it in some contests."

"I hope it will be successful."

"Thank you, Papa. I hope to publish some of my poems also."

"Victoria loved poetry," he said with a wistful smile.

She glanced over at him. "I didn't know that."

"Oh, yes, she has several books…" But Angelo looked down at his plate. Taking a deep breath, he smiled and said, "You haven't asked about my trip."

"How was it?"

His expression lit up, "Simply wonderful."

Picking at her sandwich, Mia listened as he described his cruise to the Bahamas.

"And I met a delightful woman shipboard: Margaret Vandyke. Maggie. She's Irish, with lovely long hair. Quite an interesting woman. She just finished a Master's program in writing at the University of Idaho." He beamed as if proud of the accomplishment.

"A bit old to be finishing college and beginning a career, isn't she?"

Angelo laughed, "Not at all. She's in her late fifties, but Maggie has worked all her adult years. She wanted the degree for her own personal growth."

"Sounds determined," Mia said evenly.

"Yes, yes, she is. Very determined. And interesting."

"You said that." Mia stood up and walked over to the sink with her plate. She filled a glass with water and gulped it down. "Will you keep in touch?"

"Why, yes. Actually, you can become acquainted at dinner later."

Mia set the glass down. "She's here in Austin?"

"Yes! I invited her. She'll be staying with us only a few days, and I do so want all of us to have a good time."

"Wait. She's staying here?" Mia's surprised voice grew loud, "In *our* house?"

"Why, yes. She's only out for a little more shopping, but will return shortly."

Mia dumped the uneaten food from her plate into the garbage. "I guess I have her to thank for this little spread," she remarked with sarcasm.

"I thought you would like it." Angelo's face fell.

Mia drew a breath. "I did. Thank you. I'm tired and I need a nap."

"Yes, of course. Take a rest. Shall we go to dinner at seven o'clock? We can go wherever you like," Angelo offered with a hopeful expression.

She nodded and went down the hall to the front door.

"I can help bring in your things," Angelo called.

"I can do it," Mia snapped, but then added in a softer tone, "Thank you anyway."

She retrieved her suitcases from the car and carried them to her old bedroom. She kicked off her shoes, then collapsed on the bed, her head sinking into the fluffy down pillows. Mia drifted to sleep and woke several hours later. Though she had plenty of time before dinner, she lingered too long in a hot bubble bath. Sweaty and irritated, she tried on every outfit in her suitcase but settled for a simple black sweater and slacks that fit her mood.

They went to dinner at La Traviata. Its thick, stone walls and lovely wood floors reflected a warm ambience that enhanced the delicious cuisine. Angelo had spicy lamb meatball pasta, Maggie the duck confit, and Mia the chicken Parmesan.

Maggie told long stories about the Palouse: rich, rolling hills of farm land in Washington and Idaho. She talked at length about White Spring Ranch, a National Historic Site, near Genesee, Idaho, and not too far from Moscow, home of the University of Idaho where she had studied. Maggie was involved in some projects associated with the museum being developed at White Spring Ranch and was writing an article about it for the *Smithsonian Magazine*.

Mia tried to listen politely, but she could barely resist the odd urge to suddenly hoot, whistle, or sing—an impulse she fought as a child while sitting through Mass. This dinner was no less tortuous. The intent look on Angelo's face whenever Maggie so much as moved or breathed had Mia nearly unhinged by the time her tiramisu and coffee arrived. Nevertheless, she continued to be as gracious as Angelina would have been had her grandmother not declined the invitation.

Perhaps it was only the rich food upsetting her stomach, but Mia slept poorly and woke in the morning with a groggy head. She was in the kitchen when Angelo emerged from the master bedroom. "Morning," she mumbled but did not look up from the toasted English muffin she was slathering with apple jelly.

He poured himself a cup of coffee. "What did you think of Maggie?"

"Seems a nice enough date." Mia took a long drink from her cup of coffee.

"I'm quite taken with her." He smiled and added, "If all goes well, perhaps I will ask for her hand."

"Just the hand?" she asked smartly and watched his smile fade. "Rather sudden, isn't it? I guess not for you. It was only a day before you say you married Mother."

He managed a steady tone. "Would you be so against our union?"

"What difference does it make what I think?" she snapped, but the shocked look on his face compelled her to add, "I'm surprised you're even dating."

"I am not young. I know what I want and what I need to be happy. Things happen unexpectedly; too fast life is over. Why wait?"

Mia considered this and said quietly, "I do want the best for you, Papa, whatever you think that is."

"I know, Darling Mia, as I do for you."

Their eyes met, and blinking back her tears, she nodded. Mia left her unfinished coffee and muffin and returned to her room, resignation saddling her shoulders. Sitting on her bed, she stared at the walls until she heard Angelo and Maggie go out the front door.

Mia wandered through the house. She fingered the satin cords that wrapped the living room drapes, ran her hands over the cool wood of the entry table, and studied colorful bindings of the books on the study shelves. Blue, gold, red, and black, the books were arranged in blocks of color reminding her of a quilted bed cover. Her fingers traced the gilded letters on a tome of history. Gerald loved history. But she would not think of him.

Her eyes moved along a shelf to a small gap between two volumes. She pried out a thin book of poetry by a Mexican writer. Mia read several poems and turned to the back to read the bio: Octavio Paz was born to a family of Spanish and native Mexican descent. A chill ran over her. She turned to scan the room, but there was nothing behind her except the empty wing back chairs.

Mia carried the book to her room and tossed it on the bed; she changed into running clothes and went out. Her eyes studied the neighborhood as she ran along the street. The structures seemed familiar, but there were new fences and landscaping, patios and paint. Houses change, people change. Everything changes. Change or be changed. Even death was a change: one form to another. Her mind filled with questions. What was life supposed to be about? Angelo was considering a future with Maggie. If they married, would that make Maggie Mia's stepmother? It was unimaginable. But Mia had never imagined being childless. Or tempted into adultery. Or mourning a mother. Or divorced. Or starting a new career. Who was she becoming? Who had she ever been?

Her feet pounded the pavement as she ran; her cheeks, breasts, buttocks jarred up and down. Tears ran from her eyes and sweat soaked her clothes, but she kept running and running until a blister on her heel and pain in her groin forced her back to the house.

"Is that you, Darling Mia?" Angelo called as she went inside. Her athletic shoes thumped across the hardwood floor toward the study. Head bent, eyes scanning the papers spread across the top of the desk, Angelo said, "Sit down, please."

Her feet were rooted to a spot in the doorway. "I'm wet."

He looked up in surprise.

"What is all this?"

"Real estate papers. If Maggie agrees to marry me, I may sell this house."

Mia's jaw tightened.

"Perhaps I'll move to Idaho. Or Maggie will move to Austin and we'll buy another house, some place where the past does not linger like a ghost in every corner."

"You'd sell the house?" Her eyes were wide with disbelief.

"It *was* our home..." Angelo's words faltered.

She sighed. "I guess it *was*. Now it is just a house in the midst of change." Mia sighed inwardly: change or be changed. She took a deep breath and announced, "I am not a child in need of shelter. I plan to buy my own place." She turned and left him staring after her.

*J*oyce invited Mia over to make cookies for a New Year's fundraiser. Mia brought an old cookbook she found in Victoria's kitchen and they silently went about measuring and mixing half a dozen varieties each. When the last of the dough had been rolled and cut and placed on a cookie sheet, Joyce poured them each some eggnog, and raised her glass, "To sweet involvements!"

"The sweeter the better!" Mia laughed as she scooped the excess flour and bits of dough littering the table into a waste can.

Joyce jotted down the names of the cookies that were cooling on the wire racks. Mia pointed to the ones made from Angelina's old recipe book, "Italian Almond Cookies, Amaretti, Italian Candied Fruit Cookies, Brown Sugar Squares, Fresina, and Spicettes."

"Did I see you put mayonnaise in that last one?"

"It takes the place of shortening and eggs. I promised to bring Grandmother some if the fundraiser can spare a few."

Joyce smiled and began washing dishes. "I made extras of my favorite: old-fashioned wine cookies. My edible and sweet welcome to the New Year!"

Mia began drying bowls and utensils. "I am glad this year is over!" she declared, her eyes glistening. "I don't know if I'll ever care about the holidays again. When I was little, Mother made them so beautiful, and I tried to do the same through the years." She looked over at Joyce, "All the decorating, buying and wrapping gifts—I just don't know if it was worth all the work. I did little this year, and I feel just the same—kind of empty. Where is the joy we're supposed to feel?"

Joyce replied gently, "It was a hard year. But the brightest moments for me have been doing things with you."

"I don't know what I would have done without *you*. And I really don't know what I'll do next. I told Papa I plan to buy my own place, but it may take some time."

"I have an idea: stay here! I could use another slave." Joyce scooped up a handful of soapsuds and blew them her direction.

Mia snapped the drying towel. "Sister, better watch yourself or I'll go on strike!"

"That challenge cannot be ignored!" Joyce grabbed up another towel and they chased each other through the house snapping and laughing before collapsing on the sofa.

Later, they made New Year's toasts, and unwilling to return to Angelo's house on the night of his planned marriage proposal, Mia stayed over in Joyce's guest room.

A week later, Dr. Farnsworth called. "I've gone over your work, Maria, and while I initially was enthusiastic, the story began to lose its appeal. Something is missing."

Chills ran down Mia's spine.

"I want to hear more about Rosa and how she rallied."

"I'm not sure how to get to her again," Mia replied reflectively.

"I have confidence in you. Dive in. You'll find her."

"I hope so. Thank you, Diana, for your time, and your thoughts. I'll have an updated version to you as soon as I can."

Securing a temporary job at a bookstore in a shopping mall, Mia intended to work only part-time but was asked to work many extra shifts. Unable to say no to the requests of other workers, she worked nearly full-time, but Mia did not mind. Work days were busy start to finish: manning the registers, stocking shelves, answering customer questions, and reading whenever she got the chance. Although she had worked the previous months only on writing now Mia filled every spare minute with everything but her own writing.

A coworker recovering from a mastectomy asked Mia to participate in a 5K walk/run called "Heaven Can Wait," an annual event/fundraiser for cancer research and awareness held in many cities around the country. Mia was glad for the athletic challenge and to do something to help at least someone with cancer, if not Victoria.

"I can't run with my bad knees," Joyce protested when Mia asked her to consider participating in the race. "I'll cheer you on, and I'll pledge some money, okay? Maybe next year I can do more. It'll be good incentive to get in a little better shape."

On the day of the race, Mia was passing the 3K marker when she noticed a blond woman beside her was limping badly. "Are you okay?"

The woman tried to smile but discomfort showed on her face. "My shin hurts."

"Try taking some weight off of it." Mia leaned and the woman wrapped an arm over her shoulder. "Better?"

The woman's face showed some relief. "Thank you. I'm Wendy."

"Mia." They took a few slow, trial steps with their arms entwined and soon were in a rhythm. They made good progress together.

Joyce was passing out cups of water to participants and called to Mia as they approached, "How are you doing?"

"Wendy has shin splints," Mia answered. "But she's a trouper. We want you with us next year!"

"Sure thing! You go, girls!" Joyce called after them.

*A*ngelo's house sold within a week of listing and he and Maggie purchased a house only a few blocks from Angelina. The west Austin neighborhood of Tarrytown has gracious homes, lovely churches, quiet parks, and easy access to a nearby nature preserve, museums, and some nice shopping. Angelo wanted virtually nothing from the old house but his clothes and golf equipment; he enlisted Mia's help in packing and sorting items to be kept by her, to go back to Angelina, or to be donated to charity.

Mia struggled with the seemingly monumental task. She started boxing books in the library but opened each one and rifled through the pages as if some important thing, some slip of paper, or fond memory, would be discovered. She had found nothing and was nearly finished filling the boxes when she reached the old, red atlas. Mia thumbed through the book and noticed a thin spot on one of the pages. Perhaps something had been stuck there and was torn away from that spot in the southern state of Oaxaca on the map of Mexico. She snapped the book closed and set it aside with others she would keep.

Empty boxes lined up at the ready in the kitchen, Mia opened cupboards and drawers and began sorting. She had dispatched dozens of items to their respective boxes when a well-used cheese grater caused her to pause. So many meals had been made with cheese from that grater. She could almost smell her favorite dishes baking in the oven. New smells would soon waft through the house, and some other family's favorite dish would be baking in the oven. Tears welled up in her eyes. How could Angelo just move to a new house and marry a new woman only six months after Victoria's death?

Mia took a deep breath and resumed sorting. Old placemats and table linens were placed in the donation box, but she set aside for herself several embroidered tea towels in pristine condition. She had successfully cleaned out half a dozen drawers before coming again to a halt at one of Victoria's dog-eared cookbooks of favorite Italian recipes. Mia studied the handwritten inscription on the first page: *Property of Angelina Casinelli.*

Turning the pages, she studied guides for removing stains; weights and measures; ingredient substitutions; suggested menus; first aid for poisoning; an index of Bible passages. A list of maxims stopped her cold. They were proper, polite, self-sacrificing. And they resonated with her. Had she read these words, or heard them, before? Who would pattern their life after something in a book—especially a cookbook? It was odd. Mia read the words again about the importance of admitting mistakes. Did Victoria ever admit *she* had made a mistake? At the hospital, Victoria had claimed to be "sorry for many things…what I did… and what I could not…"

Angelo seemed to understand what was meant, but Mia did not. There were many things she did not understand. She was losing both her parents. Victoria been taken away so quickly, and now Angelo was completely preoccupied with Maggie. Mia might as well be an orphan. A tear slid down her cheek and she allowed herself a self-indulgent whimper.

Mia sorted and packed and did not pause again until she'd emptied the last deep cupboard of its pots and pans and baking items. Glancing into the dark interior she noticed something in the back corner. Mia reached in and pulled out a bundle of papers. Behind it was another bundle, and another behind that one. The cotton strings wrapping the bundles were tied in single loops in the way Victoria had tied her apron strings.

One by one, Mia undid the bundles and went through her cards and letters that had been stacked in chronological order. The details of her life unfolded there in long narratives about Portland sights, the business, and the weather: especially rain. Updates of her home renovation projects included pictures, diagrams of furniture placement, and swatches of fabric. But these glimpses of Mia's life in Oregon were meager substitutes for phone calls and visits she should have shared with her parents. Her eyes pooled with tears and Mia sighed heavily. At least she had shared something with her family, even if it was not always the truth.

She pushed back her tears and examined some of the papers more closely. They were dimpled, and the ink was smeared, as if the letters had been dampened, as if droplets had been wiped away. And it was bittersweet to realize: all her letters had been saved and treasured, tied together and tucked away in the kitchen—the heart of the home.

*I*t was unusually warm for March on the day of Angelo and Maggie's wedding. The high ceilings and tinted windows of the church kept the heat at bay. Lavish bouquets of creamy white gardenias and pink roses gracing the altar and the ends of pews filled the air with sweet scent.

Mia's legs were trembling as she made her way down the aisle and stood at the front of the church. It was hard to stand still. She glanced down at her hands. Her bouquet of miniature roses matching her deep pink satin gown was shaking. She looked up at the statue of Mary at the side of the altar and beseeched her with a silent request, "Mary, help me. Do you listen? I feel so lost. I don't want to be alone."

How long did Mia look up at the pretty face with the sweetly smiling lips? It seemed only a moment but already the newly wedded couple was kissing. A sudden outburst of clapping and cheering ushered the wedding party down the aisle, and they were swept away to the reception hall. Enduring the seemingly unending receiving line, Mia fought the urge to bolt through the door. Her ears rang with the sound of Angelo's countless introductions: "My Darling Mia..." and "My Dear Maggie..."

When finally able to break away, Mia hastily filled a glass at the champagne fountain, took a sip and turned, nearly spilling her drink on a tall, rather good looking man behind her. "Oh, I'm sorry!" she gushed.

"No problem," the man grinned with gleaming, straight, white teeth.

"Join me in a glass of champagne?" Mia laughed uncomfortably.

"Will we both fit?" The man reached around her slim figure to refill his glass.

She lifted hers. "Here's to you: Mr. 'No Problem'."

"Don't you remember? We met over there," he pointed, "the line of torture. It's Kenneth. And you are 'My Darling Mia'." He flashed a smile and offered his hand.

Shaking it, she noticed his long tapered fingers and immaculate nails. "Are you a friend or a relative?" Mia asked and her face suddenly warmed from the champagne or the flattering look he gave her.

"Bride's cousin."

"Oh," she stammered, "you don't look a bit alike."

"Nor do you and Angelo. But that's a good thing," he quipped.

Mia's brow furrowed. Did she look nothing like Angelo—the only parent she had left? It was sad in a way. She took a sip of champagne.

The band broke in with a loud introduction followed by a waltz. Kenneth asked her to dance. He deftly removed the glass from her hand and steered her onto the dance floor. His eyes were on her face, and the hand resting on her waist was warm. His muscular thigh brushed against hers as they danced, but Mia did not pull away.

They sat down together to eat delicious almond pound cake with buttercream frosting. Kenneth told her he was 49, divorced, and had two grown children. He loved outdoor sports, lived in Houston, and was a partner in a legal firm specializing in big money personal injury cases.

Animated by the champagne, they enjoyed a witty repartee. Mia's eyes lingered on Kenneth's steel blue eyes and silver hair, his lean but athletic build looking quite attractive in his well-cut suit. By reception's end, they had exchanged phone numbers.

Much later that night, excited by the emotion and activity of the day, Mia struggled to get to sleep. Unable to do so, she wrote in her journal, and her words illuminated complex feelings she could not ignore.

> *Wonder where the whine went*
> *could I be merely sleeping*
> *wonder what my dreams will bring*
> *if my life is for the keeping*
>
> *Wonder what the wind does ask*
> *in whispering longing sighs*
> *Am I free to give and take*
> *with answering tender thighs*
>
> *I wait for you*
> *and long for you*
> *and I wonder*
> *when will you come rain on me*

# LADDER

A three-hour drive separated Austin and Houston, but Mia got together with Kenneth the next weekend, and any other weekend she was willing to make the trip. Their stimulating conversations were sprinkled with interesting debates; their private time was comfortable, uncomplicated, and unsurprising.

After having searched several months for her own place, Mia had finally found a condo she liked. It was newly built in the Arboretum neighborhood of northwest Austin. She closed on the deal several weeks after Angelo and Maggie's wedding. Although Kenneth made a late pitch for Mia to move to Houston, she was not persuaded to leave the city that had only just started to feel a little like home again.

The top floor condo seemed spacious and had a pretty view of acres of forest through double French doors leading out to a wide balcony. It was less than half the size of her Portland home but she welcomed its easy-care. Valerie and Tim now lived in the Tudor house on the hill, perhaps with their new little son in the nursery. Maybe Valerie's parents stayed in the guest room Victoria and Angelo had never visited. As Mia surveyed the empty condo, her mind returned to old, painful memories of when she had moved away from Austin.

*"Consider how your life will be if you marry and move far away," Victoria pleaded when Mia announced her sudden plans to marry Tim.*

*"How my life will be? Are you saying you disapprove?" Mia's tone was strident. "Why Mother? Because he's not Catholic and we're not marrying in your holy church?"*

*"I want what is best for you."*

*"I want to do this. I want the store. I can make something of it."*

*"But what does Tim give you?"*

*"A chance for my own life!" Mia snapped.*

*"You have that already," Victoria stated quietly and turned to the sink. She picked up a plate and washed it slowly, soap suds squeaking under the pressure of the dishcloth going around and around. "Are you sure a wife is what he wants and not just a worker?"*

*"I can't believe you would ask such a thing!" Mia nearly yelled and moved closer to Victoria. Her next words were fierce, "You'll see what we can accomplish!"*

*"But Portland is so far away and visits will be difficult," Victoria responded in a tone of restraint and reason.*

*"Why will they be 'difficult'? Because you don't like Tim?"*

*When Victoria spoke, her words were careful.*
*"We like Tim. But he does seem to want so much from*
*you."*

*Eyes flashing, Mia snarled, "At least he wants*
*more of me than you ever did. Why can't anything be*
*because I want it? You can visit. Or can't you pull*
*yourselves away from Grandmother, your precious golf*
*and gardening? Can't anything be just for me?" Mia's*
*voice broke at the last words, and she had turned away,*
*her eyes not seeing the shake of Victoria's shoulders or*
*the tears that fell into the sink water.*

*N*ow fifteen years later, recalling that bitter exchange, Mia somehow understood what Victoria had meant. She sighed loudly. Old memories and old feelings would do no good now. Shaking off those heavy emotions, she set her mind to measuring the condo's dimensions and making a diagram showing the placement of doors and windows.

From furniture store to department store, Mia trudged in search of things needed to make the condo a home. She had loved the traditional furnishings in her Portland house: calm, classic, orderly, and matching. But there were no unique pieces, no deviations from the standard, nothing interesting or surprising. The sunny condo called for something different. Her new life was different. Venturing over near the university, Mia passed by the coffee shop where she'd met with Dr. Farnsworth, and suddenly she had an idea.

She spent the next few hours searching through second-hand and thrift stores dotting the blocks around campus. Mia purchased a bookshelf and dresser, an old table, mismatched wooden chairs, and a long, low trunk. The large pieces would be delivered; she toted accessories to her car. It didn't matter if these items had belonged to someone else, so had she. It didn't matter if they had marks and dings, a history. She had marks and dings, a "her-story."

*A*fter laboring for weeks on the décor of the condo, Mia was finally unpacking her last box. She dug through the loose papers at the bottom for the two stones she had found high above the Columbia. One resembled a woman with gently bowed head and the other was rounded like a baby in swaddling clothes. Mia placed the stones in the niche of the hallway outside her bedroom. She dug into the box again and found the dark stone she'd picked up at the beach in Galveston. The three stones did not fill the niche, so she scanned the condo for some other item to place there.

"Aha!" Mia spied the statue of the Virgin Mary she'd rescued from a pile of forgotten items in a dirty second hand store. She set it behind the stones and stepped back to examine the arrangement.

Mary's face was pale porcelain except for her blushing cheeks the color of a Rome apple. Her lips were pink and slightly curved in a smile as if something sweet was on her mind or in her heart. Mary's long blue cloak edged in gold covered her feet, but Mia imagined pink roses rested there. She smiled and blinked back satisfied tears as she whispered quietly, "Welcome home."

Mia moved into the living room. Light filtered through the half-drawn Roman shades she'd sewn on Victoria's old sewing machine. She was not satisfied with her slightly wavering lines of stitching, but it was only her first attempt at using the sewing machine. Perhaps Joyce could teach her better techniques before she tackled the next sewing project: bedroom window coverings. Mia had just hung the last frame on the wall when there was a loud rap at the door.

Opening the door, she took a step back as Joyce pushed in with two large, brown paper bags. "Quick! These are heavy!"

Laughing, Mia grabbed one and led the way to the kitchen. She deposited the sack on the counter, turned and gave Joyce a hug. "What a surprise!"

"I'll say! Your hair looks great! But of course, you're always stunning!"

"Thanks," Mia beamed.

"I never thought you'd cut it! What possessed you?"

"'Locks of Love' and 'Pantene Beautiful Lengths'. They make donated hair into wigs for people going through cancer treatment or with other illnesses. I have to grow my hair out without color first, so I thought I'd start with a new style," Mia replied, tucking a short wisp behind her ear. "Look at your necklace. Such beautiful stones!"

Joyce smiled, "Thank you. It's from a company called "Bold, Bodacious Jewelry." Isn't that a great name? Saying *bodacious* just makes me want to laugh! The piece was made especially for me. I love the vibrant colors in the gemstones."

"Yes, they exude such a warm feeling."

"Natural stones have powers—maybe healing, maybe only enchantment." Joyce smiled and pointed to the bags on the cupboard. "I brought you a consumable condo-warming. Hopefully it will be enchanting as well."

"I'm sure it will be! It's great to have you here, but I was hoping to have everything finished and perfect before you saw it."

"Like I need perfect?" Joyce replied in a funny East Coast-sounding accent.

Mia laughed warmly. "And I wanted to celebrate your graduation by making my cheesy rice, a nice chop, fresh green beans with garlic...maybe gelato for dessert."

Licking her lips, Joyce squealed, "YUM! That would be a good celebration! I am *so* glad to be finished with school!"

Peeking into the brown sacks, Mia pulled out a bag of coffee beans, a grinder, sugar and creamer, a jar of home-canned peaches, a package of cream cheese, and a large bundle wrapped in foil.

"Oh, put that one in the oven to keep it warm."

"You know how I love your baking." Mia turned the oven to low and placed the wrapped bundle inside. She ground the beans and set the coffee to brew.

"You'll get some sweet satisfaction today! But how about the condo tour first?"

Mia waved her hand, "Here you have the kitchen: hub of all goodness."

"I love the yellow! It's so welcoming!"

Mia smiled. "I painted it myself."

"How did you get the textural effect?"

"It's a combination of color wash and rag rolled glaze."

"Wow!" Joyce nodded approval. "I didn't know you knew how to do that."

"I'm learning. Thanks to Maggie."

"Ah. Getting along now, are we?"

"Yes. She's nice, actually. I still think she's too young for him." Mia's face colored. "They seem happy, though, and we've had fun decorating their new place."

They stepped out onto the balcony. Scanning a row of terracotta pots filled with dark green plants, Joyce asked, "What do we have growing here?"

"Christmas rose," Mia laughed. "Cuttings I stole from my yard in Portland."

"I've never heard of a Christmas rose."

"There's an interesting legend about it: a country girl had no gift for baby Jesus until an angel showed her the rose that blooms in winter. There's also a touching poem about the flower and the Virgin Mary. But the plant is poisonous. In medieval times, it was sometimes used to kill, among other things."

Joyce arched an eyebrow, "Did you think about leaving a little of that juice for the man living in your Tudor house?"

Mia shook her head, "I'll admit to a fleeting thought. But I wouldn't wish harm to anything or anyone I once loved, even Tim."

"You're so good!"

Tears sprang into Mia's eyes. "Am I?"

"*I* might have used a knife to cut something else!"

"Joyce!"

Laughing mischievously, Joyce looked again at the plant and mused, "A rose that blooms in winter—like in the story of *La Virgen de Guadalupe*. Must be a sign."

"Of what?"

Joyce shrugged as she stepped back into the living room. "This is COOL! I love how the color is lighter at the ceiling and deepens as it moves to the floor. So serene. You really captured a mood with the perfect play of light."

"Thank you. It took hours longer than expected. I thought halfway through I'd made a mistake, but I kept working on it..." she shrugged with a smile.

"Magical! I'm surprised at your style though. I thought you'd go Modern Minimalist instead of Shabby Chic, but I like the rustic look. The framed sampler is charming. Did you do the embroidery?"

"No, I'm not sure who did. I'd like to learn. I did sew the window shades."

"Good job! Fun, isn't it?" Glancing again at the sampler, Joyce named various stitches: "Feather, Hem, Bonnet, Paris, Shadow, Blanket, Vandyke, Ladder, Running…" She paused and pointed, "That one is 'Cloud Filling,' also called the 'Mexican Stitch'."

Mia eyed the stitch on the sampler.

"Let's see the rest of your place." Moving into the hallway Joyce remarked, "Girl, you do have a knack."

"It's a niche," Mia quipped, and they both laughed.

"I see Mary's watching over your mother and baby stone. Where's your father? A baby needs some kind of father." Joyce pointed to the dark stone Mia had picked up in Galveston. "Is that him?"

"I…don't know…who my father is."

But Joyce took no notice of the bewildered look on Mia's face, and she moved on into the bathroom. "Pretty. The rustic ladder holding your magazines reminds me of ramshackle beach fences. Especially with the blue walls and bowl of shells and sand."

"I've been longing for the beach," Mia sighed. "Even though the Pacific Ocean was just an hour from Portland, I went only three or four times in all those years."

"Maybe a new spirit moves you. Or an old one's trying to get you back," Joyce remarked outside the master bedroom.

Opening and shutting the door quickly, Mia offered barely a glimpse of the unadorned walls and white-on-white linens. "I haven't really gotten started in there yet."

"Hmm," Joyce said in suspicious tone. "Romance is definitely lacking. Did you give all your passion to the woman in your story? You better get some sweetness back!"

"I will soon! It's in the oven!" Mia led the way to the kitchen, where she gracefully set plates and silverware on the table. Joyce pulled the foil bundle from the oven. She unwrapped the hot bread, placed it on a plate, and wadded up the foil. "Recycle that," Mia said, grabbing a basket from atop the refrigerator and holding it out.

Joyce tossed the foil in. "Did I see rollerblades in your bedroom? Those went out years ago and they were never for women my age, or yours! You could hurt something!"

"Oh, I did! Not seriously though: a bruised knee and scrapes on my hands. Next time I'll wear gloves and pads." Mia shrugged, "They were resale: only $10.00." And then she laughed, "I've found I like speed on wheels when I'm in control."

"Doesn't sound like you were!" Joyce chuckled. "Hmm, buying second hand, recycling? Lots of new things going on with you. Or, should I say, 'old' things?"

"A lesson from Ms. 'Eradicator of Plastic,' seamstress, baker extraordinaire!"

"Listen and learn!" Joyce laughed as she carried the bread and cream cheese to the table. "What else have you been doing?"

"I went to Hamilton Pool the other day. The green limestone under the water is so beautiful. And the air at the preserve was 'singing' with excitement," Mia gushed. "I even thought I heard a golden-cheeked warbler in the Ashe junipers!"

"A birdwatcher, too?" Joyce scanned the condo. "Where are your binoculars?"

Laughing, Mia poured coffee and carried the mugs to the table.

Joyce brought over sugar and cream and sat down. Her hand stroked the glowing pine surface of the tabletop. "This is just charming!"

"Thank you. I sanded and distressed it before staining and waxing it."

Cream cheese slathered on a piece of bread, Mia started eating and sighed with enjoyment. "Joyce, this bread is amazing! I could learn so much from you. Have you ever knitted baby blankets? I'd like to make some for a teen mother program."

"What a good idea! And I could teach you to quilt; it's good sewing practice. My friend Anna from the flower shop has been trying to enlist my participation in the local chapter of 'Quilts for Kids' that makes quilts to comfort children in need. And there are other groups we could look into…"

"Ohhh," Mia sighed. "I'd love that. We could get together weekly for a potluck and projects. I'd invite my co-workers, and Wendy."

"We could do other crafts: embroidery or beading!" Joyce offered excitedly, took a bite of bread and a drink of coffee. "It could be 'Knit and Wit,' or 'Bake and Boast'!"

"And we could trade recipes, techniques, gossip, whatever." Mia's eyes sparkled with excitement. "I need to keep busy. When Tim and I had the store, the changing inventory required frequent rearranging. It was a good outlet for my restless creativity."

Joyce sighed, "I loved doing the displays in my flower shop."

Smiling and nodding in agreement, Mia said, "The window displays were especially fun and rewarding: they bring gawkers in and make them customers."

"I really missed those creative challenges when I sold the shop."

"Why did you sell?"

"After twenty years on my feet and with all this extra weight, my knees were giving me trouble. My wrists and hands hurt all the time, too. The floral business is not easy. And it was even harder on me after Neil died. When a sweet young couple made an offer it just seemed a blessing. I was ready for a new career."

Mia sighed loudly, "Maybe I could use a new career. Writing is so hard!"

Turning, Joyce scanned the condo. "You've got a start on being a re-decorator; you could redo my house! Would it be expensive?"

"Doesn't have to be. You could re-purpose old items, mix up the colors, textures, and styles."

"Cool. Speaking of change, guess what I've been doing?" Joyce asked playfully.

"I couldn't possibly!"

Joyce leaned in and said quietly, "Internet dating. Oh, boy, are there some duds out there! Plenty of dudes looking for a good time," Joyce laughed. "I was meeting and greeting several men a week but no one interesting enough to go out with again. I nearly gave up but answered one last ad." Joyce smiled, "Tony. He's fun. And so sweet to me."

"What does he do?"

Joyce slathered another piece of bread with cream cheese. "He's a traveling artist and lives in a motor-home. Not sure I understand *that* lifestyle choice."

"Men are simple creatures: driven by forces found only in nature," Mia stated in a documentary-sounding voice and then chuckled.

"Men aren't the only ones," Joyce sighed. "Women need rumba, too. Not sure I can do that kind of relationship—two days together, two weeks apart."

"After so many years since your husband died, aren't you used to being alone?"

"Who says I've been alone?"

"Oh, I'm sorry." Mia frowned. "You haven't mentioned *that*."

Joyce's brows knitted together, her eyes narrowing, and she replied in complaint, "You don't ask. Isn't it something friends share?"

Mia shrugged a shoulder. "Isn't it rude to ask such personal things?"

"Would you be offended if I ask about Clamface? Does he 'light your fire'? He sounds blah, blah, bland. Maybe he puts out your fire."

Scowling, Mia replied, "His name is Kenneth. And no, he doesn't light my fire. But I don't want to burn! It's too painful. We have a fine time, and we go nice places."

"What about the important place—your heart? Think I don't see what you're doing here?" Joyce poked at the table.

Mia shook her head and shrugged. "Decorating?"

"Sanding, distressing and changing surfaces. What are you trying to get to? Who has gotten under your skin? What do you want?"

Mia rubbed chill bumps from her arms.

"You still think about Gerald, and dream about him, don't you?"

She nodded reluctantly. "But he's not the kind of person I'd...choose to be with."

Joyce raised an eyebrow. "What 'kind' is he? Minority? 'Half-breed'?"

"That sounds terrible! So not P.C. And heritage does matter. The blood of our ancestors leads us to our destiny, and I don't think..."

Joyce interrupted loudly, "Why can't you just let yourself *feel*? Is he really so different from you—just because he's not all white? Are you that prejudiced?"

"It did bother me that he's Native American. I mean... Italians are considered..."

"You're getting in deeper," Joyce warned.

"But mostly what bothers me is he's...so..." Mia struggled to find words.

"He works, gardens, cooks, cleans, reads...what more do you want?"

"But he just exists in such a small place. And he's so solitary."

Joyce's eyes rolled. "That differs from you how? You're here, laboring alone."

"But this is a city, and I'm trying to get out more. I'm working and volunteering."

"Maybe he could, too!"

"I have no right to ask that of him or even want it. He is who he is," Mia sighed. "But I do think I'd have more respect for him if he embraced his Native American roots."

"You were only with him a few weeks. He probably does all kinds of things you don't know about, and didn't ask. Maybe he's embracing his 'white' roots."

"But he…" Mia objected. "He just doesn't have much ambition."

"Too much ambition fills life with too much work. You did that! Where was the joy? And, besides," Joyce argued, "you said he refinishes and restores things. That's ambition. And something you now have in common!"

"But he…" Mia sputtered. "Gerald has hardly anything to show for his work."

"Aha!" Joyce replied loudly. "This is about money!"

Mia's face flushed. "NO! Why would it be? I have money. But what kind of life is that just existing out there near the 'End of the Oregon Trail'?"

Joyce exhaled loudly. "I'm beginning to think I don't know who you are."

Mia turned and looked out the window at the sky filling with clouds "I don't know either. If I could figure out what happened…I'd know who I am."

Distracted and only half listening, Joyce took another bite of bread. "Mmm." She glanced at Mia and offered encouragingly, "You are becoming quite the nature girl, artist, adventurer, writer…"

"That's not what I mean."

But Joyce did not notice the pained look on Mia's face. She went on to ask, "When will your *Lamentation* be published?"

"Dr. Farnsworth wants more of Rosa's rebound. I'll have to come up with something. But I…" she looked down at her hands. "I've lost the thread. And yet, something pulls at me."

"Maybe you can follow it back."

"Back where?"

Joyce shrugged, "Wherever curiosity leads."

They exchanged looks. Mia started putting dishes in the dishwasher while Joyce busied herself clearing the table. "Tony asked me to go on the road with him."

"That's good, right? You won't be missing him if you're together."

Joyce shook her head. "After Neil died, I said, 'Never again.' My relationships, however brief, have been for enjoyment. No risk, no worries. But with Tony…"

Mia interrupted, "*You* said we're here on this earth to learn love."

"Eh! Did I say that? I can go on."

"AND, you were just telling *me* I should let myself feel more!"

Joyce replied softly. "It's true. But that's the thing—I do feel. Too much! And suddenly, I want it all: commitment, security, devotion. The whole thing. Or nothing."

"I can understand that," Mia sighed.

Joyce turned and picked up her handbag. "I'm sure I'll know what to do soon enough, but right now I have to be going."

Mia followed her to the door. "Thanks for coming, Joyce; I loved the condo-warming. Let's get together soon to do some crafts!" Mia hugged her goodbye and said, "If I ever had a sister, I'd want her to be just like you."

"Me, too, sweetie. Me, too." Joyce waved goodbye from the hallway, pushed the button for the elevator and called back to Mia, "Let the spirit move you. Follow the thread, find 'who you are', and you'll be able to write Rosa's rebound as well!"

Later, as the afternoon sun softened, Mia sat down at the table. She traced her finger over the petals of the flower on her leather satchel and words were in her mind.

*Such civilized people*
*always behaving as we should*
*all the while wishing*
*we could break away from constraint*
*all the while longing to eat until full*
*to quench our thirst*
*exchanging waiting*
*for another chance at love*
*no matter where it takes us*
*no matter what turn we take on the road*

Mia sighed and more words came though she did not yet understand their significance.

*My heart seeks refuge in words*
*sweet lips whispering my name*
*calling me closer*
*ever closer*

# Zigzag

M̲ia woke the next morning in restless discontent and words echoed in her mind.

*I pray you come…*

After drinking a cup of coffee and eating a piece of cinnamon toast, she dressed for running and went out. Mia ran down the middle of the street in a zigzag route through neighborhoods to a trail at a nearby park. Finally, she circled back to her building, breezed up the stairs two by two, rushed into her condo, and before she could change her mind, picked up the phone.

"Hi, it's Mia," she said cheerfully when Kenneth answered. "I…" she breathed. "I wanted to see how your day's going."

"That it?" His voice was clipped, impatient.

"No. I, uh, just wanted to talk to you."

"Not a good time," Kenneth barked.

Her ears perked to a sound in the background. Was his pen rapping the desk?

"We'll talk Friday at the dinner I asked you to attend."

"Is that all?"

"I'm working. We'll hook up as usual this weekend," he replied flippantly.

"Just social engagements and bed?" she demanded to know.

"If you wanted more you would have moved to Houston when you had the chance. And don't raise your voice to me. I don't need it."

Her words thundered out, "I don't need *YOU* telling *ME* what to *DO!*"

Mia pressed off her phone. A tear fell from her eye, but she wiped it angrily away. She looked out to her green plants on the balcony. Christmas rose: transported from far away and now struggling to set down roots. Her mind mulled over the words of that odd thought. Switching on the radio in the kitchen, she was startled by a song that played: San Antonio Rose. The lyrics seemed especially significant and chills ran down her spine. Suddenly Mia knew what she had to do and where she must go.


"*A* holiday is just what you need, Darling. You've worked much too hard. I'm sure you'll enjoy the Botanical Gardens and Conservatory: the strolling paths and the city views from the gazebo are just delightful," Angelo effused.

"Sounds beautiful."

"Perhaps you would like SeaWorld and the zoo."

She laughed, "I think the museums and cathedrals will have more appeal. I love architecture. Especially stonework. It just...speaks to me."

"You should see the Alamo, and stay downtown at the O'Brien. It's worth every penny. San Antonio is such a lovely city," he sighed. "I still miss it after all these years."

"What compelled you to leave if you love it so?"

There was silence on his end.

Mia asked boldly, "Something to do with Mother, right?"

"We," Angelo paused, "thought it might put her mind at ease."

"I know she didn't like crowds, but there was more to it than that, right?" Mia drew a breath. "Something happened. Was there…someone else…before?"

"It was so long ago, why linger on the past? You have a lovely holiday to enjoy," he replied soothingly. "Call us when you return, Darling Mia."

She sighed, giving up the inquiry.


*D*eparting with a haphazardly stuffed travel bag, Mia headed toward San Antonio with words rumbling through her mind.


*Maybe* La Virgen *listen…*

An hour into the drive, she was sleepy and yawning; Mia spied a place to stop and went inside. A dark-haired girl behind the counter greeted her sweetly, "Welcome to the Hail Mary Coffee Shop. What would you like today?"

"Brewed coffee: large, white, and sugary," Mia smiled, handed her five dollars, and waved away the change.

Eyes sparkling, the girl pushed a steaming cup across the counter. "Thank you."

The coffee soon revived Mia's mind and she reviewed odd things that had been said in recent months. New questions formed in her mind, and she was all the more anxious to get to San Antonio. Arriving downtown, Mia parked the car and walked to the Bexar County Courthouse. She drew a deep breath, passed the stone pillars, and mounted wide stairs of the old building. Her footsteps echoed down the shiny marble hallway to the County Clerk's office. Thanks to modern technology, the record she sought was located without much trouble and a copy was made.

The marriage license application listed Angelo's birthplace as San Antonio. Victoria's listed birthplace was *Salina*, Italy. Her full name: Victoria Maria *Bartolomeo*. Walking from the courthouse to the car, Mia mulled over her questions. Why had Victoria been so secretive? What did Angelina mean by saying the wrong kind of woman, from the wrong kind of place, can bring a man down? Mia studied the paper and had an idea. She drove to the San Antonio Public Library, then asked the reference librarian for an atlas published before 1968 like the one from the Casinelli's study.

Turning to the index, Mia ran her finger down the page to Victoria's listed birthplace, *Salina*, Italy: 38.35 North Latitude, 14.48 East Longitude. Below it on the page was *Salina Cruz*, Mexico. Perhaps there was some detail she could use for Rosa's story. She turned to a map of Mexico and studied the shape of the country, the features of the land, and bodies of water to the east and west and south. She turned to a map of Italy and studied the "boot" with water on the east and west and south—just like Mexico. There was something strange about that—but she didn't know what. The fluorescent lights flickered overhead. The stale air of the library became stifling. Mia's head began to throb. Quickly copying the index page and the maps of both countries, she returned the atlas to the librarian and burst through the library doors out into the open air.

Her legs were shaking by the time Mia reached her car. She collapsed onto the seat; drawing calming breaths, she fought inexplicable tears. When she had recovered enough to drive, Mia went to her hotel. The historic lodging on the River Walk promised quiet luxury with gracious décor, and it delivered. Stripping off her clothes, Mia went to the shower. Hot water cascading over her melted away the headache.

Mia wrapped her hair in a towel, put on her robe, and settled down to drink a cup of tea she'd heated in the microwave. She flicked on the television but a few moments later clicked it off and sprawled out on her stomach with her feet dangling over the edge of the bed. She closed her eyes and drifted to sleep.

The terrycloth towel still wrapping her hair, Mia woke with its nappy imprint on her cheek. She got up and splashed cold water again and again on her puffy eyes. Mia stared into the mirror at the imprint of the towel on her face and odd words popped into her mind: *Salinas Victoria.*

Puzzled, Mia retrieved the copied pages of the atlas index and maps from her purse. She found a listing for the town in northern Mexico. Flanked with bumpy mountains, it was just off the Inter-American Highway, a direct route to the United States, and only 250-300 miles southeast of San Antonio. She sat down heavily on the bed and looked again at the map of Mexico. *Salinas Victoria. Salinas* like *Salina,* Italy. Strange. Was it a clue? Victoria loved word games. Maria was her middle name. It was a common name. Even Mia was named Maria—Maria Isabel Angelina, for an aunt and grandmothers, Angelina had said. But what aunt; what grandmother besides Angelina?

Lying back on the bed, Mia closed her eyes. Her mind wandered to her childhood home: her fingers dragged over the rough bark of her favorite tree and traced the bindings of the books in the old study. Victoria's words came suddenly to Mia's mind: "*I* have never lived on hope. I have lived on what I *plan.*" And Angelina had said, "Clever, that one: naming her life as she wished with a map." Mia dressed quickly, brushed out her tangled hair, grabbed her purse, and hurried back to the San Antonio Library.

"May I help you?"

"I was here earlier," she answered breathlessly. "May I see the old atlas again?"

The woman retrieved the book and asked, "Something I could help you find?"

"A place named Maria."

They scanned the index, but there was no listing for a town named "Maria" in either Italy or Mexico. Scanning Victoria and Angelo's marriage license again, Mia sighed aloud, "I thought there were clues in the words."

The librarian glanced at the paper and suggested, "Let's try *Bartolomeo.*"

They flipped to the index page.

Mia shook her head, "Not that one either. I thought Mother hid a clue to a previous identity in the names on the license. But without either one to go on..." She sighed turning away. "Thanks anyway for your help."

The librarian picked up the atlas and called out to Mia, "Miss, you said, 'without either one to go on'. That made me think of '*sans*', which means without."

"'*Sans*'? Without what?"

"Also, in Spanish," the librarian remarked, "*san* is the shorter, unstressed form of *Santo*, which means holy, saintly, or blessed."

Mia stared at the woman. "*San* what?"

"What did you say she did here for a living?"

"I'm not sure, but Mother might have been a hairdresser."

"There are some old family shops still in operation. Maybe someone would remember her if she was unusually pretty and looked anything like you."

*M*ia hurried out and went over to the River Walk of the San Antonio River. Cypress trees, some several hundred years old, and reaching ten stories high, could be seen from the streets above. Others, including many Bald Cypress that shed their leaves in fall, were planted when the canal was built to control dangerous flooding. Now thousands of tourists each day crowd into shops and other attractions as tour boats buzz up and down the river. Swooping birds dive for food on plates in the waterside restaurants, and the sound of people, activities, and motors echo loudly down the canal.

It was all a bit too much; Mia's head was spinning and her stomach churned. She found a table at a waterside restaurant and sat down to study a menu.

A waitress arrived for her order. "Need a minute? Tourists always need a minute."

"I'm not really a tourist. I'm here to visit..." A noisy boat passing by just then drowned out her words.

"Vista? I hear the rooms have teddy bears, a tribute to Bexar County."

But Mia's look was of confusion.

"Bexar County is pronounced like 'bear'."

Mia was shaking her head. "I'm not at the Vista. I'm at the O'Brien."

The waitress shrugged a shoulder. "Know what y' need?" But when Mia did not seem to understand, the waitress tapped her pencil impatiently on her pad, "To eat?"

Glancing at the menu, Mia sighed, "Pancake special... something for comfort."

"Special I can do. Get a bear for comfort," the waitress quipped in her most efficient voice, then snatched up the menu.

Mia's mind flashed on Gerald and how she'd taken so much comfort in his arms. Trying to fill her longing with food, she ate every bite of the tender buttermilk pancakes she drenched in melted butter and warm maple syrup.

After the meal, Mia trudged from salon to salon showing the picture of Victoria as a young woman but to no avail. She was about to give up when a beautician named Elena said her mother had owned the shop in the 1960s. Pleading for an opportunity to speak to the elderly woman, Mia managed to arrange a meeting for several hours later.

Elena greeted Mia at the door of her home and led the way to a sitting room where a frail old woman looked up with surprise. "So many years since I see you."

Startled, Mia glanced at to Elena. "Did you tell her why I'm here?"

But Elena shook her head. "Mother, may I introduce Ms. Casinelli?"

"Nice to meet you, Mrs. Salgado." Mia reached down for the aged woman's hand.

A warm smile parted the old woman's dry lips, "And you, Maria."

Mia stammered, "My name *is* Maria—Maria Isabel Angelina. I go by Mia." Showing the photograph of Victoria, Mia asked softly, "Did you know her?

Mrs. Salgado's eyes rested on the picture a long time.

"I'm sorry. She drifts off." Elena stepped forward as if to stop the inquiry.

Mia squatted down on one knee beside the elderly woman. "Did you know her?"

Mrs. Salgado seemed to contemplate then answered surely, "So far from home, so frightened, and with a baby so small."

"Why was she frightened?" Mia asked breathlessly.

The old woman raised her eyes and looked into Mia's face; she gently patted Mia's cheek and her eyes gleamed. "Nothing to fear now, little angel."

Mia blinked back tears and a flurry of questions rushed from her lips. "Did she say anything about her family? Where she came from? Who...the father of the baby was? Or...what happened?"

"I went to Mexico once," Mrs. Salgado said. "But it was not so frightening for me." Her eyes were misty; the old woman seemed to drift off and the photograph slipped from her grasp.

Elena handed the photo back to Mia. "She is tired. You see she is lost somewhere in her mind. You will get no more from her."

"Thank you so much, Mrs. Salgado. Thank you, Elena," Mia said warmly as she was leaving. But Mrs. Salgado did not look up, only kept her eyes on her wrinkled hands with skin as dry and thin as tissue paper.

# CABLE

*A*fter tossing and turning in the hotel bed, Mia eagerly downed several cups of coffee in the morning. She skipped breakfast and went out. Mia walked to the Alamo. Looking up at the surprisingly small structure, its creamy walls bathed in golden light, she felt no sense of history. Not even a sense of the great battle that'd taken place there or the lives that had been lost. But there was something else. A gust of cool wind flapped her collar, and Mia shoved her hands down into the pockets of her jacket. The scrap of cloth was there and her fingers stroked the comforting feel of its satiny stitches.

Maybe it was the throng of people pushing in closer and closer behind her, but suddenly Mia was overcome with emotion. She turned, looking for a way out of the crowd, and her eyes fell on a face at the back. Mia raised her hand and hurried in that direction, but when she reached the street, the figure was gone.

"I saw you," she said aloud. "Where did you go?"

A tourist with poufy blond hair glanced over at Mia and pulled her child closer.

Mia turned, walking toward La Villita Historic Arts Village, San Antonio's first neighborhood; she scanned the faces she encountered but saw no one else who seemed familiar. Mia drew a breath and went into an import store selling clothing and accessories.

She pulled the scrap of cloth from her pocket and opening her hand, Mia noticed a small spot of thin paper stuck to the back of the cloth. The spot's shape resembled the thin spot on the map of Mexico in the Casinelli's old atlas. She asked the clerk behind the counter, "Do you have anything made in Oaxaca?"

"I believe we do." The clerk led the way to a crowded rack and searched through the hangers. "These were made there."

Mia barely glanced at the embroidered pullover tops. She held up the scrap. "I'm looking for something embroidered like this."

Shaking her head the clerk replied, "That is such finely crafted embroidery. I'm afraid we have only the more 'rustic' imports. Sorry."

"Thank you, anyway," Mia sighed.

A few doors down, there was an old stucco cottage with painted shutters and very thick walls. The name on its wooden sign caught Mia's eye. She went inside.

Tallying receipts at an antique desk, a woman remarked without looking up, "Welcome. Nice and cool inside isn't it?"

"Yes, I love the architecture of this building." Mia moved toward the desk and her eyes glanced down at the business cards in a silver dish.

"They don't build like this anymore, but they should."

Mia nervously shifted her gaze to the face of the blond, carefully coiffed, middle-aged woman. "How long have you been in business here?"

"Over 30 years. I sell only high-end Southwest and Texas-made clothing in natural fibers, hand-made jewelry, and home items. Perhaps you'd be interested in my yellow-tagged sales of the week? Tooled silver and leather belts are twenty percent off. And these hand-painted silk scarves are thirty percent off."

"Were you here in 1968? Are you *Angelita*?" Mia asked nervously.

"No, no, neither one," the woman answered. "I opened this shop in 1971. Pretty name, don't you think? It just spoke to me. And it's been good luck; I've made a decent living, put my son through college. Now I'm helping my grandson. He's in law school. I might as well work; what else would I do? Sit around with friends and eat cake?" the woman laughed.

Mia reached for a fuchsia and green silk scarf hanging on a rack next to the desk.

"Go ahead and try it. Just stunning with your coloring," the woman said. "I'm Swedish: pale as can be. I can't compete with you beautiful Latina girls."

Mia squinted as she glanced at her reflection in a mirror. She fished out her pocketbook, paid for the scarf, and waited while it was wrapped in tissue and bagged. Wandering to the window, her eyes caught a glimpse of a figure passing by. Mia turned and headed for the door.

"Don't forget your package!" the saleswoman called.

Mia came back, snatched up the bag, and hurried out. She dashed down the courtyard after the woman she had seen but she could not find her. Mia sank down onto a wooden bench in the shade of a tall cypress. Leaves fluttered in a slight breeze. She closed her eyes, drew in calming breaths, and prayed for a sign, but when her eyes opened, nothing had changed.

Angelina had spoken many times of the stately residential area on the banks of the San Antonio River. Mia pulled out her map of the city. The King William Historic District was in walking distance, so she headed in that direction. A brochure from her hotel told of the German and French architectural influences evident in the late 19th century mansion-like homes.

Many of these had been converted into multi-family dwellings but they had fallen into neglect by the early 1900s. A resurgence of interest in conjunction with the World's Fair brought much renovation, and now the residential area was a lovely tourist attraction listed on the National Register. The district was as lovely as Mia expected, and she noted observations to share with Angelina.

Next, Mia walked several blocks over to the HemisFair Park. She gazed at the colorful landscaping and the Tower of the Americas that stood 750 feet high with glassed-in observation decks on top. It looked like Seattle's Space Needle. Angelo had proposed to Victoria here. Mia purchased a ticket and went up in the elevator.

Gripping the rail and closing her eyes as the glassed compartment silently whisked up the tower, she barely heard the elevator operator explain how the tower had been built for the World's Fair. The doors opened; Mia stepped out into the narrow observation deck and glanced down at the city where so much had changed since the tower had been built. Suddenly she reached out to a passing woman. "Excuse me. Did the operator say when this tower opened?"

"April, 1968. For the World's Fair."

"Thank you," Mia managed to say. She dug in her purse and her hands were shaking as she glanced down at Victoria and Angelo's marriage license application. The issue date was April 23, 1968.

Struggling to keep her composure, Mia hurried back to her hotel. She drew a hot bath and renewed the heat several times before her shaking had stopped. She slipped on pajamas and socks. After much nervous deliberation, Mia picked up the phone and called Angelo.

"Darling Mia! How is San Antonio? How do you like the O'Brian?"

She answered his questions and then Mia said, "I need to ask you something."

"Are you all right? You sound so very small."

"I..." she stammered.

"I hope you are feeling well enough for a surprise coming your way."

She was disturbed and shaking and unable to ask the thing screaming in her mind. Mia promised to call again after she had rested, for she was suddenly so very tired. Setting down the phone, she curled up on the bed. Tears flowed, but finally she slept.

Mia's heart was pounding and sounds were in her ears. Startled awake, she reached for her ringing phone. Her ears listened. Her mouth mumbled a response. She put down the phone and her feet hit the floor; her arms slipped into a robe. Soon there was a knock on the door. Her hands slid the chain from the bracket and opened the door. "I can't believe you're here."

Gerald smiled, and his eyes rested on her face.

"I'm happy to see you. You look good," Mia managed to say.

"Y'r hair's shorter. Makes y'r eyes stand out."

"Thanks..." she breathed and smiled up at him. "You look good."

"Y' said that." His eyes took in the room.

Mia stepped back and said, "I'm sorry! Come in!"

They moved to upholstered chairs at a small table and sat down. She pressed her shaking hands flat on the smooth, inlaid wood of the tabletop.

Their eyes met.

Her hand combed through her hair. "What are you doing in Texas?"

"Sold the bike to a guy not far from here."

"Oh." Her smile faded. Mia looked down at the table.

"But I came to San Antonio to see y'."

She drew a breath and looked up at him again. "How'd you find me?"

"Angelo."

"Oh," she nodded. "He did say a surprise was coming my way."

There was an awkward silence.

Gerald smiled hopefully. "Want to see something I've been doing?" He pulled a large envelope from his shoulder bag and spread photographs across the table.

She glanced at them. "Did you take these with your old camera?"

"I was juried into an exhibition next week with this one." He pointed to a photo of sailboards on the Columbia River with a double rainbow in a gray-blue sky.

"These are so good! How long will you be here? We could go to the San Antonio Museum of Art; there's an exhibit of diverse camera works by five photographers. I'm not sure who they are but...oh, my gosh! Are you one of them?" she asked excitedly.

He laughed, shaking his head. "Maybe someday. I've been painting, too."

"What kind of painting?"

"Murals. I started the first one when y' were there. Girl at the mini-mart's aunt."

"Oh," Mia relied nodding, "so that's what it was about."

He pulled a picture of the painted shed from beneath the other photos.

"A woman behind falling water? Or are those tears? Simply beautiful! You could put Rufus on the art map."

Gerald smiled, his warm brown eyes taking in Mia's face.

Heat moved through her with images streaming into her mind of his skin glistening in the sun and rivulets of water running down his back.

"Y' there?"

Mia looked at him and drew a quick breath. "I could use some air."

They went down the street to a café. Chatting, they ate cheese omelets, toast with blackberry preserves, hash browns, and hot chocolate. Mia finally pushed her plate aside and laughed with a hand to her stomach, "I am so full!"

"Me, too. Be right back," Gerald said getting up.

Mia looked out the window at people passing by: couples arm in arm, packs of teenagers, and singles on the prowl. But there was no one familiar.

Gerald slid back into the booth.

"I saw someone earlier today. Someone familiar." Mia shook off a chill. "Gerald, do you believe in ghosts?"

He shrugged. "Spirits at least."

"I...felt her, like a presence." Mia rubbed her arms. "And a while ago, when you were talking, the strangest sensation came over me. There's a word..."

Gerald gave her a look. "I know a word," he teased.

She blushed, shaking her head. "No, a word that also came to me when I was at your cabin; we were talking about the woman I dream and the word popped into my mind: *lil*. I didn't know what it meant but now I remember! It's from ancient history; it's a word for wind. But it can also mean ghost, or demon."

"Maybe she brings a message. Have y' asked to know something?"

Mia shook off another chill and stood up, moving toward the door. They stepped out to the sidewalk. "I've been searching..." she started to say, but a group of noisy teenagers brushed past them, and she did not finish her thought.

They stopped at Gerald's truck on their way back to the hotel. He undid clips, loosened a cable, and peeled back a tarp covering the bike strapped to a trailer.

"Ohhh," Mia sighed.

Even in the light from street lamps, the chrome gleamed and the logo on the gas tank was clear: a stunning profile of an Indian chief with his long hair streaming back.

"Just like one my dad had when I was little," Gerald said.

"It must have been difficult to get parts for such an old bike."

"Easier with Internet."

"Internet? Are you online out there?" Her eyes looked at him with surprise.

"Not yet. I use the Internet café in The Dalles."

"You have a computer now?"

Gerald nodded. "Laptop. Makes many things easier. And more fun."

She looked again at the bike. "Sad to let the Indian go."

"Y' still have this one," he answered, smiling with hopeful confidence.

As they walked back to the hotel, she stole sidelong glances at him. And when they went into her room, Mia yawned and stretched out on the bed. Gerald lay down beside her. Maybe she only dreamed how they came together: her cheek resting against the smooth skin of his muscular shoulder, her mouth falling onto the soft cushion of his lips. And maybe it was the digital clock flickering at the bedside and not sparks of their pleasure lighting the room. Maybe she only imagined floating up higher and higher and traveling with him through the heavens with the sound of music in her ears.

When sleep came to Mia, it was heavy and filled with another kind of dream.

*Kisses. So many sweet kisses. Crying. So much crying.*
*A fire raged. Someone grabbed her and ran. Brilliantly*
*embroidered cloth lay in tatters on the ground. A man*
*raised his head, and his face was as creased and*
*scarred as old leather. An old truck drove slowly down*
*a road. Trees lined a beach where a woman was*
*sewing. Searching, Mia showed the piece of cloth and*
*the picture of Victoria. She looked off in the distance to*
*a flash of light and her name was called.*

Waking, Mia sat up suddenly in the bed. A sliver of light slipped into the room through a crack in the drapery. Gerald was gone. Her heart pounded. Tears sprang into her eyes. She lay back down and cried, sobbing as if her heart was broken.

There was a noise at the door, and it opened. Gerald came in with coffee cups in hand, and she wiped her eyes. "I had a bad dream. I woke up and you were gone and I..."

He held out a cup and Mia took it, thanking him. Her eyes gleamed up at him. She drank the coffee fixed just the way she liked it: sweet and white. And then she told him of the strange dream. "There were so many images. What do you think it meant?"

He shrugged. "Haven't a clue."

Mia's eyes searched his face and words escaped her mouth. "Haven't a clue? Without a clue...without either one to go on...sans..." Mia jumped up from the bed and dug into her bag for the copy of the index from the library atlas. Between the listings Salado and San Carlos, she found San Bartolomeo, in the mountains of south central Italy. Victoria had listed her name as Victoria Maria Bartolomeo from Salina, Italy. Why had Victoria left her homeland? Why did Mrs. Salgado mention Mexico and why did she say Victoria had been frightened? Did *Salinas Victoria* have any significance?

Below *San Bartolomeo*, Italy in the index, Mia noticed two listings for *San Bartolo*, Mexico: one in the mountains of northern Mexico near Durango, and one further south near Mexico City. She looked for the towns on a map she'd purchased, but didn't find them.

"Perhaps absorbed by larger towns or the names were changed," Gerald suggested.

"Come to Oaxaca with me. We could fly to Mexico City and on to Oaxaca."

She showed him the embroidered cloth with the bit of paper on the back. "It was in the atlas, stuck on Oaxaca. It means something, something about Mother, and me," Mia answered. "I just don't know what."

"Not much to go on."

"Gerald, please. Come with me!"

He shook his head, "Can't. I have to get back."

"Oh," Mia sighed. "I forgot about your show."

"Can y' wait?"

"I don't think so. Something calls me. I have to go there."

"Do y' have someone else who could go?"

"I'll find something," she claimed, as if there were more than old threads on a cloth and torn paper to lead her.

When they had packed their things, and walked to her car, she put her purse and suitcase inside. Mia turned and looked up at Gerald.

His hand rested on top of the door between them; his eyes studied her hair, her eyes, her lips.

Her face warmed under his look. "I hope your exhibition goes well. Your photos are striking. You'll take Portland by storm!"

"Just like y' to bring up clouds," Gerald said smiling, his look a caress. He leaned down and placed his lips on hers.

Pulling away Mia said, "Gerald...I..."

He kissed her again.

Breathless, she pulled back. "I don't know what this is. There are so many things we haven't talked about."

"That what y' want? Talk?" His eyes stared down into hers and then his fingers tapped the center of her chest. "Everything y' need to know is here. Time to stop closing doors on what y' feel. We are not so different..."

Her eyes filled with tears. Mia smiled, and stepped out from behind the car door. He pulled her in close, they kissed, and she was shaking when she pulled away. "I'm so glad you came. When I get back from Mexico…"

"Y' know where to find me," he responded, his voice slow and deep. He brushed her cheek with his hand.

"I already did," she breathed, but as he started to walk away, she called to him, "Gerald, wait. Take me for a ride before you go!"

"Not safe. Don't have a helmet."

"We could live dangerously," she suggested playfully.

He only laughed, and walked away with his long pony tail dangling between his broad shoulders.


*M*ia drove back to Austin with questions on her mind. Pulling up to the curb outside Angelo and Maggie's house, she switched off the headlights. Mia drew a breath, went to the door, and knocked.

The outside light came on, the door opened, and she stepped inside. They went to the study. Angelo poured glasses of brandy and they sat down. "Was your trip good?" He raised his glass to drink.

She nodded. "I was searching for information about Mother."

The glass came down from his lips.

"Papa…" she implored with her eyes, "What happened? What frightened her so much that you left San Antonio? Did she think some danger would catch up to her? I know there was violence." Mia's voice was firm. "And there was another…"

But he interrupted, "Victoria would not speak of it. She begged me never to ask. I did not care where she came from, what had happened, or what she left behind. I only wanted to make you both safe." Angelo's face paled as if he'd said too much.

Mia eyed him and pressed on. "Grandmother said you had a high fever as a child, that you were *damaged*. She said she and grandfather waited and prayed for a 'miracle': just one grandchild to carry on the family heritage." Mia's eyes bored into him. "I carried the family name, but that's not what she meant, is it?"

His mouth stiffly delivered carefully chosen words, "We are proud of our Italian heritage. It was good to give you a sense of that." His eyes said something else.

"Grandmother said heritage matters. Religion and custom influence a life, how it is lived. The blood of our ancestors is thick with knowledge and tradition. Much sickness comes from denying this connection. Denial and secrets, like sickness, kill. She said Mother kept secrets, and that Mother was clever."

He did not say anything, but his eyes told her everything.

Mia's shaking hands raised the glass of brandy to her lips; she took one drink, and another. Truth was between them though she could not speak it, and neither could he. Finally, Mia said quietly, "I don't know who I am. I'm losing everything…"

His eyes were misty. "A sense of family is a comfort in times of need."

A tear slipped down her cheek. Wiping it away, Mia said, "I guess there are all kinds of family. Papa, do you and Maggie mind if I stay over?"

His face came alive. "Yes stay, Darling Mia, and we shall have a lovely breakfast together in the morning."

He stood and opened his arms to her. "I do love you, my Darling Little Angel."

"I'm not little, nor am I yours," she might have said, but she only hugged him and whispered, "I love you, Papa."

# STAR

*S*een from the air, the lights of Mexico City dazzled like old jewelry on dark, rumpled cloth that stretched as far as Mia could see. Though hours past midnight, long security lines snaked across the worn marble floors of the crowded Mexico City airport terminal. Travelers inched past guards dressed in intimidating black uniforms.

Mia fought an inexplicable, yet rising, terror as she handed over her paperwork and passport. Penetrating eyes scrutinized her, but after a long moment she was waved through with her papers. Joyce followed and they moved to a check out where their paperwork was stamped.

Mia walked on shaky legs into a hallway lined with small shops. She turned to Joyce and breathed, "I'm so glad you're with me."

"How could I refuse such a generous gift?"

"You said you'd wanted to come back ever since your honeymoon…"

Joyce gushed, "It will be so sweet to see the places Neil and I visited again. And what a way to celebrate my graduation!"

Mia nodded but her eyes warily watched people passing by.

"What's the matter?"

"I feel strange and my stomach is upset."

"You're probably just thirsty. Do you get dry when you fly? I sure do."

They found a soda machine. Mia deposited money, and the can dropped noisily. She flipped the top open, gulped down the citrusy soda, paused, and burped.

"Excused," Joyce laughed. "Feel better?"

Mia looked around and whispered, "I see these faces and I'm terrified. Mother wouldn't go anywhere without Papa, and someone here might..."

"Come on," Joyce said wrapping an arm around Mia's shoulder. "You'll get over the traveling jitters."

They walked to the bus terminal. Ciudad de Oaxaca, Oaxaca City, in the state of Oaxaca, is six to eight hours from Mexico City by bus. They boarded and discovered the first class vehicles are quite nice with wide aisles and large seats.

"I'll sit behind. I want my own window to watch the scenery," Joyce said.

Mia sank gratefully into a seat as comfy as an easy chair.

As soon as the bus was under way, a violent American movie dubbed in Spanish filled the large screen at the front. Ignoring it, Mia examined the food items in a plastic bag the bus driver had handed each traveler: warm soda, packaged lemon wafer cookies, potato chips, hot sauce, and a sandwich of bologna with mayonnaise between slices of thin white bread wrapped in wax paper.

Peeking through the crack between the seats, Joyce whispered, "I wouldn't eat that sandwich. Who knows how long it's been unrefrigerated."

Mia winced and put the bag down. She tipped her seat back and pulled a sweater over her chilly arms. She slept until the sun was coming up and the bus was pulling into a roadside stop. Passengers filed out to use the fly-infested port-a-potties standing in the gravel beside the road.

The bus soon departed again and Mia watched the sparsely populated countryside whiz by. Agave, a relative of the yucca found in the southwestern United States and in Texas, dotted the landscape. "I read there are over 400 varieties of agave, and many of them are used to make liquor. Mezcal is made in Oaxaca, right?"

"Yes," Joyce answered. "The flavored ones are especially delicious!"

Mia's eyes were drawn to patches of green outside the window; scrubby vegetation and wind-swept trees hovered wherever there was water. Separated by ramshackle fences of wire and wood, makeshift residences on small plots of land stretched out to distant hills. Some farmers used only hoes to till the soil. Others used old tractors or emaciated cows or donkeys to pull their plows through the fields. Peasants carrying sacks and baskets walked along the road. Mia studied the people as if looking for something—some unknown, yet familiar, thing.

The bus stopped briefly in a small village. Strip-mall businesses in concrete buildings with corrugated metal roofs lined the road at the center of town. Bright sun streamed warmly through the window. Mia had started to drift off when a woman with a cloth bundle and a tattered plastic sack squeezed into the seat beside her. The woman was dressed in a threadbare cotton dress and a soiled apron smelling of perspiration and onions. Her dark eyes glanced around.

"*Buenas dias,*" Mia said politely.

"*Buenas dias*," the woman replied. Her lips parted briefly in a shy smile showing missing and rotting teeth. She tucked her creased and soiled hands with ragged nails into a fold of her apron and glanced toward the front windows as the bus pulled out.

"Are you going to Oaxaca City?" Mia asked in hesitant Spanish.

The woman shook her head and made a reply Mia only partly understood: something about a brother, a village celebration, and a patron saint.

Mia gazed out the window at the passing countryside that was becoming greener and prettier with each mile traveled. She pulled out a book on Oaxaca she'd purchased at the airport gift shop and offered it to the woman.

Turning the pages gingerly, the woman carefully studied each colorful photograph and she smiled. Reaching the end, she closed the book and held it securely in her lap. Upon reaching her stop, the woman handed the book back to Mia and thanked her with a warm smile before getting off the bus.

Joyce leaned forward and commented, "See, not so scary. You're getting more comfortable already." Buildings and houses increased in number, and the scenery became less rural as the bus neared the city. Located in a central valley formed by converging branches of the Sierra Madre Occidental mountain range, Oaxaca City has a population of more than 800,000. It was already afternoon when the bus pulled into a bustling terminal; outside, taxicab drivers standing by their vehicles eagerly waited to take travelers to their destinations.

Joyce and Mia paused on the sidewalk outside to study their map of the city. "It's only a couple of miles to our hotel."

"Shall we take our chances with that taxi?" Mia pointed to a slightly battered but clean looking Chevy 4-door sedan with a smiling driver motioning to them. He helped carry their bags and loaded them into the trunk. Cristiano spoke some English and was a very enthusiastic conversationalist. He asked where they were from and offered that he had cousins working in Texas. He said he'd like to visit someday and asked if there were many tall buildings in Austin.

"A few," Joyce answered politely as he weaved alarmingly fast through double lanes of stalled traffic. "We have traffic jams like this, too."

"Ah! Same every city, I think," the driver replied with a smile and a long look at her in the rear view mirror. Joyce turned her eyes away and watched out the window as the car moved from an industrial area to the historic district of the city where old buildings lined the narrow cobblestone streets. The car stopped beside a stucco wall displaying an oval wooden sign with painted butterflies. Cristiano carried their bags through weathered iron gates into a covered, open-air lobby with a red tiled floor. A long wooden bench lined one side of the lobby. A tall, bar-length desk and tables displaying brochures filled the other.

"Welcome to *Las Mariposas*, the Butterflies," said a lovely gray-haired woman seated on a stool behind the desk. "My daughter and I welcome you to Oaxaca."

"Thank you!" Mia and Joyce chimed. "We're so happy to finally be here!"

The owner informed them of the services and offerings of the hotel, where to go for sundry items, and even where to find the best tamales. They were escorted past a central fountain to their room that opened onto the courtyard through curtained French doors.

The modest room had a soaring, slanted ceiling and plaster walls painted in cheerful ochre. It was comfortably furnished with two double beds, bedside tables, and a writing desk. Saloon-style doors opened into a dressing area with built-in pine shelves, and a small bathroom with a large tiled shower. Joyce turned on an electric fan standing near the door and flopped down onto one bed. Exhausted, Mia fell onto the other bed and sighed, "I can't believe we're here!"

"I KNOW!" Joyce pounded her bed with her fists and laughed.

Mia looked up, admiring the swirling design of a glass block set in the vaulted ceiling; above it was the blue, blue sky of Mexico—a sight her parents might have enjoyed. The idea excited and terrified her.

"So," Joyce remarked suddenly, "why *are* we here?"

"Just looking around," Mia sighed.

"Research for writing about Rosa? And something to do with Victoria, right?"

"And my…father."

Joyce rolled over, yawned and asked sleepily, "How is your papa?"

"Papa?" Mia drew a breath. "There's something I want to tell you…" But she paused, listening to the sound of breathing from the other bed. "Joyce?" There was no answer. Mia closed her eyes and soon fell asleep in the comfortable breeze of the whirring fan that muffled the traffic noises coming from the cobblestone street.

Tormented by her dreams, Mia tossed and turned through much of the night. She woke mid-morning to the sound of Joyce and other guests chatting in the courtyard. Mia dressed and went out. She stirred honey into a cup of coffee, poured milk over a bowl of puffed wheat, and carried both to a long patio table surrounded by plastic chairs.

"This is Blake," Joyce motioned toward the man sitting beside her.

"Hello." Mia exchanged smiles with him.

"He's an artist, from South Africa, but now lives in London. He's a muralist, like Gerald," Joyce offered.

Blake's hazel eyes sparkled behind trendy, bright blue framed glasses. He sported spiky but thinning gray hair, and his face was clean-shaven except for a tuft of whiskers in the shape of a "V" on his chin. Blake was slight of build and nowhere near Gerald's height of more than six feet. "Perhaps this Gerald and I will meet one day."

"Perhaps," Mia nodded. It was hard to imagine that possibility, but they would make an amusing sight with their opposing physiques and coloring.

"Some of us," Blake said, glancing around the table to the other lodgers, "are going on a tour of Zapotec ruins today. The van picks up out front if you'd like to go."

"Is the tour in English?" Joyce inquired.

"I certainly hope so," he remarked wryly. "My Spanish is bloody poor."

"Mine, too," Mia laughed.

An hour later, they gathered near the iron entrance gate and were introduced to a driver and their archeologist guide. Once loaded in the van and traveling, the other passengers chatted amicably, but Mia only watched out the windows. Peasants dressed in faded clothing and others in more modern fashions stood slightly apart in small groups waiting beside the road for buses. Where did they live? Where were they going? Who were they?

Monte Alban, one site of Zapotec ruins, covers a high bluff above the central valleys of Oaxaca and is surrounded by the Sierra Madre Occidental Mountains. Only fifteen percent of the ancient structures, first built 500 years before Christ, have yet been uncovered, their guide, Claudia, told them. Massive basalt stones were reordered by each generation: one level covered another and reached higher and higher. Significant designs and messages carved into the stones became obscured as the stones were realigned with each renovation.

It was the rainy season, but with less precipitation than other years, the ground was dry and covered in fine blades of sparse green grass. The midday temperature hit the mid-eighties, but there was a gentle breeze at that elevation. They sat on benches in the shade of trees that seemed part of a very old orchard while Claudia mentioned various facts. She said that when the bushes on the sides of the mountain bloomed, it looked from a distance as if it is covered in snow.

Claudia's gleaming, enameled nails and jewel-covered fingers gestured toward the weathered stones of the ancient structures. "Go. Feel. Experience."

They dispersed to wander the expansive bluff. From that vantage point, Mia could almost feel the passing of time. She could almost see the ocean and feel the pull of the distant tide. And perhaps it was only wind that called to her in a haunting, familiar way.

Returning to town after the tour, Joyce and Mia went for *comida*, customarily the largest meal of the day served in mid-afternoon in Mexico. Just a few steps down the cobblestone street from their hotel, a family style eatery with rustic wood tables covered in checkered plastic offered hearty meals. Mia ate a plate of beans, tortillas, and steamed squash with soft white Oaxacan cheese. "Delicious! I love cheese!"

"Mmm," Joyce nodded enthusiastically.

"So simple and fresh. Just what I needed. I'm feeling better. It was strange before—the contrasts: Texas has been 'civilized' less than two hundred years, but here, the civilizations date back thousands of years. The pace is slower here, but there are glimpses of progress. Did you see the woman talking on her phone at the top of Monte Alban? A satellite phone! Next to those ancient stones!"

"Let's wander a bit around town," Joyce suggested as they left the restaurant and walked down the narrow streets.

Mia snapped photos of the various buildings made of brick, concrete, or adobe. Many structures once had more stories, or perhaps would someday: metal rebar stuck straight into the air at the tops of walls and posts where destruction, or expansion, had been inexplicably halted. Doors and windows were often bricked in or re-framed with ill-fitting sections.

Spanish colonial buildings had many curved cornices and other attractive and ornate architectural features. Vegetation sprouted from tile roofs and ledges where soil had collected over time. Layers of peeling paint lent a lovely patina to the wood doors and windows in these old structures. Buildings variously painted and sized butted up against one another and signs stretching across old and new sections were often half-covered in newer paint, as if the old was being gobbled up, only bit by bit.

Every few blocks, there was a church of stucco or stone with wooden doors, curved arches, and niches adorned with saints or *La Virgen*. Electric wires attached to the old buildings intersected and crisscrossed the streets: linking antiquity with modernity.

A wide variety of languages were spoken by passersby. Modern influences were evidenced by the shiny Escalades on the streets. Wealthy, well-dressed people were frequenting posh hotels and restaurants housed in renovated ancient structures. While outside, peasants peddled both handmade and manufactured goods.

Down one block where they walked, a man lay crumpled across the narrow sidewalk. Joyce passed by, but as Mia tried to squeeze past, she heard him moan. The man suddenly raised his head, gaped at her and gasped, "*Ay, Dios! Mi esposa!*" He clutched her legs and began weeping.

"Help!" Mia cried.

Joyce turned and grabbed Mia's arm, pulling hard to free her from the man's grasp, and they hurried away.

"What was he saying?" Mia asked, still shaking from the encounter.

"He seemed to think you were his wife."

Mia shuddered. "His face and hands were hideous! Was that scarring from a fire? What a nightmare!"

They were walking quickly and soon reached the *zocalo*, the central plaza of the city. Iron benches shaded by towering India laurel trees were filled with people. Standing nearby, policemen in neat black clothing chatted with individuals but their eyes were constantly scanning the square. Vendors on mats, blankets, and at tables around the perimeter sold hand-carved gourds, food, plastic light-up key chains, ceramics, clothes, baskets, textiles, and art. A 19th century iron bandstand near the center of the courtyard sported a painted white dome shaped like a puffed shamrock.

"Too bad there's no music today," Joyce remarked. "I'd love to come back to Oaxaca for the *Guelaguetza*. I've seen clips of it on video."

"What is that?"

"Oh, you would love it! Folk dancers from all the different regions in the state come together for a wonderful exhibition. It is just stunning! Brightly colored costumes, lively music, and enchanting choreography."

"Sounds wonderful," Mia agreed. "When is it?"

"Every July. Maybe we could come next year! And maybe we could each bring someone *special*," Joyce suggested with great enthusiasm. They both smiled dreamily.

Six blocks beyond the zocalo stood the baroque cathedral, Templo de Santo Domingo. Mia paused outside to admire the creamy, aged patina of the stones and the carved wooden door. "How many people have walked through that door, do you think?"

"Thousands. Maybe millions. Too bad we didn't see the old basilica of Our Lady of Guadalupe when we were in Mexico City. You would've loved that cathedral, too."

"Oh!" Mia exclaimed. "Maybe we can stop on our way back through."

"Remember the story of roses that bloomed in December? Juan Diego's cloak with the image of the Virgin of Guadalupe is on display there. You'd appreciate the circular architecture of the new basilica that allows all 50,000 visitors a view of it."

"We have to see her," Mia whispered as they stepped inside the cathedral. She looked up and was awed by the splendor of the Spanish period religious art. Colored Biblical scenes in plaster relief and sparkling with gold covered the walls and ceiling.

Mia kneeled on a creaking bench in the chapel of Nuestra Senora del Rosario and looked up at the image of Mary. Resplendent in a glowing ivory gown covered in jewels, Mary held baby Jesus in one hand and a rosary in the other. Mia's eyes rested on Mary's sweetly smiling face and familiar words poured into her mind. "Hail Mary, Full of Grace..." Other words poured from her heart. "Mary, do you know me? Do you listen? I'm thankful for all I have: the special people and the love in my life. But I..." she whispered and tears glistened in her eyes.

Wandering over from a different chapel, Joyce slid in beside Mia on the pew and whispered, "I'll meet you outside."

Mia nodded. And then she prayed some more. When she had nothing left to ask or say, she slipped several coins into the slot of a stair-stepped metal stand of candles. She lit a slender reed at a flaming wick and passed the flame to a new candle; she watched the wax melt and drip, and a new flame flickered. Mia turned to leave but paused at a bulletin board where bits of paper and tiny objects had been tacked: beautiful and crude items served as petitions to the saints for intervention. Could presenting the correct article bring answers to prayers: little metal legs to restore ambulation, locks to seal the lips of gossipers, tiny painted hearts to bring back loved ones? How could so many laments ever be answered?

*Only I can pray...and every wish...is hope...*

Mia did not know if she had hope—but something pulled at her. She exited through the gift shop and stopped to select several postcards of the stunning interior art. Mia set her purse on the glass counter and was digging for change when her eyes fell to a display of rosaries and a silver medallion on a black velvet display card. An alert woman behind the counter presented the shining necklace for closer inspection. Mia clasped it around her neck and smiled as she glanced into the mirror at the reflection of *La Virgen de Guadalupe* hanging close to her heart.

Bright sunshine and colorfully painted buildings across the street greeted Mia as she stepped outside. Joyce was chatting there with artists displaying paintings on easels on the sidewalk. Mia waved and pointed down the street in the direction of a shop where outdoor tables overflowed with brightly colored textiles.

"I'll catch up," Joyce called.

Looking through table runners, shirts, pants, shawls, and purses, Mia searched but did not find any cloth or embroidery like the scrap she'd found in the atlas. And the shop was more commercial, less artisan, than she could imagine Rosa might have, but she noted details for later writing.

"Maybe I'd have more success if I tacked the scrap onto the bulletin board at the cathedral," she sighed to Joyce when they met up.

"Are you trying to find a match to the old cloth? I read an article once about some cotton grown here. The filaments are so small the fibers have to be spun by hand. Maybe it's cheaper now to import the yarns and textiles than to grow them. We could look up Mexican cotton on the Internet," Joyce suggested.

But when they arrived back at the hotel, Mia plopped face down on her bed. Worn out from having seen and felt so much, she fell asleep and dreamed.

*Maybe* La Virgen *smile to me…*

*I*t was late in the evening when she and Joyce finally went for dinner. Mia ordered chicken with *mole*, a complex blend of sweet and peppery chocolate. She tried to dilute her internal fire with multiple cold drinks after eating it, but her lips still burned, and her belly was hot. Unable to get to sleep later, she tossed and turned for an hour before leaning toward the other bed and whispering, "You awake?"

Joyce groaned. "I didn't even have the *mole* and I'm suffering."

Sounding deflated, Mia asked, "What if the cloth leads nowhere?"

"We're here because of it...that's somewhere. Have you found anything to add to Rosa's story?"

Mia shrugged.

Suddenly sitting up in her bed, Joyce asked, "Is Angelina the Italian version of Angelita?"

Mia only looked back at her with furrowed brow.

"If Rosalita means 'little Rosa', does Angelita mean 'little angel'? You could name Rosa's lost baby..." Joyce yawned and lay back down. "...Angelita. That would make Rosa's heartbreak so much more real." Joyce yawned yet again.

A chill washed over her. Mia breathed several slow breaths and whispered, "Joyce, about the scrap of cloth..." But there was no response from the other bed. Mia looked up at a spot of light twinkling through the glass block in the ceiling. Probably it was not the first star, but she wished on it anyway and drifted eventually to sleep.

# LEAF

*A*fter a cup of coffee and breakfast in the morning, Mia lingered with Blake at the table in the courtyard. "What brings you to Oaxaca?"

"Art and culture," he answered. "The colors! My Lord, the colors!"

"Did something particular prompt you to come *now*?"

Blake nodded slowly, "My mother passed away."

"Oh, I'm sorry. I lost my mother, too."

He blinked away tears. "Recently?"

Mia's brow furrowed. "It seems long ago."

"Mothers are so very dear, aren't they?" Blake struggled to keep his mouth from quivering. "A part of us and we a part of them, we're never really separate. I promised Mother I would come. I've admired Mexican crafts for such a long time."

They sipped their coffee and Mia asked quietly, "Do you ever feel her nearby?"

"OH, YES!" he effused, brightening. "I feel her love all around me. Sometimes her spirit hovers so close it's as if I could turn and actually touch her." He glanced around and whispered, "She's here now."

Maybe Mia sensed some energy lingering, or maybe it was only a draft that caused goose bumps to rise on her arms. "Does your mother," Mia asked in hushed tone, "ever talk to you?"

Blake laughed. "Of course! What good mother is ever silent? I am still a work in progress! Oaxaca is such a spiritual place, don't you think? I feel new possibilities all around me. And there is so much love here. Do you feel it?"

She nodded. "I feel close to some discovery, as if I'm at the edge of something."

"Jump!"

"Sounds like something Joyce would say," Mia chuckled.

Blake smiled warmly, "That Joyce! Quite a character! I'm visiting the cemetery this morning. Later there is a tour of the ruins at Mitla. Would you like to come?"

"I'll see if Joyce wants to come, but I will for sure."

Mid-morning, the three of them entered the cemetery through a wide iron gate in a high stone wall. They wandered down narrow dirt paths amid the tightly packed rows of head-stones that were carved in marble and stone or fashioned out of concrete. Many gravesites, surrounded with fences or roofed structures of metal, glass, and wood, were complete with doors and windows.

"These are larger than my flat in London," Blake remarked. "They're nicer, too."

Joyce and Mia laughed but looked around nervously when a woman with a wheelbarrow of colored calla lilies and gladiolas stopped in the path a few yards away.

"I hope we didn't offend her," Mia whispered, but the woman did not seem to be bothered for she was focused on replacing the wilted flowers at a gravesite.

Blake moved on to snap pictures of elaborate headstones and articles of tribute. He was especially fascinated by the numerous figures of Jesus hanging from the cross and the many *Virgens de Guadalupe.*

Mia stopped before a gravestone with a life-sized relief of a young woman with head bowed, face in her hands, sorrow emanating from her small form as if she were made of more than stone. Tears welled in Mia's eyes, and Charlotte's words suddenly came to mind, "A woman cry…"

Joyce looked over and murmured, "Isn't she beautiful?"

"I feel her heart breaking as if every sorrow was heaped on her small shoulders, and the tears of every woman flowed from her eyes."

"Yes. Just a child herself and with such heartbreak…as if she has lost someone very dear…a baby, she's lost her baby."

"Like me," Mia whispered, wiping away tears with her sleeve.

"Yes, like you," Joyce said soothingly. "I've been wondering: how many doctors did you see? How many said you couldn't carry a baby to term?"

"Several. Another suggested Tim might have his own fertility issues making it difficult for me to get pregnant, and that my own hormone imbalance caused the miscarriages. There was possible treatment, but it was costly and…" she shrugged.

"And what?"

"Tim said I could go through whatever testing, treatment, and torture the doctors devised, but he wouldn't. Without his participation, and support, it just seemed hopeless."

Joyce nodded sympathetically. "I meant to tell you about a program I saw: a woman with perhaps a similar problem went on a special diet. Her new doctor suggested different treatment and with luck and prayer, she delivered—not just one baby—twins!"

"Really?" More tears stung Mia's eyes.

Joyce smiled, nodding. "And maybe you and Tim were just the wrong combination. Perhaps it will be 'right' with someone else."

Mia turned and looked again at the headstone. "I did wish so much to have a daughter...but I've given up hope."

"No wonder you're miserable! Never give up hope. Hope makes all things possible. And it brings love."

"But I can't live on hope," Mia snapped.

Joyce shook her head. "You've got it wrong. You can't live without it."

Farther down the path, Blake was photographing a high arch connecting crumbling eight-foot walls when a bicycle suddenly rounded the corner and barely avoided running him over. The handsome young rider quietly apologized and smiled sweetly before peddling away, looking strangely alive and fluid in the bleak landscape of headstones.

Blake resumed snapping photos but as Joyce and Mia caught up, the bicyclist reappeared. He stopped beside Blake, placed something in his hand, then rode off. Bewildered, Blake stared down at the weathered concrete relief of an angel's face. "Why did he give this to me?"

"Perhaps an apology for nearly running you over," Mia suggested. "Or something he thinks beautiful enough to be captured in your photos."

"Maybe he fancies you," Joyce said with a sly grin.

"I'm overcome," Blake uttered, his teary eyes turning to look down the path. "Come back," he called, but the young man had vanished.

"Perhaps *he* is an angel," Joyce suggested. "God's messenger."

"What message does he bring?" Mia whispered and she shook off a chill.

They ambled silently through the cemetery and down the street; all the way Blake kept looking for the man on the bike but did not find him.

Several blocks beyond the *zocalo* at a bookstore, Mia scanned a shelf of bargain books. Her eyes were drawn to a small, bright blue paperback with a tiny image of the Virgin Mary on the spine. The cover had a red rose, the Virgin Mary, and a title in curvy letters: *Looking for Mary*. It was written by Beverly Donofrio, who had also written *Riding in Cars with Boys*, a story made into a major motion picture starring Drew Barrymore, Mia remembered.

"Find something?" Joyce inquired. "Buy it and let's go, okay? I'm really hungry."

Mia paid ninety-nine cents for the book and walked back to the hotel while Joyce and Blake went in search of food. She turned on the fan, stretched out on her bed and pulled the book from her bag. It was the writer's own memoir of how a "lapsed Catholic" with a sudden interest in collecting images of Mary, found herself traveling the world on a spiritual quest for the Blessed Mother. Mia studied the pleasant image on the cover: Mary with dark reddish hair, dark eyes, and wearing a cloak of blue. Reading it, she was captivated by the story of the Blessed Mother speaking to average people, even children. Mia closed her eyes, clutched the small book to her chest, and began to pray.

Joyce burst into the room a short while later and they ate: tamales from a street vendor, pastries and chocolates from the *pastelaria,* and bags of potato chips with hot sauce dribbled inside. "Oh, that was good!" Mia laughed, leaning back against the wall.

"My mouth is spicy and sweet," Joyce chuckled, licking salt and sugar from her fingers. "We should hurry if we want to go on the tour to Mitla."

"I can't move," Mia complained.

Joyce clapped her hands together. "Get up. Chop, chop!"

Their tour guide, Claudia, was relating fact after fact about the ruins at Mitla but Mia could not pay attention. Her eyes turned to a listless dog lying next to a tall fence of cactus surrounding a neighboring Spanish cathedral. How she longed to sleep.

When Claudia had finished instructing, Mia wandered away from the group. She examined many articles for sale at numerous craft booths but found no cloth or embroidery resembling her scrap. Spirit lagging, she returned to the van and they went on to the next stop: Santa Maria del Tule.

"*Arbol del tule* is a large ahuehuete tree, a type of cypress. Believed to be the largest in the world and older than Christianity," Blake informed as they stared up at the tree so large it dwarfed the old cathedral beside it.

"It takes thirty-four people stretching finger to finger to circle the tree," Joyce exclaimed. "Just imagine *that* 'ring around the rosy'!"

Mia studied the trunk of the giant tree. How many hands had touched that rough bark? Children had played and dreamed beneath that tree for thousands of years, but now it was surrounded by an iron fence protecting it from the hands of humans. Even the nearby highway had been moved recently to shield the aged tree from dangerous vibrations of ever increasing traffic. Mia bent down and stealthily picked up a fallen leaf she tucked into her pocket.

"It reminds me of a weeping willow," Joyce observed.

"An ancient creature with craggy skin, many arms reaching up to the sky, and knotty toes winding down through the earth. That's how I'll paint her: 'Mother of All Trees'," Blake declared.

"Something Gerald would say," Mia sighed, looking up at the branches swaying with a breeze. "I've dreamed a tree like this…two girls playing under the shelter of its spreading branches. I wrote this…" she murmured and words were in her mind.

*Ay…ahuehuete…you listen to my dreams…*

*A*s they traveled back toward Oaxaca City, the conversations in the van blended with the steady hum of the engine and Mia tuned in and out. She looked out the window to the passing landscape and wondered if there was something for her yet to discover.

Claudia said, "Oaxaca is known for its diversity of crafts. Secret techniques and skills are passed down through the generations within families to maintain the unique qualities. Some communities specialize in one main craft. We could go to the village with black pottery, or see the painted clay figures in Ocotlan de Morelos."

"I'd *love* to see those naughty girls of the night in bright and bawdy get ups," Blake pronounced enthusiastically. "But I'm sure the black pottery is quite nice."

Suddenly at attention, Mia patted his arm, "What did you say about black pottery?"

"Claudia suggested we visit the village famous for it."

"I'd like to see it. Maybe I will buy some for my condo. Can we go tomorrow?"

"It is a few miles south of here, but Claudia can't go because she's having a party for..." he looked to Claudia.

"*Mi hija*," Claudia replied. But Blake's blank look brought a loud sigh and clarification, "My daughter."

# HERRINGBONE

XXXXXXXXXXXXX

They secured a car with driver the next day and traveled to the village known especially for its black pottery. A garden of tall succulents, some reaching the roof, lined the back wall of the modest, single-story building. They stepped through the heavy wooden door to the open-air interior. Green grass and a fountain at the center lent a feeling of liveliness to the space. Tall wooden shelves lining the perimeter displayed hundreds of pieces of shiny black pottery: bowls, platters, candlesticks, vases, religious articles, and figurines.

"Look at the fine texture!" Joyce remarked examining the wares. "No wonder this is the most famous shop with black pottery."

Blake nodded. "Beautiful. I rather prefer color, but I see the appeal."

Mia picked up a bowl. The lustrous finish shined like obsidian. It was perfectly crafted. And familiar. Her eyes moved along the wall to a bulletin board where newspaper articles were posted, and she wandered over to read.

Joyce leaned over Mia's shoulder and scanned an article about the woman who put the village on the world's map. "Dona Rosa? Strange. Rosa…like in your story. "

"A common name," Blake interjected, looking on.

"Just an odd coincidence," Mia sighed. But she turned and her eyes fell to a small vase with an etched design—a flower with five petals like the one etched on the glass of her Tudor house door and tooled on the leather satchel, like the one embroidered on the scrap of cloth and on the book she had purchased. She turned back to the article, and her eyes found the name of the village: *San Bartolo Coyotepec.* Mia's voice was shaking as she said, "Mother collected black pottery like this. Maybe she meant for me to find the scrap, and this place."

"Why?" Blake asked. "What is the significance?"

"And this is *San Bartolo*—like *Bartolomeo...*" Mia mused. "Maybe Mother ..."

Joyce offered excitedly, "We could show the cloth around the village. Is the stitching distinctive enough for someone to recognize the style? Perhaps we could find the craftswoman, or the family that stitches in that manner. But why would Victoria have the scrap?"

Mia sighed, "There's something I..."

But Blake interrupted enthusiastically, "I love a good challenge!"

While their driver went on an errand, the trio traipsed up and down the streets and showed the embroidered cloth to every person they encountered, but heads only wagged. Resting in the shade beneath the overhang of a flat-roofed building, Blake pulled off a leather sandal and rubbed his foot, complaining, "My dogs are weary."

"Come on, team! Let's don't give up yet," Joyce said in her best cheerleading voice, grabbing Blake's sandal and slipping it back on his foot.

They covered several more blocks before coming to a barbershop where a man was sitting outside. He wore a long mustache, and his gray hair was slicked back with grease. His skin was wrinkled and dark, and he grinned at them with crooked teeth. The printed polyester shirt he wore was a hangover from disco days, and his misshapen herringbone jacket might have been just as old. Upon seeing the cloth, he gestured wildly, giving directions to someplace and someone he was adamant they should see.

Though skeptical, Mia, Joyce, and Blake continued walking a few more blocks. They located a residence that seemed to match the man's description. A low stucco wall lined the street; a small brown and white dog sat outside a rustic gate opening into a dirt courtyard. Baskets overflowing with fabric, a cooking fire, racks of clothing, and several small tables filled the interior of the open-air residence. A woman sitting on a stool and sewing called out, and a man rushed forward. He invited them to enter into the welcome shade beneath a corrugated metal roof.

Polite greetings were exchanged, but communication relied heavily on gestures. The man offered drinks he poured from a pitcher into plastic cups and they sat down on roughly hewn benches to sip the bitter homemade drinks.

Blake indicated an interest in colorfully embroidered articles of clothing hanging on a metal rack. Standing to show him, the woman was not much taller than when sitting for her back was hunched, perhaps from many hours bent over sewing. Her skin was very wrinkled but her hooded eyes were bright as she showed him a blouse on which she had stitched an intricate design.

"It's a *huipil*," Joyce said, "a traditional article worn by the women. Some skilled Indian craftswomen, *huipiles*, are said to stitch codes of magic and religious secrets into their designs."

A chill went down Mia's spine. Reminded of the dream with brilliantly embroidered clothes in tatters, she studied the woman's sharp eyes and quick hands. Mia reached into her pocket for the embroidered cloth and a picture of Victoria fell to the ground. The woman reached for it and her eyes grew wide. She clutched the photo to her chest and tears flowed from her eyes. She began speaking excitedly to the man who exclaimed, "*Ay, Dios! Un milagro!*"

Joyce, can you make out what they're saying?"

"'A miracle.' That was Spanish, but they're also speaking something else: maybe Mixtec, Zapotec," Joyce shrugged. "The Indians in Oaxaca speak at least sixteen different languages. Oh, wait! She said '*esposa*'; that's wife. I left my dictionary in the car. Later we can look up words we remember."

Mia listened intently to words of the couple's exchange: *primos ... bonita mujer ... Abuelita ... hermanas.*

The old woman reluctantly handed back the photo, wiped her tears, then went into a side room. They heard sounds of rummaging, and the woman returned with a wrapped bundle she placed in Mia's lap.

Mia peeled back the crumpled paper and smoothed the wrinkles of a tiny white dress embroidered with delicate stitching. "It's beautiful."

"Maybe a Baptismal gown," Joyce suggested.

Mia re-wrapped the gown and held it out but the woman shook her head and smiled, motioning for Mia to keep it. Bemused, Mia whispered, "*Gracias*. Thank you." More smiles were exchanged, but silence settled over them.

Finally Mia said, "We should go." She patted her chest to show her gratitude then offered her hand. Pressing it to her cheek, the woman smiled a sweet, toothless grin.

They went out and began walking. Mia glanced back; the dog was sprawled in the street and was sleeping.

"A man after my own heart," Blake quipped. "That grog, or whatever it was, made me sleepy." When they reached the car, he leaned his head against the seat and closed his eyes.

"What were some of the words the woman said?" Joyce asked quietly.

"*Abuelita.*"

Joyce looked it up in her dictionary. "Grandmother."

"*Primos.*"

"Cousins," Joyce answered.

"*Esposa.*"

"Wife. That's what the scary, crazy man with the scars said."

They exchanged glances. Mia said, "*Bonita mujer.* That means pretty…"

"Woman. Pretty woman."

"Oh," Mia sighed, her shoulders sagging. "Maybe that's all she meant: Mother was a pretty woman."

"What did you *think* she meant?" Joyce asked seeing Mia's abject look.

"I thought she…might have recognized her."

"Do you think Victoria has been here? Is that where she got the cloth?"

"Maybe," Mia answered. "But why did the woman give me the baby's gown?"

Joyce's eyes glistened, but she only shrugged and smiled.

Mia glanced out the window; they were passing a white Baroque cathedral with an arched doorway and red spires on either side of a center dome. Giant black pottery urns stood atop the stone gateposts of the surrounding wrought iron fence. Mia sighed inwardly. Would prayers whispered in such a grand cathedral be ushered to Heaven? Could blessings flow down to the faithful—even if all the rules of society and the Church were not followed?

*L*ate that evening, up on the rooftop of a restaurant in the historic district of Oaxaca City, Joyce and Mia dined beneath a canopy of bright stars. The food was delicious and plentiful and the setting was spectacular, but Mia was unusually quiet.

"Blake might move here," Joyce said filling the silence. "He says he's tired of 'dreary old London'. He wants to come back here to paint, and maybe open a gallery."

"Do you think he will?" Mia pushed food around on her plate.

Joyce shrugged. "He says he can afford a large house with a walled garden. And labor is comparatively cheap. He could open the gallery and hire someone to run it while he paints. And he thinks he could keep his London place, too."

"I guess it wouldn't be a bad way to live," Mia sighed. "Traveling, creating…"

"Is that a hint about me going with Tony?" Joyce raised an eyebrow, but smiled. "Speaking of work, have you gotten any new ideas for *Lamentation*?"

Mia gulped down her glass of *agua de naranha*, orange water.

"I have some. The story can't end with Rosa just work-ing!" Joyce said enthusiastically. "Agraciana said Manuel gave money to a woman in the city. Maybe there was a reason, something he wanted the woman to do. I don't mean...well, you know. Did he come back and push Rosa out from the flames? *Was* he 'etched in red' against the night sky—or was that only her delusion? Did he search for her after she ran into the night? And since Rosa's faith and hope was renewed by the love and attention of Jaime, why couldn't she also be forgiven for what she did, and what she did not do? Did she really let shame keep her from sending word to her family?"

Mia smiled at Joyce's sincere and earnest face. "I'm impressed you read it so closely. I don't know what I will write. I guess it depends on what more is found."

Joyce pushed away her plate. "Let's see what we can do." She laid out a tourist map and they peered down at it. "I heard there's a reservoir at the foot of mountains and at night you can see the city lights. Here it is: Picacho."

A tiny inset photo showed a marketplace of a nearby village where Indian women were adorned in brightly-colored, flower print scarves. "Those flowered headscarves remind me of something," Mia mused.

"Roses are a common theme in Mexico."

Mia nodded and traced her finger over a congestion of words on the map near the photo. "Joyce! The name of the village is *San Bartolome Quialana*. Like *San Bartolo Coyotepec* And *Bartolomeo*..."

Joyce shrugged her shoulders. "There are many towns of *San Bartolo* and *San Bartolome*-somethings in Mexico."

"That's right. Too many," Mia sighed loudly. "And I like your idea of the reservoir, but I would just *love* to go to the beach."

Joyce perked up. "Puerto Escondido is only an hour away by air. Maybe we could stay somewhere luxurious. And we could walk on the beach with the sand under our bare feet…"

"With water lapping the shore…"

"And wind in our hair," they said in unison and laughed.

# BONNET

The next afternoon they bought tickets and boarded the airplane for Puerto Escondido. Mia sank down into her seat and sighed.

Joyce looked out the window as the plane lifted off. "It's so beautiful down there. Look at all the little villages on the outskirts of the city." Suddenly she turned her gaze to Mia. "I almost forgot—while you were packing, I got on the Internet and looked up some places we might visit if we come back this way."

"Oh, good. We might."

"I found *San Bartolome Quialana*. The pictures on the Internet are really beautiful; it is so green in the valley at the foot of the Sierra Madre Sur. The largest peak is Mount Picacho; I think it has something to do with a devil. Maybe that's where the name for 'black stone' comes from." Joyce shuddered. "But the village has the prettiest white cathedral with three spires."

Mia was suddenly at attention. "Black stone?"

Joyce nodded. "*Quialana* means 'black stone'."

She was barely able to find her voice, "Joyce, Mother had black stones in the bottom of her black pots! I thought they were just to keep the lightweight pots from tipping over. And you said the church has three spires? Were big black pots out front like in San Bartolo Coyotepec?"

"No. But the window above the arched door was similarly shaped."

Mia's voice was barely more than a whisper, "Like a rose? Joyce! Mother said the arched door of my Tudor house with the etched rose reminded her of..." She pondered a few moments and said, "Wouldn't it be strange if the architecture of a church is part of the answer?"

Joyce raised her eyebrow. "I don't know what answer you're looking for but most answers probably have more to do with what's found *inside* a church. Maybe you just need *hope*."

Mia's eyes pooled with tears.

Joyce patted Mia's arm. "You're so emotional!"

"I feel so full of...," Mia paused, searching for the right word, "...possibility."

"As if pregnant with 'the mystical universe'?" Joyce suggested in a dramatic tone, and they laughed until tears were running down their cheeks.

Disembarking the airplane in Puerto Escondido, they were struck with oppressive heat. The daytime temperature in Oaxaca City, at 5,000 feet above sea level, was in the mid-eighties, but here on the coast it was mid-nineties and uncomfortably humid.

The small airport terminal was surprisingly sleek and modern with soaring glass walls allowing a wide view of ocean and sky. Shiny marble floors, towering green plants in huge ceramic pots, and furnishings in glass, leather and steel created a casual-chic atmosphere. They would have liked to linger there in the cool air conditioning a while, but their luggage was quickly unloaded. It was only a short taxi drive to their hotel across from a popular beach with bright sand, terrific waves, thatched cabanas, and wooden lifeguard stands on stilts. Palm trees and numerous surf shops and restaurants catering to tourists lined the road.

The staff of their hotel was courteous, but their second floor accommodations were not pleasant. The rattling refrigerator was cooler than the sweaty room but not by much. Panes were missing from the louvered windows and the overhead fan made noise but barely turned. The sofa consisted of flat vinyl cushions on a stained plywood base, and the beds were not much more than sheets covering slightly padded platforms. The bathroom was so small a larger person would barely be able to squeeze between the wall and the sink to use the toilet, and the tile floor slanting toward the shower drain smelled of urine.

"So much for luxury!" Joyce laughed. "Let's go for a swim to cool off."

They changed into swim suits, grabbed two thin towels, and headed down to the patio. Red and white umbrellas shaded pool-side tables. Blue tiles lined the pool rimmed in smooth concrete the color of sand. A crowd of palms waved in the breeze above thick green grass, and bushes full of glorious red flowers surrounded the pool area. Just a few yards away, incredible blue-green water of the Pacific Ocean rushed a sandy beach beneath a sky of turquoise.

A group of loud beer-toting young people congregated at the opposite end of the pool watched as Mia slid into the water and swam a few lengths. Joyce took only a quick dip and found a lounger in the shade.

Climbing from the water, Mia frowned at the leering looks of surfer "dudes" with bleached hair and low baggy shorts exposing tattoos and piercings. She ignored their obnoxious calls, wrapped her towel into a sarong, and dropped into a chair next to

Joyce. "I didn't like this kind of scene even when I was their age."

"Not really what I expected. I don't think the place has been updated since I was here years ago!" Joyce said glancing at a nearby wall of a building badly in need of paint.

One of the "dudes" took a fake punch to the gut and fell backwards into the pool, drenching them in a cascade of water.

"Thanks," Joyce said loudly with sarcasm, but the youths only laughed.

Mia and Joyce soon left the pool, showered, and dressed.

Joyce scanned a list of restaurants within walking distance, but surveying their less than satisfactory room, she suggested, "Let's go look before we decide."

"Good idea. We can check the menus and prices."

They walked down the beach to a cobblestone street roped off from traffic. Shops and street vendors displayed everything from mass-produced items to stunningly colorful pottery, hand-tooled leather, paintings, and pretty clothing. Mia and Joyce passed by a string of crowded restaurants but reaching the end of the block, they discovered a large thatched roof restaurant beside the beach where small fishing boats were tied up.

"Perfect," they agreed.

As they entered the quaint lobby, Joyce's eye caught glimpses of good-looking waiters in pressed white shirts and neat black slacks. "So much better than the pool!"

Mia laughed. "Oh, so much better."

Green plants and flowers in hanging baskets graced a spacious dining room illuminated by flickering candlelight. A mariachi band entertained the diners, and when they finished, American music sounded from large speakers.

Joyce and Mia lingered over their menus. A waiter recommended the octopus, and he claimed all the seafood was brought in from the boats that very day. But, unable to decide on entrees, they ordered appetizers—spicy fish paté on crisp tortillas, and large shrimp sautéed in garlic oil that were delicious, and messy.

Buoyed by the waiter's attention to her every want, Joyce smiled but was not fooled: he aimed for a generous tip from the *Norte Americanas*. "So sad. We've left Mexico for 'tourist-ville'."

Mia sighed, "It could be a thatched roof hut in any city anywhere."

"But you know what I want that I can't get elsewhere?"

"The cute guy over there?" Mia nodded toward their handsome waiter.

Joyce laughed, "No, no. *Platanos*...plantains. They're like bananas."

The waiter was called over, and he soon brought two spoons and a plate of sliced, grilled plantains topped with vanilla ice cream.

"*Muchas gracias*," Joyce smiled up at him. He thanked her for the privilege of serving them and flashed his very white teeth before walking away, oozing masculinity from every pore of his fleshy body. "Oh, my!" she laughed.

"This is heaven!" Mia gushed after a bite of the sweet and creamy desert.

Joyce took several bites. "Mmm. We will definitely sleep sweet tonight!"

*M*ia did sleep later but only fitfully and woke early in the morning rubbing her temples. "WHAT is that noise?"

"There seems to be some work being done across the courtyard."

"Why do they start so early?"

"And did you hear those dogs barking all night long? I'm so tired," Joyce whined.

"That was the worst night I've ever had to pay for! And I had a terrible nightmare," Mia shuddered. "I was standing on a rocky cliff, looking down at beautiful blue-green water. The underside of a cresting wave was smooth like glass. I was crying and…"

Joyce rolled over in her bed. "That doesn't sound so bad."

"I couldn't move; screams were in my ears, 'My baby'. Then she was gone. My heart was breaking…" Mia sobbed, wiping away tears. "I've had the dream before…what do you think it means?"

"Ohhh," Joyce sighed, her eyes also glistening with tears. "I don't know. Find your inner child. Find yourself. Find the mother in your heart?"

"The mother in my heart?" Mia ruminated, but outside their room on the landing someone shouted, "Dude! Dude!" There was a lot of commotion: doors shutting and footsteps running on the open stairs.

"Back to surfer dudes!"

Mia got out of bed. She splashed her face with water and glanced in the mirror. "I look haggard, DUDE! Look at the dark shadows under my eyes, DUDE!"

Laughing, getting up and checking her own reflection, Joyce exclaimed, "I've got *some* bags, and I don't mean luggage!"

Mia patted her shoulder. "You're lovable anyway."

"You too, kiddo. You, too."

Already it was getting hot outside, judging by their room's stuffiness. Mia slipped on a light dress and sandals and pulled her hair back into clips. When Joyce was also ready, they went in search of breakfast.

Not far from the hotel, they found an open-air restaurant. Their watery coffee was refilled many times, but Mia's eggs arrived cold and hard, and the toast was soggy. Pushing her food around on the plate, she said, "I really do not want to spend another night in that hotel. We're in one of the most beautiful places on earth; we shouldn't be tortured by beds as hard as rocks, hammers pounding, dogs barking, and idiots yelling. Even if we don't find anything better, at least we should find some-where different."

Joyce agreed. Mia packed her things and scanned a stack of tourist brochures on the table. Her eyes were drawn to a photo of a museum in town: a white cathedral with a spire topped in red on each side of a center dome, and it had an arched door but no flower design above.

Joyce dragged over her suitcase. "Find anything with hotels?"

"No," Mia sighed. "We could just go see what we're drawn to; it worked last night for dinner."

They lugged their bags down the stairs and waited near the curb for a taxi to appear, but none came. "Maybe everyone but surfer dudes and carpenters are still sleeping," Joyce remarked.

A man standing beside a white car with a logo they couldn't quite make out held up his hand as if to catch their attention. He took several steps in their direction and addressed them politely. He said he worked for the local tourist division and he could take them on a tour to the beautiful bays of Huatulco, a premier resort area several hours down the coast. "Better than Acapulco," he claimed in reasonably understandable English.

"Thank you," Mia responded, "but right now we just want to find another hotel."

He offered to take them to a place he knew with better accommodations. "Perhaps another day you go on tour?" he prodded, smiling hopefully.

"Perhaps *mañana*, tomorrow," Joyce answered, "a shorter, less expensive one."

Mia added, "Yes, perhaps after a better night's sleep."

He smiled and loaded their luggage into his trunk, and they went with him away from the main tourist area. About a mile down the road, the driver turned onto a gravel road he followed for a short distance. When he turned onto a narrow dirt road lined with tall grass, Mia's heart began to beat wildly.

Bouncing over ruts worn in the road, the car went further and further from the busy tourist area. Mia held her breath and watched expectantly out the window but breathed a sigh of relief when the ocean finally came into view. The car headed toward a vine-covered wall with iron gates and stopped next to a burgundy Suburban. As they got out of the car, a tall, sandy-haired man approached.

"Welcome," the American sounding man said smiling, offering his hand. "I'm Andrew. May I show you our accommodations?"

They hesitated. "Should we bring our luggage?"

"Ricardo will wait here with it and hope for a bigger tip. Eh, Ricardo?"

"Are you the owner?" Mia asked as they followed Andrew through the gates to a grassy courtyard.

"I wish! Just filling in for relatives who went back to the States for a few months. Seems like a working vacation!" Andrew laughed jovially as he led them to a small office with a large desk facing a row of bright windows. He handed them each a brochure and began listing the amenities of available villas.

Joyce interrupted, "Sounds lovely: too lovely for our meager budgets."

"I'll give you the tour. Then decide. No pressure."

They exchanged looks, shrugged, and followed him down a concrete walkway through the grassy area with a bubbling fountain ringed with flowers. Several small villas stood at varied angles on either side of the walkway. A bar, with a thatched roof, called a *palapa*, waited for customers. A covered patio large enough for small groups to gather offered hammocks and low slung canvas chairs for relaxing. And the view was spectacular from the cliff on which they stood. A rocky peninsula curved into the ocean and just below was a sandy beach and a stunning little bay with blue-green water.

"Incredible," they chimed and took a moment to drink in the beauty. "It *must* be out of our price range."

"We're very proud of the place, and our prices. I have a two bedroom with air conditioning and a view of the beach: eighty-five American dollars a night."

Joyce and Mia flashed smiles and replied in unison, "We'll take it!"

Returning to the waiting car, they tipped the driver generously and promised to consider taking a short excursion on another day. He suggested going to see the giant sea turtles at the marine park a few miles up the beach. "Perhaps you like to see Puerto Angel, or Huatulco," he offered, handing out his card.

"Perhaps," they both said and waved good-bye.

Joyce unlocked the door of their villa, and they stepped inside. A large fan circled overhead and open, screened windows allowed comfortable movement of air. Mia stretched out on the soft canvas cushion of the wicker sofa and sighed with giddy pleasure. "Ah, now this is more like the paradise I imagined!"

"I'll say!" Joyce sank down onto the love seat and closed her eyes.

The sound of the ocean rushed to their ears. They lounged there only a few more minutes, for the surf was calling them. They changed into swimming attire, and headed down to the beach.

Dropping to the warm sand, they sighed. Swimmers idled in the water and further out, surfers tried their luck in a succession of waves. Pushed forward, the tiny figures were swallowed up by the water and spit back to the surface, their white boards popping up like marshmallows moments later. It was an energetic display of man against nature, and it seemed nature was winning.

Joyce lay down and closed her eyes, murmuring, "I do wish I had brought a hat or bonnet."

Laughing, Mia replied in agreement, "Sure is hot."

Mia opened her satchel, took out paper, and wrote a few lines. When nothing more came to her mind, she slipped the paper into the satchel and went into the water. Floating on her back with her face turned to the sun, she called to Joyce, "Look, no hands, no feet! I'm buoyant!"

"I bet I float better than you!" Joyce went into the water, swam out a ways, dipped under, then popped right back up. "This extra layer of fat around my middle *is* good for something!"

They laughed and paddled around; the waves pushed them toward shore. Again and again they swam out and let the water push them back to the beach. Finally they settled down on the sand and basked in the sun. Stretched out on her belly, chin on a towel, hands and feet pushed down into the warm sand, Mia sighed happily. "This is so great! What a miserable night last night! And now this!"

"I KNOW! I can't believe our good luck!" Joyce replied in matched amazement.

Flipping over, Mia sat up and brushed the sand off. She scanned the beach. A dozen or more adults and children played near the water. It was a different scene than in the U.S. where the bodies would be scantily covered and the sounds of their play might be loud. These women and girls were dressed in shorts and t-shirts; even the men were discretely attired in long cut-offs pulled high up on their bellies. There was occasional laughter, but otherwise the groups on the beach were very pleasant and quiet.

"I think I'll go snorkeling," Joyce said hopping up. "Want to come?"

"No, I'm content here. Maybe later we can go climb around the point."

"Now that's an idea: tiptoeing over jagged rocks," Joyce retorted as she headed toward the office to rent gear.

"Okay, maybe not," Mia laughed. "I'll be here when you get back."

A few minutes later, in fins and facemask, Joyce returned to the beach. She tramped over the sand clumsily and pretended to trip.

Mia laughed and watched as Joyce entered the water and swam away from the shore with her feet fluttering along the rocky border of the little bay.

Waves rushed the shore and receded, leaving a wavy, bubbling line of foam on the sand. The air was warm and soft, and words tugged at Mia's mind. She jotted them down on paper and pondered their meaning.

> *My feet find the hollow of wet sand*
> *where other feet have sunk*
> *pacing of another pulls me along*
>
> *Sweat on my brow mixes in the wind*
> *with what went before*
> *and lingers still*
>
> *Water lapping the shore whispers to me*
> *we are not separate*
> *nor dream alone*
> *beneath the sky of blue*

*H* ours later, showered and dressed in bright skirts and gauzy blouses they'd purchased in Oaxaca City, Joyce and Mia went out to the courtyard bar. The handsome bartender prepared drinks and chatted amiably with the customers.

"What do you do when you're not here at the villas mixing drinks, Jorge?" Joyce asked, smiling over at him and twirling a strand of her hair.

Slyly pulling a brochure from behind the bar, Jorge slid it across to her. He lowered his voice and leaned closer. "I give Spanish lessons."

"I could sure use a brush up," Joyce cooed. When he moved away, she commented to Mia, "What is more delightful than learning a language in Paradise?"

"Learning it from Jorge, perhaps?" Mia whispered, and they both giggled.

Couples lining the bar chatted about what sights they had already seen, and where else they planned to visit. Mia gazed dreamily at pots of yellow hibiscus flowers waving in the warm breeze while the rosy sun slowly plunged behind a long finger of land.

# SCROLL

*fter a delicious meal of spicy fish at a cozy outdoor restaurant in town, they purchased coffee and rolls for breakfast, and small bottles of flavored mezcal. Back at the villa, they relaxed. "Oooh, this is good!" Joyce laughed, taking a sip of creamy almond flavored liquor.

Mia took a sip of her chocolate flavored liquor. "Don't you just love these little bottles? They're so cute! Just the right size for a sweet little buzz."

"Yep, I'm officially blissed."

Mia giggled. "Did you say 'officially blessed'?"

"Blessed?" Joyce chuckled, "Oh, how I hope so!"

The warm breeze of evening changed to a whipping wind late in the night and several roof tiles from their villa blew down to the courtyard. By morning, the ground was littered with leaves and palm fronds.

Mia woke with words in her mind.

*Maybe* La Virgen *listen...*

Joyce rapped at Mia's door and pushed it open. "Are you moping in paradise?"

"No. But I feel a little sick; maybe I had too much sweet liquor."

"Let's get coffee and go outside. That might help."

Mia donned a swimsuit, shorts, and a big yellow t-shirt. She poured herself a cup of coffee, and went out to the covered patio.

Steadying a cup of coffee while swinging slowly in a hammock, Joyce said with a grin, "Isn't this the life? Look at the view!"

"Undeniably gorgeous." Mia settled into a lounge chair and closed her eyes for a moment. She breathed in a long slow breath. "Something Mother said is troubling me. She said to remember what she loved, that there was meaning there. She loved roses, collected black pottery, had a book of Mexican poetry, and enjoyed embroidery. Mother was a good cook, but Grandmother said she had to teach Mother to be an *Italian* wife."

"Her passive-aggressive way of revealing something about Victoria she disliked?"

Mia's eyes widened. "Grandmother said, 'The wrong kind of woman that comes from the wrong place can bring a man down. When a man falls, he is not alone. Down comes his heritage, his name, his blood, his family.'"

Joyce sat up a little. "The wrong kind of woman from the wrong place? What was she insinuating?"

"Grandmother said, 'Clever, that one: naming her life as she wished with a map.' Mother never talked of her family in Italy, never went there. And Mother loved puzzles and word games; I think she came up with clues by using an atlas, and she hid them in the words on her marriage license."

"Clues to what?"

"That's what I'm trying to figure out. Mother said she did something once that changed both our lives. I just don't know what."

Joyce stopped swinging. "Is that what's been bothering you?"

Mia nodded gravely and said evasively, "Part of it." She drew a shaky breath. "There's something else I've been trying to find a way to say…"

Joyce silently observed the strained look on Mia's face, and waited breathlessly for her explanation.

"I went to San Antonio in search of information. I discovered the scrap of cloth in the atlas. And I found a picture of me at Christmas; '1968' was written on the back. I have no birth certificate. I was an unregistered birth, my parents said."

"How does that happen?"

Mia shrugged. "I do have a baptismal certificate dated December 23, 1968."

"What's strange about that?"

"I was a toddler in the Christmas picture dated 1968."

"So, someone just wrote the wrong year."

Mia was shaking her head. "Mother was exacting. And she was right. About everything," Mia barely whispered.

"Oh, come on! She wasn't perfect! She could have made a mistake."

"I got a copy of their marriage license application; it was dated April 23, 1968. Only eight months before I was baptized."

"You were premature?"

Mia drew an uneasy breath. "Mother did say I was 'unexpected' but I don't think that's what she meant. Papa said, when they met, he didn't care about her past, what had happened before, or where she came from. He only wanted to make us both safe."

Joyce gasped. "Make you *both* safe?"

Mia nodded. "And Grandmother said...he had been 'damaged' by a high fever as a child—perhaps never to father a child. Something happened to Mother before they met. Something so compelling Mother would never talk of her early life, never went back, in fact was never was out of the company of someone else. And an old woman in San Antonio seemed to know her, mentioned Mexico, and said Mother was frightened and with a small baby."

"So...you're thinking Angelo is not your father?" Joyce's eyes were wide. "Have you asked your Papa?"

"Not in so many words. But I *know*."

"Do you think Victoria left the clues for you to figure out who your father was?"

Mia nodded. "Or who she was, or both. I just don't know how to figure it out. The answer has something to do with the words on the license, the atlas map, the embroidered scrap, the black pottery and black stones, and the cathedrals."

They considered the clues as Mia ruminated out loud. "*Bartolomeo* is like *San Bartolo Coyotepec* and *San Bartolome Quialana*. The door of the cathedral in *San Bartolo Coyotepec* is straight with an arched window above it. The door of the cathedral in *San Bartolome Quialana* is arched like my Tudor house door. Both have windows shaped like a flower above the door. They could be roses; Mother loved roses. And she said my door reminded her of the door of the cathedral in her village."

Joyce added excitedly, "The two villages are only about twenty miles apart; that's not much distance to travel between, even many years ago. Not a coincidence the names of the villages and the cathedrals are similar. My head is swimming with details!"

Mia nodded dully. "How will I ever find out who I am?"

"Let's take a dip to cool our minds. We can think of it as a baptism: a beginning for the next stage of both our lives. And a new you! Whoever you are!"

The beach was nearly deserted. They swam out into the smooth-as-satin water and floated peacefully until several noisy motor boats came zipping into the bay.

"*Lanchas* rule," Joyce yelled, pointing at the boats.

Mia frowned and coughed. They swam to shore, wrapped up in towels, and Mia sat down on the sand. Joyce remained standing. "I thought we'd get cleaned up and go to town for a little diversion. Want to?"

"Sure," she answered, but Mia didn't move right away. "My stomach is upset. Must be from the choppy water and gasoline fumes." She took a deep breath and hoisted herself to her feet. Back at the villa, after she had showered and dressed, Mia felt better. They decided to go shopping.

Walking up the dirt road toward the business district, they passed small residences and a school. Several streets were crossed and then a busy four-lane highway. Long blocks of buildings of simple concrete and glass construction held many small shops with varied and discordant signage. Some signs were painted professionally on the glass storefronts; there were also wooden signs hanging from chains, and hand printed signs on paper and cardboard taped to the windows. Mia glanced at each one, as if she would see something important.

They went inside several shops. Many of the manufactured items offered for sale were imports from other countries and might have been displayed in any modern shop in any city.

Customers crowded around sale racks and attentive, attractively dressed clerks inquired as to their needs and wants.

"Just looking," Joyce and Mia replied again and again as they picked through all the shops on the first block. While waiting on the corner for a break in the traffic so they could cross the street, Joyce noticed a tiny market. They purchased sweet rolls and ate them standing out on the sidewalk. Sugar granules sticking to her lips, Joyce grinned, "I could eat these night and day."

Her mouth full, Mia chewed and swallowed. She smiled. "Uh huh, they're delicious! Just like Mother used to make for me." A strange look suddenly showed on her face and Mia said, "I think she really loved me—in her own way."

"Who wouldn't?" Joyce replied with a shrug, and they went on.

After window shopping down another block, they stopped for fruit ice on sticks, *paletas*, from a push cart vendor. "Try mine. Coconut." Joyce offered a bite and sampled Mia's. "Oooh! Chocolate's good, too. Sugar heaven!" They licked quickly to keep creamy drips from running onto their hands.

After covering yet another block, they came upon a shaved ice cart. "I'm so hot!" Joyce exclaimed with a giggle and ordered *rompope* flavor. She tasted it and grinned, "Eggnog! You should get one!"

Mia put her hand to her stomach. "I couldn't possibly! Maybe later."

They walked along and glanced into more shops and businesses. Surprised to find an Internet stop in a narrow room rimmed with leggy desks supporting old computers, Mia went inside. She paid a few dollars for Internet time and the English-speaking clerk showed her how to send an E-mail. Mia crafted a letter to Gerald and pushed the button to send it into cyberspace.

Out on the sidewalk, Joyce had finished her shaved ice and was wiping her sticky fingers with a wet wipe she pulled from her purse.

"Is Tony ever online?"

Joyce nodded. "Online, texting, calling: he's big on communication. That actually has me *almost* convinced to try a road trip. That and his..."

"Don't say it!" Mia laughed.

"Aw. And I thought you were loosening up a little," Joyce giggled. "I was going to say 'his sweetness'."

"Oh. Sweetness is good."

"Yes! And *he's* very good, also!"

"JOYCE!"

*T*hey were still laughing when they entered a large metal building: *el mercado*, a market. House wares, clothing, toys, carcasses of meat hanging from hooks in the ceiling, pirated cassette disks, textiles, fruits, and vegetables were displayed inside. Along a wall of windows, buckets overflowed with colorful flowers. Joyce and Mia strolled down the row, admiring the many varieties. Stopping at a bucket of white flowers, Mia breathed in a sweet aroma and remarked, "I didn't know there were coneflowers that smelled good."

"*Fragrant Angel.*"

She turned to look at Joyce and sighed, "It *is* heavenly."

Down another aisle, they stopped at a booth to admire hand-carved and painted wooden figures. "I read an article in *National Geographic* about these; *alebrijes,* they're called. Zapotec Indians in the Oaxaca Valley use a variety of rustic knives to carve chunks of wood, usually copal," Joyce explained. "Look at the detail!"

Mia scanned the colorful assortment of dogs, cats, turtles, armadillos, devils and...her eyes stopped on a blue robed figure with delicate wings. "Another angel."

Joyce followed Mia's look. "Angels bring messages. Maybe it's a sign."

"Maybe. But of what?"

Joyce shrugged, and continued browsing while Mia wandered over to examine articles at a corner stall piled high with finely embroidered and woven items. A pretty woman straightening the stacks pulled out a dress and draped it across her petite frame to show how it might look on. Mia nodded and smiled but kept looking. She picked through the tablecloths and runners with intricate designs and colorful borders but found nothing resembling the scrap in her pocket. Mia selected several beautiful *rebozos,* traditional shawls worn by the countrywomen and used for a variety of purposes such as covering a head in bad weather, transporting goods, or wrapping and carrying babies.

Rejoining Mia, Joyce remarked, "Those are very pretty."

"Gifts for Grandmother, Maggie, and you! Which would you like?"

Joyce pointed to a gold-colored shawl with a woven scroll design and long fringed ends. "I love that one! Thank you."

After much more shopping, they left the market. Their arms were laden with many multi-colored striped plastic bags and they dawdled.

"We have only one more day in Oaxaca," Mia sighed, her eyes scanning the residential neighborhood they were passing. "Oh, look!"

They gazed at a thatched roof fire station where helmets and slickers hung on pegs. The firemen were playing cards around a small table. A decades-old shiny red fire engine with gleaming chrome stood at the ready.

Mia's mind recalled the disturbing dream of fire. Words flowed into her mind.

*My baby...I pray* La Virgen *keep safe...I pray someday she come...*

Distracted, Mia paused at a split in the road: a dusty trail leading west to their hotel, or a paved road veering to the east.

"Let's try that one, just for fun?" Joyce asked.

They proceeded down the paved road but were soon forced to the dirt shoulder by a passing pickup truck loaded with people. It reminded Mia of another dream and her brow furrowed.

Joyce waved away a cloud of dust and exhaust. "Must be a popular beach."

Following the road through dense trees, they came out onto the beach of a small bay. Jutting rocks split the shoreline into two parts: noisy motor boats on one side, swimmers and surfers on the other. They walked past a half-dozen empty chairs and umbrellas.

"Golly, it's hot. You'd think I'd be used to the heat after so many years in Texas," Joyce said wiping perspiration from her neck and sinking down onto the sand. "I guess I'm still a Wisconsin girl at heart."

But Mia was not listening. She was watching the waves rolling in to the shore and retreating; she said suddenly, "Let's go in."

"We don't have our suits. You go ahead."

Mia kicked off her flip-flops and waded in. Her arms stretched out to the water and she swam with smooth breast strokes. "Ah, Joyce!" Mia called. "This water! It feels like I've waited all my life for it!"

Joyce grinned and sighing contentedly, she scanned the clear, blue sky.

Mia swam a long time. Back on the beach, she walked slowly and turned to see her footprints fade as the water followed her to the shore. She stretched out on the sand and drew in several breaths before asking, "What beach is this, do you think?"

Digging in her purse, Joyce retrieved a map and oriented it to the landscape, "Our hotel's over there so this must be Playa Manzanillo."

"Manzanillo Beach," Mia sighed again. "Sounds as pretty as it is."

"This little bay is called *Puerto*..." Joyce paused, "*Puerto* 'Something I can't read'-*ito*. The word is lost in the fold of the map." Tossing the paper aside, Joyce lay back on the sand and closed her eyes. "I don't care what it is; you seem relaxed finally and that makes me happy."

Mia looked out to the blue-green water like glass as it swelled and crested. It was as beautiful as a dream. A gust of wind lifted her hair. Mia looked around. "Joyce," she whispered. "Are you asleep?"

"No." Joyce yawned and opened her eyes.

"I just thought of something. The woman in *San Bartolo Coyotepec* said: *primos*. It means cousins, *boy* cousins, right?"

"Uh, huh." Joyce sat up and yawned again. "It ends in 'o', so that's masculine."

"What about the other word—*hermanas*?"

"Oh, we forgot that one." Joyce pulled her dictionary from her purse and looked it up. "It means sisters."

Mia's eyes grew wide. "Sisters? Joyce!" she said breathlessly. "Cousins? Sisters? What if...the old woman *did* know Mother? And...what if...the *reason* Mother struggled with me wasn't..." Mia swallowed hard and stumbled onto the words, "because she never wanted me...maybe it was because...*my*... mother..."

Joyce held up a hand. "Wait! I'm sorry. But I *must* have sustenance to fuel my brain." Joyce turned and looked up the beach. "Do you see a refreshment stand?"

Mia slowly shook her head.

Pushing up from the warm sand, Joyce said, "Hold that thought."

Sea birds swooped down in great arcs, diving for bits of fish being discarded by the fishing boats idling in the bay. Children were running back and forth along the water while parents lounged on the sand. Everything was in motion; even the air seemed alive.

The warm Mexican sun beat down. Mia wiped beads of sweat from her forehead and hugged her knees to her chest.

Several men approached, each asking politely in choppy English if she would like to rent an umbrella and chair, or snorkeling or surfing gear, perhaps take a boat ride up the coast to swim with dolphins, or see the giant sea turtles at the nearby nature preserve.

"No, *gracias*," Mia answered, shaking her head at each request.

Scooping up handfuls of hot sand, she studied the multicolored particles: tiny bits of coral, beach glass, and the discarded shells of sea creatures. Life was like that: a mixture of light and dark, smooth and rough, mystery and fact. Maybe all truth could not be known. Maybe some questions, like some prayers, just went unanswered.

Mia looked up to the blue, blue sky and drew in a long, settling breath.

A barefoot man dressed in loose, white clothing walked toward her. A guitar dangled from a brightly-woven strap around his neck, and his long, graying hair was blowing in the breeze. He sat down and began playing. Beautiful tones emanated from his battered instrument, and the hypnotic music blended with the sound of waves lapping the shore. Mia settled down on the sand and rested her head. She drifted off.

Mia opened her eyes and glanced up the beach. The man had finished playing and was walking away. His silhouette glowed eerily against the fading sky.

"MIA!" Joyce yelled, and raised her hands to show two large cups she carried.

Mia nodded but was distracted by something shining brightly in the distance. She stood up and began walking toward the trees near the road to the beach.

Holding out a cup as Mia approached, Joyce laughed, "I knew you couldn't wait! This stuff is irresistible!"

Mia shook her head and pointed. "Something I have to see..."

Joyce eased down to the sand, careful not to spill the cups full of frothy pink, icy liquid. She took a sip from each cup and sighed with a smile. "Don't be gone long; your yummy fruit drink will get warm. I might have to drink it!"

Mia kept walking toward the spot shining through the trees. She clutched the silver medallion of *La Virgen de Guadalupe* around her neck; her heart was beating very fast. Stepping into the trees, Mia spied a sign hanging from the rafters of a thatched roof hut. Her eyes focused in on a rose, and a name painted in curvy letters. Many colorful items were hanging from pegs in the hut and neat stacks of brilliantly embroidered articles covered a table. Beside it, a woman with graying head was bent over her sewing. She looked up as Mia approached and a sweet smile of welcome was on her face.

Taking a few steps closer, Mia asked breathlessly, "Are you *Angelita*?"

The woman's smile faded. She pointed at the bay. "*Puerto Angelito*."

Mia looked and her mind flashed back to Joyce's statement about the name of this bay: "*Puerto* 'Something I can't read'-*ito*."

The woman was saying, "When I come here…I think name…was good sign. Maybe someday…*Angelita* come…"

Charlotte's words echoed in Mia's mind: "By water, wind whisper name."

The woman blinked back tears and said sadly, "*Angelita* was…*hija*…"

*Hija*? Mia troubled over the word she'd heard somewhere before. And then she remembered; Claudia, the tour guide, had been planning a birthday party for her *hija*: her daughter. Mia searched the woman's sad but pretty face—the face so familiar—the face so much like Victoria's, and her own. Barely able to breathe, Mia plunged her shaking hand deep into her pocket and drew out the embroidered cloth.

The woman stared at the scrap on Mia's open hand and gasped, "*Ay, Dios!*" Words rushed from her lips, "I cry and wait…and I pray…but I think *La Virgen*…no listen. I think only devil answer." Tears poured from her eyes like rain. "Still I… work…and hope return." The woman clasped her hand over her laughing mouth and exclaimed, "Now I see a miracle come! It is you!"

Mia's heart pounded loudly in her ears.

"*Angelita*," the woman breathed, "*mi hija.*"

*Ay, my heart break is you*
*With you...a piece of my heart go...*
*I cry and wait and pray...*
*and every wish is hope...*
*someday you come...*
*and my heart return.*

# EPILOGUE

More than a dream, more than words in her mind, or a story she had written drew Mia back to the land of her birth. Perhaps it was magic stitched into the cloth. Or an answer to prayer. Or perhaps, it was only love that led Mia to the woman who had waited so many years to see her again. Their eyes lingered on each other's face. And then their arms wrapped around each other. Mia's head rested on her mother's shoulder and there was so much softness in the body that held her close—as if the love in Rosa's heart made a cushion of flesh.

"Are you Rosa?" Mia asked as she released her grasp.

"Rosalia."

"Ohhhh," Mia sighed and nodded her head. "I'm Mia —Maria Isabel Angelina."

"Maria? My sister…she live?"

Mia shook her head sadly. "No. She passed. Not quite a year ago."

Rosalia blinked back tears. "She have good life?"

"Yes," Mia nodded. "She lived a very good life—just how she wanted."

Rosalia's smile was bittersweet. "She have children?"

Again Mia shook her head. "Only me to raise."

"Ah," Rosalia replied knowingly. "When we young, she say she no want children, spoil her looks."

Mia's smile was wistful. "So like Mother."

"My sister have handsome husband? She marry for riches?"

"Her husband was—is—very handsome, but she married for love."

Rosalia's eyes sparkled. "Is good." And then she added enthusiastically, "I find love. Two times."

"With my father?" Mia stammered. "Who was he?"

"Mano. I call him this. He was good to me. But Mano...something happen...I never see him again. I think life no good for living. Then...another good man find me! I thank God for him! He so good to me. You see! He come soon."

Mia nodded. "Do you have...more children?"

"No," Rosalia replied sadly. "I have only one sweetness..." but then her face brightened. "You! I have you! Is a miracle!"

Mia's eyes glistened and they were both laughing when they heard someone calling and they turned to look.

"Oh, there you are! Did you finally find something?" Joyce asked as she approached and surveyed the stacks of colorfully embroidered items.

"I did!" Mia exclaimed. "I found the answer to the longing of my heart!"

*Everywhere my heart go with you...with you...I cry and wait and pray...And every wish is hope...Someday you come...And my heart return.*

# ABOUT THE AUTHOR

*S*haron Duerst lives in Central Oregon. Outdoor and creative activities shared with family and friends offer great inspiration for her writing. *Mending Stone* is her first novel.

~ ~ ~

Dear Readers:
You are important to me!
Please visit my site at www.mendingstone.com to leave a comment or to find more about Mending Stone, and other writing!

Thank you,
*Sharon Duerst*

# Discussion Questions

1. What is unique about the setting? How do changes in the setting influence the story?

2. Is there a recurring theme in the novel?

3. Can you relate to the characters? Do they seem real?

4. Are you surprised by any events or revelations in the story?

5. How has reading the story affected you/your life, or world view?

6. Does any part of the novel speak to you in ways that are surprising?

7. What do you like most about the story? What do you like least?

8. After finishing the story, do you have lingering questions or feelings?

9. If you could project the characters into a future story, what would it be?

Three Towers Press is a division of HenschelHAUS Publishing, Inc.
We are happy to review manuscripts from new and veteran authors
and offer a wide range of author services,
such as coaching, editing, design, and book marketing.

Please visit www.HenschelHAUSBooks.com for submission guidelines,
our on-line bookstore, and calendar of workshops and author events.